WAR OF MEN

A *Buried Goddess Saga* NOVEL

V

RHETT C.
BRUNO

JAIME
CASTLE

JOIN THE KING'S SHIELD

Sign up to the *free* and exclusive King's Shield Newsletter to receive early looks and new novels, peeks at conceptual art that breathes life into Pantego as well as exclusive access to short stories called "Legends of Pantego." Learn more about the characters and the world you love.

Did you know we have a Facebook group too? All the same perks as the email readers group plus instant interaction with Rhett and Jaime! The Official King's Shield Fan Club.

This one is for the fans.
*Truly, they've all been for you. Without you, these characters
wouldn't live and breathe.*

DRAV CRA
BRO
PANTEGO
THE
crowfall
west vale
THE
GLASS KINGDOM
N
grambling
YARRINGTON
troborough
oxgate
bridleton
W
E
FORT
MARIMOUNT
winde port
S
TRADER'S
BAY
nahanab
fellwater swamp
THE
WEBBED WOODS

ON'S TAIL
BREKLIODAD
hornsheim
GLINTHAVEN
YAOLIN CITY
PANPING
THE
K SANDS
ibar
LATIAPUR
HE BOILING WATERS
BND '18

PROLOGUE

The golden stew boiled within one of many cauldrons, bubbling, wafting up a mouth-watering aroma, inviting Kari Kahoru to sneak just a small taste. She moaned as the broth hit her tongue. *Perfect.* The recipe had been passed down to her by her mother, and her mother before that, and it went on like this back to even before Panping was called Panping. Now, that glorious stew simmered in her kitchen.

The Innbetween, as her inn had always been called, stood west of Yaolin City and east of the Wildlands. It was a lone beacon on the Glass Road, providing respite for weary travelers. From all over Pantego they would come, and more than a few of them had tried to steal the recipe as they swept through, and just as many had been sent packing to find somewhere else to sleep—something Kari knew they wouldn't find. Not without days of walking. The secret was locked in her mind, and nowhere else. It would only leave that vault when it was passed down to her daughter one day.

As if trying to earn it, Winimoto stirred the pot rigorously. "Like this?" her young daughter asked, barely tall enough to see over the pot's rim.

"No," Kari said. She gently slapped Winimoto's arm, then wrapped her own hands around her daughter's. "You have to tilt the spoon. Just like this. Then you properly fold in the spices. Good." Kari took another pinch of her special mixture and sprinkled the spices in while they stirred.

"What are those?"

"Ah-ah-ah, you won't trick me so easy." Kari poked Winimoto in the center of the forehead. "Only when you are old enough to be trusted with such a grand secret."

"It's just stew, Momma..." her daughter groaned.

"Just stew? *Just* stew?" Kari threw up her hands. Then she stabbed the air toward a booth just beyond the opening looking out into the dining hall. "I'll have you know that King Liam himself sat right there with Philippi Nantby the day he was named Governor of the eastern regions." She pointed again. "In the western corner, with the King's Shield all around them, the Slayer of Redstar, himself, stood guard!"

"What does that have to do with the stew?"

"Would you have said, 'It's *just* King Liam, Momma?'" Kari asked. "I sure hope not."

"I dunno," Winimoto said quietly. "He's just a man."

"Just a man!" Kari was laughing, but there was no humor in it. "Wini, we owe him *everything*. When I was a child—your age— all any Panpingese man or woman was concerned with was magic. Magic this. Magic that. Never a care for practical things, like… you know, feeding our people. From all over, they visited the Red Tower to see if they have the gift, which, of course, so few do. Some of the fools even offered their services to the mystics only to be near them. Perhaps they'd hoped some magic would rub off while they scrubbed their robes."

That got her daughter's attention. She stopped stirring and looked up, eyes bulging. "Did you ever go?"

"And what, have the old Council test me?" Kari dismissed the very notion with a wave of her hand. "It was all playing games to them. What need do we have for that nonsense, when we have this place? What do I always say?"

Winimoto rolled her eyes. "'The open road isn't safe, except *The Innbetween*,'" she droned, as she'd done countless times before.

"Precisely. We're the first thing travelers see at the border of Panping. Long before Yaolin City or even Jangat. The Gateway to our people, our culture, our everything! And *that... just* stew? It's a taste of what Panping is truly capable of when we are not worried about magic tricks."

"They aren't tricks, Momma. Hadaoto said when he visited Panping with his parents, he saw a young woman who could wield fire with her hands! And a wyvern. A real one." Her daughter swept her free hand in front of her, accidentally slapping the top of the spoon and sending a bit of stew soaring onto the counter.

Kari ran her finger through the spill, then brought it to her mouth, sucking through her teeth. "If it can't feed us, it's a trick," she said, then gently pushed her daughter's hand aside and took control of the spoon. Winimoto slinked back in shame. "Now, go and fetch the bowls. We have hungry guests."

She watched as her precious Wini crossed the room and collected clay bowls, stacking one inside another until the tower threatened to topple.

"That's enough," Kari said.

Wini whispered something under her breath.

"I heard that!" Kari scolded, absentmindedly stirring. The perfect technique came second nature to her now. The back of her grandmother's spoon made sure of that.

Her daughter came waddling back to the table, carrying a stack still far too tall for her stature.

"There you go," Kari said. "Hard work, not miracles. That's

what makes us strong. Liam woke us up to that truth, and now the farms of Panping provide more food for Pantego than any region we know of. And food, my dear, is the wheel that keeps civilization going. Without a pot to cook in, we may as well be savages."

"Or knife-ears…" Winimoto muttered as she leaned up on the balls of her feet to place the bowls down.

Kari's hand shot out and grasped her wrist. The bowls fell with a clatter, but Kari didn't even watch them bounce and roll along the floor. "Why would you say something like that?"

"I heard it... from one of the men out there drinking."

"What did he say?" Kari asked through clenched teeth, squeezing her daughter's wrist without meaning to.

"Momma, that hurts," Wini complained.

Kari let go. "What did he say?"

"Just that he wishes I was around back during the third war, and he'd have shown me what a pretty little knife-ear deserves."

"He said that about you—a child?"

"Uh-huh. Then his friends laughed and groused about 'too many laws these days.'" She reached up and rubbed the pointed tip of her ears between her thumb and forefinger. "I guess they are like knives. I never really noticed."

"They aren't—" Kari took a deep, measured breath. She didn't even realize she had the spoon in her hand and out of the stew, knuckles white like she was going to beat somebody with it. She might. She'd been hesitant to let her daughter start helping on the inn floor, and, apparently, rightly so. Most travelers were just exhausted, looking for the delights of a good meal and sound sleep. But some, Kari wanted nowhere near her paradise, or her kin.

She stormed out of the kitchen and around the bar. *The Innbetween* was as quaint as it was entirely Panpingese. A red-leafed acer tree grew from an island on a pool in the room's center, rising toward the peak of the sweeping roof. The water around it was dotted with white lilies that filled the whole dining area with a sweet aroma. Paper walls, painted with scenes of the old gods, offered privacy to some tables in the corners. The rest were laid out in a perfect grid, made from sturdy bamboo that had been there since well before Kari was born.

"Who would dare say that to a child!" she barked. Her cheeks were hot from boiling blood. However, she stopped the moment she got a look around the room. It was utterly empty even though the last time she'd checked, there were at least a dozen guests. The lute-player was gone, stool vacant. Her beloved husband tending the bar, vanished.

All gone.

"Hello?" she called, voice carrying. Never in her life had she heard the place echo around supper time. Ever since Liam's war opened trade between the east and west, bringing riches to both sides, there were always travelers on the road.

Kari slowly crossed the room, a few of the old floorboards creaking, reminding her of the task she'd been meaning to issue her husband. Stopping at the stairs, she called up to the rooms, got no answer. She didn't even hear footsteps. Walking past tables, she saw unfinished plates, undrained mugs, and worst of all, no autlas to pay for any of it.

"Momma, what's going on?" Winimoto asked, standing in the doorway leading to the kitchen, holding the swinging door open. A chunk of meat on the corner of her lip betrayed her sampling of the stew without asking. Kari let it go this time, far too concerned with other things.

"Stay there," she told her daughter.

"But—"

"I said, stay."

Kari moved back across the room, and a subtle, orange glow started to filter through the shaded front windows. It grew brighter, and flickered, like the flames in the spherical, paper lanterns hanging over the tables. Hurrying to the front door, she slid it open. The sweet scents of her garden usually awaited her there, but instead, there was something else. It smelled of cooked spices and sweetmeat.

That is not my stew, she thought to herself, *but it smells delicious.*

Spanning in either direction toward the darkening sky, the fine, squared stones of the Glass Road were a testament to the workmanship of her people. The Glass Road was always empty at this time of day, but in light of the events, something seemed especially off.

Where was everyone?

"Shinmen!" she called her husband's name. "Shinmen, this isn't funny!" No answer.

A gust of hot air drew her to the left, and she followed it around to the side of the inn where she heard whispers.

"Shi shi?" she said, but the words barely escaped her lips. She cleared her throat and said it in common, "Hello?"

The only reply was the steadily growing whispers. When she'd put the inn behind her, she could see her beloved herb garden, which helped produced flavors that'd delighted travelers for generations. However, beyond the thyme, lemongrass, and cardamom, she saw it.

People in long, red hooded robes stood in a wide circle around a crackling bonfire. They were speaking something but, from such a distance, Kari couldn't understand. She moved closer.

"Buried, not dead," they said, over and over. Each had a hand raised, with a dagger in the other already having sliced open their palms.

Kari gasped involuntarily, and every shrouded figured turned toward her, still chanting.

"Buried, not dead," they said, only now louder. Their faces weren't only veiled by their hoods, but hidden behind pure white, porcelain masks, expressionless and with a single red tear dripping from one of the eye holes. All identical. All horrifying.

They slowly approached her, robes dragging through her garden and disturbing the soil, their feet crushing her precious plants. Fear had her completely frozen, and once the circle broke, she saw that within the fire, other secrets were kept. The bodies of all those who'd been inside the inn, eating, drinking, enjoying the soft sounds of music, were arranged on the ground in the shape of a triangle within a circle. Their limbs were stretched to leave no breaks between them, their throats cut open, and each of them burned, the fire spreading into her garden now.

Kari's spoon clanked against the cobblestones.

"No…no…no…" she stammered as she recognized the nearest body, forming a point of the triangle with another. Her husband's eyes were frozen open and glassy, aimed right at her, the fire slowly charring his cheek.

She threw up, wiped her face, then threw up again. She tried to run but tripped on the step of the inn's porch. She tried to crawl, but fear had her pinned, shaking. The masked killers neared, their voices growing louder.

"Buried, not dead."

"Buried, not dead."

"Buried, not dead."

I

THE GODDESS

The Far North was bleak, white, stark, void of all life, but Nesilia could feel all of existence beneath her feet, from the halls of the Boiling Keep to the golden arches of Glinthaven and beyond. Directly below her, the squirming, writhing, and scurrying of dwarves in the many tunnels tickled her bare toes—Sora's toes. Never had she cared for Meungor's pets—the furry rodents burrowing through the rock, with no greater ambitions than gold and mead. Such short-sightedness wasn't tolerated in her own followers.

For as far as she could see, in all directions, those followers marched with her, clad in furs and painted with the blood of man and beasts. Dire wolves hobbled along beside them, starved. Some rode atop great, duel-tusked, hairy, mammoths they called chekt which only roamed the furthest reaches of the Drav Cra. The gods had another name for them, a name that, like she, had been buried and forgotten.

Five of Drav Cra's most impressive dradinengors led their little armies, all declaring loyalty to her and Freydis after what they'd all witnessed at the Earthmoot in the Buried Hollow. The rest waited in Drav Cra, preparing for the great raid to come.

Despite the bitter cold tundra north of Winter's Thumb that the Drav Cra called home, a burning fire coursed through their veins, unwilling to be stifled. The world—Iam's world—would feel their flames. The Buried Goddess would be avenged, and she'd use those deemed 'savages' to do it.

Freydis rode on the bare back of a gray dire wolf along one side of her, blood coating her eyes and lips, dripping down from the center of her mouth, over her chin and down into the cleavage of her breasts. She was pure power, concentrated into a lithe and beautiful form. Dark hair hung over her shoulders in mottled clumps, dotted with trinkets designed to channel the presence of their lady. In reality, they were useless, all of them, but the Drav Cra devotion to Nesilia was admirable, and thus, rewarded.

"My Lady," Freydis said. "Do you think it wise that we left Wvenweigard to train the children? Should I not be there to help them indwell?"

"Do you now doubt me, too?" Nesilia asked. She knew it wasn't what the woman meant, but mortals so needed the reminder.

"That's not it at all," Freydis said. "I'm sorry. I just—I simply—"

"You fault me for sparing his life." It wasn't a question. "You think I should have punished him with the other warlocks who refused to see me?"

"You did not know him, my Lady," Freydis said. "He followed Redstar—"

"Did you not follow Redstar? Here I was, believing you to be his second in command. Was I mistaken about that as well?"

Freydis opened her mouth to speak.

"You say I didn't know him—Wvenweigard… Which is it, dear Freydis—am I Nesilia, the Buried Goddess of Earth, or am I a fraud?"

Nesilia could see the flood of emotion washing over Freydis' features.

"I'm sorry, my Lady," the warlock said. "I just wonder what would have happened had Redstar stayed behind and left the fighting, conniving, and meddling to someone else."

"What would have happened," Nesilia said, "is that you would not be Arch Warlock, and you would not be by my side. You do wish to be by my side, do you not?"

"More than anything, my Lady."

"Good. I need you here. This is the work of divinity we embark upon. Wvenweigard has proven himself loyal, just as you have. Those he chooses to indwell while we're gone, will do so in your name. Arch Warlock Freydis. You like the sound, yes?"

"I…" Freydis started, but quickly settled for, "Yes, my Lady. You're right."

"Always," Nesilia said with a smile.

She had been left behind, forgotten beneath a mountain for centuries, while Iam did as he pleased. She would not see Freydis suffer the same fate. It wasn't that she held any real esteem for Freydis—but too long had men ruled under the Eye of Iam. No more.

While they marched across Winter's Thumb, another worthy ally—so far as mortals can be worthy—Aihara Na, the one these fools called Ancient One, remained in Yaolin City to oversee the training of a new batch of mystics. As her first act within Sora's body, Nesilia had dispatched of the old, set-in-their-ways Mystic Order.

Wvenweigard in the North. Aihara Na in the East. Both building an army of new and devoted soldiers.

Ancient One, Nesilia thought derisively. Nesilia had experienced festivals which lasted longer than this creature's whole existence. But that was before the feud. That was before she and

Iam set forth to create men and call into fruition the destruction of all she'd known and loved.

Love...

She shook away the thought, because with it, her host began to stir. Sora, daughter of the human King Liam and another *Ancient One* who'd died so easily... it sickened Nesilia to feel the meager emotions these beings considered to be love. They had no sense or scope for its true meaning. The flittering feeling in their bellies, goose pimples, swollen cocks, and erect nipples—these physical manifestations within their quickly dying bodies were not to be compared with eons of companionship.

Internally, she cursed both Iam and herself. Why had they even set forth to make these things. They are pitiful, weak. And she hated how much she needed them. Even in trying to bury the thoughts, they only grew, along with the taste of bile in the back of her throat.

She took a deep breath of the frigid air, pulling her to the present. As Nesilia looked around at the Drav Cra, she considered their mortality. Flesh and blood, protected by little more than animal skin and hard wood.

Aihara Na … now that was power. The old mystic may have been barely corporeal, but she had untold power. She feasted upon Elsewhere—drawing strength from the very gods which Nesilia had played a part in banishing. With neither body to slay nor blood to spill, who could kill such a thing? Though a mere child in terms of age, they were like unto gods, themselves, or as close as creation had known for these many centuries.

But for all their power, their personal attraction to this realm kept them weak, and they were weakened further by their lust for power. She found solace in knowing that this new batch of mystics would be made aware of her benevolence and they'd worship her for it.

Nesilia felt rumbling deep beneath her feet, further stirring her from her thoughts. By now, the dwarves had to know of their arrival. Unlike their kin in the Dragon's Tail Mountains, these poor dwarves lived below ground, fighting for scraps in a puny kingdom of outcasts. They would have felt the quaking of thousands of Drav Cra above.

These, Clan Strongiron, as they were called, would serve her needs either way. If they would not bow, they would break under the hand of her mighty warriors. She wouldn't even need to lift a finger. And through their kingdom, she would lead them on a path to the Citadel; to removing the upyr and their Sanguine Lords from the equation. The only beings who could possibly rise up against her.

A wedge of stone, smooth as ice, rose from the snow a short way off. Nesilia recognized Meungor's handiwork even from such a distance. A stone door, large enough to allow giants passage, spanned the width of it, and without looking, she knew the many runes that would be etched upon its face.

Meungor did so love his dramatics.

"Freydis," Nesilia said.

"Yes, my Lady?" she answered immediately.

Such unwavering devotion. If only there were enough of these ice-dwellers left to truly bring Pantego to its knees without the need of monsters.

But there wasn't. Years of stubbornness had dwindled their numbers. Without their even realizing it, decades of settling for second, third, or even fourth best had driven them to rely upon the Glass Kingdom, same as everyone else.

Where the Panpingese—like Sora, her beautiful host—and Black Sandsmen paid tribute, or even gave up ruling rights altogether, the Drav Cra submitted to the Glass in another way. If towns like Crowfall and Fessix simply stopped receiving the many goods and life-sustaining materials… or smarter yet, retreated south, the Drav Cra raiding and pillaging parties would cease being useful. In a matter of months, the whole of her devoted peoples would resort to killing one another like the Shesaitju, and worse, eating one another to survive.

"Show me how resourceful you are, Freydis." She pointed to the door. "Show me I have not chosen poorly in calling you to lead. Show me that I did not make a mistake in allowing Redstar to die so you might live in his stead."

At that claim, the shock on Freydis' face was evident until she dipped her head. It was the reaction Nesilia wanted. She hadn't truly sacrificed the existence of the former Arch Warlock, but it was important for Freydis to believe Nesilia's hand was in everything.

Before entering the boy-king Pi, Nesilia had little hope of ever escaping her tomb. Even then, she was a shell of what she'd been, constantly struggling to maintain even the slightest hold over the boy. Then, finding Sora atop Mount Lister through the break in Elsewhere, receiving the sacrifice of faith... Redstar had given her new life. That was a fact Nesilia would never let anyone know.

Freydis hopped down from her mount, running her hand through the beast's fur, then waved to a legion of Drav Cra warriors. She gave their drad orders, and started toward the dwarven gate. Moving to a hundred year old pine poking through the snow, three large men began chopping at it with sharp axes.

Nesilia watched, rapt, curious, wondering if she'd indeed done well in selecting Freydis. The warlock's dire wolf roamed up next to Nesilia, and she stroked the back of its neck, listening as it purred like a kitten in delight.

Positioning herself in front of the gate, Freydis drew her knife, slashed her palm, and rubbed her hands together. Then they shot forward, a stream of ice pulsing forth and into the center of the door. Frost gathered across the stone, coating it, until Freydis was exhausted. Then she waved the men onward, and the mighty warriors began using the tree like a battering ram. The ice cracked and chipped away, but nothing more than, perhaps, a thin layer of the stone cracked with it. Dwarven masonry was legendary—a gift from Meungor.

Blunt force, Nesilia thought, shaking her head.

The truth was, neither Freydis, nor her other warlock companions had the slightest clue just how powerful their blood magic could be if they gave it just the slightest bit more thought. In many ways, the cultists around Pantego were more knowledgeable, but far less moldable. They'd been grafted onto the tree, not like Freydis, a natural branch bearing the fruit of generations who'd worshiped the Buried Goddess. The cultists would serve their purposes, causing unrest in the major cities, drawing the Glass soldiers away from Yarrington but they'd have no place in the true fight.

The ground shook and shadow passed over her.

"Shall my chekt help them?" a muscle-bound drad asked, calling down from the back of his giant, wooly beast. Its every footstep left an imprint the size of a wagon, and its head thrashed to the side as he guided the reins.

"No, that won't be necessary," Nesilia said without looking at the hulking warrior. Then, placing a hand on one of the massive tusks, said, "Send these cumbersome beasts back west. We won't need them underground."

"Your wish is my command, my Lady," The drad lowered his head in a slight bow, then coaxed his chekt a few stomping steps away before sliding down its long fur.

Nesilia listened as the loyal chieftain barked orders, and the herd of chekt marching with them, keeping her army warm and fresh, were handed over to beastmasters to march them back west. Dire wolves snapped at their heels to get them moving faster.

"Freydis!" Nesilia called after waiting a short while longer.

The Arch Warlock turned, shoved her men aside, and strode

back to Nesilia while they continued to ram futilely at the gate. Frail as they were, Nesilia admired Iam's handiwork in this one. Her hips swayed at just the right trajectory, hypnotic in their movements. She had all the right curves. Had Nesilia not found Sora, this warlock would have been an apt choice for a host. But even her willingness didn't make up for her lack of knowledge. To think, the Arch Warlock of her people hitting a door with weapons instead of using her blood.

"Let me see your hands."

"My lady?"

"Your hands," Nesilia repeated.

Freydis lifted both hands, palm up.

Grasping them, Nesilia said, "You do not know your strength."

"We were almost through," Freydis lied.

"That door hasn't budged in nigh on a millennium—nothing you could do will pry it open. Only if the Dwarves wanted you inside, and it is the first of many. But, there are other ways. An eternity in the shadows has taught me."

"We were—"

"Quiet!" Nesilia barked, perhaps more harshly than intended. She smiled to offset the remark, but Freydis only looked down, disgraced.

Freydis winced when Nesilia's thumbnails carved deep lines into both of her palms. Blood bubbled and spilt to the snow.

Grasping Freydis' hands in her own, Nesilia weaved their fingers together, then squeezed until their forearms and elbows were stained with streaks of red. The snow melted under the heat of the blood. Once through the snow, it began melting through the stone itself.

Freydis gasped. "How…"

"It is not me, my child," she said. "This is the true power of your blood. The blood of the earth."

They descended until the ground broke through. From within the bedrock, vines carried them until they were firmly planted in the center of a dwarven tunnel, vaulted stone all around them.

Nesilia could imagine the Drav Cra thrusting their weapons into the air as they bellowed out war cries above. Releasing her grip, she pointed up where concentrated beam of light poured in.

Freydis understood, which pleased Nesilia.

She drew on her blood and took control, and the same vines which carried them down, now formed a ladder for her army to join them. Soon, hundreds of Drav Cra warriors flooded the tunnels under command of their drads.

Dust and dirt filled the air, kicked up from the ground, and falling from the ceiling as the tunnel shook with their steps. Nesilia followed behind, watching as Freydis summoned magical fire to her palm and led the way through the darkness. Sweat beaded on the skin of men and women accustomed to much cooler temperatures, but none complained, even when the tunnel graded downward at a steady slope, bringing them deeper into the earth.

A part of Nesilia grew uneasy underground, reminding her of so many years beneath the dirt—but this was her domain. She was not just the Buried Goddess… for there was a time before she was buried. The earth, the dirt, the animals and beasts, the mountains, and the sea: these were her children.

Something swooped overhead. Freydis spun, fire in hand. Another zipped by in the other direction, screeching.

"What are those… things?" Freydis asked, readying herself for a fight. One clawed at her hand on its way by, drawn to her flame. She went to immolate it, but Nesilia stopped her.

"Grimaurs. They will not harm you," Nesilia assured. "The beasts, forgotten to the darkness of the mountains, are drawn to me. All throughout the land, they feel my call, and know that I am returned."

Behind her, the Drav Cra all readied weapons. Above, the grimaurs snapped razor-sharp beaks, but made no other movement. They were long-faced creatures, half-humanoid, half-bird, grotesque with long, spindly beaks, and sharp talons that oozed a toxin able to paralyze the nerves. They were an early creation, unfinished, but precious to Nesilia.

As if suddenly recognizing her, one flew down. All muscles in Freydis' body tensed, but Nesilia held out a steadying hand, then slowly raised it, allowing the grimaur to rest on her forearm.

"Oh, how far you've fallen, nesting in the musty darkness." A look of genuine sadness rolled over her face as she stroked the rough feathers of its long neck. Now, these… these were her family. "I gave you the sky. I gave you the world, my first creations. But you weren't beautiful enough for them… for *Him*. You so challenged their small, shallow minds."

The creature squawked, and a murder of them echoed the same sound up above, before digging talons into a hanging stalactite.

Nesilia sent it flying off and continued through the chasm. More gathered overhead as she walked, following along, entering through every nook and small cavern around the greater passage.

She overheard two of the Drav Cra dradinengors exchanging words.

"Truly, this is she that even the beasts obey her command."

"Truly," came the reply.

Nesilia smiled, and pressed on.

They stopped before another dwarven gate, etched just like the one aboveground. Those closest to Winter's Thumb were especially defensive, setting their cities beyond a series of ancient gates. This one wasn't just outer defenses. Through the hole in the earth Freydis formed using the technique Nesilia taught her, they now stood before the entry to the city.

"I never understood why these foul little men live so deep," Freydis said.

"Like the grimaurs, the dwarves once lived atop Pantego," Nesilia answered. "They ruled the lands the Glass now calls home. But Iam's children are wretched and greedy, always taking what doesn't belong to them, hiding behind his name."

"Filth," Freydis agreed.

"Worry not, my child. We will liberate them, one way or another."

Nesilia motioned to the door. "The city behind those doors has access to an ancient tunnel. One that pierces the core of our world, far beneath the Dragon's Tail. The inhabitants aren't primitive as their surroundings might suggest. It is likely they know we are here now."

"Heathens. Worshipping Meungor," Freydis spat.

"Not all can be so aware as you," Nesilia said, no lack of distaste upon her tongue. "Give them one chance. If they refuse to bow after the first demand, kill them all. It's time Meungor knows he can't hide his creations in the mountains and pretend Pantego doesn't exist."

"My Lady," Freydis said, bowing her head.

Nesilia pointed to the door. "Now, it is your turn."

Freydis set her jaw. She picked at the skin on her palms, then rubbed her hands together, tearing at the already healing wounds. Blood poured out and she pressed both palms against the door. Closing her eyes, she began to chant.

"Why are you speaking?" Nesilia asked. Freydis looked over her shoulder, opened her mouth to speak, but stopped when Nesilia continued. "There's no need for words. Trust..."

"Yes, my Lady," Freydis said, then turned back to the door and closed her eyes again.

The door shook slightly, Freydis' arms trembled, and she lowered her hands. Taking a deep breath, she raised her hands once more and the door began to rumble again. Nesilia could see Freydis feeling the earth, feeling every part of the stone. No elements were needed. The earth itself, the stone, bent to Nesilia's will, and thus would bend to the will of her followers.

It cracked, vibrated, and began to crumble. Nesilia watched the smile beginning on the warlock's face as it fell, but knew it would quickly fade.

The movement had nothing to do with Freydis, but everything to do with the legion of dwarves standing just beyond the threshold. As the door opened, mine carts and towering stone edifices could be seen in the city beyond. The small army was led by one whose yellow-hair was swirled up in a knotted mess, beard long and braided.

"One chance," Nesilia reminded Freydis as she shrank to the back of the gathered army to watch her commander command.

The air was thick with dwarven confusion, which was quickly mounting upon the wings of anger.

"Who be knocking on our—" The dwarf speaking stopped as soon as he saw what lay in wait. They'd been hounded by Drav Cra raiders for centuries. Any dwarven traders and outposts, anyone who dared travel behind the safety of their subterranean city, but their home was well-protected. They weren't used to being invaded.

Nesilia smiled.

Are you watching this, my love? she said to Sora, who was now so deeply buried within her own mind that she hardly spoke at all anymore. But Nesilia knew she could see it all, that she would eventually break and become completely lost to the goddess' will. All she clung to were thoughts of Whitney saving her, the useless thief who'd tried to break into her mind.

"Tell me who ye be before we send ye to Meungor's arsehole

with cracked skulls!" The dwarf who spoke was bold, Nesilia would give him that. He was king of Clan Strongiron, a pesky little kingdom.

"Big claim for such a wee little thing," Freydis said, laughter filling the tunnels behind her. The drads arrayed themselves at her back, ready to slaughter. Dire wolves stepped up between them, their low growls trailing on even after the laughter stopped.

"Bold words for such a dumb cunt," the dwarf retorted.

Freydis glowered back at Nesilia, hoping for answers. The Arch Warlock looked enraged, grinding her jaw. Nesilia didn't budge.

Freydis turned back to the dwarven king. "We come, extending to you a hand of peace. March with us against our enemies in the south, and know riches beyond your wildest imagination."

"We got no beef with the flower-pickers. Best ye turn around before—"

The dwarf's words cut short as Freydis sliced her hand and flung a ball of fire at him.

Blunt weapon, indeed, Nesilia thought.

It took a moment for the rest of the dwarves to realize what had happened. The king screamed, then ran like a mad boar as the blaze caught his beard, and singed his clothes. Freydis raised her hand and the flame intensified. After one final outcry, he collapsed face-first.

Stubborn bunch, Meungor's pets.

As soon as reason met them, they charged with a thunderous shout. The doorway acted as a funnel, making numbers count for nothing. With her natural magic, and Sora's mystic blood, Nesilia could have slaughtered them in a heartbeat, but instead, she watched.

The Drav Cra may have had the height advantage, but the dwarves knew the terrain. Meungor's little runts bounced off the walls, rolling like boulders into the Northerners' ranks. Freydis cut herself and sent more balls of fire hurling through the tunnel, burning the dwarven front lines. Then she used vines to halt their tumbling marauders and ground them in place. Dire wolves leaped over the closest skirmishes, tearing the little men behind to pieces and tossing their mangled bodies.

Axes clashed, metal on metal, bone splitting and blood splattering. Nesilia saw enough death, but she had to sate the bloodthirsty nature of her followers, forced to live like rabble for so long. Forced to be angry by Iam's ignorance.

She raised her arms, and all at once, hundreds of grimaurs flew out of the darkness, soaring overhead. The sound was like a hurricane. They grasped dwarves by the shoulders with their talons, hauling them back over the dwarven city, and littering the passages between their carved structures with dropped bodies.

From mezzanines, and overhangs, floor to stone ceiling, the inhabitants of the city became aware of the situation. Cries of alarm rose. Dwarves started throwing things at the grimaurs, but it was useless.

And just like that, the dwarven army broke, and the Drav Cra were unleashed. They ravaged the hollow, slaughtering anything in their path while Nesilia casually strode forward, wading through the carnage. Her people tore through their structures carved into massive stone pillars supporting the great hollow. Dwarves fled into offshoot surface tunnels, into their mines, anywhere they could.

"Please, no!" A running dwarf screamed, before a grimaur dug into his back and hefted him away. Nesilia stepped aside to let them pass. Another dove out of a second-story window at her, but vines lashed overhead, controlled by Freydis, and whipped him at the building. The impact shattered his body and the stone wall.

Nesilia stopped before a tunnel leading down into the mines.

The iron ore within was precious—hence the Strongiron title of this kingdom's ruling family. However, the dwarves could only mine so deep before the heat of Pantego's core became unbearable for any mortal being. But there wasn't only iron. In the deep, ore containing silver was plentiful. It would prove invaluable in her upcoming war.

Grimaurs landed all around the maw, atop the dwarven equipment and mining carts, breaking the wood of the tracks.

"My lady, they flee like ants," Freydis said, stopping next to her and breathing heavy from exertion. Fresh blood coated her arms, down to her elbows. "Shall we send the wolves to hunt them down?"

"Let them run," Nesilia said. "A message for the Dragon's Tail."

"As you wish."

It was one that Meungor's kind would not soon forget. They would either have to join with the Glass, keep hiding, or eventually pledge themselves to her. It didn't matter which. For all his brashness, Meungor was a coward—perhaps even more so than Caliphar, if that were possible.

The dwarves inhabited her earthly domain. They'd be no concern.

"Gather the others, there is no time to waste," Nesilia said. "We move, east, through the mines. Through the heart of our world."

"What awaits us there, my Lady?"

Nesilia smiled at her. "You'll see."

She strode forward alone, steeling herself against the fear of being trapped again. She was free now and forever more. Skittering creatures moved through the shadows, their eyes glinting like tiny diamonds in the dark. Goblins. More forgotten creatures drawn to her power, like grimaurs, seen only as pests by Iam's chosen children.

Nesilia turned a corner, into the heart of the dwarven mines. Their tunnels stretched in every direction, cart tracks running through each of them. Miners and inhabitants of the city could still be heard up ahead, screaming—but the lizard-like goblins and their crude weapons attacked them from cracks in the walls, feeding on their flesh.

She headed for the deepest chasm, where a faint reddish glow emanated from the bubbling magma deep within. Where dwarves would never dare dig lest they boil alive in the heat, her magic would allow her people safe passage.

For in the east, on a long trek beneath the earth, the hidden Citadel of the Dom Nohzi awaited. The first of the fallen mystics —the one they called Mammon the Mad—had formed the upyr an age ago. The undead beings were the oldest in Pantego, living centuries more than even Aihara Na. They had taken control of the wianu, imprisoned and fed on them to draw on their power.

Nesilia would find them, and their meddlesome Sanguine Lords, and ensure that they couldn't stand in her way. Then she'd free the wianu, the most powerful of her forgotten creations— beings of two worlds, twisted to serve her from the gods she and Iam had defeated in the feud. Now they'd help destroy him, the great deceiver she was such a fool to ever love.

With them at her side, and the upyr removed from the equation, all Pantego would soon be well within her grasp…

II

THE THIEF

When Whitney Fierstown considered recovering one of his many stolen items, those he'd spent years hiding and burying all over Pantego, he figured this one would've been the easiest. However, as he and Gentry crouched in the small boat on Lake Yaolin, looking up at the cliff-side where there'd once been a small cave entrance, it became abundantly clear to him that nothing was going to be simple ever again. Now, a grand, massive structure, stood there, looming over the lake like a god.

"Shog in a barrel," he said.

"What do you think it is?" Gentry asked.

"In our way."

They looked up at what appeared to be a giant ship under construction, but more than half of it was on dry land, and the portion which extended onto the lake hovered above the water like a dragon in flight. It wasn't like a real boat being built at the docks. No, this looked… ornamental. Extravagant.

"So, now what, Mr. Fierstown?" Gentry asked.

Whitney bit his lip in frustration. He'd long since given up on trying to get Gentry to call him Whitney. They'd been together for weeks and about the best he'd been able to achieve had been 'Mr. Whitney.'

"I buried it in a cave beneath that monstrosity," he said, pointing. "Of course, that monstrosity hadn't been there when I'd done it."

Whitney thought over their next move for a bit. The artifact was easily the most accessible and valuable item he'd ever stolen and hidden in this region. He'd need it if he ever hoped to repair Lucindur's enchanted salfio, and contact Kazimir, the only being he knew who'd be familiar with the nuances of whatever existed between Elsewhere and the living world. The instrument's string had been broken by Nesilia's power and required a special type of string created from the hair of a magical beast present only in Glinthaven. An expensive item, requiring a lot of gold they didn't have.

Whitney missed the simplicity of being a thief. Warlocks, demons, other realms—it was all getting ridiculous. But, he'd been there with Sora in that realm between, and he had to get her out. Whatever it took.

Whitney considered stealing something else instead. He was, after all, in a city filled with wonders and people too rich to care if those wonders suddenly went missing, but he wasn't that simple, petty thief any longer. Even if the papers proving he'd been ennobled had been burned by that bastard Darkings, he knew it within him—he was Whitney Fierstown, once Blisslayer, now guardian to a small child and Sora's only hope of salvation.

Water lapped at the side of the boat, the waves creating a dizzying effect as the light of the moons danced across the surface. It was quiet. Although, for this side of Lake Yaolin, this late at night, it wasn't unexpected.

"It's about time to put your small size to our advantage, young Gentry," Whitney said. "You see that little porthole?"

"You do not mean for me to climb through there, do you?" Gentry asked.

"That is precisely what I mean for you to do. Then, once you're in, you need to find a way to get me in."

Gentry looked around like he was being surrounded by monsters. "There has to be another way. We did not even look."

"Do you expect a ladder and an open door?" Whitney laughed.

"What about the street?" Gentry asked. "Perhaps there *is* a door."

"And risk being spotted by the guards? Gentry, I didn't make it this far as the 'World's Greatest Thief' by getting caught."

It wasn't exactly true. Whitney had been caught and imprisoned more times in the past year than all his days combined. Not that he'd told Gentry all those stories, not yet. The Pompares had tasked him with looking after the boy. It was better to have his undeniable trust.

"This is the way in without being seen from the streets," Whitney assured him. "And here I thought you wanted to learn the ways of the world."

"I… I do, Mr. Fierstown, but I do not think I am capable of such an act," Gentry said.

Whitney waved his hand in dismissal. "I've seen you tumble around on stage better than anyone else in the troupe. I'm beyond confident in your ability to do this. Now, less talking and more climbing."

Whitney grabbed an oar and started paddling toward the ship.

A shiver ran through him that had nothing to do with the chill in the air. In an instant, the sky turned black, the sea a sickly shade of crimson. As close as they were to shore, Whitney could hardly see the city anymore. All torchlight was gone, leaving only darkness as if he were in a cave, alone, at night.

In the distance, he saw a wianu like the one from Elsewhere—

the colossal sea creature's countless tentacles and teeth sharper than any blade. Looking back, Whitney couldn't see Gentry either. Pressure under the water fought each pull of his oar, like it was hitting something solid. Whitney gripped the oar tighter. Fear, like a thousand snakes, constricted his chest.

"Mr. Fierstown?" The voice was far off, distant.

Forms rose from the midst of the water. Dark shapes wavering just beneath the surface. Specters floating in the deep. The dead in their realm. They closed in on Whitney, growing, then shrinking —ebbing, then flowing. In and out. Up and down. Whitney felt an odd sensation of longing. Longing for the darkness. The cold, wet, crimson sea beckoning him forward. If he would only take the plunge, he would be where he belonged once more.

He could be home.

I have no home…

A sound gurgled within him and then without, like a swarm of locusts on his father's farm. It festered in his ears and pounded in his chest, battling with his thumping heart for dominance. Then he realized, it wasn't buzzing… not humming. They were whispers. Whispering his name. Calling for him. Drawing him in. Deeper. Deeper.

The shapes gathered beneath him. Purple, sallow skin, vile, yet inviting, reaching out to him. They wanted him, and he wanted nothing more than to let them take him.

Overwhelming loneliness poured over him. He felt every hurt, every pain that ever was. He felt as if they'd take it all from him, like those shapes would take away the anguish of losing Sora yet again, the knowledge that he was the reason she was lost deep within her own mind, tormented by Nesilia, the Buried Goddess. They'd take from him the memories of his parents, and Rocco's death because of Whitney's impulsiveness in Elsewhere. Fake as that had been, it felt real to him.

As they drifted closer to him in the inky black, their indistinct faces took shape within the murky water. He saw the Black Sandsman he'd killed in Troborough, and every other man and woman who'd died because of him, whether directly by his hand or not.

And then he saw his mother.

Lauryn Fierstown. Beautiful, loving, kindhearted Lauryn stared back at him. Her milky white eyes bored into his. Pleading. A plump arm stretched out for him, and his heart banged harder around in his chest. Her voice called out his name in a low, mournful wail. He could smell pie, blueberry and ginger, apple and cheese…

Whitney felt himself drifting. It was so much like it had been with Sora, lost in the recesses of her mind, but even that thought was merely a sliver of a memory—so far out of reach.

Without warning, his mother vanished beneath the surface. Bubbles gurgled up as he cried out, grasping for her, feeling the water with one hand, but his other… something was holding it. Pulling him.

Mother!

"Mr. Fierstown!" The voice came again, louder this time. Closer. "Mr. Fierstown."

Whitney snapped back to reality. His head pounded. Sweat soaked him as if he'd fallen in.

"Mr. Fierstown, are you okay?" Gentry asked.

He'd been there: the Sea of Souls in Elsewhere, with Kazimir and the strange old geezer called the Ferryman. Cold, purple hands reaching up from the blood-colored waters, always grasping but never obtaining their goal. It was just like the place itself. Whitney had spent six long years there, always grasping, always trying to escape, always trying to learn a lesson that never truly came. Or perhaps it had…

"Gentry, I'm…" Whitney lost his train of thought. He clutched at his chest and the racing heart within.

"It's okay, Mr. Fierstown," Gentry said. "You do this at night sometimes."

The words came as a shock. Whitney knew he dreamed of the place, but never that he'd showed signs of it.

"Okay, well. Enough of that, don't you think?" Whitney said, wiping his brow with the hood of his cloak and forcing a smile. Their little boat was now almost directly beneath the galleon-like structure and drifting. Whitney used the oar against the wood to steady them.

Out of his peripherals, he saw Gentry eyeing him, but Whitney ignored the pitying glance. He laughed and said, "Looks like something Gold Grin would cruise around in."

"Who is *Gold Grin*?" Gentry asked.

Whitney clapped his hands together, thankful for the distraction. "Oh, sweet, innocent Gentry. Sweet, sweet, child. Grisham "Gold Grin" Gale is only the world's most renowned pirate—besides yours truly, of course."

"You? A pirate?" Gentry asked, head cocked to the side incredulously.

"For a time! The best there was. I'm credited for stealing The Sea Hawk right out from under that big brute's nose. Left him with another ship, mind you. I'm not a monster."

"Wow." All the boy's concern washed away and was replaced by the genuine sense of awe that Gentry reserved for when Whitney told him of his many adventures. He was the anti-Sora, who would just roll her eyes and assume Whitney lied about everything.

It had been too long since anyone took interest in Whitney's great moments. It felt good. Possibly too good.

Then, it felt equally awful when Whitney considered how much he'd give to see one of Sora's eye rolls again. He subconsciously rubbed at the spot on his arm where she'd always punch him whenever he said something foolish. He'd give anything to feel that mild sting again, too—all the treasures he'd ever stolen.

Whitney cleared his throat. "Alright, up we go. Those slats will be perfect handholds."

The enormous ship rose at a steep angle, and it would be difficult for anyone to scale, but Whitney didn't mention that. Gentry was a pro. He'd make short work of the climb, be inside, and find a way for Whitney to join him in no time at all. Otherwise, Whitney never would have taken him on as a companion. He had an eye for talent. Always had.

Whitney boosted Gentry, holding him high above his head. Immediately, the kid had his fingers and toes finding every crack in the ship's facade with practiced ease. It was a thing to behold.

"Got it!" Gentry whisper-shouted down as he reached the porthole and began squeezing in.

Keeping one eye on the streets above, hoping no Glass soldiers were roaming about, Whitney watched Gentry until he made it inside. Once the kid's foot disappeared into the dark hole, it was just a matter of waiting.

He let himself plop onto the boat's bench, and did the only thing he could manage to do lately. He thought about Sora. Wondered where she was, how he was going to get to her, and what he would do once he did. He thought until darker possibilities crept in. Like, what if she was already lost, and Nesilia already had taken over? What if there was no way out of her prison of darkness. What if—

"Aye! You there!" The voice nearly startled Whitney into the water. Amber, flickering light washed over his boat from above. "What are you doing?"

A Glass soldier stood, bright lantern in hand. Whitney had been so distracted in his thoughts he hadn't been paying attention.

Squinting, forearm raised against the light, Whitney said, "I— uh. Fishing! Still no crime against that, right?"

"It's past midnight! Where's your net?"

"In the water… where a net ought to be when fishing."

"Don't get smart with me, you whelp."

Just then, Gentry's head popped out from the porthole above.

"Yes sir, Mr. Guard, sir," Whitney said loudly as a warning to Gentry. "Though I've been accused of many things, smart has never been one of them. Just trying to feed my family."

"Well, do it during the day. Eerie things going on around here lately. The Governor wants the city clear at night. Go home, now. If you're here when I come back round, it'll be trouble for you." The guard didn't even wait for Whitney to respond before he turned back to the road.

Whitney breathed a sigh of relief and held up a finger to Gentry, urging him to wait until the guard had fully moved on.

The moment Whitney lowered his hand, Gentry said, "Mr. Fierstown, there's a hatch at the top of the ship."

"The top of the…" Whitney sighed again and shook his head. "What about the front door?"

"But the guards…"

"You opening the door from the inside, and us breaking in are very different things, Gentry!" Whitney was whispering through clenched teeth.

"Oh… I… Hold on." The boy's head disappeared through the porthole, and a moment later, Whitney was left alone again.

"Who doesn't check the front door?" Whitney groaned to himself.

Whitney rolled his neck and his eyes as he started rowing toward the retention wall. It was rough-hewn stone, which made climbing a cinch. When he reached the top, he peered over, searching for any sign of the guard or others. When he was sure they were alone, Whitney threw himself over the ledge and made for the front of the ship, only the front was less a ship and more a storefront with tables and chairs, benches and a fence. It looked like a proper pub with an outdoor seating area built into the low bluff. Like something eccentric he'd have seen in Winde Port before the Drav Cra and the Shesaitju leveled the place.

Parts of the building were clearly still under construction. Bits of wood and steel lay around the patio. Hammers, pry bars, and other tools as well. The door cracked open a hair and Whitney could see the white of Gentry's eye.

"It looks as if it is still under construction," he said as he opened the door fully. "I do not understand how this is where you buried this treasure."

The interior was tremendous. A bar lined the entire back, with two levels of seating extended from it within the shape of a warship's hull. The shelves were up, but no liquor or ale stocked yet, unfortunately. After the horrors he'd relived on the lake, Whitney could use a drink.

Nigh'jels—Shesaitju apparatuses, globes with little bioluminescent jellyfish swirling around within—hung from the balconies. Fish tanks lined all the walls, teeming with life. Above the fish tanks, the walls were all adorned with skulls and bones, as well as a variety of weaponry from all over Pantego. In the center, there was even a titanic circular tank stretching floor to ceiling like a column, with a small shark swimming inside. Flags hung from the ceiling at regular intervals, all black and depicting the images of chipped skulls with blood leaking from their eyesockets and mouths.

Whitney snickered. "Taking this pirate motif seriously."

"Huh?" Gentry said.

"Nothing. There used to be a garden here," Whitney said, looking at a spot on the wood floor. "Trees. Flowerbeds, tall grasses. Just over the edge, where that uhm… gilded naked mermaid statue is, there was a cave entrance. It was narrow and looked like an animal burrow carved into the side of the cliff face, but you wouldn't believe what was inside.

"What was it?" Gentry asked. His eyes were saucer-wide and even in the darkness, sparkled with intrigue.

"Well, it was… uh… a big cave. It's not important *what* it was as much as how out of place it was. I'm sure no one had been there before or since. Spanned the whole underground of this side of Panping like some kind of secret city."

"It was empty?"

"As far as I could tell at the time. I'd explored, but it was beyond huge. Looked like the perfect place to hide something valuable."

"I still do not understand why you would steal these things just to hide them."

"Anyone can obtain stuff, Gentry. And anyone can get rich doing it. This was about the thrill."

"But it helps nobody underground."

"It's helping us now, isn't it? I've sold plenty, trust me. Some men like to lock their treasures up in a vault. I prefer to spread mine out so nobody can rob me back. Anyway, I don't need to justify myself to a kid. Life is all about experiences. I thought the Glintish knew this."

"I suppose," Gentry said.

Whitney surveyed the room. He could estimate that the statue indeed rested upon the ledge, but a wood paneled floor now covered it.

"Staircase," Whitney said. "There's got to be one. Split up and look around."

It was difficult to focus on locating a staircase with so many amazing things lining the walls. Inside, the place reminded Whitney of Gold Grin's ship even more than the exterior had. Elaborate wooden cornice joined the walls to the tall ceiling above, complete with golden brackets. The balcony of the upper floor, too, was intricately carved from what appeared to be a single piece of wood on each side.

"Over here!" Gentry called. "Stairs!"

Whitney tore his focus away long enough to see the boy at the far end of the room. Joining him, they stared down into darkness below.

"Wait," Gentry said as Whitney started down. "We cannot just go in there. What if something dangerous is down there?"

"In the cellar?" Whitney laughed, then turned.

"Seriously, Mr. Fierstown."

Whitney exhaled slowly, then crossed the room and dragged a chair back to the wall. He let it make a long, groaning sound just to accentuate the action. Stepping up, he reached out and snagged a short sword on display, stepped down, moved the chair again, and grabbed a short bow and a quiver of arrows. Finally, he snatched two crossed daggers from plaques on the walls. The daggers appeared Breklian in design, dark metal with sweeping blades like dragon teeth. The sword was gilded, almost like it was only ornamental, but the weight felt right.

It felt good to have daggers again. With all that had been going on, Whitney had been forced to leave the few weapons they'd brought with them at the city gates. Apparently, the Glass Kingdom's Governor had grown strict since the Shesaitju rebellion began. Yaolin had been a peaceful city last time Whitney visited, with remarkably little crime. Now, only sworn Glass Soldiers were permitted to openly carry blades in the city.

He couldn't complain, seeing the beauties he now had his hands on. A part of him considered leaving right then and there with more of the weapons on display, but if Lucindur was right about the value of her salfio strings, he'd need a lot more. A chest of gold and jewels even. Besides, he didn't crave that thrill anymore. Selling a dozen weapons plucked out of a public place was surer to get him caught than one extremely rare item. He wouldn't do Sora any good locked up again.

"Are they real?" Gentry asked. "Not just decoration?"

"I think so. Sharp as any I've held," Whitney said, handing Gentry the short sword. "Good?"

Gentry waved the blade in the air a bit and nodded.

After slinging the bow and quiver over his shoulder, Whitney tucked the daggers into his belt and said, "Are we ready now?" He didn't wait for a reply before descending.

Darkness hit him like a fist, momentarily sending him back into the place he'd just been—souls screaming to him from Elsewhere. The feeling passed much quicker this time. He'd been out of Elsewhere for so long now, he wondered why he was now being affected so much by it.

C'mon Whitney, he told himself. *Just buckle down and save her, or you'll never hear the end of it when you both reach Elsewhere.*

As they descended, the only light was Celeste's bright light which poured in through more portholes, painting the stairwell orange, then even that was absent.

"We should have brought Aquira," Gentry whispered.

"And who else would be around to protect Lucy and Talwyn?" Whitney replied, inwardly cursing himself that the boy was right, but things were easier in a city under watch without a wyvern on your shoulder. Plus, she hadn't been herself ever since the Drav Cra muzzled her. She'd been listless, jaded, and Whitney was damned if he allowed Sora's favorite pet to get taken away from him if they were caught.

"Still, how are we supposed to see?" Gentry said, his tone betrayed the tremble of fear.

"What are you, afraid of the dark? Torches get thieves caught."

"You said it's empty."

"I said it *was* empty."

Gentry gave him a pleading look.

Whitney stifled a groan. "Wait here." He crept back upstairs to the bar, broke a nigh'jel lantern off the wall, and hurried back down. "There, happy?"

He noticed Gentry nod out of the corner of his vision.

"Always a cheap solution around the corner," Whitney said. "Let's go."

The lower level was like any other in the realm. It reminded Whitney of the Twilight Manor's storeroom, or even the cellar where he and Gentry had stayed in Grambling. There was nothing intricate or elaborate, just raw wood walls and dust. Lots of dust.

Pushing past crates, barrels, and other supplies, they reached the back wall. The wood construction butted right up against the cliff face and there, in the center of it all, was a boarded-up hole that Whitney knew very well.

"Ah-hah!" Whitney exclaimed. "As I said." He then dug his fingers under the planks and pulled, but nothing happened. Then he took a step back and appraised the situation.

Whitney put down the lantern. "Back up and give me your sword."

"What are you going to do? You can't just—"

Gentry's objection was disturbed by Whitney snatching the sword from his grip. Then, the loud *thunk* of the pommel against wood.

"Wow, that's solid." Whitney lifted and tried again, to no avail. On the third strike, he heard a small crack. It took a dozen more strikes before the pommel broke through. He shoved the blade through, held it longways, and used it like a pry bar to snap the wood further.

"Help me," he panted.

Gentry shoved his fingers through and pulled another plank. Then another. Soon they stared into a deep, cavernous hole. If the cellar appeared dark, this was the abyss. Whitney glanced down at Gentry, eyes wide with fright. He returned the sword to him, knowing how much safer it always made him feel, having a weapon to defend himself. Gentry took it back gratefully.

"You know, us bringing weapons all but guarantees we'll have to use them," Whitney said. "It's sort of how the world works."

"Yes, Mr. Fierstown," Gentry answered, his voice small and quavering.

"All right, then in we go."

Gentry carried the green lantern. It was a good thing too because, without it, they wouldn't have been able to see anything inside the caverns. The passages weren't wide, though not claustrophobia-inducing, yet. They curved up into a natural arch above them. Thick stalactites hung beyond it, many times reaching the floor like columns.

Whitney followed close behind, squeezing between one such pillar and the wall. Wet, dirty perspiration coated his back as he dragged it along the stone. Cold and damp, it reminded Whitney of Bliss's lair. A frozen finger traced the length of his spine.

Come on, Whit. Get it together. Things had been simpler back before he'd seen all the horrors of the world and beyond it. So much simpler.

"Are you sure you're okay, Mr. Fierstown?" Gentry whispered. His voice wavered slightly, but Whitney didn't know if it was still from fear or the air, growing more frigid with each step.

"Yes. Yes. I'm fine. Just fine. Watch out for that puddle." A long line of water seeped in through a crack above like a tiny river. It reflected the light of the lantern, momentarily illuminating the area brighter than before. Specks in the rock bounced the light as well, creating a prism of color that cut through the green nigh'jel wash.

They left the steady drip behind them and cut a turn to the

right. It was one of several they'd taken, and it all looked relatively the same.

"How do you know where we're going?" Gentry asked

Whitney pointed to his head. "Mind like a steel trap. It really shouldn't be much farther."

They ducked into a hole, which now did threaten to bring on the panic of being enclosed in a tight space. The last time Whitney had done something like this, there were sticky webs and soft, red blisters filled with transparent little spider babies.

Whitney cleared his throat and his mind and said, "Do you miss them?" His voice echoed within the tunnel.

"Who?" Gentry replied.

"The Pompares," Whitney said. He was the last person on Pantego to offer wisdom regarding parental figures, but the question had been ignored for so long. Someone ought to ask.

"Do I miss the back of Fadra's hand?" Gentry scoffed. There was a bite in his words that Whitney found all too familiar.

He'd spent years using that precise tone when discussing Rocco's effect on his life. As far as Whitney had removed himself from them, their real deaths, dying from the sullied water supply, had had a more profound impact than he was willing to admit out loud. He now realized he blamed himself, though he didn't exactly know why. Chances are, he'd have died from the same thing had he stayed in Troborough, but after taking care of his fake mother for so long in Elsewhere, he couldn't help but wonder if he could've made a difference.

But above everyone he left in Fake Troborough, the face that stuck with him, the moment that burned itself into his mind, was when Young Whitney broke Sora's heart by leaving.

"She loved you," Whitney said, wondering if he was telling himself that or Gentry.

A moment passed between them, splashes and trickles filling the silence before Gentry said, "I do not want to talk about this."

Whitney knew he was pushing it. Who did he think he was, anyway? *You tell jokes. Leave the mushy stuff to someone who isn't an emotional carriage wreck.* "Okay, fine. Yeah. You're right. Look, up there. That's the turn, I think."

The light from the lantern bounced as Gentry crawled behind Whitney, making it difficult for him to see his hand placement. It didn't really matter anymore; they were both already soaked and dripping from the many puddles.

Finally, the tunnel opened into a cylindrical, vertical shaft, taller than it was wide. Whitney groaned as he rose, making a vain attempt to brush off his pants. Light filtered in through a grate that opened up into Panping. Once, Whitney tried to figure out where it led, but the best he could track it was to a large temple that had once been for Ghenuah, the Panpingese God of Dark Nights. It was said he was the patron god of thieves, murderers, and debauchers of all kinds.

Of all the gods and goddesses Whitney had met, why couldn't Ghenuah have been among them?

There's still time, Whitney mused.

The ground was covered in feathers. Thanks to the lantern, they only appeared green, but Whitney thought he could see the subtle shimmer of a familiar liquid on them.

"Is that blood?" Gentry asked.

"Just chicken blood, I think.Feathers too." Many of the temples within the city were known for fowl sacrifices. As Whitney said it, they heard echoing voices jabbering in Panpingese. A second later, they were hit with buckets of liquid. Whitney looked up just in time to get splattered in the face. He wiped away the iron-tinged substance from his eyes and was met with a load of feathers floating down.

"Gross," he said, flapping his hands to dismiss some of the blood. He looked at Gentry, who had a bright white feather hanging from his nose. Whitney snickered, and they both collapsed into a fit of laughter. Then Whitney realized someone above might hear and said, "Shhhh."

He motioned to a ledge and a small alcove not ten feet above them. No ladders were leading there, but it was an easy climb after Whitney boosted Gentry up. He made for the back of the alcove, then patted through a pile of loose rock and dirt, found something soft, and grinned.

"Ah, my child," Whitney said airily.

"That's it? It's just a… a what?"

"This, young Gentry, is an enchanted robe belonging to a council member of the Mystic Order." He flapped the fabric to reveal a yellow robe with bright ornamental markings, radiant even in the darkness. If only Sora could have seen him now. He knew every time he brought up one of his hidden treasures, she thought him exaggerating. Or everyone else who'd ever said to him, "If you have that, where is it?" or, "Why not sell it?"

This is why! My own personal bank, stored around the world.

"That's going to be worth enough for Lucindur to restring her salfio?" Gentry asked, clearly unimpressed with what appeared, on the outside, to be only an overly extravagant robe. Whitney wasn't sure what it did, or how it worked, but he knew it was legitimate; plucked from the private vault beneath the mansion of a family with mystics dating back centuries.

"To the right buyer," Whitney said, still marveling at the enchanted robe.

"How will we find the right buyer?"

"Glassmen love their trinkets from defeated cultures. We'll be able to hold an auction for this thing if we wanted."

"That sounds more than a little bit dangerous," Gentry said. "What if someone just tries to… take it?"

Whitney draped the robe over his shoulder and let his hand fall to one of his new daggers. "Just you let them." He grinned. "Alright, now let's get on."

A low rumble rose just beneath the pitter-patter trickle of poultry blood still dripping through the metal grate above.

Whitney stopped at the edge, turning away from the vertical shaft and said, "Hungry?"

"Huh?"

"Your stomach is growling. I should've remembered food. It won't be lon—"

"That wasn't my stomach," Gentry interrupted.

A dozen sharp snarls drew Whitney's attention back to the feather-laden cavern. From the tunnel they'd entered, came a veritable army of hawk-faced beasts. They appeared to be half-man, half-bird, and wet-looking feathers glistened in the lantern's glow.

"Shog in a barrel." He'd seen grimaurs in person, but only ever in cages owned by curiosities dealers. They were considered rare, frightened of men, and deadly when cornered.

"M-M-Mr. Wh-Wh-Whitney," Gentry stuttered. "G-Grimaurs."

Of course, Gentry knew what they were. They hailed from the mountains surrounding his homeland and were way too far south —and in way too big a grouping. Whitney had never heard of more than a handful being spotted in the ridges of the Pikebacks by hunters after their down feathers and other rare body parts. They weren't known to gather.

Each one had a long, sharp beak extending from their predatory faces. Their feathered wings doubled as arms, almost like Aquira, and their legs and arms ended in razor-sharp talons the length of a man's forearm even though they were each only half Whitney's height.

"Get your sword ready," Whitney told Gentry as he pulled out his new short bow.

"What do they want?" Gentry asked, all his nerves from earlier seeming to have returned in full force.

"I don't know, but I don't want to find out either."

They stared up at Whitney with narrow yellow eyes. One let out an ear-piercing shriek, like a dying galler bird, and the others joined in. As Whitney watched, he neglected to consider the space above them. A grimaur's head lowered right into his field of view. Without even a second thought, as if he'd trained for it his whole life, Whitney snatched an arrow from his quiver, nocked the bow, and let the missile go. It caught the beast right through the eye and its corpse careened down and into the mass below.

The hoard protested with high-pitched vehemence. They made their way as one, clambering over one another to reach the alcove. With what Whitney knew of the creatures, none of it added up. These ones, the look in their eyes, they seemed rabid.

"Ready?" Whitney asked.

"I'm scared," Gentry replied.

"Me too."

Whitney fired down, one arrow after another. Most of them maimed or killed the smaller grimaurs, providing a bit of extra time, but the sheer number of them spelled out death. One, large and ugly, screeched toward him and sliced the bow in two with a fierce talon swipe. Whitney bashed it in the head with one of the bow halves, then drew both saw-toothed daggers, and planted his feet.

A grimaur peeked over the ledge and Gentry stabbed forward. It didn't die, but if fell backward, knocking a few more down with it.

"Good strike!" Whitney celebrated. "Try and hit it next time."

Another popped up, and Whitney drove his boot into its beak, it went down, but another grabbed his ankle and yanked. Whitney slipped, falling to his rear and bouncing before getting dragged forward. He kicked with his other foot, desperate to relieve himself of the thing's grip. Whitney closed his eyes, screamed, and slashed like a madman with his weapons.

An exasperated wheeze sounded, and hot blood sprayed his

face. He stopped moving. When he opened his eyes, he saw Gentry removing his short sword from where it was buried hilt-deep in the grimaur's skull.

"I hit it," he said.

"You sure did." Whitney scrabbled backward and got to his feet. He regarded the passage where grimaurs continued to gather. There was a demonic quality to them, reminding Whitney of when Elsewhere opened up to that horde of dark creatures and the wianu.

"Gentry, I'm not going to lie," he said. "This doesn't look good."

The kid stood, sword in hand, trembling.

"I've told you once: I have a great plan for the day I die, and this isn't it either," Whitney went on. "We're going to do something stupid. Are you ready?"

Whitney tore his gaze from the monsters long enough to see Gentry nodding.

"Right. Good. On the count of three, we are going to run, and jump over that mess. Bend your knees when you land, you hear? It'll be just like one of your shows. Got it?"

"Uh-huh," Gentry said, then swallowed audibly. "Yes, Mr. Fierstown."

Whitney quickly checked to make sure no more were close to reaching the ledge, then backed up, pulling Gentry with him. "Hold this." He handed Gentry the mystic's robe, then sheathed his daggers so he could take the boy's hand.

"One… Two…"

"Mr. Fierstown, I do not thin—" Gentry didn't have a chance to finish.

"Three!"

Whitney kicked the nigh'jel lantern at the beasts, distracting them with food in the form of the poor jellyfish within. It went dark almost instantly. Then he pulled Gentry along and, together, they leaped. His shoulder holding Gentry wrenched back and stung with pain. He wasn't sure why, but he expected the boy to be lighter. He lost his grip, but Gentry was a master acrobat. The momentum was enough for him to flip off, and use the soft, enchanted robe to make a smooth landing behind the grimaurs.

Whitney soared a bit more before falling. Hard. The poultry feathers—which Whitney now knew to belong to these foul beasts—few as they were, did nothing to cushion the impact as Whitney rolled into a rough landing and hit his back on a stalagmite.

Gentry grabbed his hands to help him back up.

"Did you just use the robe!" Whitney scolded.

"You said it's enchanted," Gentry replied.

Whitney bit back a response. There was no time to impart to the boy that value went hand-in-hand with condition.

The beasts reacted slowly—grimaurs weren't known for their smarts. Otherwise, they would have made use of their claws for more than slashing—but a few turned and snarled. Then, a moment later, the rest.

"Go!" Whitney shouted, and they took off, running through the darkness.

He could hear the grimaurs snapping and screeching behind them, and just as they reached the low tunnel they'd passed through on the way in, a talon raked across Whitney's shoulder blade. He yelped and tumbled, bowling Gentry over with him. Whitney rolled protectively over Gentry and poked and stabbed blindly, only a sliver of light from a gap above providing any ability to see. A grimaur flapped down over them, its talons ready to tear them to pieces.

A man's deep roar filled the hollow before a short, blurry shape barreled through the cramped tunnel. Then, an oversized warhammer crushed the grimaur against the wall. Whitney checked himself, patting all over with his hands. If it hadn't been for their hammer-bashing savior, Whitney would've been ripped to shreds.

"Stay here," Whitney told Gentry. He didn't wait for a response before joining in and helping the newcomer, although the dwarf—for that's what he was—didn't seem to need help.

Whitney made use of his daggers, favoring his uncut arm. He got a few good strikes in, but took another grimaur claw to the same shoulder. The dwarf handled the rest. It wasn't long before the surprise of the attack gave them victory, and the rest of the creatures fled, some even squeezing through the grate above, screeching and afraid.

The dwarf turned to Whitney and raised his hammer to his broad shoulder. "Who ye be and why did ye break into me place?" he asked.

Whitney didn't even have to think about it. He knew that voice as well as he'd have known if it was Sora or Torsten standing before him. For the dwarf was the one person on Pantego whom he was proud to say he'd known for longer—the very same who'd taught him everything he needed to know about fences and thievery the first time he'd visited Winde Port, what felt like ages ago.

"Tum Tum?" Whitney said, incredulous. "Is that really you?"

III

THE KNIGHT

"Sir Unger, are you sure they want us here?" Lucas Danvels asked. His charcoal-colored mule whinnied as a gust of cold wind tore through the canyons. It was stubborn—yet more cooperative than most of its kind.

Torsten sucked in a breath, feeling as though ice lined his lungs. He let it out with an exasperated sigh. They were in the shallow north, far beyond the Jarein Gorge, at one of the passes through the Dragon's Tail Mountains.

Dwarven territory.

Torsten knew these lands. He'd fought in these lands.

King Liam had never shown interest in conquering the dwarven kingdoms, as only men were the children of Iam, and not all Meungor's children were so eager to do business with Iam's ilk, especially a conqueror like Liam.

The dwarven kingdoms were countless, filling caverns and hollows throughout the mountains with their subterranean cities. Torsten thought he knew them all, but every so often, a new king popped up in a new hollow, deeper below ground. When it came to dwarves, only bellies filled with ale and coffers filled with gold concerned them, and the unexplored parts of Pantego always had more riches to find. At the height of the Glass, the kingdom's vast wealth allowed Liam to ally himself with the most powerful of the dwarven kingdoms. They respected a man who could fill a vault. Now, they barely listened.

"I'm not sure of anything," Torsten said.

Lucas' teeth chattered. "We're going to freeze to death out here."

"You're a Shieldsman now. You made the climb of Mount Lister in naught but the clothes on your back. You took the oath. This is nothing."

"I still say we should've brought the army."

Torsten grunted. Since wearing the blessed cloth over his eyes, he no longer wore his glaruium gauntlets. The frequent need to adjust and re-tie the thing, combined with the bulkiness of the gauntlets, had become too frustrating. Now he wore only thin gloves made from zhulong flesh, supposedly tough as iron, but, it still made him feel partially naked.

He did so now, feeling the frost hardening its wrinkles. With that, his ability to see in shades of white and black was blurred. They needed to get inside, and fast, lest he find himself blind again.

They stood on the precipice looking down into a great valley, sharp rocks rising from the snow at steep angles. Across the valley, a giant, stout dwarf was chiseled into the rock face, arm outstretched with a pointed finger. A marker.

Torsten followed it with his eyes and ran his hand along a flattened portion of the cliffside, his thumb tracing the grooves of some manner of ancient dwarven inscription. The way Celeste's light reflected off the snow, Torsten's limited vision didn't allow him to read it. Not that he could've anyway.

"Balonhearth. The Great Mountain. King Logrit Cragrock, Master of the Three Kingdoms," Lucas read.

"Good to see those evenings with Lord Brosch paying off,"

Torsten said. It was kind of the new Master of Rolls to train Sir Danvels. It wasn't often that a Shieldsman was also given the opportunity to become a scholar, but times were changing.

This wasn't Torsten's first trip to the alliance of dwarves at the southern ridge, though he hoped it would be his last.

"The door is right there. Not much of a hiding place," Lucas said.

"Look around you, Sir Danvels. Do you believe you'd have stumbled upon this place by accident?"

"Fair point," Lucas said.

Torsten circled his eyes and whispered, "Iam, we've come this far out of the way. Lives have been lost. Make it worth it."

Torsten banged on Balonhearth's massive door. "This is Sir Torsten Unger, Shieldsman and Master of Warfare of the Glass Kingdom." He struck once more, harder this time, and a clump of snow fell upon his arm. "I request audience with your king!"

"Let's head back, Sir Unger," Lucas said, after a minute or so passed in silence. He fidgeted with the mule's reins. "We outnumber Mak. You said it yourself, we can take him."

"They're dug in," Torsten countered. "A hundred men or a thousand, it won't matter at the White Bridge. And there's no time to waste preparing a siege or requesting reinforcements from Governor Nantby in the East." Philippi Nantby, the man who'd lorded over Yaolin City ever since Liam defeated the mystics, did a fine job maintaining order, but he was insufferable to deal with. A distant third or fourth cousin to the Nothhelms, he liked to imagine that meant more than it did.

Maybe it does. Only one of them remains…

"I haven't seen a dwarf in Yarrington in months," Lucas said, drawing Torsten's attention back to the present. "Maybe they're done."

Torsten couldn't help but worry the kid was right. Relations had been strained between the kingdoms for a long time. The

Crown couldn't afford payments on open trade agreements, or protection in the northwest against Drav Cra raiders. Iam's light, they'd barely found a crew willing to rebuild the crypt after Pi's resurrection. After what happened in Yarrington with the riots, it wouldn't be a far stretch to believe the dwarves had entirely written off the realms of man.

"They'll follow the gold," Torsten said instead, hoping to at least convince Lucas if not himself. "We have that now, thanks to Valin." Those words came out through Torsten's teeth. He sighed again. "If we can secure open use of this pass with King Cragrock's blessing, we can surround Mak, and shipments east to the war front can continue."

I hope, Torsten thought. However, Lucas was exaggerating. Yarrington and other cities in the Glass still had plenty of dwarven citizens who'd left their mountain dwellings behind. In addition, mercenaries, tinkers, and adventurers who swore no allegiance to any kingdoms remained.

"I still believe we should have traveled south through Winde Port and come up north from there," Lucas said.

"And strike further fear into a city which barely stands? Borrow ships they need desperately for repairs? This will work, Lucas. Trust me."

It had to work. Besides, Torsten couldn't very well admit his hesitance to return to Winde Port due to the horrid events that had taken place there at his hand and under his leadership. If he'd been stronger, Muskigo would have died there, and the rebellion would already be over.

The Kingdom needed all the help it could get now to flourish, and the Cragrocks were step one. Yarrington was secured, and Pi was finally safe from snakes in his own garden. Valin Tehr had been removed, and Lord Kaviel Jolly rose as Pi's primary advisor. Sir Mulliner always stayed at the King's side in case of an attack like the one which claimed Oleander. Father Morningweg had received the unanimous vote of every priest in Hornsheim to be named High Priest after word spread of the miracle which returned Torsten's sight and saved the Kingdom from Valin's treachery. A Master of Coin had yet to be decided on, but in times of war, sacrifices had to be made.

Most important: the war was coming to an end.

The siege against Muskigo was finally petering out after most of the afhems in Latiapur had publicly declared their opposition to the rebellion. Somehow, the Caleef still hadn't turned up, though Torsten was now sure Valin had been lying about him. The god-king was likely dead already, drowned by the weight of stones in Autlas' Inlet like so many of Valin's other victims.

Drad Mak had claimed White Bridge with what little remained of his Drav Cra horde. There, he claimed he would kill his captives one at a time until Torsten met him for battle. And so Torsten answered the call, leading a small army of young Shield-smen like Lucas and newly conscripted soldiers. The future of the Kingdom.

When the rebellion comes to an end, and the Glass' rule over the Black Sands is reaffirmed, only then could peace take hold again. Torsten would wipe Mak and his heathen murderers from White Bridge and re-open the Kingdom's primary trading route. Muskigo would then lose, and southern ship routes would open.

"Sir Unger, I—" Lucas began.

"Just be patient!" Torsten's shout carried through the canyon, enveloping them like a cold sheet of ice. A bit of rock clattered down from above. Torsten thrust his hands against the wall. "Sorry. They're just…" His voice trailed off when a low, baritone horn sounded. It came like a rumble from below, then rose gradually.

Lucas' longsword rasped free of its sheath.

"Watch out!" he cried, leaping in front of Torsten and raising his heater shield. A dart plunked off it. The thing was small—too small to be a dwarven arrow. The feathers—waldrooth pharimon —commonly known as grimaur… the same as those which had assailed them in the Yarrington markets.

Something screeched, and Torsten whipped around just in time to bash a creature aside with his fist. The force of his blow sent it soaring against Balonhearth's great door, breaking its neck.

"What in Iam's name is that?" Lucas asked, looking down at the dead thing, its limbs twitching.

"Goblin," Torsten said. "Creatures of the darkness, corrupted by the God Feud."

"I thought them unthinking beasts?" Lucas asked as another darted toward them.

"We can argue their sentience should we survive," Torsten growled as he drew *Salvation* from his back, the sword of Liam Nothhelm. He'd tried to return it to King Pi where it belonged, but the King wanted it in Torsten's hands, the hands of one who knew how to bear it, to bring justice to enemies of the Glass. Torsten felt compelled to oblige even as he cleaved the leaping goblin in two.

"Fall in," Torsten commanded.

Lucas lowered his shield and stepped back to guard Torsten. Together, they kneeled behind it, listening to the clangor as more darts pelted the metal. Celeste's light revealed hunched silhouettes dashing in and out of the nooks and crannies of the massive dwarven effigy carved into the cliffside.

Goblins scurried this way and that, quick as lightning. Hollowed out bones served as blowguns for their darts, which were sure to be coated with the toxin from grimaur talons which rendered muscles numb.

It was true, most people believed goblins to be creatures of the Wildlands—just animals and nothing more. It was a rumor spread far and wide when King Remy sat upon the throne. He believed it would steal away the peoples' fear of the things by reducing them to myth. After King Liam nearly wiped their kind off the map, it hardly mattered. But it seemed something was stirring them once more.

The northern tribes normally stayed deep within the mountains, attacking dwarven miners in the deep and scavenging their outposts. They were, in fact, irksome, primitive creatures. The size of small children, they were like lizards on two legs. If they spoke, it was in chirps and hisses—easy to mistake for animal sounds.

The mule began bucking, sending one of the goblins over the cliffside. Stumbling, the mule and the cart it pulled, nearly followed.

"Don't let the beast fall!" Torsten called out.

Lucas moved to grab hold of the mule's reins and grunted as one of the darts stabbed into the crease of his elbow. His grip on the shield lowered, but Torsten used one hand to stabilize it and wielded *Salvation* in the other. Out of the corner of his vision, he spotted movement and slashed, gutting one of the creatures midair.

Another fell on his shoulder from above. It hacked at his chest with a bone hatchet, but Torsten's glaruium armor protected him. The thing was impossibly fast, avoiding all Torsten's attempts to grab it. In less than a second, it was on his other shoulder, slashing away at a new spot.

"Get back!" Lucas shouted, stabbing at another attacker.

Torsten swung wildly at the goblin, but kept missing.

Suddenly, gears cranked, ice fell in a thick sheet, and the great doors slowly opened. Warm air pumping from dwarven forges gushed out, and a blade of light bloomed across the mountainside. The goblins scattered at the sight of it.

"Back ye vermin!" a dwarf yelled, rushing by Torsten and Lucas. He banged his axe against an iron cooking pot, the *clang* echoing loudly. A few more dwarves followed him, doing the same. The goblins screeched and howled as they retreated. The one on Torsten's shoulder leaned in front of his face, wearing a mask that looked like it belonged to some terrible bird. Torsten saw into its eyes, filled with nothing but darkness. The spawn of evil. Then it leaped off him and clambered up the rock face and out of sight.

Lucas dropped to a knee, panting, and let his shield drop. He tore the dart from his arm and vigorously rubbed the wound.

"Ye'll be fine, laddie," one of the dwarves said as he slapped Lucas on the back. "They make 'em from grimaur toxin, but it'd take a fair bit more of them little darts to take down a man yer size."

Torsten stabbed his sword into the snow, leaning on it to gather his breath. "What were you all waiting for?"

"Never good news when a Shieldsman arrives at our doorstep." The yellow-bearded dwarf stuck out his hand. "Brouben Cragrock, at yer service."

"One of King Logrit's sons?" Torsten asked.

The dwarf nodded, then with a chuckle said, "Some lands, they call that a prince."

"Sir Unger, at yours." Torsten shook his hand. For such a small man, Brouben had a grip like a zhulong jaw. "The Light of Iam shines upon our meeting."

"I say all the gods have shogged off." He and the others started inside without warning.

Torsten looked to Lucas, and they exchanged a nod before following. Lucas patted the mule, took its reins, and led him in, the cart's wheels creaking as he did. The doors had opened just enough for the cart to fit, then slammed shut the moment they were in, earning a stuttering exhalation from Torsten's young ward.

"Sorry bout the goblins," Brouben said as if they were his fault. His voice carried down an impossibly smooth stone hall.

Torsten was larger than most men. He'd often been called a half-giant—a bit of an insult, but that was long before he'd taken up the shield. Big as he was, the immensity of the tunnel system made him feel like a dwarf himself. But wasn't that like the dwarves? Always eager to show off their ingenuity and masonry skills; compensating for their height.

Torsten found it challenging to see with mere torches for light, but he let his blindfolded eyes focus on the gentle bumps and lines along the ground.

"Not the first time dealing with them," Torsten said. "But since when do they venture into the light of day?"

"They been crazed of late," Brouben said. "Last few months. Attacking higher up than usual, in bigger groups than usual. More reckless than usual—ye can imagine that. Ye ain't the first flower-pickers they tried to shuck off on the way up the Dragon's Tail."

"I've not heard a word of that."

"Of course, ye ain't. Ye men are too busy killing each other to worry about us stone folk up here."

"I'm sorry if that's the way you feel," Torsten said. "But I promise, it isn't true. You may not be the Children of Iam, but Meungor refused to betray him in the feud."

"Aye, instead he hid down here." The dwarf laughed. "Meant nothin' by it. Weird things been happenin up north, right about the time those cultists ravaged your city. Right about the Dawning. Ain't been to Yarrington since I was this tall," he raised a flat hand to his already low-to-the-ground hip, "but I was sorry to hear it."

"Thank you," Torsten said, sincerely. "We're doing what we can to recover. With your help—"

"I have a cousin on Daemon's Spike… East Vale, actually. Yer Glintish, aye? Just a stone's throw from yer people."

"I'm from Yarrington," Torsten said, a harsh edge to his tone.

"Whatever ye say. Besides all that, he—my cousin that is—

told me of a shog shuckin grimaur infestation nested in their Great Hall! Loathsome beasts damn near ate half their foodstores."

"Up from the depths?" Lucas asked. "All the stories I read said they'd burrowed into the caverns."

"Usually keep their distance from people too, dwarves or flower-pickers." He shrugged stout shoulders. "Strange, all of it, ye ask me. Just last week, our scouts spotted a flock of somethin flying northeast, full speed. Most say they were wyverns, but I say grimaurs. Just cus the grimarus ain't been seen in a while don't mean they're gone. Most think I'm crazy for thinkin it, but wyverns by the hundreds is crazy, too. And there were hundreds. Ain't seen so many in me life. My father either."

"Goblins, grimaurs… What do you think is causing it?" Torsten asked. He didn't have to, but he did anyway. It was clear, now, that the dark magics performed by Redstar atop Mount Lister hadn't only hurt Yarrington. It'd rippled to the North, stirring monsters forgotten from the older, more violent age of the God Feud.

"Questions like that be for the tinkers," Brouben said. "I just head where the fightin needs me." He stopped at the start of a massive set of stairs and spread his arms wide. "Welcome to Balonhearth, Sir Unger of the Glass."

Torsten noticed Lucas' eyes go wide as the city's Great Hall loomed before them. Columns as thick as thousand-year-old trees rose to the height of the lofty, vaulted space. Behind it, the great hollow within the mountain extended, its sides and bottom carved with homes for the countless citizens. An entire city, underground. Veins of iron shimmered all around in the stone.

Stairs snaked up and down in every direction from the entry chamber. Massive fire basins hung over the sprawl like tiny suns illuminating it all. Carts on tracks zipped all around, using slopes and dips to propel themselves, and allowing dwarves to traverse the districts easily. Some vanished into deeper caverns, down into the mining trenches.

"So, what brings ye to Balonhearth; to me Father's city?" Brouben asked.

"Actually… *he* does. I need to speak with your king," Torsten replied. The sense of awe faded quickly for him, unlike Lucas, whose eyes darted this way and that, a dumb smile staining his face. Torsten had been here before, though years ago, and it was bigger now. The vast hollow had been expanded, and more carved, stacked homes descended into the deep, into the shadows.

"And here I hoped ye were just weary travelers desirin a samplin of dwarven hospitality."

"I wish that could be said."

"As ye can imagine," Brouben said, not skipping a beat, "with all the yiggin strangeness going on in this place, the King's very busy."

"And I'm not here to waste his time. Lucas." The boy was too busy staring at the city to move. "Lucas," Torsten said a second time, nudging him in the side.

"Sir?" Lucas said, snapping out of it.

Torsten gestured to the mule's cart, and Lucas hurried to it and threw back the tarp, revealing a chest with the seal of Valin Tehr: a bushel of grapes.

Brouben's eyes lit up. "Well, why didn't ye say so. This way, Sir Unger."

They were led toward a wood-and-iron track running alongside the main staircase. This one was bigger, meant for more than mining carts. Torsten heard it before he saw it: a wooden platform powered by two burly dwarves working a seesaw apparatus twice their size.

"Up ye go," Brouben said, waving them along.

Torsten followed, but he could hear Lucas swallow audibly. "It'll be fine," Torsten told him.

"I'm not worried about me…" He patted the mule and urged it up onto the platform. The thing gave more than a little resistance, neighing and tossing its head, but eventually, Lucas managed to load both it and the cart. A dwarf locked the gate, and before anyone said a word, the platform took off.

Torsten's stomach dropped as the track curved around a column, then led them so close to one of the hanging basins, he could feel the heat of the flames. There really was no end to dwarven ingenuity, even though he couldn't understand why they made it so hard on themselves. Bridges were strung between clumps of houses carved into stalactites. To Torsten, used to the disciplined order of Yarrington's streets, it all seemed like chaos.

The platform cut sharply. The mule stumbled, and Lucas grabbed onto Torsten's arm like a child riding a horse for the first time. He promptly coughed and removed it, and Torsten thought it best not to draw attention and embarrass the kid. Instead, he watched a group of dwarven miners in a square down below, burning a pile of goblins who'd clearly ventured too far beyond their home. Now it was his turn to cough, but for a much different reason. The smell was intolerable, like seared hair mixed with goat shog.

"Embarrassing," Brouben said, waving a hand in front of his nose.

They turned again, headed straight toward a colossal statue of a dwarf's head bearing a winged helm—the crown of Balonhearth and the Three Kingdoms. An intricately carved beard fell down from his broad chin. Torsten felt as if he could make out each individual hair in the curls that cascaded down a stalactite. As if supplying life to the whole city, fresh water—likely melting snow from the peaks above—ran from a slit just below the statue's open mouth and pooled prodigiously in a pit below. The track passed through the mouth and stopped within a wide, domed chamber.

Rising in intervals, thick columns along the edge were

sculpted in the form of Meungor the Sharp Axe, god of the dwarves and lesser giants. Each one hoisted a battle-axe to support the ceiling.

Just as Torsten had been in the city before, he'd also stood before this throne. And, as remembered, Clan Cragrock couldn't help but display their wealth in ludicrous fashion. Curled like a sleeping dog, the skeleton of a dragon wrapped the circumference of the circular room. Its spine—each vertebra a step—from its long pointed tail to its head served as the path up to the throne where an oversized seat forged of iron and festooned with gold etchings sat between two curved horns. The skull faced the entry, each fang as tall as Torsten and just as wide. A fire basin crackled within its fearsome jaws, sending plumes of smoke billowing from its nostrils.

And beyond the cage of its ribs was a barred gate into the Iron Bank itself, guarded by four dwarves in spiked armor. These were no ordinary dwarves. The clanbreakers were specially trained with the sole purpose of defending the Three Kingdoms and the Iron Bank, and no one knew how many of them there were.

Within the Iron Bank, amongst all his gold, iron, and jewels, the King made his home, like a greedy dragon in the stories of yesteryear. Hoarding. Possessed by riches. Straight through the gates, encased in an altar shaped like Meungor's axe, rested the greatest of all riches, a red stone that glowed so bright, it was said that staring at it could blind a man. The Brike Stone. The solidified heart of the dragon he sat upon, said to be the last ever to soar through the skies of Pantego.

"Sir Torsten Unger, is that ye?" King Lorgit Cragrock asked. His voice was soft, weathered by time. As he rose from his chair, he groaned. The dwarves lived a long time, but Lorgit had lived longer than most. A long, gray beard unfurled down to his waist, partially obscuring glinting chainmail emblazoned with the symbol of his kingdom, an iron watchtower split by an axe. Every link in his armor was crafted from gold—not a very strong material, but with the clanbreakers standing guard, it was doubtful the King would see any trouble unless he went looking for it. His winged helm, also gold—and likely worth as much as the Glass Castle—sat crooked atop his head.

Now there's a crown Whitney should have stolen, Torsten thought to himself, against his better judgment.

Finally, a vermillion cape wrapped once around his throat and trailed behind him. Torsten noted the different fabrics sewn onto its end. The dwarves had a custom: when a battle was won, the losing king would be required to forfeit a portion of his train to be added to the victor's. King Lorgit's train was very long, indeed.

King Lorgit strolled down the dragon's back, taking his time and letting each agonizing step fall ever so carefully. Yet another thing about dwarves Torsten couldn't stand: they were never in a hurry to accomplish anything. From rebuilding the Royal Crypt to their own mines, they knew how to milk payment, chiseling away, perfecting every little detail beyond the scrutiny of even the most well-trained eye.

"It's me, Your Highness." Once the King had made it all the way down, Torsten struck his chest and bowed his head. Lucas fell to a knee, an action that would have been customary before a Glass King, but Torsten gave him a kick to stand. Dwarves saw it as an insult from men; forcing themselves to a dwarf's height.

"Been too long, old friend!" He grabbed Torsten and pulled him close. Very little of the old man's face showed behind his beard and bushy brows, but what was there was wrinkled as centuries-old leather. He had kind eyes for a conqueror, though it had been many years since he'd waged war against his brothers and seized control of the three great subterranean cities.

"Too long, indeed," Torsten said.

"What's this?" The handsy king flicked Torsten's blindfold. For a moment, it rose above one of his eyes, and Torsten was thrust into darkness. Torsten straightened his back and readjusted it.

"A gift from Iam," Torsten said. "Helps me see."

"Ye a priest now?" King Lorgit asked, then with a laugh, said, "Father Unger?"

"Shieldsman, he claims," Brouben chimed in. "Never seen a knight who blinds himself though."

"His natural vision was stolen from him by unholy magic," Lucas said. All heads snapped toward the boy like they'd forgotten he was there. Lucas cleared his throat and continued, "The… uh… blindfold was blessed by our new High Priest, and offers sight."

"That true?" King Lorgit said. He leaned up on the balls of his feet to get a better look at it like he was evaluating a newly discovered vein of gold.

"In a way," Torsten said, pulling away. "But that's not why I'm here."

"Straight to business!" King Lorgit laughed, then patted Torsten on the back. "Always with ye flower-pickers. Come, let's sit. Been a long time since these old bones hoisted an axe."

"Shog shuckin lucky for our enemies," Brouben remarked.

King Lorgit led Torsten toward the dragon's ribs. "Who's the kid?" he whispered.

"A new recruit," Torsten said. "We have many these days after… well, everything."

"I can imagine. I was heart broke to hear news of Liam dyin, and now his beautiful wife. I would've come for the funerals, but aye, I ain't one for travelin these days."

"I understand," Torsten said. "And so does the Crown."

"I trust the crew I sent ye to fix yer Royal Crypt performed as expected? 'Twas me own ancestors built that place, ye know. I'd hate to see ye men let it rot." He chortled.

"Payment was difficult, but the job got done."

"I hope that's not why yer here—" His voice cut off abruptly and his breath became labored.

"Father," Brouben interrupted. He hurried forward and helped lower his father onto one of the dragon bones, positioning Lorgit's long cape so it wouldn't catch on anything.

Just then, the doors to the Iron Bank swung open and a new face entered.

"Father!" the newcomer said, deeply concerned.

"I'm fine, Al," the King said, then he exhaled as he made himself comfortable. "Sir Unger, this be me other son, Alfot-drumlin—ye can call him Al."

Torsten dipped his head respectfully.

"I understand the difficulties yer kingdom has been through," the King continued. "Dead Kings, rebels, those paler-faced north-erners, but ye know better than anyone. If ye can't pay, we can't help ye. That goes for any of ye flower-pickers comin here with shallow promises."

Torsten's eyes would have narrowed if they could. He took a seat next to the king and said, "Has another of us come here?"

"Yuri Darkings came, oh… three months past. Beggin the help of my army, but only on the promise of future wealth." His laugh, punctuated by a sharp cough, echoed across the throne room. "Can ye believe it? A loan, like we'd be trustin a man who betrayed his own."

"Bastard…" Torsten grumbled. He couldn't wait to end this rebellion and get his hands on the man who'd killed Wardric and freed the Caleef. He was about to scold the dwarf for not informing the Crown about those talks, then realized that Yuri offering on promised wealth meant he didn't have much at hand. And it also meant that he was without the full support of the Black Sandsmen, who were often too stubborn to ever ask for help from others. The Shesaitju certainly had the wealth to recruit mercenaries if they wanted to.

"That's why yer here, ain't it?" King Lorgit asked after a brief silence. "To *borrow* a chunk of me army, same way Liam loved to do."

Torsten sighed. "Am I so transparent?"

"Yer kind always are. But ye can't hardly pay for repairs to a crypt. I be glad we have peace, but me and Liam—we had our deals. This new king… just a kid… don't know Liam's son, don't know a soul on his Council, savin yerself and Kaviel Jolly of Crowfall. That one's had more than his fair share of run-ins with me cousin Thakmuck Greythane up north even of here. Not to mention rumors of yer young king's… uh, shortcomins."

"Are greatly exaggerated," Torsten said through clenched teeth. "The work of Drav Cra warlocks who have since been driven away. But King Pi understands that a relationship with the Iron Kingdoms is crucial. And so, we bring you this gift."

Torsten nodded toward Lucas, and the young man stirred from staring at the dragon's enormous teeth. He dragged the tarp off their cart and fumbled through his satchel for a key. Then, he threw open the chest, revealing a pile of gold bullions. It was only a third of what had been requisitioned from beneath the Vineyard after Valin's betrayal was revealed. The rest had gone toward rebuilding Dockside, Winde Port, and funding other facets of the war effort. A fresh start for the royal coffers.

King Lorgit's dark eyes glinted like two obsidian stones. He stood, ignoring his son's protests, and approached the gold, as if drawn to it by some unseen force.

"Yuri Darkings brings promises," Torsten said. "I bring proof of our willingness to work with your great kingdom once more. Under Liam's reign, we all saw wealth beyond measure, and, of course, peace."

Lorgit ran his hand lovingly atop the pile of gold. Torsten half expected him to lift one and hug it like his own darling child.

"All of this as a gesture of faith?" the King asked, breathless.

"Consider it an advanced payment in hopes of a lasting alliance. All we need in exchange is a portion of your army and open passage through this route. Together, we can surround White Bridge, eliminate the Drav Cra presence choking our kingdom, then bring an end to the rebellion in the south."

Brouben joined his father in admiring the gold, and they exchanged some hushed whispers. Lucas stepped back and offered Torsten a questioning look.

Minutes passed. Torsten waited calmly, tapping his foot. *Dwarves are never in a hurry.*

Finally, King Lorgit exclaimed, "And a fine gesture it is! Killin Drav Cra, why didn't ye say so? Ever since ye lot shooed them pale bastards, they been raidin my people. Me other cousin Muzmol Strongiron was murdered by a crew of 'em just the other day."

"And we hope to work together with all the northern kingdoms to end that," Torsten said.

"Bah, that's their problem, ain't it just? Ye save all this here for old Cragrock only—the Iron Kingdoms alone." He turned, grinning from ear to ear, all the wrinkles on his face deepening. "Me boy here will march with ye and free White Bridge. He's been achin for a real fight."

Brouben shrugged. "Goblins go down too easy."

"And the Black Sands?" Torsten asked.

"From what I hear, that war's endin. But if it ain't, they'll learn how quick dwarves can tunnel under a wall." Lorgit laughed. "Meungor's axe is yers, but only under one condition."

Torsten bit his lip. *Always something else with dwarves.*

"Ye send me younger son, Alfotdrumlin, back to Yarrington to serve as yer temporary Master of Coin," King Lorgit said. "Ye flower-pickers keep throwing away gold on bad deals. It makes me stomach roil."

"I'm not certain, I—"

Lorgit smacked his younger son on the back. "It be all numbers with him, ever since he was a boy. Won't even touch an axe." The young dwarf blushed. "But he won't be the first son I sent out into the wild to learn a thing or three. He'll get yer coffers back in order so we can keep this... arrangement... going."

"King Lorgit," Torsten petitioned, "I'm not heading back to Yarrington. Your son won't be safe—"

"Nonsense. Ye take the boy as far as yer goin." He snapped his fingers, and the two spike-armored dwarves marched over. "The clanbreakers'll take 'em the rest."

After a short hesitation, eyeing the strange dwarves, armor covering every inch of them, Torsten said, "Very well, King Lorgit. I will draft a letter for King Pi and the Royal Council. Though, it might take more than a few words to convince them. Betrayal runs deep in that position."

"Bah, he's as loyal as a mule." Lorgit laughed yet again and slapped Lucas' mule on the backside.

"Father..." Al grumbled.

"As Master of Warfare, in these perilous times, I'm certain they'll heed my recommendation," Torsten said, "until we find a worthy successor ourselves. Our king is eager to learn from worthy men—or dwarves—and build a fruitful alliance between our kingdoms." Torsten stood, approached King Lorgit Cragrock, and stuck out his hand. "May the Light of Iam extend into the mountain deep."

Lorgit gave the gold one more stroke, then took Torsten's hand, and they shook. "And may it keep Meungor's axe sharp."

IV

THE REBEL

Afhem Muskigo Ayerabi felt the cool air beneath him as he climbed one outcrop to the next, all the way up the bluffs which enclosed the city of Nahanab. He did his best to ignore his groaning stomach and strained muscles.

They were starving. Months under siege now, and still, there was no sign of reprieve.

Even with the Glassmen's Northern allies disbanded and their forces cut in half, there was still no way out. More ships had arrived to block the bay. Archers from Panping had been summoned, and every night or so, they fired over the walls of Nahanab, pounding away at Muskigo's dwindling forces. Siege weapons ravaged the walls, and the buildings within were leveled. Had the city not been enclosed by tall, natural cliffs, he and his men would have fallen already.

Despite the many calls to the capital for help; for assistance from the afhems who hadn't yet joined Muskigo in this rebellion, none had come. This was their last attempt to disrupt the siege, Muskigo's last chance to get word out to Latiapur. The Glass had thwarted all his messages, by courier or bird, ever since he got Yuri and Farhan out.

They were on their own.

That's what I get for trusting a traitorous pink-skin like Yuri Darkings.

His strong fingers used a small jut of rock to heave himself up. From so high, he could see far to the south, black sands reaching out eternally. To the north, the M'stafu Desert and the coming together of the Kingdoms, black and white sands intermingling in a way neither side had seen in years. Stifled screams drew his attention to the left, where one of his best soldiers faltered and plummeted. His gray body vanished in the darkness before the soft *thud* signaled an impact that no man could survive.

Muskigo winced. They couldn't afford to lose a soul now.

He sucked in a shuddering breath and returned his eyes upward. He and a hundred of his best men were about three quarters of the way up the cliff on the north side of the kingdom. These were good men—warriors who had been with him since he'd stepped into the sands of Tal'du Dromesh, and claimed the Ayerabi Afhemate.

The plan was simple: they would reach the top of the cliff, move in behind the Glassmen, and raid their camp, taking out their stores and as many soldiers as they could. But climbing so high without nigh'jels to illuminate the path provided a significant challenge. Doing it with barely an ounce of food or fresh water in their stomachs, even harder.

Even the moons offered no aid. As if Iam were defending his chosen people, a thick blanket of clouds obscured them. The God of Sand and Sea, however, kept the wind calm, at least. Trader's Bay was still as a northern lake. All Muskigo could hear was the sound of hands and boots scraping rock, like countless tiny spiders clambering up a wall.

"Afhem Muskigo," Impili Mansoor said as he skittered down the wall. It was so dark, Muskigo couldn't even see the grisly scar wrapping his commander's neck like a snake. With Farhan Uki'a gone, and still no word from him, Impili—a man who'd be ready to claim an afhemate for himself if they survived this—was Muskigo's second.

"What is it, Impili?" Muskigo asked, short of breath. Saujibar, the oasis he called home, was in the deep desert, where there were no tall cliffs to climb, only rolling dunes and the occasional pit lizard. He was better suited to zhulong-back than mountain-scaling.

"They have sentries posted along the ridge," Impili said, air whistling against his broken front teeth. "A collocation of soldiers, heavily armed. If we don't take them out fast, they might alert the camp."

"They thought of everything, didn't they?" Muskigo grumbled. There was one thing Muskigo had learned over these past months—the Glass was not as fragile as he'd once believed it to be. "Have the archers at the top first. We need to take them out with one shot each. How many?"

"Twenty. Maybe more."

"We move fast and quiet," Muskigo whispered.

"Yes, my Afhem."

Impili climbed away. He had long limbs and thin fingers, a man built for climbing, having grown up in this region.

Muskigo's afhemate was unique in that way. Whereas most afhems led men who'd rarely even traveled outside their lands, Ayerabi boasted warriors from all seventy-nine afhemates. When he'd taken a stand against Liam, all those years ago, in Tal'du Dromesh, he'd inspired others to forsake their leaders, to flock to him. It had given him the strength to mount this rebellion without waiting for approval from the cowards and sycophants who called themselves afhems these days; who surrounded the Caleef and kept themselves fat off trade with the Glassmen.

Muskigo exhaled slowly, his stomach rumbling again, then continued the climb.

It took an hour longer for all his men to reach the ridge just below the crest. Luckily, no others fell. Pulling them into a line along the edge, a hundred meters above Nahanab, Muskigo looked from side to side at all his bravest men—or at least those that yet lived. A break in the clouds and Celeste revealed all. Sweat glistened on their brows and backs. Their ribs showed as their muscle tone gave way from malnutrition.

Each one bore countless scars from countless battles, thanks to countless decades of fighting amongst their own people while their rulers watched from their Glass Castle. He was glad his men now had some scars courtesy of the real enemy—the men who'd pounded their fathers into submission and made them bend the knee.

Even the sight of them now filled the pit in Muskigo's stomach.

Muskigo slowly rose to peek over the ledge, which was about chest high. He saw the Glass sentries, camped in the moonlight at the summit, huddled around small, crackling fires to combat the chill of the desert night. Most were there, a few others paced along the plateau, longbows slung over their shoulders.

From this vantage, Muskigo could also see lights from the Glass blockade on Trader's Bay, and the dark streets of Nahanab behind him. Even most of their nigh'jels were starving and had to be released back into the bay where they would likely die from cold. Muskigo's army had been forced to camp in the markets— but now, most of those who still remained, fit within the walls of the late Afhem Dajani Calidor's mansion.

Civilians kept to their homes, more of a drain on supplies than anything. Muskigo had long considered sending them out, but he feared what the honorless Glassmen would do to them. All he needed were the fishermen who trawled the city docks, just outside of range of the Glass ships. They couldn't get much, but anything was better than nothing.

Now, Muskigo was in charge of all of them, from warriors to withered old men. All people without afhemates, their leaders dead in battle. After Winde Port, he saw his great victory unfurling before him, and now it seemed hopeless. His fight—once a valiant plan designed to free all the Black Sands—had been reduced to saving those who remained.

Muskigo raised an open hand to the side. A slight rustling sounded as those of his men armed with blackwood longbows drew their weapons and cautiously rose. He peered over the ledge again. The Glassmen sat around a fire with a series of spits turning above. It looked and smelled like rabbit.

"Gotta piss," one of the Glassmen above said, his voice carrying on the still air.

"The gray men ought to be thirsty," another answered pointing to the ledge.

They all shared a laugh, then the guard strolled toward the edge of the cliff overlooking Nahanab, right toward Muskigo and his men. Muskigo motioned for his men to draw back into hiding and bit his lip. He kept his hand open. His men leaned back, each carefully drawing a second barbed arrow to hold in their mouths while another remained nocked. One lost a grip, and his arrow clattered down against the cliffside.

Muskigo froze, grimacing and holding his breath. A moment passed, but the Glass soldier didn't seem to hear as he shuffled to the ridge and unbuckled his belt.

"Long way down," he muttered, kicking a pebble. "If only me mum could see me now, looking down on savages."

Muskigo closed his fist. At the same time, he reached up, grabbed the man's ankle and dragged him off, no hesitation. His archers sprung up, steadied their bows and let loose, then immediately loaded the next and fired.

Muskigo rolled up and drew his sickle-blade. The very same he'd claimed from the undercroft of the arena when he'd earned his nickname as the Scythe. The Glassmen went down one after another, with expert precision.

One of the soldiers on the other side of the narrow plateau took a barbed arrow to his quad and collapsed, but he didn't lose grip on his bow. The Shesaitju archers lost view of him behind the campfire, but Muskigo took off. The Glassman crawled for the fire to ignite an arrow. He aimed it toward the sky, but Muskigo threw his weapon and caught the soldier's arm in the sickle-blade's curve. The arrow sputtered only a few meters up, then toppled straight to the ground.

Muskigo launched himself, catching the man's head between his legs and twisted down, snapping his neck. He rolled over, retrieved his weapon, and whipped around to observe his men's handiwork. His archers had done their jobs, disabling the enemy counterparts. The rest of his men killed the Glassmen while they were down. Impili knelt near a pink-skinned soldier with a hand over the man's mouth. The whole thing had happened quickly and silently, there'd barely been time for anyone to scream.

Muskigo and Impili exchanged a nod, then the former turned toward the enemy camp. The rocky landscape extended for miles around Trader's Bay, even more treacherous on this side. He spotted ropes, which the Glassmen had used to climb up, leading to a lower plateau, then another. The Glass army's camp rested in a clearing east of the city, with another rock formation at their backs to defend against a rear attack. Torches dotted all the high points nearby, making them impossible to sneak up on. But, as Muskigo watched, the clouds rolled back in, more oppressive than ever. It would cover their advance. In light leather armor, speed was their ally. They could get in, inflict havoc, and escape back up the rocks before the Glassmen knew what happened.

"Fire is their signal," Muskigo said to Impili. "That one tried to send a flaming arrow up, no doubt to inform the others of attack. Make sure this does not happen."

A few of them carried what little whale oil they had left from Nahanab's stores—the kind the Glass loved trading for so they could burn their torches and campfires all through the nights, fueling their weakness. As soon as they torched the enemy camp, a handful of couriers would use the distraction and ride to Latiapur. Muskigo would beseech his peers one last time to stop suckling at the teat of the Glass Kingdom and its new boy king, and claim the freedom that was rightfully theirs.

One last courier was to go to Saujibar, Muskigo's afhemate, to find his daughter Mahraveh and her caregiver Shavi. The message was for them to travel somewhere far. He knew what would happen if his failure became complete. The Ayerabi Afhemate would have to pay. The Glassmen wouldn't show mercy after Winde Port, and his own people would have to prostrate themselves to earn favor.

Muskigo's family and his most loyal followers would join him in death.

Our fathers surrendered, he recalled. *I cannot.*

"What are your orders, my Afhem?" Impili asked, tightening his grip upon a long spear, the blade made from the sharpened rib of a zhulong. Seeing it froze Muskigo momentarily. His daughter had always favored polearms to make up for her stature. As the days under siege ticked by, he started to fear he may never see her again, that he'd never get to hug her again, or even scold her, and see that impetuous smirk she wore after being caught breaking one of his many rules.

My little sand mouse.

"Afhem Muskigo?" Impili said.

"We'll use their path down and follow it," Muskigo said, burying the fond memories of Mahi deep where he buried any other happy thing. There was no room for softness in war. "We'll take out that post overlooking the western side of their camp."

"That close?"

"The weak Northerners and their fire. We'll spill the coals over their tents and set the blaze. We'll hit them with every arrow we have to keep them from dousing it, then fight from the high ground and retreat back this way."

"The narrow inclines make their numbers meaningless," Impili offered. "A few of us, we can hold them off."

"If it comes to that," Muskigo said.

Together, they turned and saw their men crowded around the Glassmen's small camp, pulling the rabbits off the spits. They didn't even appear to care that they hadn't fully cooked. Upon noticing Muskigo, they stepped back and bowed.

"You first, my Afhem," one said.

Muskigo stared at the food as he stepped over. There wasn't just rabbit. There was bread and dried meat, too. He hated bread —that Northern food which was as soft as they were. Grown without struggle, not hunted or pulled from the Boiling Waters, but still, nothing had ever looked so appetizing.

"No," Muskigo said, fighting every survival instinct he had. He had to think back to when he was young, just of age, shortly after Liam took everything from him, how he crossed the heart of the M'stafu with nothing but the clothes on his back, only to see if he could.

"Eat your fill, all of you," he went on. "I'll take the scraps. Be fast. Then, we move as swiftly and quietly as the shifting sand."

Muskigo's feet were cut and battered by the time they made it to the outcrop overlooking the camp. They'd been calloused by sand, though, not enough for this, and they needed bare feet to feel every nook on the sheer rock face. A fall to either side spelled certain doom. The God of Sand and Sea certainly didn't intend to watch Muskigo torn apart by sharp rocks.

He was pleased with his plan. His men had eaten—not enough, but it would be better than a battle with starved bellies and wounded hearts, and they'd even saved him a large portion despite their own hunger.

As Muskigo watched the sentry post they targeted, he felt better than he had in weeks. He knew the Glass commander—this new Wearer of White named Nikserof Pasic, couldn't garner that kind of respect from his men. Maybe Torsten Unger, but Muskigo had broken him at Winde Port, and he'd do the same to Sir Nikserof if given the opportunity. He'd break all of them, and show his people what true strength was.

"We're in position, my Afhem," Impili said.

"Why are you still here, Impili?" Muskigo asked.

"Me? I—I'm sorry if I've offended you—"

"No, no. Not like that, my friend. Here, with me. Fighting this impossible battle, when so many of our people seem like dogs, eager to eat scraps off the floor."

Impili stared at him. His hard face was made harder by more than just the lumpy scar up his neck. His front teeth were broken from a helmet to the face many years before. He had so many signs of past injuries, it was impossible to know in the limited light which of them were merely wrinkles, and he'd earned each of them serving Muskigo without question.

"Where else is there to be, my Afhem?" Impili shrugged.

Muskigo smirked. He took his old friend by the shoulders and gave him a firm shake. "And that is why we fight rather than bow to cowards. Caleef or not." He unlatched his sickle-blade from his back and eyed his men. Fear showed on none of their faces, all of them ready to die if God commanded it.

Not today, Muskigo thought.

He waved them along, and they skirted down the ridge like a pack of desert wolves. The Glassmen had grown too comfortable in their luxurious tents, around their warm fires, drinking, carousing, and playing their silly card games. This was war, and they thought they had time for games of chance.

None noticed as Muskigo and his men descended upon their most vulnerable point. They likely didn't even know it was the weakest, with influence over their entire location.

Muskigo stayed low, pushing his muscles to the brink of exhaustion. He was first down to the flat, first to sneak up behind one of the watchmen, cover the man's mouth, and slash his throat. Only, as he brought the soldier to the ground, there was no warmth of blood, nor muffled gurgling. Just dead weight.

Impili and the others made quick work of the rest while Muskigo flipped the body over. His eyes went wide. The man's skin was gray but robbed of color, and it stunk like old death. The moment Muskigo inhaled, he fought every urge to vomit. It was a Shesaitju corpse dressed in Glassman armor.

One of his own.

"Impili, fall back to the ridge," Muskigo ordered. "We have to go."

He stood, but it was too late. All around them, the green glow of nigh'jel lanterns rose. Tongues trilled, warriors howled, and they found themselves surrounded by Shesaitju warriors with barbed arrows trained. It was too dark to see their tattoo, to tell which afhemate's marking they wore on their necks. Not that it mattered.

"We've been betrayed," Impili growled.

"Back to the ridge!" Muskigo shouted.

Again, he didn't hesitate. He didn't allow heartbreak to slow him. They raced back up the incline. Bowstrings thrummed, and the ambush commenced. Muskigo deflected an arrow right before the barbs shredded his face. Others howled in agony.

A Shesaitju warrior and a Panpingese archer charged down a hill, side by side. Muskigo made short work of both, leaving a string of their entrails on the red rock. His men fought at his side, desperate to push their way back up. Arrows rained down from behind.

"Impili!" Muskigo shouted as he noticed his commander dash back toward the campfire.

Muskigo rolled, then followed, gutting another traitorous Shesaitju on his way. A spear zoomed at his head as he came to his feet. He twisted and slid just in time, feeling the gust of wind from the weapon. He hooked it with his sickle-blade and brought it down to use as a vault to launch himself over the man. Landing feather-light, his blade whipped around and slashed the man's neck as if the thing had its own mind.

Impili used his range to repel a group of attackers by the fire.

"Keep them back!" Muskigo ordered. He then returned down the incline, arrows from Panpingese archers *clanking* off the rock, *zipping* overhead. The easterners were once known for their accuracy, but Muskigo was grateful Liam had killed off most of them in his conquest.

Muskigo shouldered a Glassman in the back and sent him colliding into another, sending them both tumbling over the ledge. Screams echoed through the city below, and more screams rose to meet them.

"Muskigo!" Impili shouted and tossed a canteen filled with highly flammable whale oil.

Muskigo caught it, bit off the stopper, and dumped the oil all over one of the planted, rotting corpses. "Your death will not be in vain," he whispered before he and Impili pushed the corpse through the campfire. It ignited, then rolled over the ridge and into the Glass camp below. It stopped at one of the supply tents, causing it to erupt in flames.

"That should send the message," Muskigo said. "Regroup at the top. Find another—"

Impili suddenly pushed Muskigo with the butt of his spear. For a split second, which felt like a lifetime, Muskigo thought his betrayal was complete, that his closest friend, the second in command of his forces, had joined with the other traitors. Then, a Shesaitju arrow raced up from the main camp at incredible velocity. Even with Impili's quick thinking, one of the barbs caught Muskigo's cheek, and the force spun him around. His foot slipped, and his fingers just missed clasping Impili's spear before he lost his footing and tumbled ten meters down the incline.

Muskigo landed at the edge of their camp, face bloodied, arms bruised, facing a wall of Glassmen. These didn't appear like they'd been busy sitting around, playing cards and waiting out a siege, but were prepared for battle. Muskigo recovered quickly. He'd learned long ago, when he mastered the black fist, to conquer his pain, to be as a stone in Boiling Waters.

"Muskigo!" Impili called down amidst the echoes of more fighting.

"No!" Muskigo shouted. He didn't need to look up. He knew the loyalty of his afhemate, and that Impili would gladly leap to his death in service to his afhem. But he also knew he would never ignore an order. "Go back. Defend the city at all costs."

Muskigo spat out the fresh blood filling his mouth from the gash in his cheek. He slowly swept his foot across the patted sand, drawing a line, and extended his curved blade. All the Glassmen arrayed before him were painted in the light of the growing fire, wielding blades and shields, no bows, no arrows. That meant they wanted him alive.

"Afhem Muskigo, you are defeated!" Sir Nikserof, Wearer of White, called out, smug look on his pink face. The coward wore more armor than any man should ever need. Muskigo wasn't surprised, considering he let his men do all the dirty work for him while he sat on his tall steed at the back of the ranks.

"You hide behind a shield," Muskigo bellowed. "Face me, coward!"

"Did you really think you could take us all alone?" Nikserof asked. "The arrogance of you heathens never ceases to amaze me."

"Give your men the order to stand down, and I'll show you arrogance."

"Didn't you look closely at the bodies we left for you? Didn't you recognize them? They're from your precious Saujibar. *You* got them killed. Now your own people want you dead. Lay down your blade, Muskigo. It's over."

He didn't let the revelation settle. If those men were from Saujibar, it would be something to deal with later. Now, there were more pressing needs.

"It'll be over when your boy king loses his head!" Muskigo shouted, charging straight at them. Their spears met him, but he leaped, slashing down with his sickle to push aside the shafts. In their metal coffins, they were too slow to keep up. He landed in the heart of the ranks, carving a circle with his blade and knocking legs out from under those closest to them.

He snapped a spear in half with his foot and wielded it in his offhand. Not that his was inferior. Masters of black fist trained so they could fight with any weapon, in either hand. The moment he wielded the new weapon, it became an extension of him.

He carved out a throat with his sickle, then threw the spear straight at Nikserof's horse. A whinny sounded, followed by the *thump* of it collapsing.

Muskigo crouched, his sickle-blade held out.

As one, the Glassmen shuffled back. They were scared. Their armor might as well have been musical instruments as they quivered. Muskigo positioned his foot under a fallen longsword and flipped it up into his offhand without ever breaking eye contact.

"That's enough, Muskigo," a deep, basso voice spoke. Even with the crackling fire and the din of the battle above, Muskigo thought he recognized it. Then, his enemies parted, and through them, appeared a familiar face—a man who looked more like a boulder: Babrak Trisps'I, a powerful afhem commanding the largest land army left in the Black Sands.

"Babrak," Muskigo spat. It was hard for him to speak that name without venom. They'd had their share of feuds ever since Muskigo became afhem. His refusing support for a rebellion and now fighting alongside the Glass army was merely the last straw.

The big man lifted a warhammer off his back, then tossed it to the side. He raised his arms and showed his empty palms.

"How many more must die, Muskigo?" Babrak said.

"Was this you?" Muskigo asked.

Babrak frowned. He was a good actor, but Muskigo saw right through it. He knew the man wanted to grin from ear to ear. He'd hated Muskigo ever since the woman he'd considered his own chose Muskigo over joining his harem.

"Unfortunately, I know all your tricks," Babrak said. Not a full admission, but not a denial either.

"You would dare throw in with them?"

"And you haven't?" Babrak barked. "I met your Darkings *toy*. He's as unimpressive as your daughter, Mahi."

"Don't you dare speak her name!" Muskigo stomped forward. The Glassmen around him shuddered and raised their weapons higher.

"Enough games," Sir Nikserof said, recovering from his fall to walk up beside Babrak. "You promised me the rebel, and you delivered."

"You're a coward, Babrak," Muskigo snarled. "Always have been."

"I'm giving you a chance to save the rest of the fools who joined this war against the will of the Caleef and the greater afhemdom."

"They would gladly give their lives," Muskigo said, though he had to admit, he wasn't sure.

"And what of your daughter and Shavi?"

"I fight so they don't need to."

"Too late Muskigo," Babrak said, shaking his head in mock sympathy.

"What are you talking about?"

"He means that they're dead," Nikserof said. "You taught them to be fools."

"Watch your—"

"Like you," Nikserof continued, "they refused peaceful surrender. But it can end now, without more bloodshed. You've already lost. The sooner you accept that the sooner we could all be back to paying tributes to the King with gold instead of lives."

"No…" Muskigo squeezed the handle of his weapons so tight his nails dug into his palms.

"It's true," Babrak said. He removed a long braid of hair from his belt and tossed it at Muskigo's feet. With the tip of his blade, Muskigo lifted it and gave it a whiff. The scent—her scent—transported him to days gone by when he'd held her, kissed her head. It was a father's instinct, and it had awakened fire within, blood stirring like a sandstorm.

"No!" Muskigo roared. He leaped at the nearest soldier, bashing him in the face with the butt of his sickle-blade. With the sword he'd stolen, he slashed at anyone who got near as he continued to smash the man's face into a bloody pulp of red and loose teeth.

Mahraveh.

She was everything.

The very reason he fought.

So she could grow up in a world where the fathers of her generation weren't cowards who sacrificed everything to kiss the Glass boot and lose what it was that made them Shesaitju.

Mahraveh.

"No!" He cast his weapons aside and punched, one quaking fist after another into what was now a corpse, his face so mangled, Muskigo's fist pounded the rock beyond. Blood coated his gray skin until the surrounding Glassmen grew the nerve to grab and pull him off.

He'd been fighting nonstop for months, but he couldn't fight them. Not anymore. His muscles were too weak from malnutrition and overexertion. And his heart… he could no longer feel it beating.

V

THE THIEF

"Who in Meungor's name are ye?" Tum Tum asked, pointing with his hammer.

For a heartbeat, Whitney was confused. How did his friend not recognize him? Sure, it was dark, but dwarves could see well in the darkness. Had he changed that much since Winde Port? Then a tickle against his ear—the one whose lobe he'd lost the last time he'd seen the dwarf—reminded him of the blood and feathers covering him.

"Tum Tum, it's me. Whitney." Whitney brushed furiously at his face with one hand, trying to uncover it enough for his friend to be convinced.

"Well, stab me with the fiery end of a sharp poker. Whitney Fierstown! Back from the dead! Get yer arse over here!" The next instant, Whitney was wrapped in a crushing dwarf hug that robbed him of what little breath he had left after the fighting.

Pain shot up his neck, and Whitney pushed off.

"What, are ye mad at me?" Tum Tum asked.

"No. That thing must have gotten me good." He turned and tried to view the scratch on his shoulder, but to no avail. It was too dark, and the angle was wrong. A second later, the dagger he held in that hand slipped through his fingers with a clank.

"I can't… uh… feel my arm."

Tum Tum picked up the dagger. "Ye takin things that don't belong to ye again, Whitney?"

"Tum Tum, my arm," Whitney said, more urgently.

"Oh, keep a hold of yer trousers. They're grimaurs. Haven't ye read? Their talons paralyze. Glintish doctors make a nice little cocktail out of em." He pointed to Gentry. "Don't this one know?"

"I grew up on the road Mr…"

"Tum Tum," the dwarf finished for him.

"Is anyone else going to worry about my arm!" Whitney shouted.

"Quit bein a baby. One of me workers got a scratch the other day. It passed in, oh… a few hours. Knocked him clean out though. We'll head upstairs to me bar and wash it out."

"Your bar?" Whitney slurred.

"Aye! Everything on the other side of this here tunnel. C'mon." He waved them along, and only had to crouch to pass through the opening. Same with Gentry. Whitney pretty much had to crawl with one arm, and all the while, he could feel his head getting woozier.

"How's the robe," Whitney asked Gentry up ahead.

The boy unfurled it a bit. Whitney couldn't see much in the darkness, only the glimmering embroidery, getting blurrier by the second.

"It's… uh… fine," Gentry said. Before Whitney could respond, Tum Tum reached back and helped the boy through the rest of the way.

He then extended his hammer to drag Whitney along, and Whitney hugged it with his good arm. Tum Tum pulled him through puddles, around stalagmites, up small inclines, and finally, they could see the soft moonlight blooming down a ways, through the broken wall they'd passed through.

"Sorry about the wall," Whitney said.

"No bother," he said. "If a fool like ye could break through, so could them beasties. We'll build it stronger. Yer lucky I came down and heard screechin. Takes a bit to chase them off."

They reached the break in the wall, and Whitney lost his grip on the hammer. Gentry bent down to examine him. "Mr. Fierstown, you don't look so good."

"I'm fine."

Whitney pulled himself to his feet and staggered through the opening, but Tum Tum helped him, wrapping one of his burly arms around Whitney's waist. Once inside, he peeled back Whitney's shirt. Whitney couldn't feel the action in the slightest.

When they made it back upstairs to Tum Tum's bar, the dwarf said, "That's a mighty fine scratch ye got there. We'll need to get that cleaned, no biggie." He helped Whitney up the stairs. "By Meungor, when did ye get so heavy?"

"I've been working out," Whitney said.

"Found someone new to impress, eh?" Tum Tum shut right up the moment he said it. He turned to Whitney, scratching his beard as if to say he was sorry.

Whitney nodded. He couldn't expect everyone to walk on glass around him.

"Who's the boy?" Tum Tum asked.

"An apprentice of sorts."

"Ye never will learn."

Tum Tum groaned as he helped Whitney into a plush seat at one of the tables upstairs. Whitney leaned forward. His head felt like an anvil. He now felt the venom from the talons in his neck, slowly making its way to his head. He felt sleepy and squeezed his eyelids tight and shook his head to try to wake himself.

"All right, shirt off," Tum Tum said.

Whitney swatted at his hand. "Only for ladies."

"Ye ain't pretty enough for any dwarf. Let's go." Tum Tum grabbed his collar and yanked the shirt, pulling it down his numb arm. Gentry sat across from them, eyes rapt with fear.

Whitney heard a *slap*. "Feel that?" Tum Tum asked. Gentry winced from the sound.

"Nothing," Whitney replied. All he could sense was the pressure of Tum Tum's fat fingers as the dwarf examined his back. "So, how in Elsewhere did you afford this place?"

"After ye disappeared—where did ye go, anyway? Sora send ye out?"

Whitney groaned. "A story for another time."

"Well, Sora was a gods-damned mess," Tum Tum went on. "Didn't leave the captain's quarters on that upyr's corsair ship for what felt like years. We were about as shog shucked as ever I been, and then Gold Grin Gale sailed up."

Whitney ran his working hand through his long hair, then dragged it down over his face and pinched the bridge of his nose with a thumb and forefinger. "Gold Grin?"

"Aye." Tum Tum laughed. "Weren't so much an attack as a rescue as I recall it. We were fit to die on the sea, no qualms about that. Headin for choppy waters in a tiny ship, angry Shesaitju fillin the seas. Gold Grin rode in and saved the day. Fine fellow, he is."

"Grisham "Gold Grin" Gale?" Whitney asked skeptically, overly pronouncing every syllable.

"The very same. Invested the gold after sellin their treasures to help me own this fine establishment—*Gold Grin's Grotto*. Ain't be no finer pub in all of Panping when it's done."

"I knew this place looked familiar," Whitney said under his breath. He had to admit, now with the torches lit, adding to the nigh'jel lanterns, and the gentle glow of Celeste's light through the many portholes, the place was impressive, all bronze-studded leather and mahogany… Gold Grin's style, indeed. Construction hadn't yet been completed, but it made Tum Tum's old place, the Winder's Dwarf, look like a hole in the wall—which it was.

"It's really a great looking place, Mr. Tum Tum," Gentry said.

"Just Tum Tum, lad," Tum Tum replied.

"Don't bother," Whitney mumbled.

"Aye, well, this is me place now. Glad ye like it. Wait til ye see it with all his golden trinkets brought up from the chests downstairs."

Whitney nearly choked on his next breath. A treasure chest would have spared them a visit into that nest of foreign beasts.

"Don't get any ideas, ye old thief." Tum Tum laughed. "Been chore enough tryin to clear out the nest of those fiends ye ran into. I keep demandin the city watch do somethin, but they don't believe me. 'Grimaurs don't come this far south, and they don't like flocks.' Bah, the fools."

"Well, I'm sure they won't cause much of a problem after what we did to them," Whitney said, words slurring even more now.

"We?" Tum Tum cocked one of his bushy eyebrows.

"Yeah, yeah. I helped. Ouch!" Whitney's head snapped around so fast, he wound up seeing double. Tum Tum stood behind him, holding a flask upside-down, the contents poured all over his wound. Numb as he was to contact, that sting was deep in his tissue.

Tum Tum grinned. "That ought to clean it out."

"You're a right piece of shog, you know that?" Whitney said. "I still can't move my arm."

"Can't make time jump forward."

Whitney exhaled through his teeth, and after letting the pain settle, said, "So where's Sora now?" He knew, but he hoped against hope he was wrong, that maybe Lucindur's magic wasn't all it was cracked out to be, and Sora was still here, in Yaolin, waiting for him like he'd once hoped.

"Even if ye could ask Iam, I doubt he'd know," Tum Tum said.

Whitney swore, then looked at Gentry who was obviously becoming used to Whitney's poor language choices. The kid didn't even look up from where his finger traced a line of wood grain on the lacquered countertop. He seemed disturbed by the whole scene and thankful not to watch.

"Be right back to patch ye up." Tum Tum disappeared behind the bar to rummage through his disorganized belongings.

"And a drink!" Whitney called to him. Shouting made his head feel light. He leaned into his palm, then tilted to face Gentry, who still avoided eye contact. "I'm sorry for getting you wrapped up in all this."

"Why?" he asked. "This is the most fun I have ever had in my life."

"There's nothing fun about almost dying, do you hear me?" Whitney slammed his hand on the table. Right after it was done, he knew who he'd sounded like. Next, he'd tell Gentry that it was safe on a farm and that there was no need to adventure through forests with knife-ears.

Gentry shrunk back. "Okay, okay! I just…"

Whitney wished he could take it back. "I'm just supposed to keep you safe," he said. "What happened tonight was the furthest thing from that. Look at me, I can't move my yigging arm."

He let out a mirthless laugh.

Gentry smiled along, but it was just for show. "I have always been under Modera and Fadra's boots. It is nice to be… free."

Whitney wasn't sure if it was the toxin flooding his thoughts with negativity, but he couldn't help but feel Gentry was becoming too much like Young Whitney for his own good. How many times had Whitney said those words while traveling

Pantego, thieving?—or 'scoundreling' as Sora had so eloquently put it. He stared down at an empty mug. It was a fine reflection of that life. Empty. Leaving you disillusioned just long enough for reality to hit once again.

"Yeah, I get it," Whitney admitted. "Probably better than anybody. But I've been lucky so far. We both got lucky tonight. I don't know if you've thought of this, but what would've happened had we'd made it to that tunnel?"

Gentry just blinked.

"You remember how difficult it was to get there the first time?" he said. "Do you think those grimaurs would've had that much trouble?"

"I suppose not," Gentry admitted. "Gods, we almost died."

Whitney mimed hammering, clicked his tongue, then said, "Nail on the head."

A few long seconds passed in silence. Then, Gentry looked up. "Mr. Whitney, I… uh… I have to show you something."

Before Whitney could respond, Tum Tum burst back in, lugging what looked like a fisherman's tackle-box. It landed with a *clatter* and a *thunk* on the table.

"Alright, ye dolt," he said. "Lost me chance to sew that ear back on, won't be losin another chance to stick ye with a needle."

"Thanks, but no thanks," Whitney said, eyeing the contents of his box.

"Don't ye be a girl." Tum Tum patted the bar top. "Ye owe me for breakin that bow. Gold Grin said it belonged to some huntress in Crowfall. Beautiful like ye wouldn't believe—his words, not mine."

"Gold Grin says a lot of things."

"Yer one to talk. Now, lie down, and have some whiskey." He placed down a full bottle. The stuff looked too pricey for Tum Tum's usual stock. "It'll be over before ye know it.

"Go on, Mr. Fierstown," Gentry said, lowering back down. "It does seem really bad."

"You better know what you're doing," Whitney conceded, laying his torso across the table. The dwarf grunted and wasted no time. He was just about to stick the needle in when Whitney protested. "Hey, hey! Whiskey first, you villain."

Tum Tum laughed and slid Whitney the bottle. It went down like fire but soon after, the room was spinning even more. Whitney didn't even care that a sharp piece of metal was piercing his flesh over and over again. Before he knew it, Tum Tum said, "Done," and helped Whitney to sit up. "How's that?"

Whitney stuttered through a response, but he couldn't string the words together. Grimaur toxin and expensive whiskey weren't the finest combination for remaining cognizant.

With a laugh, Tum Tum said, "Gentry, let's get this drunkard upstairs. Let him get some sleep. Guest rooms ain't done bein furnished yet, but the first room has a bed. Then, ye come back down and have a bite. Gotta test the stew on someone."

Morning came too quickly, and it wasn't even the sunlight pouring in through the room's small, circular window that woke Whitney. Downstairs, he heard voices. Familiar voices. Voices that made no sense being downstairs.

He cast the blankets off and stumbled out of the room and down the stairs. His head throbbed, and his legs barely worked. Each step sounded like thunder to his sensitive ears, and the whole gathering below stood, silently waiting, until he made it to the main level.

"Ye look like a giant ate yer lunch," Tum Tum said.

"Then I look like I feel," Whitney said with a smirk. He took in the room, and as he'd thought, Lucindur, Talwyn, and Tum

Tum all stood in the middle of the ship-like pub, chatting away like it was nothing more than a day at the park.

"How…" Whitney said.

"Gentry retrieved us early this morning," Lucindur explained. "And it's a good thing too. We were worried."

"Nothing to worry about," Whitney said, wincing as he rolled his shoulder. The ache was incredible enough to almost make him miss being numb. "We're here. Got what we came for."

"Whitney, I know you're in a hurry to find this Kazimir fellow," Lucindur said, "but you're in no shape to be traipsing around Pantego, or even Yaolin City for that matter. Look at you. Besides, Tum Tum was just telling us a bit about the last time he saw you with Kazimir, isn't that right, Tum Tum?"

"Aye, and now yer what—best friends with the bloodsucker?" Tum Tum questioned.

"It's not like that. We were… imprisoned together," Whitney said.

"That what ye call six years in Elsewhere?"

Whitney shot Lucindur a poison-laced glare. "Anything you didn't tell the dwarf?"

"He's your friend, isn't he?" Lucindur asked.

"Of course, he is. But you didn't know that. Not with sincerity. I could have been acting—I do that too, you know."

Whitney finished crossing the room. It was slow, but he finally sat on one of the cushioned chairs, grimacing as he grabbed his shoulder.

"Oh, you poor thing," Talwyn said, rising from her seat and throwing herself on his lap. Whitney groaned, but she didn't care. She placed her hand near his shoulder wound. Then, she touched his earlobe—or the place where his earlobe had once been. "Tum Tum told us how you lost this, too. And you… telling us you slipped up while shaving."

"I—" Whitney said before Lucindur loomed over them.

"Tal," Lucindur said, "you're probably hurting him. Get up."

Talwyn huffed but listened. When her back was turned, Whitney mouthed the words "Thank you." Lucindur offered a smile.

"What were you thinking?" Lucindur asked. "Grimaurs, with Gentry? How is this any way to honor Modera's final request?"

"Whoa, wait a minute. You think I *knew* there would be yigging grimaurs in Panping?" he said. "When's the last time you saw them farther south than Glinthaven?"

"The *nobleman's* got a point," Tum Tum said. "Heard whispers of goblins raidin the priests' storehouse in Hornsheim, too, and Buried Goddess cultists caught sacrificing some girl at *The Innbetween* just west of here. Strange happenins ever since Redstar died. Only a matter of time before the trees start turning against us, too."

"That's not even funny," Whitney said.

"Did ye really talk to her like the musician says?" Tum Tum asked.

"Who?"

"Her."

"Nesilia?"

"Didn't know ye were on first name terms, but yeah, she be the one I meant."

"I don't know. It was Sora. It was Nesilia. Something bad is happening, and I don't know what to do except find Kazimir."

"Ye think ye can trust a damned upyr?"

"This one?" Whitney asked. "Unfortunately, with my life."

Tum Tum scoffed and moved back around the bar. He offered Whitney a cup of tea and some sort of doughy and sticky pastry. Whitney took them both, then asked, "Where's Gentry?"

As if the question had summoned him, he stepped through the doorway with Aquira perched on his shoulder.

"Aquira!" Whitney shouted. "There's my girl." The wyvern

lifted her head a bit to look at him but didn't soar over to greet him like she would have before the Drav Cra hurt her. Her head sank back down.

Gentry cradled something in his hands and wore the saddest look Whitney thought possible.

"What is it?" Whitney asked him.

"The… It's just that… Well, the—"

"For the sake of all the gods in Panping, spit it out."

"The robe got destroyed while we were running from the grimaurs. I could not tell you earlier. I tried, but then you were getting stitched up, and then you were drunk and asleep, and Tum Tum was feeding me stew, and I was so tired. This morning, I tried to take it to a tailor, but as soon as I showed her, she shooed me and told me never to come back." He said it so fast it forced him to take a deep breath when he'd finished. He held up the robe and displayed it. A handful of slashes adorned its once opulent fabric—one pulled straight down the front, neck to ankles. If that wasn't enough, the yellow mantle was now red with blood.

"Oh, shog…"

"I am not sure it is going to be worth nearly what you thought it would be. I am sorry, terribly sorry." Tears welled in the poor kid's eyes.

"Yigging Exile," Whitney swore again.

"I am so sorry," Gentry muttered again and again.

"Sorry? What are you sorry for?"

"I should have kept it safer."

"Oh, right," Whitney said. "You should've risked life and limb during a grimaur battle to keep safe a yigging robe." That brought a smile to Gentry's face. "I'd say you did just fine by staying alive." He nodded toward his own shoulder. "Did better than me, anyway."

Lucindur stood and hugged the boy. Aquira perked up again, but only momentarily before dropping back into her listless state.

"But what are we going to do?" Gentry asked. "How will we buy Lucindur's strings?"

Whitney eyed Lucindur for a moment. Her look was one part commiserative; two parts *Yes-Whitney-what-are-you-going-to-do?* She didn't have to say it out loud.

"That robe's not the only thing I've stolen over the years worth enough to cover the cost and more," he said. "I'll travel just northeast, there's a ring buried beneath a tree—"

"That what this is about?" Tum Tum broke in. "Ye trespassed on me property over that stolen rag? Aye, how much ye be needin?"

"No, that's quite all right," Whitney said, while at the same time, Lucindur told him the number.

Tum Tum whistled. "And that be for strings for the instrument ye told me about. The one that can help young Sora?"

"The very same," Lucindur said. "And enough to help our troupe get back on its feet."

Tum Tum scratched his wiry black beard, then snapped his fingers. "Be back in a jiff."

"Tum Tum, wait," Whitney said, but the door behind the bar was already swinging shut. He turned to Lucindur. "How could you do that? You barely know him? I'm not borrowing money from a friend!"

"Whitney, look at this place." She gestured around. "It's clear he has enough to lend. Perhaps even give."

There wasn't one bit of untruth in her words. His eyes were drawn immediately to the large golden mermaid statue once again. But still, it felt wrong.

"This isn't Glinthaven," Whitney said. "Everything has a cost."

Tum Tum returned and tossed a bag of coins over the bar to Whitney, so he had no choice but to catch it. "Probably can't help yer troupe, me lady, but that be enough for the strings."

"Tum Tum…" Whitney said, words trailing off.

"Don't ye start with me. I'd be dead wasn't for ye and Sora. Ain't got many friends in this world, and ye be one of the last who ain't a pirate. Take it. Find the upyr or whatever you think ye need to do. Just save Sora. She's a good lass. The only ye've ever loved, I think."

Whitney heard a soft gasp upon hearing the word 'love.' He glanced back and saw Talwyn with her hand over her mouth. Lucindur tried to whisper something to her, but she brushed by and rushed upstairs.

Whitney knew there wasn't much to be said. Dwarves were stubborn as mules. And even more so, they loved their gold. Hoarding it, trading it, showing it off. When one willingly decided to give gold away, that it was a gesture not to be taken lightly.

Instead of wounding his friend's pride, Whitney settled on, "Thank you."

"Yes, thank you, Mr. Tum Tum!" Gentry exclaimed. His whole expression went bright. Whitney had never seen him so excitable.

"I'll pay you back, Tum Tum," Whitney said. "I promise."

Tum Tum waved in dismissal. "A promise from you ain't worth enough."

"That might be the truth. But, truly, you have my word." Whitney tossed the bag in the air and caught it again.

"Whitney, just do what ye need to. Gold Grin's got so much stashed away and nothin to use it on, he won't know the difference. Vanished anyway, the bastard. We set all this up, gettin along great, then he and his crew sail off one night and haven't sent word since."

"He's probably chasing some woman across the map again," Whitney remarked.

"Consider this his punishment," Tum Tum joked.

Lucindur moved in front of Tum Tum and curtsied with the grace of a seasoned performer. "Thank you, my new friend."

Tum Tum took her hand and kissed the back of it. "Happy to help, me lady. Keep anything extra, and for yer troupe, there be a whole mess of dead grimaur downstairs. Their talons and feathers especially get a small fortune at a shop east side of the city. I'll tell you where."

"Your kindness knows no bounds, master dwarf," she said, pulling her hand away.

"Happy to do more if I can." He shot a familiar look over at Whitney. It was the same way he'd looked at plenty of women over the years. Whitney shook his head.

"Tum Tum, after all these years, you're still out of your yigging mind," he said.

VI

THE KNIGHT

T he familiar, musty smell of the Yarrington Cathedral was a welcomed aroma. Torsten sat on the front pew, flanked on both sides by the whole of the Royal Council. Directly beside him, King Pi picked at a hangnail. The room was dead silent as anyone bearing significant names or titles sat behind them, watching as Father Dellbar Morningweg stared up at the prismatic light filtering through the ceiling above the altar while sisters of Iam doused him in luminescent paint.

"Can I be honest with you, Sir Unger?" Pi leaned over and asked.

As soon as word spread of how his blessed blindfold gave Torsten the sight to uncover Valin Tehr's treachery, the choice for Father Morningweg to be named High Priest was abundantly clear. God's Mirror, located in Hornsheim's Abbey, reflected a beam of light, visible in the night sky all the way from Yarrington, signaling to the world that a unanimous decision had been made. Every priest sanctified by Iam cast their ballots to anoint the former Father of Fessix to be Dellbar the Holy, High Priest of all Pantego.

"You can always be honest with me, Your Grace," Torsten replied.

"I was beginning to question if Iam was still with us."

"With everything that's happened to you," Torsten said, *"to this kingdom of late, I understand."*

"I was considering removing the High Priest from my Royal Council and renouncing the Church of Iam as an extension of the Crown. All it seems to cause is trouble."

Torsten swallowed back his suddenly dry throat. "We cannot let the actions of a few taint our minds. Your father—"

"Was a great man, Sir Unger. I know. I've never felt what he claimed to have though. We all hear stories of being touched by Iam. Feeling his presence. Knowing he's there. Not me. Maybe it's Redstar's fault, but even before... Wren's sermons have always been a chore. I'd rather have been studying."

"And judging by your skills with our language and knowledge of our history, you've accomplished plenty of that." Torsten chuckled. "Your Grace, I have been to every corner of this world. Fought and converted heretics. Seen miracles. I've spoken the very words you've just quoted... I've found, there isn't a person in Pantego not seeking faith in something, looking in all the wrong or right places. It's what we do while we're here on this plane. But sometimes, if we're patient, the light presents itself when we least expect it."

"And it has," Pi said. He laid his small hand upon Torsten's. "In you. I allowed Valin to deceive me, just like Redstar and the Buried Goddess."

"That wasn't your fault, Your Grace. It was mine."

"No, Sir Unger. You stopped him. I've been told many Council members thought you went mad from blindness when you killed my uncle, but I didn't. I could hear my mother telling me to trust you. Iam returned your sight, so you could save me yet again."

Torsten's eyes couldn't tear, but he tried not to let the stone in his throat show. He knew the risks he'd taken that night, killing a member of the Royal Council at the foot of the Glass Throne. A part of him never expected to walk out alive and truly, he was lucky an arrow didn't bury itself within him at that very moment. Even if it had, Torsten would have been proud if separating Valin Tehr's head from his body was his final service to the last of Liam's line.

"It is my sworn duty to protect you," Torsten said. "I will never stop until my time here is over, and I find myself at the Gate of Light, Iam willing."

"It should be you, up there," Pi said, nodding toward Father Morningweg's ceremony. "The orepul. *Mount Lister. Valin. It was your persistence which showed me Iam."*

"I am honored, Your Grace. You have no idea. But a man of the cloth should not have seen the things I have. Done the things I've done. I felt doubt too, Your Grace. Thought we were forsaken. But I know Iam is with us now, and I am happy to serve as His sword."

"And what if I want a world where he doesn't need a sword?"

"Then my time here is done." Torsten turned to the young king and smiled. "Trust in the new Holy Father. Much as I love and miss Wren, there's never been a priest like Dellbar the Holy. In more ways than one, He'll need you as much as we need him."

"The reading is beginning," Lord Kaviel Jolly leaned over and whispered, making no effort to mask his annoyance. It was rare to hear a man so comfortable with taking that tone with a king, but Torsten knew that was exactly what was needed. King Pi, finally, was in good hands. Unorthodox ones, perhaps, but good none the less.

"Shog shuckin…" Alfotdrumlin Cragrock cursed as the mule beneath him momentarily lost its footing on a bit of stray rock.

Torsten was stirred from the memory of his last day with King Pi before setting off to be the Sword of Iam once again. From atop his tall chestnut mare, he glanced over at the young dwarf riding beside him, on the inside so Torsten was nearest the ledge. Age was a difficult thing to determine when it came to the dwarves. Truth be told, Torsten hadn't ever seen a baby dwarf, but he'd heard tales of them coming out fully bearded, male and female alike.

However, this one, judging by his lack of patience and proneness to sudden outbursts of anger, was young.

"You're in control of the beast," Torsten instructed, "not the other way around."

"Easy for ye to say," Al grumbled.

As they moved to reach Torsten's camp set up on a plateau just west of the Jarein Gorge, it wasn't lost on him how blessed he was. Months being led around like an old blind wretch, now the light of dawn guided him, and it was he who now did the leading once more.

He'd never seen the gorge walls in such a way. Not painted with the beauty of countless shades of reddish stone, but instead, with light. Through his blessed blindfold, Torsten could see the way it played across the crags; a dance with shadow. He wondered if this was how Iam once saw the world he helped create. Such purity. Such grace.

One night spent in a dwarven inn had him more well-rested then he'd felt in ages. Salted pork, water so pure it could only be drawn from melted snow traveling through kilometers of natural filtration to finally settle in the deepest subterranean trough. The bed barely fit a man his size and was firm like dwarves like it, but after shoving two of them together, Torsten slept as soundly as he could ever remember having done. For so long, his Kingdom felt on the brink of destruction, but that deep-seated fear was dwindling.

Oleander's death wasn't in vain. It helped remove snakes like Valin, and insert trusted lords like Kaviel Jolly at King Pi's side. With the boy no longer worried about his mother's condition, Torsten had left him in Yarrington in a better place than ever. Ravenous in his studies of both history and scripture. The priests had returned from Hornsheim, and fresh faith, Torsten knew, would do good for both him and the realm.

Even now, Torsten wished he could've stayed at Pi's side, guiding him, but he couldn't deny Mak's challenge and let more people die. Torsten had killed Redstar. Now, the last of the deceiver's ilk would fall. Reacquiring the trust of Liam's old dwarven allies would ensure that.

Brouben traveled east around the gorge with Lucas. Torsten looked back at Brouben's younger brother Al, covering his eyes against the rising sun. Sweat poured from his forehead like he'd never felt such warmth. A clanbreaker walked on each side, decked out in their spiked armor, faces as hard as the stone which they called home. Two more went with his warrior brother, around to the east gate of White Bridge.

"So, is this your first time outside your kingdom's walls?" Torsten asked.

Al nodded. "My father thought it was time for my Commute."

"Ah, that's right," Torsten remembered. When all dwarven men celebrated the arrival of their manhood—the day they could heft the weight of Meungor's axe—they spent a year outside the three kingdoms. They were meant to learn everything they could about the world, gathering information on future allies or enemies. Some found the life beyond the mountains so enticing, they'd leave and never return, making their homes in places like Yarrington which was accepting of all races and peoples as long as they bent the knee to the king and bowed their head to Iam.

"No better place to learn about Iam's world than Yarrington," Torsten said.

"Is it this hot?" Al asked. "And this bright?"

Torsten chuckled. "You'll get used to it. Your father raved about your skill with coin over supper. Our coffers could use the expertise."

"Are ye sure he wasn't talking about Brouben's fighting?"

"I'm sure."

"That's a first," Al grumbled.

Torsten could see the lines of regret written all over the young dwarf's face. "Trust me. Warriors like your brother and me are as common as house rats. Bright minds like yours? Now, those are the ones who truly bathe in Iam's light. You'll get along well with our King. Barely thirteen and his mind is keen as any grown man I've met."

Al nodded but said nothing. His gaze darted up as a flock of gallers flew overhead, then back down as wind rattled a lonely tree along the winding road.

"They're not dangerous," Torsten said.

"I think I prefer goblins," Al replied, then shuddered. "What happened to yer last Master of Coin, anyway?"

Torsten winced as he pictured his blade cleaving Valin Tehr's head from his shoulders, then the body of his fellow Shieldsman Wardric, murdered by Yuri Darkings, Valin's predecessor.

"The position comes with many… pressures," Torsten said, trying to mask his true feelings. "Greed takes a heavy toll on men. There's a lot to learn, but I think you can help us find someone worthy while making great strides, yourself. King Liam's often declared the importance of a fruitful relationship with our dwarven friends. We won't ignore it again."

"Halt!" someone shouted.

Torsten looked up and saw a dozen Glassmen, bowstrings pulled taut from the ridge above. Behind Torsten, dwarven hammers and axes slid free, but Torsten knew the clanbreakers wouldn't even need those weapons. Al panicked, and so did his mule, causing the beast to dart forward, and him to roll off its side. All his compressed, dwarven muscle resulted in a *thud* and a grunt that echoed across the gorge.

"Sir, sorry sir!" said Sir William Marcos, who led the unit. He waved for the others to lower their bows.

Torsten ignored them and went to help Al, but the clanbreakers didn't back down a hair.

Al cursed in ways Torsten's human ears didn't understand as Torsten helped him to his feet. Sir Marcos skidded down the rocky slope to join in.

"Is that how ye greet all yer guests out here?" Al grumbled.

"My humblest apologies," Sir Marcos said. "Some goblins tried to raid our supplies overnight."

"Goblins again. This far south?" Torsten questioned.

"Scared off easy down the cliffs, but not without some of our spiced meat."

"They're a pain these days," Al said. "But the grimaurs are worse when they sneak in through the upper tunnels and lay eggs."

"Well, my friend, I can assure you that we have neither in Yarrington," Torsten said. He placed his hand on the dwarf's shoulder, noticing how slender it was. A life without mining or wielding an axe had certainly stunted his growth.

"Now, come," Torsten said. "I'll have a cart prepared for you. Rest here the night, and you can depart with morning's light. I'd have you escorted by some of my finest men, but I think your guards will do just fine."

Only now did the clanbreakers stow their weapons once more.

"By the time you reach Yarrington," Torsten continued, "word of your father's desire will have reached the Royal Council. You'll be welcomed with open arms."

"Isn't that great for father?" Al shrugged Torsten off and continued up the path on his own.

"Pretty proper for a dwarf, isn't he?" Sir Marcos asked when Al was out of earshot.

Even without eyes, the look Torsten shot young Sir Marcos had him slinking back.

They're the best we have, Torsten reminded himself.

They reached camp shortly after sundown. A legion of the best soldiers and Shieldsmen Yarrington could afford to lose awaited—young, green soldiers like Sir Marcos. Half had been transferred down from Crowfall now that the Drav Cra raiders in their homeland seemed to be avoiding the Glass Kingdom at all costs. Now, Torsten knew, they were focusing their wrath on northern dwarven kingdoms. Additionally, spring was rapidly waning to summer, and the Drav Cra tended to remain above Winter's Thumb during the hottest parts of the year.

Torsten looked around. When he'd first received his blessed sight, the strange effect the firelight was having on the men would have made him a bit dizzy, but now he was used to it. Two hundred men, and a dwarven contingent just as large accompanying Lucas.

All reports on Mak's movement with his remaining warriors after their defeat outside Nahanab told him the Drav Cra dradinengor had fewer men than he; that Torsten should have enough to reclaim the heart of the Glass Road which connected all of the kingdom, from Yarrington to Yaolin City, and even south to Winde Port. Word from Sir Nikserof was that their siege would end soon. Muskigo's supplies were running out while more and more potential allies abandoned his cause, and no Caleef surfacing to help turn the tide either way, no matter how many search parties scoured the land.

"Sir Unger!" Dellbar the Holy called over. "The blessed Shieldsman returns."

Father Morningweg, now the High Priest of Pantego sat by a pot of porridge being warmed by fire, entertaining a group of soldiers. The way his words slurred and his head tilted—Torsten could tell he was drunk, as usual. His breath reeked all the way through the ceremony that had named him High Priest. Torsten remembered Pi recoil from the stench as they embraced.

Dellbar Morningweg stood, nearly tripped over a log, and was steadied by a few soldiers. Ale sloshed out of his tankard and onto his hand and sleeve.

The men laughed and slapped one another's backs.

"Never met a priest like him!" cried one of the Glass soldiers.

"He's like one of us," said another.

There is no priest like him, Torsten thought.

"And you return with dwarves," Dellbar the Holy said. "So, it seems once again, Sir Unger has good fortune."

"Your Holiness." Torsten bowed his head and circled his eyes in prayer. "This is Lord Alfotdrumlin Cragrock, son of King Lorgit Cragrock." Between getting used to calling Morningweg by his new name and title, and trying to recall Al's full name, Torsten's head swam. However, he had been sure to get it right as anything else would have been highly insulting to the dwarven prince.

Al didn't say a word as the High Priest circled him. Dellbar's chain made up of a dozen Eyes of Iam jangled, and his bright white robes dragged through the dirt as he moved. His eyes were bloodshot, beard unkempt. If ever there was a man who didn't appear holy, here he was.

"Scrawny for a dwarf, isn't he?" Dellbar the Holy remarked.

"Excuse me?" Al questioned.

"Your Holiness." Torsten clutched him by his loose sleeve and towed him to the side. As he sucked in a breath to talk, the stench of alcohol wafted over him. "I thought we discussed your drinking," he whispered.

"We discussed a great many things on the way here, Sir Unger," Dellbar said, then lost balance for a moment.

"You're High Priest now. People look to you for guidance. All of these men."

"And I'm one of them. Here, here!" He raised his ale and cheered, and soldiers joined him. He went to take a drink, and Torsten tore the mug from his hand.

"Your Holiness, people expect—"

"What?" Dellbar interrupted. "I'm sure old Wren was sober, and all that got us was Redstar in the Glass Castle." Torsten's lips narrowed to a bitter line. Dellbar stared for a few seconds before he smiled and patted both of Torsten's shoulders, having to lean up on the balls of his feet just to reach.

"Sorry," he said. "But this was my state when I blessed that cloth which made you see again. Clearly, it's how Iam wants me."

A handful of responses reached Torsten's lips before he sighed. "Surely, you should return to the capital now? Perhaps you can accompany our new ally. As High Priest, one of your many responsibilities—"

"Is to be where Iam asks," Dellbar interrupted again. "I apologize Sir Unger, but I hadn't spoken to our great Lord in many years. Then, the first time I do, I find you. We can't possibly know his will, but I know that Iam wants me here by your side. We owe it to ourselves to find out why." He flashed another crooked grin, then used the distraction to swipe the ale from Torsten's hand.

"We're headed to war, Father. It's no place for a man of the cloth."

Dellbar, like all priests of Iam, had removed his eyes. He no longer wore a blindfold like Torsten now wore, but even still, it was as if the man looked directly into Torsten's soul. "There are tales of Liam's wars," he said, "when the priests marching with the army called upon Iam's protection against the magics of fallen gods, when they received his light to their very hands to shield his people."

It wasn't a lie. Torsten had been at war with Panping when Liam led the charge. He hadn't been on the front lines, but he'd seen it. He'd always wondered if it was just the confusion of war that made him see what he'd wanted to see, but this confirmed it.

"And here you are, a blind man with sight." He raised his own hands. "And here I am, alive, despite what happened to my home. We don't go seeking miracles, Sir Knight. They confront us when we least expect it."

The High Priest raised his tankard, then staggered back to his seat. Torsten stared, dumbfounded, unable to argue. The Church of Iam Torsten knew was formal, refined; a reflection of their God himself. He remembered being a child growing up in grimy Dockside, and how, when he stepped into a church, it was like being transported to another world, a better world.

To him, it was inspirational. But as he watched the way his men caroused with their High Priest, he couldn't help but wonder if the time for a priest *of* the people instead of just *for* the people had come. Perhaps, this would be the cure for those who'd turned to blood magic and cults, to false gods or none at all.

"I like your priest," Al remarked on his way by. "Do they all drink like dwarves?"

"He's one of a kind," Torsten muttered.

"Meungor would be proud."

Al's mood brightened for the first time since leaving his father's halls. He joined the men and downed an entire tankard so fast Torsten wasn't sure how it was possible. The soldiers cheered the dwarf on, offered him another, and again until his beard was dripping wet.

"If Yarrington is like this, I'll be happy as a goat on a spit!"

A smile touched the corners of Torsten's lips, but he didn't let it last for long. Then, turning to the east, toward their objective, he watched a pillar of smoke cut the moonlit sky, rising from the area of White Bridge. He hoped it wasn't what he feared, for the Drav Cra burned their dead, turned them to ashes and spread them across the earth.

Torsten inhaled deeply, unsure if the smell of cinder and the faintly sweet scent of burning flesh was just his imagination or not. Then he shouted, "Warriors of the Glass Kingdom! Our brothers await us across the White Bridge. It's time we rid our lands of murderers and heretics. Find your peace with Iam, with yourselves, for in the morning, we march. And, in truth, I know not what awaits us."

VII

THE DAUGHTER

Mahraveh al'Tariq hung onto the mast of her new fleet's flagship, the *Shavi*, with one arm. The cool breeze kissed her half-shaved head. She still wasn't used to it, or the many tattoos inscribed along it and her neck marking her as the new al'Tariq afhem, which still felt like her skin had been burned by fire. She'd taken the name as well, as was custom—a fresh start.

She extended her spear with her other hand, its razor-sharp tip cutting through the thick layer of fog settling in all around them as they neared Trader's Bay. Wisps of gray and white swirled about it, creating a trail as if a spirit followed along with her. She knew the souls of those lost rested in the current beneath the creaking wood of the vessel. However, she couldn't help but picture Jumaat up here with her.

She'd been awaiting the fog, sitting on the coast of the Nipaval Islands, her new home, letting the waves run against her thighs, asking the God of Sand and Sea to cover their approach to Trader's Bay with Siren's Breath.

Finally, he'd obliged.

She could hear the rhythm of oar-men rowing below her and

around her from the fleet she'd won in Tal'du Dromesh. In addition to those dozen, more ships had been delivered by the Jalurahbak Afhemate, when their afhem, Tingur, declared his allegiance.

She wasn't sure exactly what awaited them at Nahanab or in the bay, even so close as they were. The Glass had tightened their grip and kept messages from coming in or out. Mahraveh wasn't even sure if any of the letters she'd sent reached her besieged father. Even Yuri Darkings' birds or spies couldn't seem to break the defenses.

Mahraveh glared down at the 'expert on Glassmen.' Yuri stooped over a map on the upper deck. Every time he spoke, she considered having him tossed overboard. He may have accomplished his goal by escaping with Farhan to bring Muskigo's plight to Latiapur, and Mahraveh's ears, but the wrong man died that day.

As if reading her mind, he looked up, eyes like a diseased vulture. He waved for her to come down, and she made no effort to hide her annoyance before sliding down the mast and dropping to his side.

"What is it?" she asked.

"If I had to guess, their blockade will start here," he said, pointing to an area of the strait that led from the Boiling Waters into Trader's Bay.

"And what do *you* know about these waters?" Mahi spat. She rattled off a few insults in Saitjuese so he wouldn't understand.

Yuri bit his lip, then glowered down his nose at her. From that angle, he really did look like a vulture. Mahi couldn't understand why her father would ever have chosen to work with the man. And still, despite his many promises, Caleef Sidar Rakun had yet to be delivered safely to Latiapur.

"I grew up on these waters, my *Afhem*." Yuri spoke the title like it were a curse.

"My Afhem, they're ahead!" Bit'rudam shouted from the bow. They were the same two words, but from Bit'rudam's mouth, they sounded so much different. He was young, like Mahi, but experienced in naval combat. He'd been the member of her new afhemate to escort her home after her victory; a loyal follower already, though probably not the best in a fight. He was too reedy, like Jumaat.

Mahi collared her pink-skinned advisor. "Get inside and don't come out," she ordered. "For reasons I don't understand, my father wanted you alive, and so, you'll stay that way."

Yuri whipped around to face her. Even the thought passing through the man's head of aggression toward her brought the unmistakable rasp of swords sliding free. She stifled a sneer. All her life, even as Muskigo's daughter, it took all her effort to garner attention, and when she did, it was to pull her away from some danger unfit for a *lady*. Now, she had it and their respect.

"Of course," Yuri said, offering a scant bow. "These days, I'm too delicate for fighting, anyhow." He swept into the ship's upper cabin, his long robe swishing at his back. He'd performed his duty in providing insight into the Glass fleet tactics and the region. Mahi was done with him, and she hoped, when her father was free, he'd be done with him as well.

A concern for another time, she thought.

She turned to Bit'rudam, and through the dense fog, offered him a curt nod. He brought two fingers to his mouth and blew. All around, loud whistles sounded from the silhouettes of the Shesaitju ships sailing alongside them. The heavy pounding of drums reverberated the deck beneath Mahi's sandaled feet. It was a signal, but more than anything, it was meant to induce terror upon the enemy. One of her father's many lessons was that in any battle where the sides were evenly matched, it is the more fearful party that loses.

Mahi pushed her spear down and vaulted up onto the quarter-deck. The ship's helmsman held them steady, but the day was calm. Perfect for battle.

"Afhem Tingur!" Mahi called out to the ship alongside them.

Mahi wasn't sure how a man so plump and out of shape had ever claimed an afhemate; perhaps he was born into it. Regardless, he was the best ally she had, and his men loved him enough to never have turned on him, even after decades. Afhems weren't known for their soft-spoken kindness, after all.

"My ships are prepared, Afhem Mahraveh," Tingur replied, moving to the railing. "On your signal. May the Eternal Current guide us!"

Mahi waited a few long seconds, focusing on the sound of the water pounding against their hulls. Then she raised her hand, and said, "No, may it drown them," before she thrust it forward.

The driving rhythm of the drummers hastened, and Mahi turned to watch as they pressed through the orange-tinted fog, growing brighter with each beat of the drums. Water splashed. The persistent patter of oars, faster and faster.

They'd spent the entire journey planning for battle—Mahi's first real battle. Tal'du Dromesh was simple—not easy, but simple nonetheless: kill or be killed. But this was different. For years, she'd found herself sidling up as close as she could to her father and his commanders, listening to their legend of battles led by great afhems, or those about how King Liam got lucky in defeating them. Now, she'd have to glean strategy from every one, every story.

Her heart rampaged against her ribcage as the moon's soft orange glow became a searing assault upon her eyes. The natural fog turned to a very unnatural smog. Before leaving Nipaval, her new island, she'd confiscated every ounce of flammable whale oil from her many fisherwomen. Now, saturated with the stuff, Afhem Tingur's rickety old ships sailed straight for the Glass blockade.

Somehow, she knew it was what her father would do.

For the Glassmen, fire was crucial to life. It kept them warm in their oversized houses and illuminated dark places. For Mahi's people, it was a weapon.

Thank the God of Sand and Sea for fog, Mahi thought again.

By the time the warning horns of the Glass army sounded, Mahi could already see the tremendous shadows of their warships —big, bulky, not meant for maneuvering in such tight confines. They were meant only to intimidate and sink deep into the water so the soft pink-skins could hide from the sun in their cabins.

"Raise sails!" Bit'rudam shouted.

The *Shiva* lurched as her men raised sleek, angled sails. They couldn't carry their ships as fast as the Glassmen's, but they allowed for far better maneuverability in places like the rocky southern coast and now, Trader's Strait. Shouting rang across the waters, stirred by racing and turning vessels. Heavy crossbows fixed to the Glass ships' bulwarks rained down upon Mahi's burning ships.

Once close enough, and sure the heavy vessels would collide with Glass galleons, her oar men abandoned their positions and dove into the water. Shesaitju could handle a swim, especially these men from the isles. Their leather armor was lightweight, flexible, not hard steel that would sink them like rocks.

The three flaming missiles rammed into the Glass warship at the center of their formation. Wood snapped and creaked, a sound like the gates of exile itself bursting. Mahi could feel the heat of the rising blaze even from where she stood, watching. Many creatures of the sea died for the oil which ignited it, now not in vain. She said a silent prayer, thanking the Eternal Current for its costly sacrifice.

All the other Glass ships turned to take advantage of their artillery, just like Mahi, Bit'rudam, and unfortunately, Yuri had planned. Their captains, clearly in a panic and used to calmer seas, misjudged the depths and the mistake caused the racket of more splitting wood and gurgling water.

The first part of the plan had worked. The Glassmen had spies and dignitaries all over the Black Sands. Even the blind missionary priests at the churches they built throughout the region couldn't be trusted. It would all be enough to know about Mahi's victory in the arena, but Glass women were weak. They'd underestimate her. She knew they wouldn't expect her to charge head-on, and her gambit had provided the advantage.

The fire pushed the enemy fleet apart and allowed Mahi's to sail straight through. Soldiers leaped into the waters on both sides, some burning alive. They met Mahi's own men in the waters, those who'd powered the flaming rams. There, they wrestled, the Shesaitju warriors claiming victory over most. Once through, Mahi's ship turned one way, Tingur the other, and they were able to coast along both flanks of the enemy ships at the same time.

"Shields!" Mahi shouted as they grew close enough to fall under arrow and bolt fire. She wore a buckler on her left forearm so she could wield her spear with two hands in battle. Less protection, more speed. She needed it, considering her slight build. Men scurried about the ship with their round shields raised, climbing the masts and booms, ready to swing over and board the enemy vessel. Others swarmed in the water, already climbing up the enemy hulls. Arrows slashed down at them and stained the water red.

Mahi watched the fighting unfold as well as she could through the smog. Thousands of men in leather and steel, dancing around the decks of ships on both sides—leaping, climbing, swinging, all while fire raged at their backs.

"My Afhem!" Bit'rudam shouted. His shield raised in front of her and an arrow clanged off before it could reach her.

Mahi snapped into action. After the first of her warriors mounted the enemy warships, others fired up barbed arrows attached to ropes. They stabbed into the enemy deck, and dozens more of her men scurried upside-down along them like ants, scimitars between their teeth. Not her. She bounced up and tip-toed along the rope toward the aftercastle.

She felt like a child again, trying to peek in on her father's meetings in the bazaar. At least, that is, until she saw the face of a Glass soldier on the other side of a rail. He slashed at the rope. It frayed, didn't split, but it was enough for Mahi to start losing balance. Another swipe and the line snapped free, but it was too late. She pushed off with one foot and flipped over the soldier. He turned just in time to meet a kick, delivered right to his jaw that tossed him over the railing.

Mahi felt the rumble of footsteps behind her and ducked. A longsword raced overhead. She heard it connect with wood as she rolled right, then popped up, thrusting her spear into her attacker's chest, under one of her knees. The *Scorpion's Sting* strike. Her father's terrifying second in command, Impili, taught her that move. She remembered how her chest stung after his training polearm prodded her.

The soldier collapsed at her feet, and she took a beat to measure her surroundings. The Glass warship was massive, like its own little floating village. Tiered decks, more sails than seemed necessary—maybe it all made sense in the bitter north, though she doubted it. Here, it just seemed pretentious.

The fighting continued to rage as her men boarded the warship from both sides, same as they had the rest of their vessels. The Glassman fell behind shield walls and guarded access to the lower decks, but they were no use in naval battle. Mahi grabbed hold of the jib, pulled herself up, and ran along the boom. She drove down amid their formation, breaking the shield wall so her warriors could penetrate the enemy defenses.

She pushed herself straight up with her spear before the Glassmen could do anything about it. Their blades slashed against its shaft, but the blackwood was sturdy as iron and held as she flung herself back to her own ranks. Bit'rudam grabbed her hand to steady her, allowing for a slingshot around him to join back in the fray.

In the arena, she recalled being terrified. Now, she understood all those times her father rode off to war against, or earn the allegiance of, some afhem. She felt that thrill of being on the brink between life and death, because she knew she was better than the warriors across from her. Her body twisted and bent, dodging their blows, swift and pliable as a sand snake.

Glass soldiers fled the lower decks to escape their flooding ship only to meet death above. It was turning out to be a massacre worthy of Mahi's father's name, and judging by the pained cries of Glassmen filling the bay, the situation was the same all over.

Then Mahi heard a drum—one of their own pounding frantically and without rhythm. She swiped her spear in a wide arc to keep any attackers at bay, then sprung toward the railing. She looked down and saw Yuri Darkings at her ship's aft, having stolen a mallet from a warrior.

"From the bay, you damned fools!" he screamed, pointing. "From the bay!"

Mahraveh followed his finger, and through the heavy mixture of fog and smoke, appeared countless tiny shadows. Oars flapped like dragonfly wings over the reflective water. Carved figureheads only made them seem more like monsters, and none of them bore religious symbols of Iam.

"Drav Cra!" Mahraveh turned and shouted. "Drav Cra, port side and forwa—"

A rogue arrow struck her in the shoulder just before she could raise her arm-buckler. The force knocked her back, and her spear slipped from her fingers and clattered onto the *Shiva's* deck as she flipped over the railing.

Cold water hit her, stealing her breath away. The two ships—

one hers and one belonging to the enemy, rose up on their respective sides. Like mountains, they cast shadows over her, leaving her in near-total darkness.

Her back smacked against debris and she twisted, desperate to find her bearings, but the Bay sloshed in response to the giant vessels at war, and she plunged beneath the surface. Blood swirled out from her shoulder, bright lines of pain coursing through it when she banged into another drowned corpse. Her lungs started to sting, and splotches of white closed in around her vision. She'd been so surprised by the arrow and the fall, that she hadn't had a chance to even gather a lungful of air before finding herself lost in the waters, and what little breath she'd had was driven out by the impact.

With the smoke and the fog, she couldn't quite tell how far the surface was. She kicked as hard as she could and used her buckler to propel her, but she grew fainter with every motion, and as confusion beset her, she feared she might be swimming deeper.

A spear poked through the water and slid under her waist. It left a shallow cut on her arm on its way by. However, it didn't pull back for another attack. She wrapped herself around it and felt the world rising to greet her. She gasped and pawed for the side of her ship with her free hand. Her fingers slid between two blackwood planks. Before she knew it, she was being heaved up onto the deck, then rolled over onto her back, She coughed, water sputtering from her lungs.

Yuri Darkings stooped over her, hands hovering above her shoulder wound like he wanted to help but wasn't sure how to. Shoving him aside, she rolled to her knees and wiped spit from her mouth. The arrow still poked out of her shoulder. She snapped it off at the shaft, then stretched out the wound.

"My Afhem," Yuri said.

"Give it here." She ripped her spear out of his hands and used it to get to her feet. Yuri stood nearby, baffled until she said, "Thank you."

She thought she saw his rigid features ready to soften, then he scowled. "I told you they'd reuse the Drav Cra ships! It's what those people do. Assimilate."

"*Your* people."

"Not the way they see me."

Mahi grunted and staggered toward the ship's mast. Drav Cra longboats raced toward them. Tens of them, and Yuri was right, they weren't manned by their builders, but more of the Glass army coming from the direction of the ravaged Winde Port docks. She remembered Yuri bringing them up while they planned this attack. He was convinced that when the Glass army betrayed their allies over Drad Redstar's misdeeds in Yarrington, that they'd do whatever it took to conserve ships in order to help with reconstruction efforts in Winde Port. She'd dismissed him, but he'd been right. The Glass didn't just defeat their enemies, they absorbed everything they had.

I should've known better after all Father taught me.

"Stay behind me," Mahraveh told Yuri.

"They'll destroy our ships!" he protested.

"Then it's a good thing my father is on the land."

Drav Cra Longboats were explicitly built for ram-and-board tactics. They were smaller, with only a single sail and hard, iron prows designed to break ice. Like giant spears skimming the water. But those prows broke ships as well, and while some sailed crooked due to the inexperienced pink-skins controlling the oars, there were enough to make a mess of things.

Yuri muttered a handful of curses and backed away until he could go no further. Mahraveh stood alone with her spear ready. Tendrils of fire caught in the water from oil or debris curled around the enemy vessels. Mahraveh wasn't sure if they'd intended to wait so long, sacrificing so many of their men, so that this new force could catch them spread out, but it worked.

From all positions, her people realized the situation and cried out orders. Afhem Tingur, himself, called attention to their flank. The pace of drumming shifted. Arrows from archers still positioned on Shesaitju ships zipped toward them—bolts from the mounted crossbows on the Glass ships as well.

Mahraveh held onto the mast as tight as she could while Bit'rudam and other soldiers swung down to stand at her side. She could practically see the whites of the enemies' eyes. Anger, terror—there was a mixture of all of it.

The world exploded around her as the first longboat rammed into the *Shiva's* side. The hull shattered, splintering below, and sending Mahraveh stumbling to the side. The planks making up the deck rippled, then rose to a point and split. Eerie silence bombarded her as drums stopped. Mahi's fleet on the bayside of the blockade was punctured. Glass soldiers poured onto the ships. No need for ropes or climbing; Mahi's ships were low and easily board-able. In the first phase of the battle, she'd had the upper hand, now things were equal.

In any battle where the sides were evenly matched, it is the more fearful party that loses.

She was afraid…

A fearsome army stood in wait while fighting still raged from the enemies remaining on the warships behind her, but her people were built for the sea, not theirs. Her people had their sea legs beneath them.

"The Glassmen think they rule the sea!" Mahi shouted, steeling herself in the face of her enemies. "But the sea is ours! Let the Eternal Current swallow them all!"

She charged forward, Bit'rudam and the others at her side, the damaged ship rocking as they moved. Then again, as shields, spears, and blades clashed.

VIII

THE REBEL

The Glassmen had Muskigo chained to a post in the heart of their camp. Wrists, ankles—everything. He knew he could escape if he wanted to. He'd been in worse, and the broken bones in his limbs which it would take to wriggle free would heal, same as they had the last time, and the time before that.

But his heart wouldn't.

"Where is her body?" Muskigo asked.

Like the changing of the tides, so went his will to fight. Mahraveh's braid lay at his feet. It took all his willpower not to stare at it. And he knew it belonged to her, that couldn't be faked. His darling impulsive daughter was dead.

"Given over to the Current," Babrak replied from his seat on a barrel, just beyond spitting distance. Muskigo knew because he'd tried. A circle of Shieldsmen surrounded them, ready to kill Muskigo if only he gave them a reason.

"That wasn't your right," Muskigo said.

"Well, you couldn't be reached, now, could you?" Babrak taunted.

Muskigo bit back a flurry of curses. "It was you, wasn't it? You told them where she was? Where I lived?"

Babrak sighed. His voice went soft, like a friend breaking bad news. "I didn't even have the chance, Muskigo. There are plenty in the northern sands who've suffered, thanks to your unsanctioned war. We're just… cleaning up the mess."

"Pis'truda!" Muskigo spat. "By negotiating with *them*? What did they offer—to make you the next Caleef?"

"Do you really think so lowly of me? There is only one Caleef until the God of Sand and Sea chooses the next. They offered peace."

"Yes, peace has been so kind to you," Muskigo said, eyes lowering to regard the rival afhem's rotund belly.

"It has been kind to us all."

"Tell that to my daughter!"

Babrak stomped closer until their noses were only a centimeter away. "Your daughter died because when the Glassmen came to bring her here as leverage, she fought back. Gave them no other choice. She died for the same reason your wife did—because she had you in her life."

"Why don't you unchain me and say that again." He knew Babrak was just trying to get under his skin. He'd never forgiven Muskigo's wife, Pazradi, for loving Muskigo instead of him. And none of the ever-growing harem of women Babrak kept around since seemed to satiate him.

"Please." Babrak slapped him lightly on the side of the face a few times with his giant hands. Then he smiled. "You're scrawnier than ever. I'd snap you like a twig."

Taking advantage of Babrak's closeness, Muskigo spat at him again. This time, it landed squarely in the man's eye. Babrak didn't budge, not even as he wiped it away. He just kept smiling.

"No wonder none of the others came to my aid," Muskigo said. "Don't you understand what I'm after? We have the men.

Years of *peace* helped our numbers grow, and so now, we can rectify the errors of our past. We can stop fighting each other and instead, drive the pink pigs out. Even the Drav Cra united under a single leader."

"And now the Drav Cra are destroyed. You've always had vision, Muskigo, but that's all you are, a dreamer. Eventually, the Glass will tear themselves apart under their boy-king, and you'll get your dream. Why should so many of our people die for nothing?"

"To prove we are worthy of something."

"Something?" Babrak chuckled. "Ever since Liam buried our fathers, have our lands not flourished?"

"While they indoctrinate us with stories of their false god."

"So, we suffer a few churches in our cities, and we nod as their missionaries try to enlighten us. A tribute every season. It is what Caleef Sidar Rakun agreed to long ago. It was not your place to forsake our God for your own vengeance."

"I forsake nothing!"

"It's fitting though," Babrak continued, "that the great Muskigo Ayerabi, undefeated in battle, would be undone by none other than himself. Isn't it clear by the lack of support that you stand alone? The Current doesn't flow at your back, Muskigo. It piles sand in your path."

"Or perhaps you and your army are just eager to grow fatter sitting in your halls while the Caleef remains lost out there, thanks to them." Muskigo nodded toward the Glass soldiers.

Babrak threw his hands up in frustration and turned away. "You're exhausting. But I'm done arguing. It's time you take credit for all those who have died on your behalf. And not only our people, but theirs. We held an alliance—"

"Alliance," Muskigo scoffed. "As I recall, payment only went one way. We are their whores."

"Whatever you call it, it was law, signed between the Nothhelm Dynasty and our Caleef. How many have died on all sides? What you did to Winde Port will take years to repay. It was your own pride that caused this, Muskigo. And now it's over. We have bad history between us, but we are both Shesaitju. I have come to present an offer."

"You mean they sent you to me like a good, loyal zhulong?"

"The new king wants peace more than anything," Babrak said. "This offer comes only once. Their Wearer of White has already agreed to it. If you reject this offer, then the man you are, so much as I already despise him, is worthless. You are to present yourself before your followers and commit the mortal sin. You will claim responsibility for this rebellion, and you alone. You will take your own life, outside of battle or tribute."

"And?"

"And all of your followers will be spared. You sought to shoulder a burden our people never asked for. Our Caleef is missing because of it. Countless are dead. At the least, use this opportunity to spare the people inside Nahanab who were blinded by your greed."

"They'd rather die," Muskigo said.

"Then show them there is a better way." Babrak knelt, his zhulong skin armor squeezed tight against his oversized body. He scooped up a handful of black sand and let it trickle through his fingers. "Look, it is dry. It sifts like salt through my fingers. Must it be soaked in blood for you to come to your senses? For centuries, we have sacrificed our own upon these sands. For strength. For honor. To be as powerful as the sea and remembered in every grain of shifting sand. But there is strength in a long, fruitful life. There is truth in their light."

"Will you wear their white robes and burn out your eyes, too?" Muskigo snapped. "You are many things, but I never figured a coward to be among them. You're as soft as you look."

"It is true, I have sat in their churches. Listened to their priests. And have I been pulled beneath the sand? Have I been drowned? The light touches even the furthest sea. Pantego is changing. The old ways are just that… old."

"If your father—"

"My father is dead. As is yours." Babrak stood and brushed the sand off his knees as if he were allergic to it. The sight made Muskigo feel ill.

"Now." Babrak clapped his hands. "This offer won't last forever. Deny it, and the city will starve until the Glass can retake it. And they will… with ease. The foundations for new peace will be erected upon your followers' corpses. Or, they can be the ones laying the stones."

"You really think the pink-skins can be trusted?" Muskigo scoffed. "They'll kill them all."

"The marks of their afhemate will be burned off, but they will live. They will help construct a proper cathedral to Iam in Lati-apur and re-establish the trade that has left our great city the jewel of the South. It's all agreed upon."

"They are warriors. They'll never accept being markless!"

"Make them, or send them to the Current with your daughter. The choice is yours." Babrak turned and left the circle of guards. The men parted for him like he was one of their own.

"Babrak!" Muskigo screamed. "Babrak!"

He pulled at his shackles until his wrists bled and his muscles burned. Then his body collapsed, and he found himself staring straight at Mahraveh's braid.

He'd never been drowning before, but he imagined this was what it felt like when Caleefs passed and tributes threw themselves into the Boiling Waters, water filling their lungs unless they were the one to return blessed with the essence of the God of Sand and Sea. It was like Muskigo's heart and mouth were at war with each other.

"I should have brought you with me, my little sand mouse…"

he whispered. "Why did you fight? Why didn't you stay quiet and return to me?"

But he knew—his daughter had always been like him. It wasn't her fault she was conceived in the wrong tide and born a girl. She had a warrior's spirit and would have happily fought at his side, if only he'd asked.

His only solace was in knowing that she'd died as the fighter she'd always dreamed of being; that the Eternal Current would let her strong soul feed the waves that carve the earth, and not damn her to the ocean floor with the bottom-feeders.

But he also knew that time on Pantego was precious. The souls of the sea may have built the land, but the living shape its destiny. Her time was cut short because of him. Now, his afhemate would join her.

A sense of dread stole over him like never before. He wondered if this was what it meant to lose. He'd won the heart of his wife, Pazradi, from Babrak. He'd won his afhemate on the sands of Tal'du Dromesh. He'd grown his following and legend enough to launch a rebellion against those pis'trudas in Yarrington when so many others refused. He'd made the Glassmen tremble at Winde Port, destroyed the heart of their greatest warrior, Torsten Unger.

For what? he wondered.

A tear rolled down Muskigo's cheek and splashed down in the sand beside Mahraveh's hair. It stung against the countless cuts on his cheeks. He'd learned the ancient art of the black fist from the monks in the Eastern Ridge—turned his body into stone like the rocks in which they called home. Now, he may as well have been made from it.

He hadn't cried since the day his wife passed. He recalled the way young Mahraveh looked at him that awful day, like he was pathetic, and from then on, had vowed never to shed a tear. Yet now, she couldn't see. The sand was for the living, and she was beyond it.

Muskigo Ayerabi, the Scythe of Saujibar, had failed. Lost in battle for the first time. And the shame was unbearable.

IX

THE THIEF

"Just draw a little blood," Lucindur said, handing Whitney a small belt knife. It reminded him of Wetzel's blade that Sora carried around with her.

"What? Cut myself? Why?"

"When we found Sora, you'd needed something that belonged to her," she said. "That was Aquira. Unless you've got a lock of his white hair in your pocket, the only thing you have is a shared blood pact, correct?"

"I suppose," Whitney grumbled.

"Okay, so draw a little blood. Right there, on your arm." She pointed.

Whitney set the tip of the knife against his skin and took a shuddering breath.

"Would you like me to do it for you?" Lucindur asked.

"I've got it. I've got it."

Whitney winced as blood trickled from the wound on his arm.

"That's enough."

I suppose this is how Sora feels, he thought.

"The bond is so strong through Elsewhere, I can feel him even without the blood," she said.

"Then why did you make me cut myself?" Whitney complained.

"Take no chances when it comes to Lightmancery. You wouldn't want to be lost within forever, would you? Okay, now, just as before, close your eyes," Lucindur said.

They sat together, just she and Whitney, in the middle of the lower level of *Gold Grin's Grotto* surrounded by boxes and crates. Not ten yards away stood the now patched-up hole where Whitney and Gentry had encountered the grimaurs.

Whitney had to chase away a few more when he and the others gathered the bodies. Better that they be used to help the troupe than rot in a cave, driving away Tum Tum's patrons with their stink.

Could they really have anything to do with Nesilia? he wondered.

Tum Tum had mentioned it. And Whitney had spoken with the goddess, felt her evil enveloping him and Sora. Torsten thought he'd put a stop to whatever it was a goddess might've been up to atop Mount Lister, but more and more, Whitney encountered evidence to the contrary.

"You've got to clear your mind," Lucindur said. "We will not be successful if you are preoccupied."

"My mind is clear," Whitney said.

She smacked him on the hand.

"Lying won't help either," she scolded. "Think about the one called Kazimir and no one else, and let us hope he is truly in Brekliodad."

Whitney had no clue where the upyr would actually be. The last time he'd seen him was in Elsewhere, and there was every bit the chance he'd be there still. Would Lucindur's song drive Whitney straight back to that damnable plane? If it did, he might never escape. Or, he might have to relive all those awful moments over and over…

"You're not listening, Whitney Fierstown," she said. "Clear. Your. Mind. Think of nothing but the goal."

"I am trying." Whitney rolled his neck. "Okay. Kazimir. Kazimir, you white-haired freak. Where are you?"

"Ready?" Lucindur didn't wait for a response before she started plucking the strings of her newly repaired salfio. It took her an entire day to get them and cost all but a single gold autla at the bottom of Tum Tum's pouch. Whitney had stressed he go with her, keep her from getting fleeced, but she insisted that the Glintish trader wouldn't bring out the good stuff if a southerner were present. Instead, he had the awesome pleasure of cleaning out grimaur corpses.

The gentle tones of her instrument echoed throughout the ship, bouncing off the wood, creating an almost choral effect. She started slow, gaining confidence in the new strings. The melody picked up, and so did her willingness to pull at them with all the strength they required.

Finally, she started singing and focus flooded over Whitney.

Let your mind be opened,
eyes be opened.
Let the winds of eternity
bring upon them clarity.
Your eyes can't see
but your mind is free
to travel Pantego
wherever he may be.
Light upon stars
dancing afar.
Demon of Elsewhere
Pale of skin and hair
Upon song and light
give us sight.

Just as it had been in the graveyard when she'd played, magical embers began to swirl around them, and even with his eyes closed, he could see the light in the room seemed to drain away as if the portholes were being covered by drapes. There was only them. *Their* light.

> *See what you came to see.*
> *See with your soul, not with your eyes.*

Whitney felt himself falling, careening through dark space. Emptiness and nothing. The pit in his stomach rose to his throat, and his next breath smelled familiar. Dirt, stale water, horse shog. He opened his eyes, feeling hard earth beneath him. Bleary eyes opened to a wattle and daub home surrounded by a wooden fence. His parents' old house looked the same as it always had. Fear choked him. The thought of spending another six years in this place nearly drove him to the edge of insanity.

Then, Whitney spotted him: a sallow-faced demon, looking very confused.

Kazimir started screaming and kicking at the ground. That was when Whitney understood. Kazimir had been summoned here, just as he'd been.

"Who are you yelling at?" Whitney asked.

Kazimir spun and pulled a knife. "You."

"Me," Whitney said with a smile. "Not very nice getting snuck up on like that, is it?"

Kazimir lowered his blade slowly, then confirmed Whitney's thoughts. "Well, if you're here, at least it isn't Elsewhere again."

"Or did we never leave?"

Kazimir pursed his lips, scoffed, and turned away. "I don't have time for your games."

"No, wait. Please." Whitney rushed to meet him, hands palm out and pushing at the air.

"I haven't felt magic like this in a long time, thief," he said. "How are you doing this?"

"I need your help," Whitney said.

"Not interested," Kazimir answered.

"Kazzy, old friend," Whitney said, flanking Kazimir, trying to keep him from wandering away. "You know I wouldn't do this if it wasn't important. Please."

The upyr seemed to mull over the statement for a minute before saying, "You have thirty seconds. You robbed me of a grand feast. Who knows what my apprentice has gotten herself into."

"It's about Sora."

"I promised you I wouldn't touch the mystic, and I did not. The Sanguine Lords taught me my lesson for pushing beyond their will. Whatever happened to her, it was not me."

"No, no. Look… do you know where we are?" Whitney asked, changing tacks.

"I know where I was before you brought me to this trash-heap you call home."

"I didn't do it. Not really. A Lightmancer connected our minds."

That seemed to pique Kazimir's interest. A light twinkled in his soulless eyes and was gone the next instant.

"You believe me?" Whitney asked.

"A Lightmancer? Are you insane? You mortals won't be happy until all magic is snuffed out, but *they* were wiped out by the mystics for a reason.

Whitney tried not to show his surprise at Kazimir knowing about them. *Of course, he knows,* Whitney thought. *He knows everything about magic. That's why I came to him.*

"Well, this Lightmancer did the same for me and Sora after you and I returned from Elsewhere. I spoke with Sora, but I couldn't find her."

"Fooling with Lightmancery twice?" Kazimir stalked forward. Whitney had forgotten how terrifying the upyr could be when he tried. "Do you realize what other beings might overhear us?"

"None of that matters. The Lightmancer she… she showed me where Sora is, trapped in her own mind, caught between Pantego and Elsewhere, she said. Nesilia was there. The Buried Goddess. Controlling her body."

Kazimir's expression rarely shifted, but for a fleeting moment, Whitney could see it. Fear flashed across his features. It happened the moment he'd brought up Nesilia, as if he, too, knew her plans for returning weren't through. And if that was true, and she had Sora under some spell… Whitney couldn't even imagine.

"She's possessed a mystic? Clever girl. Always was. Never one to give up." A finger prodded Whitney in the chest three times as Kazimir said, "Just. Like. You."

"Possessing, or whatever, I don't know what exactly it is, but Sora needs my help, and you are the only one who knows what it's like to be stuck between realms."

"I cannot help you," Kazimir declared as if doing nothing more than ordering a drink at the local pub.

"You said it yourself! You've been to Elsewhere a hundred times, and you've escaped just as many. You live between realms, close your eyes, and see the other. I need to know how to get her out."

"I cannot help you," Kazimir repeated.

Whitney's mouth opened to speak, but nothing came out.

Can't help? He has to help. This was Whitney's only plan. His shot in the dark. And he'd done so much to get to this moment. To think it was all for nothing…

"I don't think you understand—"

Whitney's words were cut off as Kazimir's cold hand wrapped around his throat. Sharp fingernails dug into the soft flesh behind his ear, and Whitney thought he felt warm liquid seeping from the spot.

"I understand perfectly," Kazimir hissed—another reminder that this was an upyr and not someone to be trifled with. "You want me to entangle myself in the affairs of gods. I will not. Unless you have a blood pact to make, release me from this spell so I can return to my apprentice."

"Fine," Whitney croaked, and Kazimir dropped him.

"Goodbye, Whitney Fierstown. It has been good knowin—"

"I hereby… uh… invoke the Sanguine Lords for… uh…"

"What are you doing?" Kazimir demanded.

"The only thing I know how. Taking a leap."

"Stop it."

"I want to make a blood pact. Now."

"You don't know what you're getting mixed up in. The winds are changing on Pantego. Powers are shifting. Now is not the time. Our work was invoked upon the blood of kings, and now our presence is remembered. This is a war of men, do not get the gods involved."

"The gods are already involved!" Whitney shouted.

"This is foolishness."

"It doesn't matter." Whitney's usual bravado was gone. All that was left was desperation. "This is my only move. If you won't help me by choice, I'll make you. If a blood pact is the only way, I want to do it."

Kazimir growled low and fierce, then knelt before Whitney on one knee. He grimaced the entire time. Whitney looked around, confused until Kazimir finally started speaking.

"Beseech the Lords, and be warned, if they reject your target, your life will become forfeit." Kazimir didn't look up as he spoke. Under his breath, he added, "You better know what you're doing, thief. Even I can't predict anything anymore."

"I don't. Not one bit." Whitney forced a grin. He'd gotten

more and more used to doing that since Elsewhere, pretending he was enjoying living.

He cleared his throat, spread his arms and said, "Oh, Lords of Sanguine, or whatever, I beseech you therefore by the power vested in me, to kill Nesilia, the Buried Goddess."

Whitney couldn't remember if there were birds chirping or leaves rustling before, but if there were, the birds died, and the wind quit.

Kazimir's eyes rose ever so slightly. They weren't soulless any longer. "You stupid, stupid man." The upyr's body went stiff, back straight, arms stiff, chest stuck out. He shook three times before his head drooped, and he collapsed to his hands and knees.

"The Sanguine Lords…" Kazimir's words hung in the air for a lifetime.

Whitney stood in hopeful anticipation, unsure of what he'd truly just done. His whole life had been built on one principle: Plan, abandon, improvise. He'd had a plan, and that was to get his supposed friend, Kazimir to help. Whitney couldn't blame Kazimir for saying no, but when he had, Whitney had no choice but to abandon the plan and improvise.

"…accept this offering." Kazimir stood, eyes filled with pity and scorn. "You've damned us all." Grabbing Whitney's arm, Kazimir drew a deep cut before he could protest.

"Ouch!"

Kazimir let the blood fill a vial he pulled out of the folds of his cloak. "Blood given, for blood required. If you back out, change your mind, or otherwise thwart my efforts to fulfill this blood pact, the order will hunt you to the ends of the world. They will find you anywhere with this. Do you understand?"

Whitney nodded.

"Use words, thief."

"I understand."

"I do not think you do." Kazimir turned to walk away when

Whitney grabbed his arm. Kazimir reared back and punched Whitney hard across the jaw.

"You fool!" he roared.

Whitney rubbed at his chin but somehow didn't fall over. "What in Elsewhere?"

"Besides the fact that you just asked us to claim the life of a goddess? This pact you've made contradicts one we already have."

"What? How?" Whitney asked.

"You believe Nesilia has possessed Sora's body. To kill her, I will have to destroy that which she possesses."

The words hit Whitney like a tidal wave. Fear punched him harder than Kazimir had. Regret, anguish, confusion, and every other unpleasant emotion he'd ever known.

Kazimir merely laughed a humorless laugh. "Her blood drove me to betray the Sanguine Lords' will, got me sent to Elsewhere, and now, they ask for it. What madness have you created?"

Whitney swore but maintained his composure. "And what would you have done, oh, great upyr?"

"Anything else," Kazimir whispered. "But what is done is done. The will of the ancients is clear. Balance is broken and must be restored. There is no going back. You have shown them the path."

"So, what—you're going to kill Sora?"

Kazimir leaned into his hand and rubbed his temple.

"Kazzy—"

"Don't call me that."

"Kazimir, we made a deal in Elsewhere. Our own blood pact. Maybe your—whatever—Lords weren't involved, but that has to mean something. Weren't you punished because you killed as you pleased?"

"This is beneath their gaze. That wasn't. Don't presume to understand our ways."

"I'm not. I'm not." Whitney moved right in front of him, forcing Kazimir to meet his eyes. Standing tall and proud, Whitney said, "I don't care what you say. You showed me in Elsewhere that buried somewhere deep in that pale, muscular chest is a heart… it's not beating, sure… but you're a good man."

Whitney pounded a closed fist on the upyr's chest and earned a glower that at any other time, might have made him shog himself. But, right now, Sora's very existence was at stake.

"I know what I saw in you," he continued. "There has to be another way. An exorcism or whatever the old priests talk about."

"This is the Buried Goddess, not some putrid demon spirit," Kazimir scoffed.

"Even still. Kill Sora's body, she can just possess someone else. That can't be the way. Look into the big old tome of magic you call a brain, and we'll figure something out. I'm the best thief there is. About time I try to steal someone's body back, right?" He laughed nervously. "Right?"

Kazimir released a low growl. "You are correct. We made a deal. A blood pact. Perhaps the Sanguine Lords are still punishing me, leaving me no options, but I will not be exiled to Elsewhere again."

"So, you won't kill her?"

"I won't kill your blood mage friend unless there is no other choice."

Whitney was halfway toward embracing the upyr, but he caught himself, and stepped back, shifting his feet. "I knew I could count on you."

"Thank only the Sanguine Lords. If this is their wish, it must be for good reason. Questioning them is another path to Elsewhere." Whitney opened his mouth to speak, but Kazimir clutched his shoulder. Even in—wherever they were—Whitney could feel the pressure against the grimaur wound and grimaced. "But know this, Whitney Fierstown. If there is no other way to destroy her than sacrificing the body she possesses, your friend will be happy to be killed. Any fate is better than watching horrors through closed eyes for all of eternity."

"We'll find a way," Whitney said assuredly. Then he swallowed hard. "What now?"

"Wait where you are."

"That's it? That's your grand wisdom?" Whitney scoffed.

Kazimir stared at him, quiet until his shape began to vacillate.

Darkness crept in upon the corners of Whitney's vision. "Kazimir?" he said. His voice echoed as if he were within a deep, lonely chasm. The darkness closed in, and he spun in place, heart beginning to race.

"Kazimir!"

Suddenly, Whitney sat in *Gold Grin's Grotto* once more. Lucindur was already lighting a pipe filled with manaroot. This time, she had a second one ready for Whitney. She looked exhausted, but at least her strings hadn't broken again.

Whitney coughed. His throat felt unbelievably dry. His head pounded, though, and hadn't stopped since gaining the grimaur scratch. He reached for his shoulder instinctively and gave it a rub.

"What did you see?" Lucindur asked after some time had passed. She broke a piece off a loaf of bread and handed it to him, which he gratefully accepted. Hunger hit him like a hammer to the gut.

"Him." Whitney lay on his back, chewed, and stared at the wooden planks above. It helped fight the nausea, fixating on one spot. He noticed Gentry peeking over the railing down at them, and the boy quickly retreated out of sight.

"Did he agree to help?" Lucindur asked.

"No… not exactly," someone said. The voice was deep and guttural, the accent thick as old blood.

Lucindur's coal-dark skin paled at the sight of Kazimir, who, somehow, now stood in the center of the room. One moment, Whitney blinked, the next he was there, standing next to a woman, her skin and hair white as the tundra. Her mouth was covered by a metal muzzle, not unlike the one that had adorned Aquira's face only days earlier. Her eyes, dark and menacing like Kazimir's, shared none of his years of wisdom.

They reminded Whitney of how Kazimir looked when he'd hunted them in Winde Port—fueled by power and the desire for how Sora's blood could help him walk in the daylight.

"Th-this is…" Lucindur cleared her throat and straightened her spine. "This is Kazimir?"

"In the cold, dead flesh," Whitney said. "Don't know who she is."

"Sigrid, my apprentice," Kazimir answered. She stared at Whitney, and though he couldn't tell with her mask on, it seemed like she was panting wildly. Her pupils filled the entirety of her irises, black as night. All Whitney knew is that he was wrong. Kazimir had been a blood-hankering lunatic in Winde Port, but she looked unhinged.

"Apprentice?" Whitney scoffed, forcing himself not to stare at her. "Never would have thought anyone would trust you with an apprentice."

Kazimir cleared the distance between them faster than a fly could flap its wings. He leaned in close and said, "Do not undermine me. I have no pact against breaking your friend's bones."

Whitney tried his best to stand his ground. He knew from his time spent in Elsewhere that the blood pact was meant for the target, and no others were to be taken until their blood was spilt, but that didn't mean Whitney trusted Kazimir to obey the rules.

"You said you didn't agree?" Lucindur said, breaking the tension. "Then, why are you here?"

"The Sanguine Lords have accepted the offer. Therefore,

through Elsewhere, here beside the offering do I appear." His words were solemn and felt rehearsed.

Lucindur looked between Whitney and Kazimir. "Offer? What offer?"

"This *fool* made a blood pact." All pretense of memorized words fled, and Kazimir emphasized the word 'fool' with a poke to Whitney's chest. At the same time, Sigrid circled up behind him. He thought he could hear her sniffing. "Almost as foolish as what you just did for him, Lightmancer."

Whitney put on a crooked smile. "What did you want me to do? He said he wouldn't help."

"A blood pact on who?" Lucindur asked slowly.

Kazimir turned from Whitney and paced, making clear effort to skirt around a blade of sunlight filtering in through an open porthole. "As Nesilia walks Pantego, there is no balance," Kazimir said. "There must be balance. Balance is everything, lest the Culling comes again."

"You took out a blood pact on a goddess?" Lucindur asked, disgust dripping from her words.

"So what? I helped kill a goddess before, no matter who believes me. It can't be that hard."

Kazimir's head turned. If looks could murder, Whitney wouldn't just be dead, his bones would have turned to dust. "You didn't kill a goddess—you killed one stripped of her power. Power is everything, and Nesilia has no lack of it. Not after her scion, Redstar, reminded the world of who she was."

"Does it not bother you at all that an evil goddess is roaming the world, seeking vengeance on whatever and whoever?" Whitney asked.

"Even in success, the stakes are high. Thousands will die. Failure… it could mean the end of everything. The rising of the dead again."

"You really are dramatic for an immortal. What if we do nothing? We fail by not trying." Whitney didn't say that failure meant losing Sora—he couldn't—but he knew it did. Nesilia didn't seem like one to let her hosts go when she was through with them. King Pi got lucky.

"I've seen it all before, thief," Kazimir said.

Whitney had a retort ready until Sigrid appeared in front of him. Her black lace was stained with blood. He knew the upyr couldn't teleport except, apparently, when a blood pact was made, but the way she moved, she might as well have. She was panting, he could hear it through her muzzle. She just stared at him. Creepy.

"Mortals rise and fall," Kazimir went on. "Gods and goddesses have their feuds. When they are through having fun, the upyr remain. The Dom Nohzi still remains."

Whitney stepped to the side, away from Sigrid, and shook his head. "This is different." His words hung there like a stubborn mule begging to be kicked. Kazimir didn't respond.

"What is the price of this blood pact?" Lucindur asked. "My people tell many stories of the upyr, each more horrifying than the next."

"Are they? And my order tells of the old Lightmancers who robbed kings of their minds; who'd inspired so much slaughter. My kind are, at least, honest about what we are."

Lucindur turned her eyes to the ground. "Ours is a dark history, yes. But no art should be forgotten. An ageless one should agree, I think."

"Indeed."

She repeated the question: "What's the price?"

"Riches and gold, fame and fortune, they pass like the rising tide, but power… power is all the Sanguine Lords judge. If the gods roam the world once more, the balance of power is tipped, and the scales threaten to break."

Suddenly, Lucindur's hand went to her mouth. "Whitney, this means…"

"No," Kazimir said. "I cannot kill Sora. There are other… complications."

There came a muffled voice from the center of the room. They all turned to Sigrid.

"*Otkryt*," Kazimir said, and her muzzle fell to the floor. "Behave."

"I have no such pact with the human, neither do the Lords," she said. Her voice was ice and steel. "I'll devour this Sora, and we can go home."

"*Blizklos*," Kazimir snapped. The muzzle reappeared over her mouth, and she snarled. "Know your place, young one."

"So, you're not going to kill Sora, but you have to kill the goddess inside of her?" Lucindur said. "What do you plan to do?".

"Yeah," Whitney said. "Please tell me you had some time to think on your teleportation over here."

Sigrid feigned a lunge at him, and Whitney staggered back.

He held his chest as he caught his breath. He'd seen so many horrible things, enough not to be afraid of much. But something about immortal beings who feed on blood always got to him.

"Can you tell your apprentice to stop doing that?" Whitney said. She traced his back with her index finger, causing him to shudder. When he whipped around, she was no longer there.

"She's learning the true nature of men," Kazimir said.

"She's playing with her… food," Whitney amended.

"Can you two focus for one minute?" Lucindur asked, stomping on the wood floor.

Just then came a growl. Two eyes appeared over the railing. He heard Gentry whisper something incomprehensible, then Aquira swooped down at Kazimir. It'd been a long time since Whitney had seen her so furious.

Her throat swelled, then fire lanced out at Kazimir. He drew one of his many knives just as fast, spun and pulled up his cloak, dispelling the flame. Aquira slashed the side of his neck on her way by. Sigrid, with impossible speed, moved to defend her master, and swatted Aquira so hard, she cracked the floor upon impact.

The little wyvern didn't give up. Then, Whitney remembered that the last time she'd seen Kazimir. he'd been immensely more evil. Aquira reared back and blew flame again, searing the side of Sigrid's face and heating the metal of her muzzle.

"I knew he couldn't be trusted!" Tum Tum shouted, leaping over the staircase banister, warhammer raised high and already crashing toward Kazimir's head. The upyr caught the dwarf by the hand and slammed Tum Tum down. Simultaneously, Whitney dashed in front of Aquira before she razed the entire pub.

"Enough!" Lucindur bellowed. She strummed a hard chord on her salfio and, as if by magic, everyone stopped. "I never wanted to use my ability, and now, for you, I have, and all you want to do is argue?"

She stared straight at Whitney. He looked from side to side. "Me?"

"Yes, you," Kazimir added.

"Get off me, monster!" Tum Tum snarled. He shook free, then ran across the floor to a crate that'd caught fire from Aquira's spray. He swore as he patted it down with a tarp he'd pulled off another.

"I'm so sorry, Mr. Whitney!" Gentry said, at the top of the stairs. One step down and he froze in his tracks. The way Sigrid ogled him, like he was a fattened hog—that would have given young Whitney nightmares forever.

"Back upstairs, Gentry," Whitney said.

"Yes, child. And take that infernal beast with you." Kazimir regarded Aquira, who dug her claws into the floor and snapped her jaws.

"I know what you must think, girl," Whitney said, "but he's here to help bring back Sora. Do you remember her—Sora?"

The wyverns head cocked, then she stopped growling.

"Yeah, exactly," Whitney said. "We need him. *She* needs him. It will all make sense soon."

Her ferocious glare lasted a few seconds more, then she flapped up to the bottommost railing post of the stairs. Sigrid watched her every move, and Aquira perched to glare at all of them. It was like being surrounded by misbehaving children, Tum Tum included.

"She understands?" Kazimir asked.

"I think so," Whitney said.

"Interesting."

"Now that everyone is relaxed, I'd like to hear the upyr's plan," Lucindur said. She crossed her legs and sat, her instrument laid across her lap.

"You don't have to be a part of this anymore, Lucy," Whitney said.

"I opened your minds to each other through Elsewhere, and a blood pact was made on a goddess. I think if any creature under her command overheard, I'm already very well involved." There was no missing the frustration in her tone, as if Whitney could have predicted any of this. He was a thief—the fact that he was the greatest in the world notwithstanding—and now people thought he was supposed to know everything?

"I have no idea how to destroy Nesilia," Kazimir admitted.

"So I did all this for no reason?" Whitney asked.

"I didn't say that," Kazimir said. "I believe I know where to start. But it won't be easy.

"Never is," Whitney said.

"Please, Kazimir. Enlighten us," Lucindur said.

"We must go to the Red Tower. Inside, there is a pool."

"The Well of Wisdom," Lucindur offered.

"Yes. If there is anywhere in this world that can tell us how to separate the two, it is there. She and Iam exiled many of their kin during the God Feud. The Well does not forget."

"That tower was abandoned long ago," Lucindur said. "How do we even know the Well hasn't dried up?"

"If this realm yet stands, the Well is not dried up. And no… the tower has not been abandoned."

"How do you know this?" Lucindur asked.

"It may not appear with luster as it once had, but I assure you… I can feel its power even now. My people, the Dom Nohzi and the Mystic Order… they are two sides of the same coin. Their blood, calls to my kind. If the Buried Goddess can be stopped without taking Sora's life, our only chance is in that tower. So much began there."

Whitney stood and clapped his hands. "So, let's go. I have a boat just outside."

"I told you, it won't be easy. Balance must be maintained. Nesilia is likely already aware of your plan, and she is not going to lie down for it. Have you noticed anything strange lately?"

"Strange how?" Whitney asked.

"The mortals have been all but pounding at the doors of our Citadel. If they'd had eyes to see beyond the rocks and trees, they'd have already found it. The goddess stirs, and so do the minions who serve the darkness she seeks."

Lucindur and Whitney exchanged a worried look. "The grimaurs," they both said.

Kazimir tilted his head.

"Last night, we were attacked by grimaurs," Lucindur said.

"In Panping?" Kazimir asked, eyes narrowing.

Whitney pointed to the boards on the wall. "Just beyond there."

"This is not good," Kazimir said. "I knew this place smelled… off."

"Hey," Tum Tum remarked, still tending to the damage.

Sigrid began speaking again, but the muzzle kept it unintelligible. Kazimir raised a hand to quiet her and said, "Nesilia is gaining power once more, and if we are not quick to act, the world will be overrun."

There was a crash upstairs, followed by a scream, sounds of struggle. Aquira snapped to life and swept up to the main level.

"Gentry!" Whitney shouted as he rose and darted for the stairs. When he reached the top, he froze. Gentry stood, bloody sword in hand. Aquira landed on his shoulder, embers flaring around her mouth, but she was too late. The boy stared down at a figure in dirty, red robes wearing a white mask, a red teardrop painted on the left side. The attacker gripped a knife, hand still twitching.

The front door was ajar, and beyond it, the sound of chaos reigned. Whitney ran and stopped in the doorframe. Beyond the front patio, more red-robed figures frolicked through the streets, laughing and rioting, all wearing those infernal masks that Whitney hoped never to see again.

Nesilia's cultists had come out to play, and where they played, the world fell into ruin.

X

THE DAUGHTER

Gentle waves lapped at a tiny beach carved into the rocky coast along the mouth of Trader's Bay. Mahi crawled, feeling the black grains of sand scraping her knees. Every breath was a struggle. Fighting in Tal'du Dromesh never lasted long but real war... she now understood her father when he called it a 'test of endurance.'

She flipped onto her back, struggled to prop herself up with an elbow, and observed the watery battleground. The fog had lifted, but thick pillars of smoke still swarmed as the slowly sinking warship burned, passing the fire to other damaged ships and debris.

It wasn't Mahraveh's intent, but the strait would be blockaded by the debris for a long time. Only three of her own ships survived the onslaught of Drav Cra longboats, and none of the Glass Kingdom's had. They were piles of charred and split wood poking through the water like an archipelago of destruction. She saw the *Shiva* among them, just a torn sail flapping in the wind.

Longboats slid onto the beach one at a time, Mahi's people covering them like barnacles, even hanging off the sides. Their victory had been found in numbers. The reinforcements from

Winde Port had provided a scare, but the Glassmen couldn't maintain their formations on the shaky decks of sinking ships where they were so clearly unaccustomed to sea battles.

In the end, Mahi's fleet may have been in shambles, but her army wasn't. And her main concern was eased when she saw Afhem Tingur being helped off a longboat onto the beach alongside his men. She couldn't afford to lose her most potent ally, not yet.

The warriors began to celebrate as more and more of them reached black sands. They hollered at the battleground, calling upon the love of the God of Sand and Sea as so many tributes of life sank to the depths. All that death would become a haven for fish and coral—a new reef. The creatures of the sea would grow and feed the Shesaitju—a cycle of life offered by a merciful god.

Mahi whispered a prayer as she let the wet sand fall through her fingers in clumps. Then, she spotted Yuri seated alone on a rock. Really, she heard him first as he hacked and coughed uncontrollably. His fine robes were in tatters and sopping, his gray hair a wild mess. And his hands… they shook like a man who'd never seen battle before, like a proper Glass Lord who'd stay seated safely by his coffers while sending good, young men off to war too many times to count.

Mahi wanted to spit his way, but instead, found herself overwhelmed with pity.

It's not his fault the Glass made him this weak, she thought.

She stood and approached. "Thank you, Lord Darkings," she said, leaning on her spear like a crutch.

He peered up at her, forced a nervous smile, then continued to stare blankly out at the devastation while he returned to his coughing fit.

An army is only as strong as its weakest warrior, Mahi reminded herself. Another of her father's innumerable lessons, even though he had no intention of her forsaking her duties as a woman and turning to the sword.

"Many more would have been lost without your early warning," Mahi said, moving into his line of sight. "Maybe I underestimated you."

"As if I care how a child estimates me," Yuri grumbled and turned away.

"This *child* is all you have." She tracked with him, and her arm shifted in a way that made her shoulder burn. She clenched her jaw.

"You should really have that attended to before we continue," Yuri said after a short pause. "It was an astounding victory, but remember, it is only the first, and now we're without a fleet. Nearly one thousand of your army is dead."

"How do you know that?"

"Setting straits ablaze may be your specialty, but numbers are mine. We're still in a good position, but unless Nahanab is a massacre, you'll need the support of more afhems to fight further."

"What if they just… leave?"

"Who?"

"Your pe—the Glassmen," Mahi said. "What if we steal their taste for battle and they give up; let us go."

"When I knew the boy-king—Pi—he was tainted, bloodthirsty, willing to lock the Caleef away, as you well know. But children are malleable, and I've been away too long. So who knows how he is now? Look at you."

"What about me?"

"When I first saw you, I thought you were useless."

Mahi could feel her face turn to stone.

"Now, wait—wait," Yuri said, stern. "First impressions aren't *always* the most important. Let me continue. I wondered, 'This is the child the legendary Muskigo Ayerabi—the Scythe—has sent us after?' However, you're more than a complete waste of life, which is better than I could say for my own flesh and blood who can't even properly rescue a frail Sidar Rakun."

"Are you saying he's dead?"

Yuri rolled his shoulders, and his gaze lilted toward the ground. Mahi didn't know him well, but he was always confident. Always scheming and purporting that he was steps ahead until now.

"Frail does not mean dead," he said. "However, I truly, have no idea. It's been a long time for them not to have been sighted. Knowing my son, they were probably murdered in their sleep by bandits and left on the roadside to rot in the sun."

"Do all Glassmen so hate their own blood?" Mahi asked.

Yuri sighed. "Not all."

"I want the truth. Was he ever actually with the Caleef?"

"Do you really think I would sacrifice everything I have on a lie? Look at me, girl. Sitting on a beach in rags, covered in blood from battle."

"It's not your blood," Mahi remarked.

Yuri ignored her. "You think this is where I expected to be as my life dwindles toward its inevitable end? Hitched to a girl fighting her first war and a son whose own daughter fled to Hornsheim rather than be associated with him? Whether or not Bartholomew lives, my good name will die with me."

"Good name…" Mahi laughed. "Yuri Darkings, why are you here? You've done enough. When my father is free, I'm sure he'd be happy to provide you a home and protection until that day…" She was going to say, 'until the day the Current takes you,' but he was pink, no matter his supposed loyalties. "…when your life does, finally, end."

Now, Yuri scoffed. He stood, threw his arms up, and walked away. As he went, he declared, "Like I said, not a complete waste of life."

Mahi hurried after him. "What are you talking about?"

"And here you go, chasing me along like a dog in heat."

"I only came over to thank you!"

Yuri whipped around, face red with anger. As if materializing out of the air itself, warriors flocked to Mahraveh's side, just as they had earlier. Bit'rudam appeared and stuck out an arm in front of her, his teeth clenched like he was about to tear into Yuri's throat.

"More men rushing to your aid. Your *father* will grant me asylum. Your *father* will drive the Glass Kingdom away. Until you children stop needing us, you're just anchors. You are an afhem, same as he is."

Mahi pushed Bit'rudam's arm out of the way and stepped forward. "And what would you have had me do?"

"Be something fresh, because Iam knows I've seen enough of the same damn men die and be reborn. The warlords, the idealists, the lunatics. Your father fought his illegal war. He had the entire world holding its breath, and then, he failed like every other worthless rebel since time began. I've watched how your people work. I've noted every detail. That is what I do. It's my greatest skill. Your father never lost, until he did. But you haven't."

"My father has accomplished more than you ever—"

"Don't even finish that. Because all your father has accomplished is on the battlefield, and unless you people realize there are other routes to greatness besides spilling blood, you'll always have nothing more than this small corner of Pantego. Great as Muskigo Ayerabi may be, he brought death to many families in the Black Sands who wanted none of it. The Shesaitju will never follow him as your leader."

"The Caleef leads our people," Bit'rudam said.

"Gods and powerful men..." Yuri's lip twisted. "Is there anything that holds us back more? You want to defeat the Glass Kingdom? To take back the Black Sands for your own? It's about more than burning down churches and winning one battle. You need to *earn* their respect."

"I thought you supported this war?" Mahi asked.

"I do." Yuri sighed. "I do. Ignore me. It's just—you just remind me of someone I knew. Someone who failed me before she could make her mark on this world. She would have been on that ship, headlong in the fray as well."

"It's where an afhem belongs."

"You belong alive, Mahraveh al'Tariq," Yuri said, voice soft. "Not fished out of the water by a failed politician."

"*He's lost it*," Bit'rudam whispered to Mahi in Saitjuese. "*I've seen it. Men in their first battle, losing their heads like they've been baking in the desert.*"

"*I've lost nothing!*" Yuri snapped, in rough, but understandable Saitjuese. Mahi's eyes went wide, along with Bit'rudam and all the soldiers around her. Yuri sneered. "Yes, that's right. I've been here long enough, and I'm a quick study. I hear it—all of it. And I am still here."

"Well, perhaps this is where you should stay," Mahi said. "Watch over this beach so nobody can get behind us."

"Gladly." Yuri pushed by a warrior and reclaimed his seat on the rock. "Just you don't get yourself killed with that shoulder. Beat the bastards and let them run. Don't give chase. Sir Nikserof Pasic is crafty. I've watched him train. Don't let him draw you in, even if he uses your father."

"Afhem Mahraveh, we found a passage!" one of her warriors shouted down from a rift in the cliffside.

Mahi stared at Yuri while the Glassman made himself comfortable. The man perplexed her more than anything, but kernels of truth always seemed to come from his advice. She couldn't help but wonder what woman he could have possibly known that would have been like her. She'd never heard of any pink-skin female soldiers. They kept their women locked up tighter than even her own people.

When she turned away again, her shoulder pain flared up, and she had to lean on her spear. The shaft wobbled until Bit'rudam steadied it.

"We must seal that, my Afhem," he said. "Come. Sit."

He led her to a piece of driftwood near where a camp was being set up to hold the supplies they'd been able to salvage. A group of wives and daughters trained in the healing arts were there, helping mend minor wounds. It was where Mahi belonged, or where she'd always been told she did. She couldn't imagine a turn in her life that ever would have led her to washing blood rather than drawing it.

She just couldn't understand what Yuri was trying to say. He didn't want her to fight, yet, unlike so many others—her father included—he wasn't recommending she stay in camp either.

"He's a strange, strange man," Bit'rudam said as he crouched to examine her wound.

"I seem to attract them," Mahi said softly. She was referring to Jumaat, but Bit'rudam cleared his throat, and his gray cheeks went purple. "Sorry, I didn't... I... Sorry." She reached out and touched his forearm.

"You never need to be sorry, my Afhem."

"Have the others tended to first," she ordered. "Then we'll march."

"Did you ever hear how I grew up?" Bit'rudam asked, not bothering to provide a proper segue.

"Should I have?"

He shook his head with deference. "On a trading ship. My father sailed across the Torrential Sea to Yarrington in service to our last afhem. Back and forth a thousand times while my mother cared for my younger siblings. Whale oil in exchange for weapons, as there is no iron on our—your—island chain."

Mahi sat up. "You've been to Yarrington?"

"Seen it from afar. The Glass Castle is so tall, on cloudy days, the spire vanishes in clouds. My father always said it was their kings compensating."

Mahi smirked. "So did mine. I—" She squealed as Bit'rudam suddenly tore the broken arrow out through the back of her shoulder. She squeezed his arm so tight her nails left deep crescent-shaped imprints, but he was stronger than he looked on the outside.

He laughed and juggled the bloody projectile once. "Youngest on the ship meant I took care of the crew. Sick, injured—my mother taught me what to do. Hold this here." He took her hand, filled it with a piece of cloth, and placed it over the exit wound. It was an awkward angle, but she managed. "Pressure stops the bleeding."

He fumbled through a satchel, then removed a curious-looking sea urchin. The tips of its spikes glowed the same color as a nigh'jel. He then drew a knife from the back of his belt and sliced off one of its spines.

Mahi rotated away as he approached her, holding the spike by its sharp end. "*Hess tu wima*—they live only around our isle," Bit'rudam said, clearly noticing her confusion. "They use seaweed wraps in Latiapur, not us. It might sting a little, but it cleans better than anything in this world."

He held the barb in front of her wound, then stopped. He looked up, and Mahi hadn't yet noticed how pretty his eyes were. Deep gray with flecks of gold, like sunlight on a rainy day.

"May I?" he asked.

She nodded, and he slowly tilted the barb over the entry wound. A trickle of its venom, or whatever it carried, splashed on the injury, and it felt like fire. She clenched her eyes, then watched through squinted eyelids as the rent flesh bubbled.

Finally, the injured area turned a lumpy white, but the bleeding stopped.

"Amazing," she said, breathless through gritted teeth.

Bit'rudam lay his hand on the center of her back and gently tilted her forward to do the exit wound. Mahi squeezed her own thigh now. The pain in cleansing was worse than the wound itself. It seared, and she felt it bubbling while it coated her wound and stemmed the bleeding.

"Good as new, my Afhem," Bit'rudam said. "And ignore the old pink-skin. Ignore everybody. Just lead. We are your afhemate. Anything you ask of us, it will be done." He flashed her a smile, then used the flat side of his knife to brush any excess toxin from the skin around her wound. He wiped it on his sleeve before stowing the blade in a sheath at the small of his back.

Mahi watched him walk away toward the passage through the bluffs, noting the way the sun glinted off his wet arms and back. Out of the corner of her vision, she noticed Yuri looking back at her. He shook his head like he was ashamed, then averted his gaze.

Mahi bit her lip, grasped her spear, and stood to follow her people.

Ignore everybody, she thought. *Just lead.*

Now those were words she could live by.

XI

THE KNIGHT

The Glass Road slashed along the Jarein Gorge, winding along the cliffs and crags like a serpent. It was a haven for bandits and smugglers who used the gorge's caverns and offshoot trails for their nefarious gains. No longer. Torsten and his legion passed by travelers and tinkers; traders heading east who were now blocked. Dozens of people camped, waiting.

For centuries the White Bridge had served as a crucial strategic point, as well as the straightest and safest land route across the gorge. The mountain pass was treacherous, as Torsten had learned, and beyond the realm of the Glass, but the ancient structure was built with glaruium-reinforced stone, said to have been constructed by ancient dwarves themselves. Unbreakable.

"Will you destroy the heretics like you did Redstar?" a woman on the side of the road asked. She clutched a small child to her breast.

"The bodies…" another cried. "It's wrong."

Fearful muttering abounded, but Torsten kept his head high as his horse threaded its way through. He had to maintain an air of confidence, for their sakes as well as for his men. It seemed every battle he'd entered over the past year, the warriors at his side were younger and younger. This was no different. Many, including Lucas, were new recruits, or converted guards.

"Worry not, fair citizens, Iam is with you now," Dellbar the Holy said as he pushed his horse to catch up. He hiccuped. "We will purge the darkness from this land."

Torsten glared back at him. "That's enough, Father Morni— Your Holiness," he said, struggling to mask his displeasure. The man reeked less of alcohol, at least, which wasn't saying much. "You're to stay here. Calm these people."

"The men—"

"Prayed with you before we left," Torsten cut him off. And it was quite a prayer. They'd circled atop the plateau beneath the noon sun, when Iam sees all, and Torsten hadn't witnessed an army so stirred by faith since the days of Liam. He too felt a lightness in his heart. Like they were protected. Dellbar had a theatrical quality to him with which Wren couldn't compare. Even inebriated, his charm was undeniable.

Dellbar remained quiet for a few long seconds, face aimed at the ground. "Drad Mak was there," he uttered. Torsten noticed his fingers beginning to twitch.

"What?" Torsten replied.

"When I was still just Father Morningweg in Fessix. When Redstar came to my home and slaughtered everyone. Mak was with the raiding party. I want to feel his fear when you beat him."

"Your Holiness—"

"Please, stop with the formalities…"

"Never. It is who you are. It is who Iam has called you to be. You are my High Priest. Regardless of what you've done or what has been done to you, these people need you now," Torsten said softly. "The Glass Kingdom needs you. I once allowed vengeance to cloud my judgment. You mustn't. Vengeance is a tool of the Buried Goddess. We seek justice."

Dellbar the Holy sucked in air through his teeth, then hung his head. "Just promise me you'll end this. Put that sight Iam gave to you, instead of me, to good use?"

"I can only promise that Drad Mak will not leave that bridge," Torsten said. "He is beyond saving."

"Well then, Sir Knight, may Iam guide your sword, and this blind man to a drink." He swung his legs over his horse's side, taking no care for the condition of his luxurious robes. Droning sounded from the gathered travelers as he walked amongst them. They bowed, circled their eyes in prayer.

A light kick sent Torsten's horse onward, leading the battalion. When they turned the next bend, he was as sure as ever that this was no place for priests. The two manmade watchtowers flanking the gate stretching across the west side of the bridge were wrecked. Piles of loose stone and smoldering wood that still smoked. Torsten was thankful the smoke wasn't from pyres, but that gratitude was short-lived.

Along the path, men were affixed to crudely constructed wooden Eyes of Iam. Their arms and legs were spread across the circle, nails through their wrists and feet, holding them secure. They were all stripped naked and left out in the sun, their skin now blistering and crisp. That, combined with the blood smeared across their bodies and faces, made it impossible to recognize any, but there were women amongst them. It wasn't just soldiers.

Most of the unfortunate victims' chests still heaved, heads swaying slowly from side to side, alive. Torsten heard a few retches from the soldiers at his back in response to the sight. The contents of his own stomach turned over, too, but he held it down.

It was Winde Port all over again, when Muskigo set Glass heads on spikes, only this… this was far worse. The victims were in unspeakable agony, all while being used to taint Iam's holy image.

"The savages…" Sir Marcos spoke, breathless. Bold and

defiant in training, the truth of war had a way of humbling those types of men. Though he wasn't alone in his words, most had been rendered silent.

Torsten noticed the light of a flaming arrow lance across the gorge on the east side, signaling that Lucas and the dwarves were in position as well. He couldn't help but wonder if they were greeted by the same gruesome scene.

"By Iam… This ends today," Torsten declared.

"Sir, wait—" Marcos didn't finish before Torsten spurred his horse toward the bridge's gate. Alone.

Torsten would never un-hear the moans. They assailed him from all directions, making Muskigo's treatment of his captors seem tame. He recalled riding up to the gates of Winde Port, and offering a duel, failing to convince Muskigo to spare thousands of warriors' lives, but this time he wouldn't. He couldn't.

Mak and the other Drav Cra had been allies, and Torsten cursed himself for ever helping let such barbarous people into his kingdom. Anyone capable of such savagery deserved nothing but the executioner's block. No more would suffer for his failure, for not having done what was needed the moment those heathens stepped through the Glass Castle gates.

Torsten adjusted his blindfold and knew Iam had punished him enough for those very same failures. No longer.

"Drad Mak!" Torsten shouted through the closed gate. He noticed Drav Cra slinking through the ruins of the watchtower, ready to chuck spears through his chest. He knew that Muskigo had too much honor to do that at Winde Port, but with these people, he wasn't so sure.

Dismounting his horse, he gave her a light slap and sent her running back toward his men. He wouldn't let the savages prove their true nature by slaying her. Then, from the scabbard on his back, he drew Liam Nothhelm's sword… now Torsten Unger's sword, *Salvation*. He let his finger trace the gold-threaded leather, and strode forward.

"Mak!" Torsten yelled again. "You asked for me, and here I am!"

Wind howled through the gorge, carrying with it whispers in Drav Crava.

Torsten's thumb rubbed the Eye of Iam on *Salvation's* cross-guard. "Come out here and face me, coward! There's nowhere to run now!"

"Sir," Sir Marcos said, walking up along side him. "What are your orders?" A cluster of Shieldsmen accompanied him, raising large heater shields in front of Torsten.

Torsten whipped around to glower down at the young Shields-man. "Help these poor souls down and get them to his Holiness." Though all priests were trained in the healing arts, Torsten wasn't sure Morningweg's drunken, shaking hands were the best choice, but he was all they had.

"Sir," Marcos said, edging up closer, "you're within their range. We must fall back."

"I gave orders, Shieldsman," Torsten said. Then using Queen Oleander's words, he said, "Follow them, or I'll find someone who will."

"They'll kill you."

"Then, that is to be my fate." He gave Marcos a light shove, then pushed through the wall of shields. A couple of his men protested but could do nothing to stop him. He wasn't sure what he'd do when he reached White Bridge until that moment, but now it was evident, he had to end it before any more Glassmen died. He had to take that chance.

"This is our fight, Mak!" Torsten roared. "Face me alone and end this."

The great, wooden gates creaked, gears *clanked* along, and they slowly opened, revealing the stone of White Bridge, too covered in dust and ash to fulfill its namesake now. It looked like a war had been fought atop it. Stone was scorched, rubble everywhere, and bodies littered it, both Drav Cra and Glassmen.

At least a hundred living, breathing savages arrayed themselves in lines down either side of the bridge, leering at Torsten as he approached. Some snapped their jaws like rabid wolves, while others whispered vulgarities. All were painted with blood and soot. Impure. Unholy. Between them, more Eyes of Iam stood with Glassmen nailed to the wood, clinging to life.

In the center of the Bridge, an encircled triangle was drawn in blood—the symbol of the Buried Goddess. Mak stood at the heart of it all, his milk-white skin stained with blood from his chin down to his muscle-bound chest. He wielded his great battle-axe with two hands against his body. A skull, eye sockets dark and empty, was fastened to the dual blades, facing Torsten, staring him down like death itself.

Mak's warriors chanted in Drav Crava. Torsten understood none of it, and he didn't care either. He just walked forward, through the gate, listening as it ground shut behind him. He heard the now-distant shouts of his men, but there was nothing they could do.

"About time you showed," Mak shouted, his voice returning ten times as it slapped against the gorge walls. "I was running out of people to display for your arrival. It's like art, no?"

"You're surrounded, Mak," Torsten growled.

"Can't bear to look at me when I drive my axe through your skull?" Mak taunted. "Look at him, blindfolded, ready for an execution."

Torsten wasn't surprised that Mak hadn't heard of Torsten's vision loss atop Mount Lister. He was too busy slaughtering people who couldn't defend themselves throughout the eastern plains.

"There's no getting out of this," Torsten said. "Surrender, or die."

"Skorravik awaits me," Mak said, pounding his chest with one hand. "As it did for those you betrayed. Slaughtered in their sleep!"

Torsten did his best to ignore the ravenous warriors on either side of him, even as they snarled at him, still snapping their jaws. His focus was singular, Mak the Mountainous, the one who'd crucified all these citizens of the Glass all around them. Torsten's blood boiled like it never had before. Redstar, Muskigo, Valin—they'd all had motives. They'd all had reasons for their cruel actions, but not Mak. This was pure evil.

"Redstar deceived us," Torsten said. "We did only what was necessary."

"Hypocrites and cowards, all of you!" Mak snarled.

"Says the man who did this to innocent people." Torsten gestured to one of the crucified Glassmen. "How many are just farmers? For Iam's sake, there are women!"

"Tits or not, one Glassman is the same as the next," Mak replied. "The Buried Goddess judges you all 'guilty.' It is your turn to be forgotten."

"Don't hide behind your fallen goddess, Mak! Her return has been thwarted. This… monstrous act. It's all you."

"What gives you the right to judge—leader of backstabbers?"

Torsten hadn't noticed they were circling each other like two bulls ready to charge. "You would have turned on my people if the tables were turned. That was war."

"And this is personal." Mak slowly extended his arm and let it fall, so his giant axe touched the ground, then continued to walk the bloody circle, letting the blades scrape across the stone. "This circle… it opens our hearts and minds to Skorravik, through the depths of the earth, to our Lady."

Torsten stopped at the circle's edge, now only a few meters

away from Mak. In his peripherals, he noticed that the Drav Cra had closed in behind him, blocking any chance of retreat. That was okay. Torsten had no expectation of leaving that bridge alive. His only hope was that Iam would allow him to kill Mak first, to save the rest of those crucified on the bridge from a horrid fate.

Perhaps this was a trap, but as Torsten squeezed the grip of his sword, felt the cold Eye of Iam at the cross-guard, he didn't think so. He knew warriors, knew how the great chieftain Mak claimed never to have lost in combat. Torsten was a man of Iam, yet, more than anything, he was a warrior. He knew the pride of men like Mak who saw nothing save for their own legend.

"It's blood on stone," Torsten spat. "Nothing more."

"Within these sacred bindings, none may interfere," Mak replied, brow narrowed to a point. "In here, it is you and me. You shall perish, and then, my fallen warriors will drag you down to Skorravik, and you will feel the pain of their swords. They will cut your skin, over and over, for all of eternity. Their reward will be your torture. Skorravik!"

An earth-shaking response came from every Drav Cra warrior on the bridge. "Skorravik!"

"And if you die?" Torsten questioned, doing his best to ignore the pit forming in his gut.

"They are sworn to their drad. Only another of my kind can claim this axe, and you will never be Drav Cra."

"You demanded I come. Here I am," Torsten said. "I will face you, Mak, if you give me your word that if you die, they will all surrender and return home. No raiding, no pillaging. They will go back to your ice."

"If I die, they will join me in Skorravik. We are one."

"That's not an answer."

"Then you aren't listening to my words," Mak said, slamming his axe on the stone. "The Fyortentek clan can have no dradi-nengor if yours are the hands which claim me. If I die within this circle, they cannot retrieve my body or this axe. They will have no drad. If I die, they do as well." He snickered and looked around at his people. The savages were so close to Torsten's back now he could smell them. "But do they seem afraid? Only you should be."

Torsten bit his lip. "I'm done living with fear." He stepped over the bloody line and into the blasphemous circle. He only hoped that within the symbol, Iam wouldn't have to see what he was going to do.

"You holy men," Mak scoffed. "Remove the trappings of your God and look upon me with your eyes."

"Iam is my eye," Torsten said.

Torsten shifted his feet to prepare for a frontal attack. All he could do was trust that this Drav Cra custom wasn't one the heathens at his back would betray. He couldn't take his focus off Mak. He'd forgotten how massive the man was, larger even than Torsten, and that was saying something. One blow from his battle-axe, and even Torsten's glaruium armor wouldn't hold up.

"They say you are the greatest warrior in all your kingdom," Mak said. "From what I have seen, perhaps only the biggest fool."

"Enough talk, Mak." Torsten brandished *Salvation*, twirling it once in his hand. "You say you're ready to die. I'm here to help."

"The halls of Skorravik will rumble when I deliver your head!"

Mak charged like an enraged zhulong. The centuries-old bridge vibrated beneath each of his tremendous feet. Yet somehow, for all his weight, he moved with remarkable agility. Torsten got his blade up to parry a downward strike, but the blow was so powerful it sent deep reverberations down his limbs.

Rolling out of the way of another wild swipe, Torsten dropped into a defensive stance on the other side of the circle. The Drav Cra onlookers cackled like ravens, cheering on their invincible leader. Torsten was used to being the strongest side of any fight, but that wasn't the case against Mak.

The man charged him again, wielding his axe in a way no man should've been capable of. It was like he was on manaroot or fueled like an upyr by the blood covering his face. A berserker. Torsten deflected, evaded, but every chance at an opening closed fast. The man's oversized weapon had too great a reach.

Torsten's heel slid across the bloody circle. In almost an instant, the tip of a spear slashed the back of his leg. Mak wasn't lying about what would happen if he stepped outside its boundaries.

Mak's axe cut air toward Torsten's skull, and Torsten ducked beneath it back into the circle. Whipping around, Mak brought it hammering down. Torsten raised *Salvation*, and any other blade might have shattered from the blow. It was still enough to send Torsten's knee to the stone.

A notch in Mak's axe locked with the Eye of Iam on Torsten's sword. The hulking man had leverage. Torsten watched the sunlight glint off the blade as it neared his face. His muscles were strained to their limit.

"I hoped for more," Mak said through clench teeth.

Torsten found the moment he was waiting for. Even the slightest distraction. He rotated his grip, allowing his sword to come free and bashed Mak in the hip with *Salvation's* sharp, dragon-shaped pommel as the axe glanced off his pauldron. Then he went to swing up, but Mak grabbed him by the back of the head, roaring as he flung Torsten across the circle.

As he did, Mak's thumb caught the knot in Torsten's blindfold, and it ripped free. Torsten tumbled, and when he came back around, he did so completely blind, the world nothing but blackness again. He patted the stone, searching frantically for it. It had been easy to bite back fear when he knew what was in front of him. But now…

"Your eyes," Mak said, incredulous. "And here I thought I'd finally found a worthy opponent."

Torsten raised *Salvation* in front of him, staying low, feeling out with feet for the strip of cloth that had changed his life. Suddenly, Mak's axe smashed against his sword and knocked Torsten back to the ground.

"Did Drad Redstar do that to you?" Mak laughed. His warriors joined him. "Made you just like one of your priests, did he? How poetic. I supposed this will be a mercy then!"

Torsten rolled to the side just in time. Mak's blade caught his shoulder cape and tore it in half. Slashing blindly with *Salvation*, Torsten prayed, but Mak snatched his wrist and yanked the blade free. It clattered harmlessly, then scraped across the stone. As Torsten crawled for it, a massive hand gripped his ankle. He kicked free, felt the hand again, and kicked free once more.

Another chortle. "Like a pig scared of slaughter, look at him. Pathetic."

Torsten found *Salvation's* grip and swung low, striking only air. He was disoriented. All the ruckus around him, and being spun around, he wasn't sure which side of the circle he was on. Only because a spear hadn't jammed into his throat did he even know he was still *in* the ring.

"Go on, stand, little piggy," Mak said. "Don't be afraid. A blind man to fight for his blind kingdom. Does this amuse you, my Lady! Are you watching from below?"

Torsten found his footing, but his muscles seared. He'd trained for much of the trek from Yarrington to get back to the warrior he was, but a real fight was different. His own men didn't strike with such wild abandon, nor were they as strong.

He could feel his heart bobbing in his throat. His hands quaked, and sweat poured down his back.

"*An anxious warrior is a dead warrior,*" Sir Uriah had once told him. "*Any man with a brain should be afraid in the midst of battle, but the moment you show fear, the enemy's got you. If you've lived a life in the light, then the Gate of Light awaits you. The outcome of war is not in your hands, so why should they quake?"*

Torsten breathed out slowly, let his grip tighten, so *Salvation* became an extension of him. For months he'd toiled around Yarrington, blind as one of Iam's priests, atoning for his sins. He'd learned to trust his ears like he'd never had to before.

Focusing on Mak's ragged breathing, Torsten straightened his back. The savage was winning, but lugging around so heavy an axe had him winded enough to identify over the others. Considering his style, no opponent had likely ever lasted this long against him.

Torsten tuned out everything but those labored breaths, letting their harsh language and jeers blend like running water.

"Are you praying?" Mak asked. "Do it louder. We'd all love to hear."

Torsten ignored his words but focused on the sound of his voice. Slowly, he paced sideways, careful to keep his balance centered. Mak gave his axe a few negligent swings, startling Torsten. He blocked, but Mak was feigning the blows, toying with him.

"I wonder, will you be accepted at your Gate of Light after I nail you to his image?" Mak asked. "I saved a special statue just for a man your size. Perhaps we'll carry it right to the Glass Castle. Show your puny king the worth of his men."

Torsten kept pacing. His blood had stopped boiling, now it was a fiery inferno. He knew what Mak was doing, trying to get a rise out of him, make a show of it, but he refused to give in. Torsten never thought he'd admit learning something from Whitney Fierstown, but that thief taught him how to handle goading better than anyone could have.

"Sir... Unger..." a frail voice spoke from over his right shoulder. Torsten wasn't sure why he listened, but something about the voice sounded familiar, made him feel at ease. It came from outside the circle, and as Torsten forced his focus onto the area, he heard strained breathing, lungs just about ready to collapse.

"Follow my voice…" the man rasped. "The cloth…"

Hands and blades accosted him as he moved over the line of blood. Most couldn't pierce his armor, only the weak spots. But as they came at him, a stiff breeze kissed the back of his neck, and he felt something soft brush against his hand—cloth.

He stopped resisting and allowed the savages to shove him forward. He fell to hands as he did, clutching the blindfold. His forward momentum was stopped by a massive fist smashing across his jaw.

Torsten sprawled out. Thankful for his zhulong-leather gloves, he let the cloth roll around in his fingertips, feeling every fiber. With his other, he swung *Salvation*. Mak kicked him in the stomach, rolling him onto his back. Torsten swiped again, but Mak's boot smashed down on his weapon hand. Once. Twice. Again, and the blade came free from his battered fingers. Another kick to his ribs kept him from regaining the sword.

"So, this is the sword which slew the Arch Warlock Redstar."

As Mak taunted, Torsten slapped the blessed cloth over his face. He didn't tie it, there was no time. But suddenly the world was painted with shades of white and gray, light and darkness. He could see Mak turning the sword over in one hand, admiring its craftsmanship.

"That is the sword of Liam Nothhelm the Conqueror," Torsten snarled. "And it should never be wielded by the likes of you!"

Torsten popped up. The moment he did, the clothe moved and was blind again, but he'd seen enough. He caught the heathen by surprise and drove his shoulder into Mak's arm, driving *Salvation* to gash Mak across the chest. Torsten grabbed the sword by the blade and wrenched it toward Mak's throat. Then, wrapping his other arm around Mak's forearm, he pinned the sword securely in place.

The flat pressed against the drad's throat, choking him, the edges digging into his jaw and collar bone. Mak swung madly with his axe, but Torsten was too close for him to have a clear angle. He was, however, still able to batter the blade against Torsten's calf, but couldn't put enough force to get through the glaruium armor.

Torsten fell back with all his weight. Mak was enormous, too big to drag fully to the stone, only to his knees, but Torsten kept pulling, crushing his trachea. And now that they were low to the ground, Mak's axe was useless. He elbowed Torsten in the chest plate.

"My throat won't be cut again!" Mak roared. He swung his head back and caught Torsten in the nose. Torsten knew the sound of breaking bone when he heard it. Blood poured into his open mouth, but he ignored it. Then Mak reached back, grabbed Torsten by his pauldrons, and flipped him over him. The blade jerked up and sliced through half of Mak's jaw.

Torsten landed hard on his back. The wind gushed out of him like water through a broken dam. He'd trained for worse. Survived worse. Coming to his senses, he listened for Mak's breathing, then thrust *Salvation* forward.

He felt it sink into flesh a short distance, then it stopped. The blade vibrated, but as Torsten pushed, there was resistance. Mak grunted from exertion. He'd caught it between his hands before it skewered him fully.

"Is that your best try?" Mak growled, his voice garbled by his mangled jaw.

Torsten threw all his weight behind the blade. Sinew split. The coppery smell of fresh blood reached his nostrils. Mak redirected him, then one of his fists pounded Torsten in the side of the head.

Though dazed, Torsten didn't allow his grip to falter, and the blade sunk in deeper before Mak got a second hand back on the blade. Judging by where Mak's voice came from, and their position, it was somewhere in the middle of his torso.

"Your plague on this land is over," Torsten said. "It's time you join your goddess underground."

Another punch crashed into Torsten's face. Still, he held steady, and the blade plunged deeper, tearing muscle, scraping through bone.

Mak screamed, primal, agonized. More warm blood sprayed Torsten's cheeks. Punch after punch landed upon Torsten's jaw, each one weaker as the blade sunk farther. If Torsten had his natural vision, he would have been seeing stars by then. He could hardly hear himself think as the blood pounded in his ears.

Then, the resistance stopped. Bone cracked, and the blade pierced through Mak's spine. Torsten slid forward until the hilt stopped against the Drad's chest. A few more futile punches hit Torsten's shoulder, but he twisted the blade, and Mak's head fell against his shoulder.

The entire bridge went silent. It felt as if even the air stopped moving. All Torsten could hear was the drad dying, sucking in breaths, laborious as those of the people he'd crucified.

"It is finished," Torsten rasped.

Mak laughed, and a chill that had nothing to do with the weather spread across Torsten's body.

"You think she's defeated?" Mak asked. "My Lady has a message for you. She… she's returned already. You failed… You're all just… too… blind." A long exhale escaped his lungs, the kind Torsten had heard too many times in his life when all air vacates the lungs, and a soul's time on Pantego ends. The full weight of Mak's head collapsed to Torsten's shoulder.

He tore *Salvation* free and moved aside. Mak's limp corpse thundered against the stone. Torsten tried to stand and found himself too weak to do anything but crawl. Murmuring in Drav

Crava sounded. Their leader was destroyed, and no matter what arrangement was made with Mak, he'd been in situations like this one. Desperate men made bad decisions.

Torsten pawed with his free hand, searching for the blindfold. As he found it crumpled on the stone, the hum of swords being drawn reverberated. He dropped his own momentarily so he could tie on his key to sight. He took up *Salvation* and raised his eyes, prepared to defend himself, to cry out for his men to begin their two-pronged assault.

Instead, he saw the hundred or so Drav Cra warriors raise their own weapons to their throats. "Skorravik!" They all shouted. Then, every single one of them drew deep, red lines. No hesitation. No lingerers.

Their blood poured upon the White Bridge, running through the grooves in the stone and through the drains along the edges. The bridge would never be white again.

The sight stole all the energy Torsten had. *Salvation* slipped through his battered fingers as he looked around, seeing the Drav Cra drop one after another, giving their lives over to a forgotten, fallen goddess.

Torsten watched them until his gaze froze upon one of the crucifixes. The soldier who'd helped him was nailed to it. No ratty beard or overgrown hair could mask what he saw. The shades of light and shadow which comprised his vision, didn't lie.

Rand Langley, disgraced-knight-turned-Redeemer, raised his head and stared straight at Torsten.

XII

THE THIEF

Tum Tum stood at the door next to Whitney now, warhammer back in hand. Talwyn returned downstairs to comfort Gentry, who'd had just experienced the first time he'd ever taken a life. Lucindur joined her.

Whitney could remember his first time quite well. It was central to everything he'd experienced over the past year. He'd just stolen the Glass Crown from King Liam's own head. It had been so easy—the old bugger died, his head lolled, and off rolled the crown, right to Whitney's mud-crusted boots.

The dwarf presently standing next to him was the precise opposite of the drunken, waste-of-breath Grint Strongiron who'd challenged Whitney to steal that crown in the first place. It had taken a long time, but Whitney finally realized there was no one to blame for that moment but himself. He'd happily snatched up the crown with dreams of being some kind of hero to the people of Troborough. Visions of him tossing riches onto the dirt streets and watching from high up on his well-groomed steed as the children, faces dirty, and clothing tattered grasped for the autlas now made him sick to his stomach.

In a stroke of luck or misfortune, it had been the exact

moment that Whitney arrived in Troborough to boast, gloat, or otherwise rub the news of his success in the squat little dwarf's cock-eyed face, that the Shesaitju arrived to burn his hometown to the ground. It was funny in a sick sort of way how long ago that seemed, how insignificant that moment had become in the light of it all—but it wasn't.

That was the day Whitney took his first life. Sure, he'd told tales before of great exploits he'd done with sword and spear, but they were all fabrications. That day, he'd shot a man straight through the heart.

Now, Gentry was experiencing the same disgust in himself that Whitney had. The only difference was that Whitney'd had a lifetime of lying to himself and others to mask his true emotions.

Kazimir appeared behind Whitney and sniffed the air. "This is the distraction we need."

Sigrid went to charge by him, but Kazimir barred her with his arm. She didn't relent until he shoved his forearm beneath her throat and slammed her against the wall. The sounds she made under her muzzle… Whitney wasn't sure who the good guys were anymore.

"Meungor's axe, what are they?" Tum Tum asked.

"Cultists, devoted to Nesilia," Whitney said. "Apparently, Torsten and the Shield didn't kill all of them."

"An idea cannot be killed," Kazimir said. "Her followers have vanished, they were forgotten, but they were not gone. It was they who stole my apprentice's mortal life." He whispered into her ear, something in old Breklian. It seemed to calm her a bit until he could back away.

Whitney covered his ears against a hair-raising screech. They hurried back to the stairs leading into the basement and saw the re-patched portion of the wall, and a claw poking through.

Sigrid unclasped the crossbow from her back, bolt already loaded, and took aim, pulling the trigger just as the fearsome head of a grimaur burst through. The bolt buried itself between the beast's eyes. More scraping sounded, then another talon appeared.

"Oh, gods," Lucindur said. "I told you I shouldn't have used my power again…"

"We don't have time for this," Kazimir growled. He pushed passed them and across the pub.

Whitney followed just a step behind, and they went out onto the patio.

Celeste and Loutis, Pantego's twin moons, hovered above, illuminating the scene before them. As a cultist dragged a young lady down the street by her hair, Kazimir unsheathed one of his many blades and flung it with a movement casual enough to be found at a family gathering. The blade sliced through the cultist's neck and he or she dropped like a discarded apple core.

Sigrid lurched forward, compelled toward the fallen body. Then, just as quickly, turned on Whitney, whiffing his shoulder where the fresh wound was stitched. He backed away and turned back inside.

"Lucindur," he said, "bring Gentry and Talwyn upstairs. Tum Tum, chase away the grimaurs and keep them and your pub safe. This place will be as defensible as a small fortress once they're gone."

"And what are ye gonna do?" Tum Tum asked.

"The two upyr and I will break into that wizards' tower. Huh, well that's something I never expected to say."

"They are not wizards," Kazimir corrected.

"Potato, potahto."

"I'm coming with you!" Gentry said, breaking free of Talwyn. Tears filled his eyes.

Whitney knew he didn't have much time, but he moved to the boy, kneeled, and held him by the shoulders. "You've helped enough, Gentry. I promise, you're the best sidekick this thief's had yet."

"Really?" Gentry said softly.

"Of course."

Another demonic screech was followed by snapping wood. Whitney only felt the gust of wind as Aquira blew by his face. Whether she was inspired to help him or Gentry, he didn't care. No sooner had a grimaur bounded upstairs, than it was turned to ash by her flame.

"Look after them!" Whitney called to Aquira. He stood and passed Tum Tum on the way out. "Don't get yourself killed. I won't be here to save you this time."

"Har, har," Tum Tum feigned a laugh. "Go find what yer lookin for. Sora needs ye this time. I'll protect em." He lifted his hammer and charged down the stairs, screaming like a lunatic. They were in good hands—safer than Whitney knew he was about to be in.

Joining Kazimir and Sigrid outside he closed the door, and said, "We ready?"

"We must be. Fate is on our side, clearing the way," Kazimir replied.

"Tell that to the people who live here."

The upyr ignored him, then led the way out onto the stone-paved street. In the distance, they could hear the cultists ululating, and see the results of their blood magic as the streets of Yaolin City were turned into their own playground. The city guard marched on them, but Yaolin had been peaceful for decades. They wouldn't be prepared for this level of chaos.

"She heard you, she heard you!" one chanted as he frolicked by, shooting fireworks into the sky. A bolt from Sigrid's crossbow pierced his throat and shut him up.

Avoiding them, Whitney dashed around the side of the building and down the cliff face to the small boat he'd tied up. From there, he could see the Red Tower silhouetted against the cold, gray sky. Also visible under Celeste's orange glow was the other half of Yaolin City—its many tiers and waterfalls, but also several small fires blazing, and plumes of smoke snaking up along the coast. Bells had just begun ringing from various places, and Whitney could see little lanterns bouncing along the streets— more guards heading toward the activity.

She heard you... that cultist had said. *Did I call them here?*

The dark thought stopped Whitney at the shore. Kazimir jumped onto the boat. Sigrid shouldered Whitney in the back and knocked him forward. He recovered in time to get over the rail and onto the boat in a move that he hoped looked smooth.

"You rowed last time," Kazimir said as he grabbed the oar and plunged it into the water.

Whitney smiled rather smugly before lowering himself onto the bench. His rear felt something soft, and he hopped up, rocking the boat.

"Sorry," he said, turning to find Sigrid already seated. Taking the bench across from her, staring into those rage-filled eyes, Whitney almost wished he was rowing.

"You're pretty in the moonlight," he said.

She hissed, a noise Whitney was becoming accustomed to hearing.

It was true, though. He wondered what she'd looked like before she'd taken on the pallid, pasty features of a bloodless upyr. Her stark white hair, though wild and unkempt, framed her heart-shaped face as well as any goddess. Earlier, when the muzzle had been removed, Whitney had seen her full lips... covered in dried blood, sure, but she was beautiful.

"You've got something familiar about you... in the eyes," Whitney said.

"Does it please you, taunting a woman to speak who cannot?" Kazimir asked.

"Can't you take that thing off her?"

"I've lived centuries, and the blood of your Sora drove me

mad. This is her first time near mystics. A lesson that must be learned, but one I will not take lightly."

"You're strange people, you know that?" Whitney said. Kazimir grunted in response.

Whitney took the ensuing silence to study his surroundings. It wasn't like what had happened in Dockside or Winde Port. Yaolin wasn't burning, exactly, but hundreds were suffering from the cultists' bout of chaos. He could hear the screams. The *clanking* of metal as soldiers put the uprising down.

When Whitney and the troupe had entered Yaolin, there'd been more ships posted guard. No doubt, they were keeping an eye out for a surprise Shesaitju attack from the water. The entire world was going to shog, and now, it seemed like they were all focused on the wrong thing. Glass ships throughout the lake came to shore to offer arms in assistance, leaving their path to the Red Tower unbelievably clear. The water ahead of them was still as ice, except in the distance where a large ship cut through the waterfall pass like a theater curtain.

"Was this my fault?" Whitney asked.

"Even *you* can't be that vane," Kazimir replied, pushing the oars. His inhuman strength had them gliding across the lake so fast, they'd look only like a blur from land or watchtowers.

"You. Her. Everyone said Lightmancery might bring unwanted attention," Whitney said.

"You think a song summoned a hundred of Nesilia's most dedicated followers to the streets?"

"I don't… not think that."

"You don't write the fate of this world, Whitney Fierstown."

Whitney brushed sweat from his brow and swept damp hair off his forehead. "She warned me."

"Iam himself could have warned you, and still, you would have done the same. Mortals are simple creatures. They do simple things. Perhaps, your actions inspired Nesilia to send her followers after us. Perhaps they were always going to attack. Gods are at play now. It's beyond anything we can predict."

"And yet we have to kill her?" Whitney asked.

"Now, you see my dilemma."

Sigrid's crossbow clicked, and she let a bolt loose. A screech above was followed by a grimaur splashing down into the lake right next to them. Whitney's heart skipped a beat as the water hit his cheek. He glanced back at Sigrid, whose eyebrows lifted like she was grinning.

They'd made it all the way to the island in the center of Lake Yaolin, the foundation of the Red Tower. Whitney didn't experience the taunts of the Sea of Souls again, probably thanks to Kazimir's rowing speed, or maybe the upyr, himself, had scared them away. Still, Whitney counted himself lucky, hopping out of the boat as soon as it reached dry land.

"Do not touch anything," Kazimir warned, causing Whitney to freeze and hold up his palms. "Everything is magic. Enchanted to kill you. To the outside world, the tower is dead. It has been for a long time."

"Sounds… delightful," Whitney said. "I can't imagine why King Liam would've wanted this place destroyed."

Whitney peered up at a series of terraced layers made from smooth red stone. They looked like giant serving plates stacked upon one another. Carved bands of bas-reliefs depicting men and women in robes marked each landing, portions aged and worn by the weather. As high as he could see, bare plants and twisting vines grew, void of all color, lifeless as the tower itself appeared to be. No guards or posts were on the small isle either, as if there was nothing to protect against. Usually a good sign for a thief.

"Do not let appearances fool you," Kazimir said as if reading Whitney's mind. "This place is teeming with life and magic. By Elsewhere, I can almost taste it." He turned to Sigrid. "Stay with me, child. If I knew it was this strong, I would have left you chained in the Citadel."

Thunder boomed and a flash of lightning sprawled across the night sky like an elaborate root system. Maniacal laughter echoed across the open waters as more cultists filled the streets. Whitney fought the feeling of dread that swept over him. He stood on an unfamiliar island inhabited by mystics that, history told him, were evil. Alongside him, his allies, were two murderous, blood-drinking upyr.

Gods and yigging monsters…

Presently, Sigrid trained her crossbow over the bay, tracking what was either a stray grimaur or a giant bat.

"Don't be wasteful," Kazimir said, lowering her weapon. She hissed again in response.

Whitney put a little distance between himself and Sigrid, stopping at the edge of a still pool. Dead husks of tall trees rose up from within its depths. It was like this across the whole island, pools and lifeless trees at the base of the tower.

Out of the corner of his eye, Whitney spotted Kazimir approaching a bronze gate. A large gem was set in its center: red as blood. Kazimir slipped between two clay statues set before it, each depicting an armored Glass soldier holding a spear.

"What are you doing?" Whitney whispered.

Kazimir didn't answer but put the palm of his hand against the red stone. When he pulled it away, the gem glowed, revealing a smear of blood on the upyr's palm. The gate clicked and swung open ever so slightly.

"How did you—" Whitney began before Kazimir cut him off.

"As I said, the Order and my Citadel have a long and sordid history. Our magic may appear different, but it comes from the same place. The same gods. I have likely broken many of our ancient agreements just unlocking this."

"Aren't you afraid the Lords will cast you back into Else-where?" Whitney asked, stepping a few paces closer.

"It is not the ire of the Sanguine Lords which concerns me here. The blood pact must be rendered."

"So, do we just stroll in like we own the place?" Whitney asked. He was used to having to break into places, but he certainly wasn't opposed to the straightforward approach, considering his company.

"We will likely have to slaughter everyone inside," Kazimir replied.

Sigrid let out a soft moan.

"You're kidding, right?" Whitney asked, but Kazimir was already walking toward the front doors. "He's kidding, right?"

Sigrid responded by nudging past him. He wasn't sure what salivating sounded like through a muzzle, but now he thought he knew.

After passing through the gate, guarded by statues that looked as if they might come to life at any moment, they stopped at two wide, double doors. They were made of bronze inlaid with an elaborate filigree—leaves, swirls, and the like—easily three heads taller than Whitney. Despite the state of disrepair the tower stood in, the doors were polished enough to see his reflection. He noted, his was the only reflection that could be seen and gulped.

A thin film of light shimmered in front of them like a blanket hung out on a line. As Kazimir reached for one of two rings, Whitney said, "Are you sure we should do this?"

Kazimir spun on Whitney, fast as the lightning still corus-cating across the sky. "You made the blood pact—twice. Now, we must do whatever it takes to fulfill them both, or the balance will break. This is the only way. If you die in there, that only makes it easier for me."

"You really are a peach, you know that, Kazzy?"

Kazimir bit into his wrist, drawing a bit of blood with his

fangs. Then, he grasped a ring with his stained hand, and a wall of light seemed to shimmer, then break away. A deep tone resonated.

Sigrid stepped to him, tilting her head in confusion.

"Their wards can't stop the fallen," Kazimir said. He rubbed his hands together, smearing the dark blood, then grabbed the other ring. Again, the sound shook Whitney to his core.

"Are you doing it right?" he asked.

Without answering, Kazimir threw the doors open wide, breaking the locks. Light poured from the inside out, and Whitney immediately understood that the upyr spoke the truth: magic within this place was alive and well.

The floors, shiny gray marble, matched a staircase which bordered the wall in a wide spiral ascending toward the top of the tower and dipping below their current level as well. The center of the floor bore a strange symbol. From the angle, Whitney had trouble seeing it, but it appeared to be a large circle with wavy lines extending from it in all directions. Then, as he edged inside, he saw it with clarity.

"Wianu…" he whispered. The creature that nearly killed them for a second time in Elsewhere. The giant octopus-type beast with razors for fangs and whiplike tentacles.

"Yes… history," Kazimir said without exposition.

The place was opulent, to say the very least. It was the opposite of Barty Darkings' mansions, both of which had a gentle air of sophistication. Gilded handrails and picture frames, trinkets made from precious gems—Whitney couldn't help but laugh.

"What is so funny, thief?" Kazimir asked.

"Their people are living in ghettos in Winde Port, yet there's enough gold to house them all for a decade right here in this entryway."

"The world is unfair. Get used to it," Kazimir stated without emotion.

"Oh, trust me. I am."

Sigrid stalked around the room like a wolfhound. In that moment, watching her, Whitney realized how bad an idea this all was. Somehow, in his obsession with finding Sora and releasing her from the Buried Goddess, he'd forgotten exactly how crazed mystic blood made the upyr.

"Maybe we should go—" Whitney started. He was abruptly cut off.

"*Aihara Na!*" It was as if Kazimir's voice was magically amplified in some way, though perhaps, it was just how the tower carried sound.

"What are you doing?" Whitney whispered.

From above, a voice spoke.

"The Well predicted I should expect unwanted guests, but a Child of the Night is not what I'd have guessed." The voice carried authority with it, reminding Whitney of the times Nesilia had spoken to him, only, this voice was older, less sultry.

Kazimir's gaze snapped toward the stairs. Whitney followed it there. He couldn't hear who he assumed to be Aihara Na descending, but he could see her. Her yellow robes dragged along the marble steps, but there was no *clack* from shoes, as if she were gliding. Her wrinkled face and thin, hard eyes spoke of a lifetime of experiences, but just as Whitney could see her, he could see through her, to the stone walls. She was ethereal, spirit-like.

"And, so, the witch shows herself," Kazimir said, drawing two knives. He fell into a battle stance, keeping Sigrid behind him, and Whitney had his back against the wall without even realizing.

"Where are the others?" Kazimir asked.

"They showed a lack of…" She rubbed her thumb and forefinger, and electricity crackled around it. "Perspective."

"A shame. I was hoping for a fight."

"Don't let me disappoint you." The old, spirit-woman smiled, the creases around her thin lips deepening. She turned to Sigrid and said, "You brought a pet, upyr?"

"A child."

"Kazimir, what's the move," Whitney whispered.

"Kazimir?" Aihara Na spoke, somehow hearing him from across the room. "I'd have expected the eldest of you, Vikas, but your name precedes you. Not quite first generation to have known the thirst, but close enough."

Kazimir grunted.

"With a reputation as such," she went on, "I would not expect you to be so foolish as to come here."

Kazimir spread his arms wide, as if wanting his cloak to spread and reveal the seemingly self-replenishing stock of knives he carried at all times. "We seek only to gaze into the Well," Kazimir said. "It need not concern you. Allow us, and we'll be on our way."

"Allow an abomination—a half-life such as yourself to gaze into the holy waters? You must be losing your mind in your old age."

"No," Kazimir snarled. "I've merely gained perspective of when a fight could be avoided. We have no quarrel with you."

"The fallen mystics made your kind in darkness," she spat. "We always have a quarrel."

"Not today. Our enemy is yours as well. The Buried Goddess returns, and she will devour all the magic in Pantego. That means you."

"This one is Whitney Fierstown," Aihara Na said, ignoring Kazimir. Whitney swallowed hard, and before he knew it, her ethereal body wound around him, taking stock. "Yes," she spoke. So close now, the undertones of her voice sent a chill through him. "It is you. The one Sora could not reject. The one who made her weak when she should be a queen."

Whitney's eyes lit up. "You know Sora?"

"Of course, I do," Aihara Na said. "I trained her, helped her embrace who she was."

"Was?" Whitney said.

"Well, she isn't quite herself anymore, is she?" She started to cackle.

"How do you know that about her?" Whitney shouted, swinging at her but feeling his hands pass straight through her.

Before Aihara Na could respond to the attack, Kazimir pushed him out of the way. Whitney hit the marble floor and slid a meter before stopping.

"You would dare align with Nesilia?" Kazimir said, realizing the truth about a hair slower than Whitney had. At least, that's what he told himself.

"Why wouldn't I?" Aihara Na replied. She sees the worth of this Order when all the mortals have done is break it. You should see that, too. What love have you for them to travel here with this thieving whelp?"

"I'll give you 'thieving whelp,'" Whitney grumbled as he got back to his hands and knees.

"What, did she tell you, she'd restore your Order to its former glory?" Kazimir scoffed. "Are you too lonely here, old woman? She will break everything in the world, you along with it."

Aihara Na drifted back across the room, near the stairs. Suddenly, other Panpingese men and women in yellow robes—at least twenty of them—slowly inched their way down the stairwell. These mystics were young, however, and completely physical, unlike Aihara Na.

Sigrid armed her crossbow, ravenous, panting through her muzzle, Whitney presumed due to the allure of mystic blood more than anything, judging by her eyes. He wondered if this 'Aihara Na' woman even had blood.

"Tell your people to leave," Kazimir ordered, "or their blood will coat the floor like carpet. It's obvious they haven't refined their power. What a sad Order this has devolved into."

"You'll find that by my hand, they learn faster!" Aihara Na bellowed.

Kazimir whispered something almost imperceptible and waved his hand.

The next moment was a complete blur. Aihara Na raised her hands, then sent a bolt of electricity at Kazimir. He moved with the grace Whitney had seen him use in Elsewhere when Fake Darkings and his thugs had attacked his parents' home. Somehow, he drew two knives and crossed them to block her magic. The energy teemed around the metal, but still sent him sliding.

The muzzle dropped from Sigrid's mouth, and she was unleashed. Bolts lashed out from her crossbow with impossible speed and precision.

Fire, lightning, and all manner of elements flashed from the hands of the mystics moving down the stairs. They all aimed at Sigrid. Unlike Sora's blood magic, they all chanted in an ancient-sounding dialect to draw on the magic, though, none of their words matched. It was all enough to have Whitney's ears ringing.

Immediately, he knew he was useless here. He backed away, slowly, to duck and take cover behind a large ornate statue of an animal—or a god—he wasn't familiar with. His back bumped into someone—a yellow-robed mystic. He whipped around with a dagger, catching her thigh. She looked down, then glared up at him. Her arm twitched, ready to immolate him, but a blade burst through her sternum first, and she dropped.

Sigrid standing behind her, licking her lips.

Whitney barely saw it happen before she was gone, carving her way up the stairs. The elements struck her, burning and freezing and damaging her skin faster than it could heal, but it didn't stop her. He'd never seen anything like it. She was blood drunk.

Whitney ran to the stairs, which led down deeper into the Tower and ducked down. From there, he watched Kazimir and Aihara Na in the center of the room. The former darted this way and that, running on walls, leaping. Where Sigrid was a tornado of rage, he was pure grace.

Aihara Na spun, too, casting spells at Kazimir in rapid succession, every element Whitney could imagine, even mixing them. Kazimir darted by her, slashing her ethereal body across the waist. Blood didn't draw, answering Whitney's question, but a wisp-like substance did, and her cries indicated that it, indeed, hurt.

"Foolish upyr!" she roared. "You cannot kill me."

She built up energy in her palms, and then electricity lanced out, catching Kazimir as he blinked across the wall, sending him to the floor, smoking.

"Everything can die!" Sigrid hissed.

Whitney leaned out to look up and realized that most of the mystics were dead. A couple gurgled their final breaths, crossbow bolts sticking out of their chests like pincushions. One heaved, Sigrid stooping over him and ready to drink.

Instead, she leaped to defend her maker, blade in hand, clearing more of the room than should've been possible. She landed on Aihara Na's back and drove the blades into her. Her corporeal state flickered as they drove in, then out again and Sigrid passed through to hit the floor.

Aihara Na screamed, then called forth fire to her hands. A pillar of it coursed down into Sigrid, burning her clothes, singeing her skin. The stench was rank on the air. Sigrid squealed and flailed, but Aihara didn't allow herself to be struck, or for the fire to relent. Sigrid's skin melted away, revealing her muscle and half her ribcage.

Whitney wasn't sure what he was thinking as he bolted out of his cover, straight at the all-powerful mystic who took on two upyr like it was some mere bar fight. But he slashed at her. Unlike

Kazimir or Sigrid, he had no powers, or whatever upyr magic it took to be able to strike her, and again, his hands passed right through, and he slipped on the blood-slick marble.

He did, however, earn Aihara Na's attention. She stopped pouring fire over Sigrid and turned to him, her spirit-like body seeming to grow before him. Sigrid crawled for the corpse of another mystic.

"You insignificant little insect," she said. "Nesilia will reward me for your head."

She raised her hand, and another bolt of pure lightning burst from her fingertips. Whitney slammed his eyes, shut but couldn't help himself when he didn't get zapped. He peeked through his eyelids to see Kazimir in front of him, and his cloak pulled up like a shield. The energy absorbed into the fabric, leaving only a thin swirl of smoke hanging in the air.

"A Son of the Night protecting a mortal?" Aihara Na said. "Now, I've seen everything."

For the first time since they'd met, Whitney saw Kazimir look weary. His eyes were somewhat lagging, and while he wasn't panting—Whitney was pretty sure he didn't have to breathe—his chest heaved.

"I'll slaughter every last mystic in this tower," Kazimir said. Even his voice was raspy.

"And I'll find more," she said. "The Dom Nohzi will meet the fate they so deserve."

She extended her hand, and it became a blade entirely made of fire. Whitney was spellbound by it. She swung down at Kazimir, moving as fast as he did, putting him on the defense. Whitney would've helped, but his feet felt like they were sunken in mud.

Bashing at Kazimir, Aihara Na beat him backward until his back was against the wall. She knocked a knife from his hand, then slashed his chest with the burning blade. His back slammed against stone. She gripped him by the throat, her hand becoming digits again but still wreathed in flame. His skin burned, sizzling, then healing on repeat.

"I have no weaknesses," Aihara Na said. "But you do."

She reached into his robes and removed a dagger Whitney hadn't seen before. It was heavily engraved with what looked like Drav Crava and gleamed, made of silver. She grinned as she sent it plunging toward his chest. His hands shot out to grab her by the wrist, and his touch turned her arms physical, but her figure seemed to waver around them, pushing through.

"Maker!"

Whitney heard Sigrid but didn't see her. Only wind gusted by him before she was soaring through the air. Half her body was burned to the bone, but her eyes still glowed, powered by fresh mystic blood on her lips.

She crashed down on Aihara Na, driving her fangs into her back. The ancient mystic pulled away and howled in agony. Sigrid didn't pass through as Whitney had. She'd bought Kazimir the time needed for him to duck out of the way of the silver blade, and he too plunged his fangs into Aihara Na's neck.

More of the whitish energy surged out of her, and the mystic collapsed to her knees. Her lower body still waffled like a spirit, but their attack made the top half physical. She continued to cast spells with shaking hands, damaging the upyr , but now with mystic blood, they healed fast enough to withstand the assault of elements.

Kazimir tore his fangs away. His eyes, normally a soulless black mass, now radiated white.

"Sigrid, child," he said, "close your eyes with her, all the way."

"You said never to do that," Sigrid argued, still wrestling with the mystic.

"I will bring you back from Elsewhere."

Aihara Na's fire-covered hand pushed at Kazimir's face,

burning off his pale skin, hot enough to reach bone and sinew almost instantly. He fought through it and bit her again. Sigrid did too.

Whitney watched, dumbfounded, and then, at the same time, the two upyr closed their eyes. For an instant, they were gone. Whitney was halfway toward running to where they'd been when they reappeared, on their knees.

Kazimir held Sigrid in his embrace, holding her tight as her eyes were wide, brimming with terror.

Aihara Na was gone.

XIII

THE DAUGHTER

Nahanab. She was a port city if ever there was one. With direct access across Trader's Bay and up the Jarein Gorge river system leading to Yarrington and Panping, the city had flourished under the thumb of the Glass Kingdom. Their major outlet into the Black Sands.

At least, it was until Mahi's father burrowed within its walls.

No city had received the Glass' influence like this one, which also came with their scorn. Mahi could see it as they ascended over the rocky terrain overlooking the city. A handful of spires from churches dedicated to Iam rose above the low skyline, constructed with black sandstone. Large libraries could be seen too, which were all likely to be filled with tomes of Glass history as well.

The shrines to Mahi's own god sat along the waterfront, half-submerged so the seaweed, nigh'jels, and other blessed life of the water could drift in and out. Unlike the rest of the peninsula, Nahanab's shores mingled with the M'stafu desert. The columns were the fingers of a Siren, made from petrified sand; the rare white grains glinting in the sunlight. Some were crumbled, others decaying. All were forgotten, neglected.

In its center, she could see the afhem's palace, still standing, which was a good sign.

Nahanab, like all cities, was named for its first Afhem. Now ruled by Afhem Dajani Calidor, the Calidor Afhemate looked after the city; a group which had thrown support behind Muskigo early on, and Mahi could only hope that Calidor and her father were still alive.

Mahi crawled up to the ridge looking down over the valley within which the city was situated. A fortification extended between two natural cliffs, protecting a mass of stacked clay buildings and stone monuments. She'd been there before with her father and remembered how the bazaar bustled. Now, it was ripped to pieces.

On the west side of the city, the docks had little more than tiny fishing rafts moored or floating loosely in the water. Mahi was glad, and prayed thanks, for the constant fog which plagued the bay. It would mean anyone on the lookout would yet to see the smoke from her battle to the south. Her men had been methodical, ensuring that no survivors made it through—not even a galler.

On the east side, a number of soldiers moved away from a vast army camp. A line of them marched through the opened gates of Nahanab like conquerors. The Shesaitju archers along the ramparts weren't even firing upon them.

"Is that—" Bit'rudam started.

"Father," Mahi finished for him. Even from so far away that he was the size of an insect, she recognized him. She could never forget the white tattoos coating nearly his entire body, marking his afhemate and many victories. Not an afhem alive boasted more.

Presently, her father wasn't fighting valiantly for the city. Instead, he was chained to a cart being rolled into town by Glassmen. Shieldsmen in shining, white armor marched on either side of him—but not only them. Shesaitju walked among them, including a leader Mahi would know from an even greater distance just by the size of him. Afhem Babrak walked, chatting with Sir Nikserof, Wearer of White and the man responsible for murdering Shavi and so many more in Saujibar.

"What is this?" Bit'rudam questioned.

"I don't know," Mahi replied. She might as well have struck like a sand snake. Her fingers dug into the rock, her knuckles going pale as ash. Her arm had been feeling better, hardly feeling the pain as she climbed through the labyrinth of rock up to their position, but now, she squeezed her fists so tight, her wound burned from the exertion.

"Is he captured?" Afhem Tingur asked, panting as he reached the ridge. He collapsed on his back to catch his breath. Unlike Babrak, he wasn't a giant, merely out of shape.

"Babrak is with them," Bit'rudam said.

"That fat, slob of a zhulong!" Mahi cursed in Saitjuese. "I didn't think even he could stoop so low."

"That is insulting to zhulong," Bit'rudam said.

"With Muskigo's army broken, and you on Nipaval, not a soul exists to challenge Babrak's power," Tingur said.

"Well, unfortunately for him, I'm not on my isle any longer."

Mahi went to stand, but Bit'rudam tugged on her arm. "Look," he said, pointing at the Glass army's camp. "They're completely exposed and relaxing in victory. If we move down that ridge, attacking them from the southeast, we can overrun their position."

"They have my father," Mahi said. She paused, remembering everything Yuri had said to her in his fear-addled rant. She shook her head. They may have been equals now, she and Muskigo, but he was still her father. "I can't leave him."

"Of course, my Afhem," Bit'rudam replied. But for the first time, she could hear a hint of disappointment in his tone. "Perhaps we can climb down, then pick them off from the rooftops."

Mahi's gaze darted between the city and the Glass encampment. Muskigo was being rolled through the central avenue now. Ayerabi warriors and Nahanab civilians flocked to watch, emerging from damaged homes, sticking their heads through shattered windows, though none attacked.

Mahi knew that all members of an afhemate would give their lives for their afhem, fight tooth and nail to free him. The only reason they wouldn't was if the afhem had ordered them not to. That meant her father wasn't just captured, he had surrendered. The very thought made Mahi's chest constrict.

"My Afhem, what is your will?" Bit'rudam asked.

The camp was still well-manned, but Mahi's forces had the element of surprise, and they could strike fast. If the Glass' armored horse cavalry didn't have a chance to mount and charge, the advantage belonged to Mahi.

Closing her eyes, she listened to the gentle whistle of the wind, hoping to hear the whispers of the Sirens upon it. What she heard wasn't gentle at all. A distant rumble broke to the south, and she opened her eyes to see the darkening storm clouds far across the desert. Never a good omen in a place where rain was scarce. When it quieted, she heard only the thumping of her own heart.

"Afhem Tingur, lead our armies down that ridge and drive the heathens out of their own camp," Mahi ordered. "Move fast and destroy everything they have. Hit the stables first. Don't want them fleeing like the cowards they are."

"What about you?" Tingur asked.

"I'm going after my father."

"Mahrav—" Bit'rudam caught himself. "My Afhem. Lord Darkings spoke like a mad boar, but his advice that you stay alive is worth taking into consideration."

"His concern, as well as yours is noted," she said. "But if they see a force coming, my father is as good as dead. If I go in quietly, I can free him. Or at least convince him to fight back. I don't know what Babrak told him, but if he sees me, I know he'll fight. We can catch the Glass army between us if we time it right."

"Or, you die, your army breaks, and we hand them the city's defenses as well as this coast's best water access."

"Then I'd better not die."

Mahi used her spear to stand, but before she could take a step, Bit'rudam moved in front of her, fell to his knees, and bowed.

His voice rose, muffled. "If this is your will, my Afhem, then I beg of you, do not go alone. I have watched you fight, from the arena to the bay. You are exceptional, but your style is still raw and overly aggressive for your stature. Not to mention your injury."

Afhem Tingur swallowed audibly, and Mahi stared at him, aghast as his bluntness.

"I do not mean to offend," Bit'rudam went on, looking up at her now. "But I loyally served Afhem Awn'al al'Tariq. It was only by the hand of God that I was not on the ship when his life was taken. But I knew him, and I know when he pushed through that storm, it was nothing except pride."

"Saving my father isn't pride," Mahi said, a harsh edge entering her tone. "I don't care what you or anybody thinks. He fought for us when nobody else would, fought for the soul of our people."

"You misunderstand. I only mean it is prideful thinking you must do so alone." Bit'rudam stood. Then he stomped on the ground and barked commands in Saitjuese. In an instant, a dozen warriors flocked to his side, drawing scimitars, fauchards, and other such weapons, and placing them on the ground before her. Then, spitting in their hands, they bent and ran their fingers through the dirt beside their weapons.

"*One Current for al'Tariq!*" they chanted.

Mahi scanned them. They were fearsome warriors by appearance, each of them far larger than Bit'rudam. She didn't know their names, barely knew much about her new afhemate since they'd departed Nipaval so quickly, but that was what it meant to be afhem. She didn't need to know their names—they were all one.

"I was a child when your father stood in defiance before King Liam on the very sands where you purchased our love with the blood of your enemies," Bit'rudam said. "The Glass will cower like rats before you."

Mahi nodded, then she turned to Tingur. "Can you handle this?"

"I may not look like much anymore, little lady, but there was a time this hammer was feared by pink-skins," Tingur said, lifting his weapon. It was unique, something she'd never seen before—a staff about half the length of the man, with a solid hammer on each end. "Aren't many left alive who can say that."

"And I'm honored to have you at my side." She spat in her hands, then lowered herself to the ground and ran her fingers across it. "May the Eternal Current guide you."

"And you, Afhem Mahraveh." He returned the gesture.

When he stood, his smile went all the way to his eyes. His back straightened, and he began to speak with a confidence she hadn't heard since she'd met the aging afhem. For a moment, she understood why his name was featured in stories about the last war with King Liam.

"When you find your father," he said, "tell him it should have been me in Tal'du Dromesh that day, but the glory is his. He'll know what it means."

Tingur waved for his forces and waddled off. Bit'rudam relayed Mahi's orders, and her afhemate went with him. It was a steep climb down, but they could handle it. Everyone knew what was at stake.

Mahi, Bit'rudam, and the others, however, faced much more

challenging terrain. The bluffs closest to the water were jagged. The warriors treated her like a child, or something precious, fragile to the point of breaking. Every step she took was guarded by one of them in case she slipped.

"I can handle it," she snapped at one as he took her arm.

"One Current," Bit'rudam reminded her as he hopped down behind her.

She clenched her jaw and watched him go by to aid another of the warriors. It was then she realized they were all helping one another. They weren't just babying her like everyone had when she was a child.

She felt ashamed. "Thank you," she said to the warrior. Then, once she was safe upon the next step, she turned and offered her spear to the warrior behind her.

"One Current," she repeated.

One by one, they made it to the lowest flat and the stark cliff-face falling toward the Nahanab valley. Mahi took note of the footprints in the thin layer of sand. Some areas of the black were darkened by what appeared to have been blood. Embers from a campfire swept along in the wind.

"Our people were here," Mahi said.

One of the warriors ran his forefinger through a bloodstain and touched it to his lips. "That's Glassmen all right," he said. "You can tell by how sweet it tastes."

"They do love their cakes," Bit'rudam said.

They all shared a laugh.

But not Mahi. She stayed low and perched over the edge of the ridge. From the vantage, she had a clear view of the city. Everyone gathered in the bazaar before one of the Glass churches which lay straight across from Calidor's palace.

Considering the state of the place, Calidor, himself, had to be dead. When news reached Latiapur, there would be a massive turnout of warriors seeking the afhemate. Tal'du Dromesh would be on again. Her father's rebellion left a number of afhemates leaderless. There would be tournaments for months, meaning Latiapur would be desperate for food and supplies and the trade which they'd been cut off from, giving Babrak more power.

No region was more desirable than one of the walled cities along the Black Sand's western coast. Those afhems tended to gather the most wealth and live the longest, provided they didn't join open rebellions. Mahi couldn't imagine what Babrak's city looked like now that he'd exploited the missing Caleef and manipulated a group of scared afhems unsure of what to do next. Abo'Fasaniyah was positioned on the largest island southeast of Latiapur. It was heavily guarded on the west by not only other small islands but the ancient Intsti Reef as well, making ship-faring all but impossible if the captain weren't intimately familiar with the region. A perfect throne to grow fat on.

"We can hit that spire with a boarding arrow," Bit'rudam said. "Slide down fast and find your father. But that's sandstone. I don't think it will hold unless we hit the blackwood over the bell."

"It's a long way off," a warrior remarked.

Mahi scowled at the holy sanctuary of her enemy and extended an open palm. "Give me the bow." A moment later, she held the longbow along with an oversized barbed arrow with a rope tied to it.

"Keep a hand on it," Mahi said. She lifted the bow, notched the arrow and exhaled slowly. Bit'rudam was saying something, but she ignored him.

Just like shooting pit lizards on the dunes, she told herself.

The bowstring snapped, and the arrow soared across Nahanab. She could hear nothing except the rope unraveling from the arms of the warrior next to her. The wind picked up, and the arrow waffled momentarily, then stabbed into the spire's pointed roof. Mahi released a mouthful of air.

"Well done, my Afhem!" Bit'rudam patted her on the shoulder. The others echoed similar sentiments.

"I'll hold it steady while you cross and swing in after," the warrior holding the rope said. The distance expended most of the line, so he carried it to the nearest outcrop of rock and sidled up against the face on the other side to help him sustain their weight.

A bout of raucous cheers erupted from the heart of the city. Good or bad, Mahi couldn't tell from where they were.

She unhooked the spear from her back, barred it across the rope and leaped from the ledge before she could think twice. A few months ago, she was skipping rocks with Jumaat in Saujibar's oasis. Now, she zipped over Nahanab, wind and sand scratching at her half-shaved head, seeing a new city from above.

Her feet hit the surface, and she skidded. Her head came inches from slamming into the bell. Even still, she sent a roosting galler squawking and flying away. It startled her, but before she jumped and perhaps hit the bell this time, Bit'rudam touched down next to her and extended a firm hand.

The rest of the warriors bunched up around the columns. The one back on the ridge swung off with the loose rope, landing on a stack of clay homes connected by a series of ladders. He'd have to keep an eye out from below.

Mahi moved around the bell to obtain a better view of the bazaar. What she saw took her breath away. Sir Nikserof and Babrak stood on the grand stairs of the bastard church staining her lands. Babrak wore her father's sickle-blade on his belt.

Shieldsmen, Glass soldiers, and Panpingese conscripts surrounded them. Shesaitju bearing the markings of both her father's and Babrak's afhemate watched from everywhere else along with Afhem Calidor's men who inhabited and saw to the wellbeing of the city.

Her father knelt alone at the top of the church stairs. Before him, a ceremonial dagger lay atop a white blanket. The blade was obsidian glass, and an empty blown-glass sphere built into the hilt was filled with sand.

The Glassmen couldn't have known such a custom, which meant it was Babrak's idea. It was a blade born from the rock of mount Kal Driscus in the eastern Black Sands, a volcano made dormant when the God of Sand and Sea tamed the region so his chosen people could inhabit it. The body of any killed by the dagger would be burned and the ashes placed into the glass container.

It was a sacrifice of the soul intended only for the worst Shesaitju criminals whose shame was irredeemable. In the worst cases, it broke an afhemate. When an afhem was cursed to never join the Eternal Current, his followers' bond was broken, and they were all left markless. Then, a new afhemate would rise from the ashes.

"What is he doing?" Bit'rudam asked, his voice shaky. Like Mahi, he'd probably never seen such an act. It was something out of legends.

"Why would he do this?" asked another.

But Mahi saw. Gripped in her father's hand was a long braid of hair—her hair. She recalled the ceremony after her victory in Tal'du Dromesh when the other afhems shaved her head so they may tattoo the mark of her new afhemate. She recalled how Babrak watched from a distance, a sneer across his face.

Now she knew why. Only, he was more treacherous than Mahi could have ever imagined. He'd clearly convinced her father that she was dead. Broken him. Cut off from all the news from the region, why wouldn't he believe it?

"It is time, Muskigo," Sir Nikserof said, projecting loud enough for the entire crowd to hear. "Let it be known that this is your will and that I, Wearer of White of the Glass Kingdom, in the name of Pi Nothhelm, the Miracle King, first of his name and friend to the Black Sands, will honor it." He raised a piece of parchment. Some sort of agreement that was too far away for Mahi to read. "May Iam have mercy on your soul."

"Iam has nothing!" Muskigo snapped. "You will face judgment for your crimes. All of you. Soon, your kingdom will plunge into darkness. My only wish would be that I get to watch."

"But you won't," Nikserof said. "Even your own people forsake you. Your own god."

"We are with him until death!" a voice shouted from the crowd. Mahi recognized the man it belonged to by the scar covering his neck. Impili Mansoor, one of her father's most trusted friends and warriors. His *most* trusted now, with Farhan dead.

Impili rushed Nikserof, sword drawn. Shieldsmen stirred to stop him, but they didn't need to.

"Stop, Impili," Muskigo said, raising a hand, and Impili obeyed in an instant.

Impili was restrained, shoved to his knees, and disarmed. Tears welled in the corners of his eyes. Mahi never thought that such a ruthless, fearless warrior even knew how to cry. His lessons when she was younger were always the most painful. She resented him at the time.

"It is clear from everything that has happened that the Current was not with you on this quest," Babrak addressed Muskigo. "You must see that now."

"I only hope that you will find yourself staring down at a dagger like this before your end," Muskigo said. He faced the crowd. "The Current has stranded me, my loyal afhemate, but you shall endure! Your feet shall tread this sand and one day, I swear it, you will have a chance to free us once more."

"Enough," Nikserof said. "Let's get this over with before our king changes his mind."

Muskigo didn't respond, only slowly reached out and let his fingers graze the blown glass pommel of the knife. His other hand clutched Mahi's braid against his chest.

"Back up," Mahi said to the other warriors.

"What's the plan?" Bit'rudam asked. "We must move quickly."

"Father thinks I'm dead."

"But news of your victory must have reached here."

"Yuri's birds haven't returned in weeks. They've been isolated. He can't know."

"How can you be sure?" Bit'rudam asked.

"I know my father." Mahi circled around to the backside of the tremendous, bronze bell. A thick rope attached it to the spire, but it was nothing her spear couldn't handle. "I am the snake only because of him."

She slashed the rope, and the bell dropped with a deafening clang. Bit'rudam and the others quickly understood her intent and pushed it once it was loose. It slid off the spire and smashed down into the Eye of Iam sculpted in the clerestory of the church's front façade. It bounced off and nearly crushed Sir Nikserof, who dove out of the way. Though a cluster of his men weren't so lucky.

"I'm coming father," she said, then let out a roar.

XIV

THE REBEL

Muskigo extended his hand and touched the cold, metal grip of the instrument of his eternal damnation. A life dedicated to battle, to upholding the honor of his people—he couldn't believe this was how it would end.

But there was one thing Babrak said which had resonated, even beyond all the lives Muskigo's rebellion had cost. Under the Glass, his people had stopped slaughtering one another over old feuds, and their numbers swelled. He couldn't let all the thousands who still believed in him enter the Eternal Current before their time. He knew their hearts, and even as they would hate him for this surrender, they would have purpose when the Glass once again pushed too far.

Like any strong leader, he could shoulder that hate. He'd failed them enough already.

Looking up, he saw all the pleading, gray faces. His people. The sight of his friend Impili manacled like a stubborn beast, broke his heart. Of all of them, he wouldn't understand. Muskigo remembered when he'd found Impili, the son of a broken afhemate, face bashed in by King Liam's army. Barely alive. None had ever been prouder to wear the Ayerabi mark.

From the humble little town of the humble afhemate Muskigo had won, he'd built an army to be feared. Now the Ayerabi would die with him. There would be no tournament celebrating his life and those who'd come before him. He'd be a scribble at the bottom of the history the Glass Kingdom wrote for him.

Forgotten…

"My little sand mouse," he whispered, squeezing Mahraveh's braid to his chest. "I know that from beyond, your heart will inspire others to come."

"You're doing the right thing, Muskigo," Babrak said. "I will find a place for these people in Abo'Fasaniyah after their service to the Crown is complete. I swear it."

Muskigo's fingers wrapped the knife's handle, and he slowly lifted it. In truth, it was light, but to him, it felt like hefting a zhulong. He could see the oversized afhem in his peripherals, watching like a wolf circling injured prey, waiting to feed on the scraps.

"Even markless, they will die before turning to you," Muskigo said.

Babrak grimaced and crossed his arms. "Then they're as foolish as you are."

"Quiet, Lord Babrak," Nikserof said. "He's doing the honorable thing for once."

"Yes, listen to your leash-master, *Lord* Babrak." Muskigo spat the title like he'd just sucked sand snake venom from an open wound. He got one last smirk in at Babrak's expense, then raised the dagger to his chest. Protests rang out from the crowd. Each one felt like a hand upon his own, tugging the blade away. He had to persevere.

Clang!

A deafening sound above made him wince and stay his hand.

Then it sounded again, accompanied by the *crack* of fractured wood and stone. He looked up and saw the church bell tearing through the front of the structure.

Sir Nikserof dove out of the way right before it hit the street, bounced again, and crushed a handful of Shieldsmen. Muskigo heard iron rending, then the shadow of the church's Eye of Iam cast over him. He didn't have time to get to his feet or even move. Instead, he covered his head and dropped into a fetal position. The crystal effigy of his enemies' god shattered right behind him. Large chunks of stone rained down around him, keeping Babrak and the others at bay. His head may have been protected, but it didn't keep his legs and back from getting battered. One rock fragment twisted his ankle hard. Another knocked the wind out of him. He crawled to avoid a larger chunk that would have pulverized his head.

"Where do you think you're going?" Babrak demanded. His foot fell upon Muskigo's back, bearing the entirety of his immense weight.

"Traitor!" A voice pierced the chaos. A familiar young woman's voice.

Muskigo rotated his head and saw her sliding down one of the cathedral's side-struts, landing on the second-story roof. Mahraveh—his only beloved daughter, a gift from the woman he loved who was cast into the Current far too early.

Only, this wasn't the daughter he'd left behind. She wore zhulong-scale armor and a frilled skirt of the finest craftsmanship. Her spear was one he'd never seen her with before. The shaft was simple but hard blackwood, and the steel blade emerged like a sharp tongue from a carved iron snake constricting the top.

Yet it was her face that revealed to him the truth. It was no longer the face of a child, but that of a warrior who had seen death, dealt death, too. Any Shesaitju worth his salt and sand could see that in a warrior. And her beautiful hair was shaved off to reveal a head covered in tattoos much like his own; only bearing the mark of another afhemate.

She flicked her spear up into a throwing grip, then launched it straight down. It caught Babrak on the hip and sent him stumbling back, away from Muskigo. Muskigo shot upright, but pain flared in his ankle, and he stumbled, settling against the church wall.

Barbed arrows slashed down from the cathedral spire. Nikserof and his Shieldsmen fell behind a wall of shields. Members of Muskigo's army forsook the ceasefire and leaped into battle against the Glassmen. Those who followed Babrak ignored it all, rushing instead to protect him.

"You meddlesome child!" Babrak shouted as he lifted the warhammer off his back.

Mahraveh landed beside Muskigo, retrieved her spear, and only then as he saw the sweat glistening on her now-toned arms did he believe he hadn't already died and was seeing visions. A father knows his daughter, and this, undoubtedly, was her.

"You're alive?" Muskigo asked, his voice quaking.

"I am," she said. "I'm here."

Muskigo couldn't help himself. He threw his arms around his daughter and squeezed, even leaning on her until his injured ankle made him flinch back. As he saw her neck, he blanched. A crashing wave. She hadn't abandoned him for another afhem. She *was* Afhem al'Tariq.

"How is this—" he said before she cut him off.

"I'll explain everything after." Mahi pushed him away. "For now, we've got to get you to safety and finish this."

"How adorable," Babrak said, then spat blood. "You couldn't just sail off into the sunset and leave the Black Sands to the men, could you, girl?"

"And let you sell us out?" Mahi retorted. "Traitor."

"How is it that none of you have brains enough to understand! The Black Sands will grow rich under the rule of the Glass. Then, when we are stronger…" Babrak let the words linger, looking to Nikserof who was too busy being battered by Mahi's troops to care. "Wealth is all they value. It's all they respect. How has your pink-skinned dog Darkings not taught you that yet?"

Muskigo regarded the braid still clutched in his left hand. Then the ceremonial knife in his right. He knew better than any that no warrior should enter battle when they were injured. When only rage fueled them.

But rage was all that Muskigo felt; all he had left.

He threw the braid aside and darted at Babrak, knife flashing. "You honorless pig, I'll cut out your tongue!" Babrak shoved his men away and met Muskigo head-on.

As expected, Muskigo lost his footing on his bad ankle, and his knee scraped the stone. Babrak's warhammer smashed down, but Muskigo rolled out of the way and lashed up, cutting Babrak across the left tricep before building distance between them. Waiting for the right opening with only a knife designed for a willing victim as a weapon, he flipped his wrist, testing the weight of the thing.

"Father!" Mahraveh shouted.

Muskigo shot a glance over as he ducked out of the way of another of Babrak's mighty swings. Having freed themselves of battle, Sir Nikserof and Shieldsmen charged as well, but Mahraveh met them with her spear. Nikserof's heater shield deflected each of her lightning-quick strikes, but she knocked him off balance. His eyes revealed his shock at being attacked with such ferocity by a woman. Muskigo couldn't help but feel the same way. He'd never seen his daughter move so fast or with such precision.

"My Afhem!" A warrior from atop the church leaped down to Mahraveh's side. Others followed, all to face her Shieldsmen attackers. They all fought together, all bearing markings like hers.

"I should have killed her when I had the chance!" Babrak

swung again. Muskigo evaded the blow, and the hammer broke open the corner of a building, sending tiles raining down from above.

"You couldn't if you tried!" Muskigo feinted left, then snapped in the other direction and left another shallow cut on Babrak's arm. The enormous man clearly hadn't yet realized that Muskigo's left side was compromised.

He's too busy hoarding gold and eating sweets to train.

Babrak reared back and threw his warhammer at Muskigo, who dodged left, placed too much weight on his hurt ankle, and slammed hard against the sandstone as his leg gave out again. Babrak then drew Muskigo's own sickle-blade and slashed.

Muskigo got the knife up to parry, but the incredible force of Babrak's swing knocked it from his grip. Babrak went to swing again. Muskigo now had nothing to defend with, so he grabbed Babrak's forearm and held. However, his opponent had greater raw strength and all the leverage.

"Traitor!" A fauchard jammed into Babrak's side.

Babrak abandoned Muskigo, tore his arm free, and slashed to the right. He cut open Impili's chest, revealing a long line of red and pink muscle and torn sinew. Muskigo snatched the knife off the floor and stabbed Babrak through the forearm.

The big man howled, dropping the sickle-blade, then limped back into the waiting arms of his afhemate, who no longer spectated now that Impili had joined the duel.

"My Afhem, we must retreat!" one of them said. "We have lost the advantage."

Muskigo wanted to give chase, but even as he tried to rise, his battered body betrayed him. His knees hit the stone, right beside his sickle-blade—a weapon he barely deserved any longer. Never in his life had he lost a fight, no matter how injured he was.

Until then.

"Defend him!" Mahraveh yelled. "Defend Afhem Muskigo!"

Her warriors had blades at Sir Nikserof's throat and forced him to the ground. His face was bloody, and his formerly pristine armor was now dirty and dented. Mahraveh twirled her spear overhead, then went to stab it down through his neck.

"No!" Muskigo rasped.

She froze just before dealing the killing blow. Her shoulders heaved as she held in unbridled rage. He'd never seen her like this, like a rabid animal—blood drunk.

"He killed Shavi, Father. He killed everyone!"

Muskigo's chin hit his chest. It was as Babrak said. The Glassmen really had taken Saujibar. Shavi had cared for his family since the day he'd become Afhem, but he knew she'd have died well with the Current if Mahraveh still lived.

"I know," he said. "And he'll pay."

"The Glassmen are tricksters, my Afhem," said a warrior with Mahraveh. He was so young, Muskigo wondered if he was even old enough to fight, though he supposed rules and traditions no longer meant what they had before his rebellion began. "We should end him before he poisons us all."

"We can use him," Muskigo said.

Mahraveh's arms shook as she fought every urge to run him through. Muskigo understood it. He'd felt that rage for his enemies more times than he could count. He'd felt it when he and Sir Unger plunged into the icy depths in Winde Port's canals.

"Mahraveh, you are, apparently, now my equal. I no longer command you. But you will always be my daughter. I implore you, control yourself—not for my benefit, but your own."

She bit her lip.

Muskigo could practically see the scenarios running through her head. He knew she'd be seeing his crimes in Saujibar. He knew blood would be washing over her vision. She looked at Muskigo for barely a heartbeat, then turned back to the Wearer. In a motion, swift as a sand snake, she used the tip of her spear to unseat the man's helmet, then spun her spear and bashed Sir Nikserof across the skull, knocking him unconscious.

Sand mouse no longer, Muskigo thought.

Beyond her, the bazaar had turned into a bloodbath. Warriors, markless, women—everyone was a target as the Glass army fought through, shouting for retreat with their leader captured.

It could be declared a victory, though Muskigo wasn't sure he'd want to call it as such.

Bloody streams ran across the sand and the stone. Gallons of it. Impili gurgled nearby, rasping for those final breaths before his soul joined the Current. Fighting raged between two sides, scraping to survive, and Mahraveh left Nikserof with her followers to join in. She took control immediately, barking orders and giving some semblance of strategy to the chaos caused by Muskigo's ineptitude. As a father, he'd never been prouder. As a leader, a part of him wished he'd jammed the ceremonial knife straight into his own heart.

XV

THE THIEF

"**W**hat in exile just happened!" Whitney shouted, pulling Kazimir and Sigrid apart after watching them vanish into thin air and reappear just the same. Sigrid snapped weakly at him, but Kazimir held her back.

Then Kazimir guided her to the floor. Her chest rose and fell rapidly. It was ghastly, ribs sticking out and bent in ways that seemed unnatural, but there was no blood. Her nostrils flared, and her face was contorted. It was fear, rage, pain, hunger—everything terrible Whitney could imagine all at once.

"Guh," Whitney dry-heaved.

"The Ancient One is dispelled for now," Kazimir said. "No thanks to you."

"Hey, I saved her." Whitney pointed a dagger at the rattled upyr. Then he shook his head. "That doesn't matter. What do you mean, dispelled?"

"I told you, when an upyr closes their eyes all the way, they see Elsewhere."

"You don't blink?"

Kazimir leered at him. Whitney recoiled. He hadn't noticed that. How hadn't he noticed that? He supposed he'd always been so disturbed by Kazimir's dark, soulless eyes he hadn't even real-ized part of the creepiness of it was him not blinking.

"So what?" he said. "You dropped her into Elsewhere, just like that?"

"Her essence is trapped in Elsewhere, not her. She's in between. But she isn't like us. She won't stay for long. The power of this tower and the Well will draw her back."

"Soooo, she's a ghost-woman?"

"Only an old wretch who refuses to die," Kazimir said. "One who sucks the power from all others who may hope to have it. And she calls us cursed."

Whitney rubbed his face. "I hate magic."

Sigrid tried to stand, and Kazimir rushed to help her. Half her body slowly reformed, but it was taking a while. Both of them seemed about ready to faint. Whitney didn't know an upyr could be damaged so thoroughly. Sigrid's eyes remained fully open, but they focused on nothing.

"She okay?" Whitney asked.

"She's too young to carry such power with her to the other side, but she'll be fine," Kazimir said. "Now, let's move before Na returns. I don't think we can face her again and survive, not like this."

Whitney put his hands on his hips. "Kazimir, scared. I never thought I'd see the day."

The upyr grunted and shoved by Whitney with Sigrid on his arm. Whitney followed behind.

"So, where is this Well?" Kazimir asked.

"At the bottom," Kazimir said, cryptic as ever.

He led them just like he said, to the very bottom of the stair-case winding down through the tower. They'd descended so many floors, they must have traveled well-below sea level. They even passed one all-white room that extended endlessly in every direction. Any other time, Whitney might have been drawn to enter, learn what treasures might lie within.

Another couple of flights brought them to a small round chamber before two tall, glowing, stone doors. Moss pushed through cracks in the floor, water trickling along in them, disappearing beneath the doors. And in the center of it all, stood another mystic in yellow. The young man looked like he couldn't have been a day older than Whitney had been when he'd left Troborough. His skin was smooth—not even stubble. Scars showed at the part of his chest just below his neckline, like something had been jammed into him.

"You can't be here," the man said. Just as he was about to cast a spell, his head snapped back, and Kazimir appeared behind him as if from nowhere. One of his many daggers pressed against the mystic's throat. Sigrid lay on the end of the stairs, more coherent now, but still weak.

"Open the well," Kazimir demanded.

"You have no idea what you're doing," the young mystic growled.

"Would you like to test that?" Kazimir yanked back on the kid's chin, and a thin line of red appeared on his neck, but he said nothing. Kazimir, on the other hand, looked, like he'd just stepped into a Westvale brothel. The thought of the scent of blood overwhelming someone with such force made Whitney sick.

"I wouldn't test him," Whitney warned.

"It doesn't matter," the young mystic said. "I can't open it."

"Then I'll break it open." Kazimir threw the mystic down, then moved to the door. He touched the handle, but as soon as he did, something shot him backward. His face scrunched like he'd never felt such pain.

He raced forward to try again, holding on longer, and pulling with all his supernatural might. The stone didn't give, even an inch. Then he was repelled again.

"Why are you here?" the mystic asked, coughing.

Kazimir was back on him in a flash. "Ah," he said, dragging his finger through the young man's blood. The mystic winced as the upyr dug a sharp fingernail into the wound, then brought it to his lips. Kazimir moaned and said, "I have my own questions for fate. I must gaze upon the waters."

"Only the Ancient One may enter."

"Is that so? Well, that's an issue, because she's taking a nice visit to Elsewhere now. And the rest of your brethren who stood beside her, they're gone, too." Kazimir made a spectacle of looking around the room. He dragged the mystic's head, mimicking his own. "I don't see anyone here either, except you. Perhaps you could open the doors. That would be rather helpful to us all."

"Be exiled to Elsewhere, you twisted perversion of life!"

"I am going to kill you, mystic. You cannot change that. However, you can determine how long you will suffer before you die. I have had centuries to learn the limits of a man. One thing is certain, you will let us into the Well of Wisdom."

Whitney had seen enough. He approached them. "Kazimir, we didn't come here to torture anyone."

"You are here only because, in the Well, your connection to the girl might provide answers!" Kazimir snarled. *"This* is precisely why I am here, to fulfill the will of the Sanguine Lords. This isn't Elsewhere anymore, thief. We are not friends."

The words cut Whitney deeper than he imagined they would.

He cleared his throat and said, "This one doesn't need to die, too." He turned his chin, remembering all the dead bodies upstairs. He thought it'd affect him more, all the death. But he'd seen so much of it over the last year, it was like he was numb to it. He hated that about himself.

"We've already won," he said. It didn't feel like winning.

Sigrid sauntered forward and eyed the young man under

Kazimir's knife. He, on the other hand, couldn't look away from the right side of her chest, still burned down to sinew. Grotesque.

"You are welcome to turn away and go wait with the others," Kazimir said to Whitney. "But while we are here, I make the rules. You chose this."

"And I thought you weren't supposed to kill for pleasure anymore," Whitney protested. "Get a hold of yourself, Kazimir. Up there was defense, but do you really want to get exiled again? He's a kid."

"Trust me, thief. More than anybody else in this realm, the mystics in this tower deserve every pain they suffer. The Lords know that, and they guide my hand."

"They're renegades!" the young mystic forced out as Kazimir crushed his throat. "I'll never help you."

Kazimir glared down at the boy, smiled, and said, "You will."

Whitney wasn't totally delusional. He knew his six years spent in Elsewhere was mere minutes to Kazimir. The upyr had never told Whitney how old he was—claimed he, himself, didn't know. Come to think of it, Whitney knew very little about the man.

Gods, Whitney thought, *he isn't even a man.*

That thought helped as he watched the creature poke at the boy's neck with his dagger tip, over and over again, little beads of blood forming and taunting Sigrid.

The scene brought back terrifying memories for Whitney. His first encounter with the upyr had been with Sora in the Panping Ghetto district of Winde Port. They'd stumbled upon Tayvada Bokeo, a wealthy merchant and prominent name in the city, tortured, blood pouring from his body. Then, Kazimir appeared from the darkness and stole Sora. For how short their reunions had been since then, that might as well have been the last time Whitney had seen his friend.

Friend.

A strange word—one that carried far too much baggage for Whitney's weary mind to process.

"So this is it, huh?" Whitney goaded. "A thousand years on this world and the only power you have to get answers is to torture a kid?"

"My name is Kai T'zu," the boy spat.

"Pain is a great motivator, Kai T'zi," Kazimir said.

"So is money," Whitney interjected.

"Not for a mystic."

There was truth in those words. The mystics couldn't have wanted for much considering the opulent tower. Whitney just didn't understand why the Glass Kingdom hadn't stripped the place to its bones after they won—made a fortune to stock their coffers selling it all to dwarves for gold. But the way Kazimir spoke about the mystics, like they were more wicked than even him, maybe King Liam and everybody else had been scared of what might happen if they had.

"Let me get him talking, Maker," Sigrid pleaded. With every passing moment, her strength returned, along with her lust. Watching her face, every bit as horrifying as a dire wolf, Whitney wished Kazimir would put her muzzle back on. If at one time she had been a normal woman, there was very little of her left.

"You do not possess the necessary restraint," Kazimir told her. The dagger bit deeper now, and Kai still didn't even flinch.

"You know," Whitney interrupted, "as someone who's been tortured—many times—I'll tell you that if he hasn't spoken yet, he is very unlikely to. I've heard torture is the least effective means of obtaining answers."

"You've never been tortured by me," Kazimir said, eyeing the tip of a blade and moving toward Kai. "Now shut up so I can concentrate."

"If you don't call six years stuck with you in Elsewhere torture, I don't know what is."

Kai's head was bright red, not just from the blood. Whitney could imagine the anger and the embarrassment… that in itself must have been torture. With one hand, Kazimir ripped open Kai's robe, revealing a cluster of scars that almost looked like a sundial. Then, he softly dragged the tip of the dagger to his shoulder and slowly pulled, drawing a thin line of red across one. Still nothing. No response.

Kazimir did it to the other shoulder.

"I do not know what you expect from me," Kai said, staying brave.

Kazimir didn't respond, just drew another line, and then another. As the blood leaked out, Kazimir licked one of the wounds. His eyes sparkled, and Sigrid looked absolutely rabid. When she approached, Kazimir said, "No, you've had enough. This is part of your training. You must learn to resist."

She let out a low growl but backed away.

"Have you ever heard of death by a thousand cuts?" Kazimir asked Kai.

"Seriously?" Whitney said.

Kai grunted but didn't further respond.

"I will stop at nine-hundred and ninety-nine," Kazimir went on. "Then, once you heal, I will start again. I know how to keep you alive. You will only sleep long enough to keep your body functioning. You will eat the bare minimum. I have all the time in the world."

"I don't," Whitney snapped. "Sora is out there somewhere, possessed by the yigging Buried Goddess, and you want to take your time?"

Kazimir spun around and threw one of his daggers. It literally shaved Whitney's hair just above his already damaged ear.

"I am warning you," Kazimir said, "I do not miss my targets. The next one will be your eye. Or maybe I'll leave you here, let the Ancient One have her way with you upon her return."

Whitney knew enough about the blood pacts to know Kazimir couldn't outright kill him without risking angering the Sanguine Lords and their desire for balance or whatever Kazimir called it. But looking at Kai in Kazimir's grip, bleeding, Whitney didn't want to push the upyr. He hated everything that was happening, but if it meant saving Sora, he could live with hating himself for all eternity.

"S-Sora?" Kai whispered. "Did you say Sora?"

Whitney ran to the kid. "Yes. Sora. You know her too, like Aihara-whoever?"

Kai blinked. "Yes, Sora Nothhelm. She was here. She… it was her."

"Let him go! Let him go, now!" Whitney demanded, turning on Kazimir.

"He is lying."

"I am not lying," Kai said.

"He is not lying," Whitney said just after, mimicking the boy's formality. "Look, you wanted answers. This is what we get. Don't be pissed that I got them and you didn't. Why are you being such a shog? Showing off for your new girl—"

Whitney knew he'd gone too far even before Kazimir's knife tip nearly touched his eyeball. "I warned you," he said, low and menacing.

"Look… I just want Sora back." Whitney backed away slowly. "Please, Kazimir."

He wasn't used to begging, but he didn't care this time.

"Information about Sora won't open the Well," Kazimir said.

"It won't hurt either," Whitney countered.

Kazimir muttered under his breath. Then, the same knife that had just been a hair's breadth from Whitney's eye now rested securely back in its sheath, and Kazimir released his grip on Kai. The mystic toppled to the ground.

Sigrid stalked behind Kai, inhaling deeply. Whitney could see the desperation in her eyes… she needed that blood like he needed Sora. Her entire face had healed now and with it, all the dread of her expressions. Whitney had to move fast before she lost control like Kazimir had in Winde Port. He'd had centuries of experience and still could barely handle the power emanating from Sora.

"Sora… you said she'd been here?" Whitney asked.

"If these walls hadn't already been red, they would be from all the blood she spilt in these hallowed halls. But… that wasn't her. That wasn't Sora Nothhelm."

"Why are you calling her that?"

"Calling her what?" Kai asked.

"Nothhelm."

Kai's brow furrowed in confusion. "She is the bastard daughter of Ancient One Sora Sumati and the former King of Glass, Liam Nothhelm, birthed after they fell in love in secret. It is known. Aihara told us all. She was to return the Mystic Order back to prominence."

Whitney's breath was gone, fled from the room like a dog used to being beaten. It didn't make any sense. Sora was just an orphan entrusted to the crazy badger Wetzel. She'd grown up in Troborough. She wasn't a princess or a mystic. Was she?

Whitney knew there was something special about her. He'd seen her wield unbelievable power to defeat Redstar, and then use that same power to burn down Winde Port—power she'd only begun to scratch the surface of, power that made what he'd just seen from the other, now dead, mystic acolytes seem like child's play.

"You're lying," Whitney said. "Liam and all his Shieldsmen hated mystics and magic more than anything. Trust me, I've seen it."

"Now you believe him a liar?" Kazimir said, reaching down as if to grab Kai and start torturing again.

"I do not lie," Kai answered.

Whitney looked quickly to Kazimir, and Kazimir stopped, returning the gaze. Whitney registered something in that glare.

"You knew?"

Kazimir just stared.

"You yigging knew? And you didn't tell me? Sora is the daughter of a yigging king? *The* yigging king?"

"How would this knowledge have helped you?" Kazimir said. "She was hidden, forgotten by a king whose mind was lost, and a mother who'd died birthing her. A life for a life. Of course, the Sanguine Lords knew. She is part of the balance."

"Am I just 'part of the balance?'" Whitney demanded. He scoffed. "Do you realize how much easier this would've been if someone knew that? The Crown would've had whole armies out here searching for her instead of just me and couple of undead people."

"She is illegitimate. She would just as soon have been hanged by the Queen Mother than honored."

"You don't know that," Whitney said.

Kazimir stepped toward Whitney. "She was hidden away with a broken mystic exile. Never to be found or discovered. Only meant to be forgotten. It is no wonder the Buried Goddess was drawn to possessing her. I should have never let her go. At least with me, her power could be worth something."

Whitney opened his mouth to speak, but nothing came out. Learning that old Wetzel was more than just a mad hermit practicing blood magic was the least of it. What Kazimir said about Sora was true. He knew it was. He knew that if everyone in the Glass were as pious as Torsten, they would never have suffered the existence of a bastard born out of wedlock—beyond the blessing of Iam's holy union. Not to mention a mystic. They were all taught to hate mystics, that they were perversions, even while their king loved one over his own wife. The hypocrisy of nobles never ceased to astound.

Kai was still on the ground. Whitney turned back to him and said, "What do you know?"

Kai eyed Kazimir nervously.

"He won't hurt you," Whitney assured him. He had to really struggle not to let his anger ooze into his tone. He wasn't even sure who he was angry at. The world, maybe. A world that had cast Sora away to his tiny corner of Pantego to grow up with a worthless badger, when she should have been so much more.

"Just tell me everything you know about her," Whitney went on.

"Sora was very kind to me," Kai said. "The only reason I am speaking to you at all now is because I know that what returned from within the portal was not the Sora I'd met. Now, I know why. If what you say about Nesilia is true, we are all in very grave danger."

Kazimir approached the two of them and tore a strip of cloth from the boy's sleeve. He wrapped it around Kai's wrists, binding them together.

"What are you doing?" Whitney asked. "He's helping."

"You may be convinced, but I am not," Kazimir said. "To know the truth about Sora, it means he has Aihara Na's trust now. And I definitely do not trust a mystic, let alone one throwing in with the Buried Goddess. Until we are in the Well of Wisdom, this one is not free. But perhaps, now that he's proven so helpful, I will spare his life."

Kai looked up into Kazimir's soulless, unblinking eyes. Whitney watched, impressed. Kai still didn't show one bit of fear.

"I'm telling you the truth," he said. "Sora was a guest here not long ago. She learned within the tower under Madam Jaya's tutelage. She healed me. She was kind. Very kind."

Whitney felt a sudden surge of jealousy but pushed it back

down. Her words in Elsewhere and in her Nowhere soothed him. *I love you, Whitney. I have since the beginning.* A bastard princess loved *him. And they say fairy tales don't come true...*

"Then, when she met with the Council," Kai went on. "I don't even think they knew I was there, listening from behind the heavy doors. She stood up to them like no one I'd ever seen. When she destroyed her bar guai, she disappeared. I think that's when it happened. When everything changed."

"What is her bar guai?" Whitney asked. Even Kazimir seemed to be unclear over what he meant.

"It is magical essence from past mystics, stored within discs and worn about the neck. It's merely a vessel to help acolytes channel their blood's power. Mine was only just removed after its power was drained, but Aihara Na says I'm the most talented."

"So the mystics discovered a way to store their power before their souls passed on to Elsewhere?" Kazimir said. "Interesting. You see, Sigrid? There are new lessons every day, no matter how many centuries you live."

She licked her lips in response.

"Well, Sora hadn't trained enough to use magic without it, like any of us acolytes, but she'd clearly always been able to do incredible things," Kai said. "Once it was discovered who she truly was, we understood. Her mother was known to be more powerful than even Aihara Na."

"So, this bar guai thing," Whitney said. "It stores magic. Could anyone use it?"

Kai shook his head. "Only those predisposed to a bond with the magics of Elsewhere."

Whitney swore. When he turned away, he saw Sigrid on her hands and knees lapping up Kai's spilled blood from the ground, like nobody would realize.

"*Blizklos,*" Kazimir uttered, and as if from thin air, the

magical muzzle appeared on Sigrid's face once more, keeping her from her truest desire.

I know the feeling, Whitney thought.

"I don't know how she disappeared that day, or where to, but when Sora returned, she was different," Kai continued.

Whitney knew where. It was Elsewhere she'd gone to. She'd gone to save him and instead, ended up possessed by the Buried Goddess herself. He knew, because now as he looked around, he recognized the red stone of the tower. He'd seen it there, behind her as she was torn back through the rift, and a circle of mystics chanting around her.

"Sora came back and she…" Kai had to take a breath. "She killed every last one of the Council. Everyone but Aihara Na, the Ancient One. They said the future required it. That the old Council was too set in their ways to find our new future. That Sora was meant to rule over all Pantego, and we would help her get there so that men and mystics could live in harmony again."

"That wasn't Sora," Whitney said. "She would never kill anybody who didn't have it coming."

"It is so very obvious now," Kai said.

"So, Nesilia and Aihara Na decided to rebuild the Order with ones so young as you?" Whitney said.

Kai nodded. "She took the time to train us all beyond the need of the bar guai. There were hundreds of eager acolytes serving within the tower. Only a fraction could survive the stress… They weren't gifted enough, but I was. I think Sora's presence helped me, Aihara Na said I was the first to join the new Council."

"Then I will ask again," Kazimir said. "Can you open the Well of Wisdom?"

"I… I never have. But I can feel it. Ever since I'd entered, the last day of my training, it has been calling. I believe it wants me to return. Aihara Na never told me what to do next. Only to stand watch here, even as I heard the screaming upstairs."

"Good," Kazimir said. "Then I won't ask again. Open the doors, or I will make you."

"I—"

"Please," Whitney whispered.

"Aihara Na helped Nesilia slaughter your entire Council," Kazimir said. "You must see that now, as now I know why the Sanguine Lords accepted this responsibility. A second Culling is upon us with such power in her hands."

Kai's brave façade fully broke. "You don't know what she'll do to me…"

Kazimir wasn't willing to argue. He strode over, grabbed Kai by the back of the neck, and forced him to face the door. "The Buried Goddess returns again, and her followers have gone mad. They burn and pillage the city, knowing they'll die. Not caring. She will plunge Pantego into darkness."

"At least you'll be able to walk outside then," Kai spat, one last shot at defiance.

Kazimir shoved Kai's face against the wall. Sigrid perked up and watched, a sparkle in her eyes. "Open the doors so we can return balance!"

Kai craned his neck to survey his captors. "If this is true, and Nesilia has indeed returned, we are in far more danger than any of us knows. If you're lying…"

"Then, either way, Aihara Na kills you for failing when she returns. I watched the third Panpingese war, boy. She isn't known for her mercy. And neither am I."

"Why open it, knowing it will be the last thing I ever do."

"If you really help us, it won't be," Whitney assured. Kazimir glared, but Whitney didn't back down. "It. Won't. Be. All her life, Sora knew that she didn't belong, and now we know why. That's worth something, even if nobody else cares because her blood isn't pure. They threw her out like trash. But me and her, we found where she belongs."

"Let me guess, with you?" Kazimir said.

"No. Wherever she damn well wants to be. Now, Kai is going to open that door, and we're going to get what we need to save her." He pulled Kai free of Kazimir and set him before the doors. Then he sliced his bindings. The young mystic stared at him, confusion mounting as he rubbed his sore wrists.

"I don't know what to do," Kai said. "I've only watched the Ancient One."

"You have to try," Whitney said.

"Do it," Kazimir said, more firmly.

Sigrid lurked up behind him, close enough that he had to feel the chill of her upyr presence. Kai stretched his arms, then raised one. Kazimir flinched, ready to cut it off if the boy tried any magic, but Kai didn't. He placed his hand against the stone, muttered some words, but nothing happened. He shook his head, squeezed his eyelids. "I can feel it beyond the doors... so much power."

"Power that is unhelpful unless these doors are open.." Kazimir gave the kid a shove.

"You know I am a mystic of the New Order? I can—"

"You can do nothing," Kazimir stated. "You've already proven that. I do not fear your magic, child. Open the doors so we can be done with this."

Kai drew a deep breath and tried again. It took several minutes, and then the faint blue light glowing around the edges of the door began to pulsate and intensify. Kai spoke more boldly now, words Whitney didn't know, in a language he didn't recognize. Blood leaked from one nostril, then the other. The doors shook but didn't budge.

"Give me your dagger," Kai strained to say.

"What?" Whitney asked.

"Give it."

Whitney handed over a dagger and backed away, out of range.

He didn't trust the young mystic that much. But, again Kai didn't try anything except to cut his own palm with the blade, letting the blood squeeze out like Sora used to do. Then his chanting grew louder, echoing throughout Whitney's entire being. His eyes started to glow. He squeezed his bloody hand and shouted one last time.

With a sudden boom, the stone doors shook hard, dust falling from the frame and the room beyond was revealed.

It was a stark difference from the all-white room just a few floors above—dark walls, the smell of mold, and a bubbling pool of steaming blue liquid. The pool was surrounded by overgrown moss sprouting white lilies. The squeal Sigrid made at the sight of it… she had to lean against the wall seemingly just to control herself in its presence. Kazimir too regarded it with a level of awe Whitney didn't think him capable of.

Whitney, on the other hand, felt nothing. While the others stood around with their jaws hanging, he stepped forward. "This is it?" he said. "It looks like a bathhouse in Latiapur. All that's missing are the whores."

"You should know that appearances can be deceiving," Kai said. He was on his knees, panting. Dark bags wrapped his eyes as if he hadn't slept in days. He sluggishly turned his head to Kazimir. "I don't know how this will help you, but I've done my part. Promise me this one thing… you will stop her, no matter the cost. I don't believe Aihara Na is in control any more if Sora is who you say. The Buried Goddess has deceived us all."

"You are right. You've done your part." Kazimir nodded, then turned to Sigrid and said, "Take him."

"What? No, stop!" Kai rasped as Sigrid's cold, pale hands grasped his shoulders. He flung a weak spell at her chest. Her pale skin bubbled, then slowly began to heal as she sneered. He was far too weak to damage her.

Whitney ran back to them. "Kazimir, you don't need to do this!"

"You don't know what needs to be done, thief," he said. "As long as this pathetic new band of corrupt, untested mystics lives, none of us is safe. They aren't worthy of Elsewhere and will only breed darkness as their ancestors did. Sora's father killed the last that were."

Whitney watched Sigrid drag Kai from the room, screaming up the stairs. The lust for his blood, which she couldn't sample with her muzzle, had her even more powerful. Whitney paled to think what she'd do to him after fully indulging.

"Says the assassin upyr," Whitney said. "He helped us. You don't need to hurt him."

Kazimir removed his long cape and tunic, then began undoing his belt. "Sigrid only means to watch him. She cannot feed."

"I just met her, and I already know you can barely control her!"

"I got you to play along in Elsewhere, didn't I? Enough of this, Whitney Fierstown. If he tries anything, she will do what is needed, and she will guard us if there are more of his kind hiding. For now, we enter those waters before Aihara Na returns to this realm, and you will learn, perhaps, that sometimes the truth is better off forgotten. As it was for Sora."

XVI

THE DAUGHTER

Mahi hurled her spear and took out a Trisps'I Shesaitju riding bareback on a zhulong. The force of the throw knocked him off and into a wall. She grabbed hold of it as she ran, spun around it, and used it to launch herself onto the back of the frantic beast.

It bucked and kicked, but she leaned forward and whispered calming words into its ear.

"Take Babrak down!" she yelled, kicking the zhulong in the haunches. It barreled forward through a Shieldsman, leaving the man screaming and writhing on the road. An arrow raced by her face as she watched, and plunged into the chest of another enemy ready to trip her mount with a spear—as if such a beast could be thwarted in such a way.

A glance up revealed Bit'rudam darting across the rooftops, following her route, letting arrows fly like a guardian Siren watching over her, refusing to let another afhem die.

On the streets before her, the city's markless populace threw themselves into battle. One leaped from a window onto the mounted Glassman in front of her. Another was trampled trying to stop one. Thousands of feet rampaging through Nahanab coated the city in a thick fog of dust, the coppery smell of blood and rotting flesh permeating it all.

Mahi slashed down at a Glass soldier and whipped around a corner onto the city's main avenue. There, she saw Babrak, far up ahead near the gates, ripping one of his own men off a zhulong. Then, he forced the same man to help lift his bulbous, injured rump onto the saddle.

"Babrak!" she roared, leveling her spear in his direction. He was surrounded by his men, in full retreat alongside the Glass army.

"My Afhem!" Bit'rudam shouted down from his perch above her, drawing her attention. He peered off into the distance, to the south, brow furrowed, visibly perplexed. "That is a sandstorm on the horizon. We must find cover!"

Mahi shouldn't have been surprised. Thunderstorms were rare in the Black Sands, and they usually meant a sandstorm would soon follow, though it was impossible to predict exactly where and when they'd strike. They were a shifting of the tides, said to be stirred by the Sirens. She couldn't imagine a worse time for one.

Ignoring Bit'rudam, Mahraveh pressed onward, pushing her zhulong as fast as it could go in Babrak's direction. The giant afhem finally finished mounting his own ride and raced out ahead of his forces like the milksop he was. But under his weight, the beast couldn't move as fast as Mahi's.

Weaving in and out of his forces, deflecting blows, dodging men, she pressed toward him. She wasn't here to kill her own people, only the man who'd poisoned their minds with lies about how being subservient to the Glass would somehow help them.

Babrak passed through the city gates where a wall of enemies funneled to block her path. Mahi pulled on her mount's mane, and its enormous claws dug canals into the sandy street as it turned. Its long, spiked tail smashed against the Glassmen, shattering several shields into splinters. Spotting a ramp, she prodded the zhulong up and toward the city's fortifications.

Archers from her father's afhemate dotted the ramparts, firing down into an obtrusive smog upon the enemy forces with the few arrows they had left. From above, the city was a cloud of kicked-up dust, as was the expanse of land before it.

Across the clearing, Afhem Tingur's battle with the other half of the Glass army raged in their camp. Spreading fires merged to catch tents. Footsteps from men and fleeing horses echoed like rolling thunder.

To the south, Mahi saw what Bit'rudam was talking about. A thick line of black grew across the rocky horizon, blowing in from the southern lands. It was a wall of whipping sand that would slice the skin right off the bone without prejudice.

"Mahraveh!" Bit'rudam yelled from across the wall.

Ignoring him, she stuck her spear down into the base of the ramparts, using the momentum of her zhulong to spring off and over. She could see the large shadow of Babrak in his retreat. Her zhulong crashed through the stone parapet, squealing as it plummeted.

Mahi soared through the air, locking in on the shape of the man who'd been so cruel to her, and had now committed the unspeakable betrayal of a fellow afhem to foreigners. They were the kind of betrayals that had allowed Liam the Conqueror to plow through her people in the first place. All the old rivalries and infighting.

The world slowed as she soared through the air. Babrak looked over his shoulder but didn't look up. He hadn't even seen her before the spear stabbed down into his lower back, further tearing open a wound he already had. He bellowed like the beast he rode but didn't falter. Instead, he clutched the shaft of Mahi's spear with one hand and swung at her with the hammer in his other. Still gripping her spear, she planted her feet on the haunches of the sprinting zhulong and ducked out of the way.

Her weight tugged at Babrak, wrenching the spear, tearing flesh.

"The storm," Babrak gasped. "Even God wants me alive. I… am… salvation."

"You are the past!" Mahi dipped under another of his swipes. "You are nothing!"

With that, she ran up the back of the zhulong, twisting her spear's blade, then tearing it out of Babrak's flesh as she flipped. Blood soaked the zhulong's rear, and her feet landed there, slipping, fighting to stay on. Just as she was about to jam her spear into the base of his neck, the flat of his hammer caught her in the gut.

Already unstable, she flew back, losing every ounce of air in her lungs as she hit the ground, rolled over onto her chest, gasping, sucking in sand. She coughed and heaved, but couldn't catch her breath. Footsteps and hooves pounded by her, lost in the fog. Enemies, allies—she couldn't tell and neither could they.

And then came the blackout. She tried to rise, but grains of sand sliced across her cheeks like tiny knives. The sandstorm was unstoppable, moving faster than any she'd ever seen, and all the shouting and the din of battle was lost in it. All she was left with was howling wind and screams that were probably her own.

She tried to stand, but a horse barreled into her and knocked her aside. A heavy hoof pressed her back into the ground, again driving the air away. She was blind. Couldn't even open her eyes against the onslaught of sand. More hooves connected with her shins and ribs, and as she lay there, wondering when a retreating foot would crush her skull, she couldn't help but wonder if Babrak had been right. If this was meant to be where she fell. If the Current demanded it.

Someone grabbed her wrists. Her light body was heaved up

onto a set of strong shoulders, and her savior dashed back toward the city. He slammed into warriors retreating in the opposite direction, absorbed the brunt of others bashing into him. All while sand assailed them from every angle. Mahi couldn't even draw a breath without feeling like it was filling her lungs.

Then doors slammed behind her, and her rescuer collapsed to the ground inside what appeared to be a guard post along the city walls. Mahi rolled to her back, coughing up sand, wheezing as it scratched her throat.

"My Afhem!" Bit'rudam quickly kneeled by her side and held a leather canteen to her lips. He gently tilted her head back and let the cool water fill her mouth until it couldn't any longer. She rolled onto her hands and knees and coughed up a gob of black liquid; a mixture of sand, water, and bile.

"Breathe," Bit'rudam said, rubbing her back. She struggled to hear him over the door being battered by the storm. "Let it all out."

Coughing again, she looked up at him. His hair was let loose, braids now a wild mess that fell over his shoulders. Sandy blood covered his face and arms, making his skin seem even darker.

"Was that you?" she asked. "That saved me? Carried me?"

Bit'rudam shook his head, and she followed his gaze toward Afhem Tingur, sitting opposite her. His men catered to him as he, too, coughed uncontrollably, soft belly spasming. His armor was in tatters, his hair and face coated with sand.

"No problem at all," he grated, waving a dismissing hand before she could say anything. "I couldn't leave you out there."

"I…" Mahi paused to breath. "Almost had… him."

"I saw." Tingur released a pained laugh.

"The moment Afhem Tingur spotted the sandstorm coming, he and his men abandoned the camp and headed for the city," Bit'rudam said, sounding displeased. "It opened an escape route for Babrak and the Glass army. Thanks to him, they'll live to fight another day."

"Thanks to him," Mahi said. "I live."

Bit'rudam looked as if he were biting back a response when Tingur said, "A good leader knows when to retreat for the sake of his people."

"That's what you do, right?" Bit'rudam said. "It's why you're still alive. I know the stories, how you didn't show to support your brethren in their final battle against Liam, when even Babrak did."

"Every day, I regret my choice, just as I'm sure many afhems do."

"Your regret means nothing!" Bit'rudam barked. "We had them!"

Tingur seemed to reclaim his energy as he slammed his fist on the wall hard enough to shake dust from the ceiling. "I will not be scolded by a boy who's just feeling guilty he left his own afhem out there to die!"

"I would have—" Bit'rudam froze and sank back.

Mahi could see the wave of emotions playing across his features.

Tingur was right, and Bit'rudam knew it.

"It's all right," Mahi said. "We survived, and that's all that matters. Babrak might never make it back to Latiapur after what we did to him."

"We had them, my Afhem," Bit'rudam said. "We had them blocked."

"And our God saw differently," Tingur said. "As he tends to do." He scooted up the wall to sit upright. "I've never seen a sandstorm sweep in as fast as that."

"What does it mean?" Mahi asked.

"Who are we to know?"

Mahi nodded in agreement. Then, she crawled across the floor and took Tingur by his hand. "Thank you, my friend. For everything."

"If we do not stand together, we'll drown together," Tingur said. "I see that now, thanks to you and your father. Our enemies may have escaped, but this is a great victory, Mahraveh. It will be remembered for generations, and it's all because of you."

"What we did, we did together."

Bit'rudam stood, presented himself before Tingur and bowed his head. "I apologize for my outburst, Afhem Tingur. You made the correct move to preserve numbers, and I am beyond grateful you've supported my afhem."

"It's war, boy," he chuckled. "We take it in stride, or we die." He stuck out a hand, and Bit'rudam helped him to his feet. Though, in truth, Bit'rudam's small frame did very little to aid.

"Well, they didn't all escape," Bit'rudam said as he helped clean Tingur off. "We have their Wearer of White prisoner. He's with Afhem Muskigo."

"Ha!" Tingur exclaimed. "Then we have nothing to worry about. The Glass don't see failure as we do. They'll do everything they can to trade for the holy Shieldsman. How the tide shifts, lady Mahrav—"

"Afhem Mahraveh," Bit'rudam interrupted.

"Yes, yes. Of course. No insult intended."

"We still have a way to go," Mahi said, ending the squabble. She squeezed by them to the door. The racket of the wind was beginning to die down, and she peered through the cracks. "The storm's moving past."

"They never last long," Tingur said.

After a sound of agreement, Mahi said, "We'll need to return to their camp and salvage any food and water they left behind. We lost a lot of supplies in the bay. We'll need more no matter what comes next."

"And what will we do next?" Tingur asked.

Mahi bit her lip. "I'm not sure. Our victory will gain us support, but I need to speak with my father."

"With all due respect, my Afhem," Bit'rudam said. "You rescued *him* from shame beyond redemption."

Whipping around, her withering scowl made Bit'rudam sink back once again. "And so I should ignore his input?"

"I'm not saying that."

Tingur stepped forward. "I believe he's trying to say that we have the advantage now. If we delay, we risk losing it. And the more of us making decisions, the more delay. I saw it myself in the war against Liam. Every single Glass soldier followed his will as if it were their own, while we all bickered over which strategy was best. Then we awoke having lost."

"Well, my father has fought in more battles than we've had years," Mahi said, looking at Bit'rudam. "His strategy will be best."

"Of course, my Afhem," Bit'rudam said, bowing. "Let us return to the bazaar and—"

From outside came the low hum of a horn. It sounded like a naval call from the Nahanab docks.

"What is that?" Tingur asked.

Mahi swept out into the streets, not waiting to find out. The storm was dying down, wisps of black sand flowing here and there, carrying cloth, parchment, and loose armor. Bodies covered the streets from every side, the blood beneath them, so coated with sand it seemed like volcanic rock.

Mothers cried, warriors bid farewell to brothers in arms—all the gray dead would be carried upon the Eternal Current soon, and they'd earned it, rising up against Glassmen and traitors, taking back their ravaged city when all seemed so lost.

As Mahi crossed the bazaar, she saw locals tearing apart what was left of Iam's church after she'd dropped the bell onto it. From within, they dragged the statues out by ropes, broke the stained-glass windows depicting all the made-up stories Glassmen told to feel significant, pissed on the graves in the yard surrounding it.

Mahi searched for her injured father amongst the masses, didn't see him. The horn bellowed again, this time louder, and drew her forward through a colonnade that opened to the docks. They were in shambles, naturally, abused by the Glass fleet before they'd established their barricade.

Then she saw him on an overwatch in the distance, leaning on his sickle-blade like a cane. Mahi started off toward him, then spotted Sir Nikserof to Muskigo's right, tied to a post. A few of her father's men circled him like hounds, spooking him, and laughing when he flinched. His mouth was stuffed with cloth, and he'd been stripped of his armor. The silk tunic beneath was shredded, and his soft, pink skin was coated in tiny cuts like he'd been left out in the sandstorm. Probably had.

Mahi's fists tightened. It was less than he deserved for slaughtering innocents.

"Daughter!" Muskigo shouted down without looking, as if he could feel her presence.

She shook away her rage. *We'll use him, like they use us. Father is right.*

Leaping onto a half-sunken pier and mounting a flipped boat, she reached him fast, and went to embrace him, but received no such affection in return. He was busy staring at a small cluster of Drav Cra longboats in the midst of docking at one of the only piers left intact.

"Father, what..." Mahi's words trailed off. Yuri Darkings stood on the bow of the lead longboat, rowing toward them. The entire harbor was now full of the green-glowing, nigh'jels. Thousands of them, flocking around the boat as if Yuri's very presence was enough to beckon them. Yuri stared over the rail of the ship, features contorted by fear as if the harmless beings were something to be afraid of.

In the distance, Mahi thought she saw sand and salt swirling up from the bay in the shape of a woman. She thought she saw the face of that same Siren who'd claimed Jumaat's life instead of hers, but when she blinked, the vision was gone.

"I ordered him to stay at the beach," Mahi said.

"I figured he'd wasted away in the desert after I never heard from him and Farhan," Muskigo said.

Hearing the name of her father's loyal servant, Farhan made Mahi's heart skip a beat. She'd always been partial to him. Now, he and Impili—her father's top commanders—were gone. Both dead. "Farhan, father…" She paused to take a measured breath. "He died in Latiapur."

"Latiapur?" Muskigo said, dismissively. "There is no fighting within those sacred walls but for Tal'du Dromesh."

"Farhan tried to stop Babrak from attacking me, and the fat brute threw Farhan through the Sea Door."

That finally gained Muskigo's attention. His hand cupped her jaw, and he stared straight into her eyes and her into his. How she'd missed the strength of his glare, irises like storm clouds ready to drown the desert. Only, now, there was something missing in them. Something she'd never seen before.

Fear? she wondered. *Doubt?*

"That beast touched you?" Muskigo said, lips trembling with rage.

"He's done far worse. He parades around the Boiling Keep as if he, himself, were the Caleef, chosen by God. He uses the Serpent Guard like a personal shield. Nobody touched him after he murdered Farhan. Nobody cared. He has most of the afhems under his thumb."

"Not all of them," Afhem Tingur said from behind her, winded from climbing the steps to the overlook. He stopped at the top for a breath, Bit'rudam standing in his shadow.

"Old friend," Muskigo said. He limped over to his fellow

afhem, and they embraced. "I see you finally got off your fat rump and joined the fight."

"I'm sorry it took me so long, Muskigo. I grew so accustomed to peace."

"Too many of us had, it seems."

"Your daughter made me see what a fool I was," Tingur said. "You should have seen her in the great arena, Muskigo. It was like watching you all over again. More, even!" He slapped Muskigo on the back. An unmistakable twitch of uncertainty flashed across Muskigo's features—Mahi knew her father well enough to know the look. Then, he smiled and turned to Mahi.

"I look forward to hearing all about it," he said. "My little sand mouse, an afhem." He gave her shoulder a shake, and she blushed. "Not so little anymore, I suppose. If only I'd taken you with me, perhaps we would never have wound up here."

"I—" Mahi began before Tingur cut her off.

"The Current takes us where it will, old friend," he said. "You know that. But whatever has happened, here we are." He gazed off toward the dwindling sandstorm. Then he raised his arms. "Even the winds are behind us now!"

"They are. We have the Glassmen on the run again." Muskigo nodded toward Sir Nikserof. "We can use him to press our position. I'm proud of you, Daughter. For what he's done, a lesser person would have killed him on the spot."

Mahi didn't respond. Hearing Nikserof Pasic's name drew her gaze back toward the pitiful man. The very sight of him made her stomach turn over.

"He's not a king," Tingur said.

"No, but with Sir Unger removed, he's the closest they have to a leader," Muskigo replied.

"You haven't heard," Tingur said. "Sir Unger isn't dead or imprisoned any longer. He slew the Drav Cra called Redstar, his own ally, lost his vision, and then regained it. They believe he was blessed by Iam. They're calling him their Master of Warfare but, with Nikserof captured, he'll be Wearer again. And he'll be out for blood."

Muskigo's eyes glinted with desire. "Good. Next time, I'll break him beyond repair."

"Father!" Mahi shouted. All eyes snapped toward her, and she pointed at Yuri's longboat, now docked. The Glass Lord carefully disembarked, taking care not to sully his robes more than they already were. He wasn't alone.

A frail, emaciated man followed behind him. Women from the al'Tariq held his skin-and-bone hands, leading him out onto the dock. Rags were his only dressings, with leather blankets draped over his shoulders for warmth. The nigh'jels followed beneath him in the shallow water, surging against the blackwood planks of the dock, pushing liquid through the cracks.

Silence overcame the outcropping overlooking Trader's Bay. Mahi couldn't speak, nor could anyone else.

The man beside Yuri wasn't that old, though not young either. It was tough to tell, considering how skinny and feeble he was. His knobby knees seemed to quake like a newborn calf as he walked.

And his face… perhaps that was the most confusing of all. It bore the look of a man who'd been pampered all his life—soft, even with the sharp edges of his cheekbones poking through skin. There was an almost childlike fear, which reminded Mahi of the first time she'd ever trekked out into the desert alone, when she felt the first pang of hunger and realized how narrow the chasm between life and death really was.

Mahi heard her father swallow the lump in his throat, then he fell to his knees and kowtowed. "The Caleef. He returns to us."

Tingur joined Muskigo soon after, then Bit'rudam and the others. Mahi's army followed, and the local markless did, too. Then, the only ones left standing were Mahi and Yuri Darkings.

He, because he was a foreigner, and she, because she'd never seen Sidar Rakun before. Her father had never taken her to those meetings.

All she knew was he was meant to be painted black, naturally, by the blood of the nigh'jels who helped the chosen Caleef survive the Boiling Waters. And he was meant to be garbed in gold, face covered by beads; unworthy of being looked upon by mere mortals.

All she saw was a starving, pathetic man covered in cuts and bruises.

XVII

THE KNIGHT

"You did a fine job not dying, my friend."

Torsten's eyes opened to find Dellbar the Holy seated at the end of his bed. White robes, spattered with red draped off his slender shoulders and his hands still showed the stain of blood, dried chunks of it bunching under his fingernails.

"Are you—" Torsten asked.

"I'm fine," Dellbar said. "We all are, thanks to you. That was a brave thing you did, shouldering the battle on your own. Foolish, but brave." He popped the top off a leather flask and threw back a sip, then held it out for Torsten.

He stared, wordless.

"Oh c'mon, live a little." Dellbar pawed for Torsten's hand with his open one, found it, then placed the flask inside.

"Some priest," Torsten said. But he lifted the flask to his lips nonetheless. Then, drawing a deep breath, said, "Iam forgive me," before downing a mouthful. He expected to retch from the bitterness, but Dellbar had exquisite taste. Honeyed wine, probably a vintage older than either of them.

"Good, right?" he laughed. "You think I'm the first priest who liked a drink here and there? Found this bottle in the crypts below the Yarrington Cathedral."

Torsten took another sip, then wiped his lips. He couldn't remember the last time he'd imbibed, even so little, but with aches in places he didn't know could ache, he took one last sip before Dellbar could grab it. Besides, he was thirsty. So dreadfully thirsty.

"It is not the occasional drink I worry about," Torsten said, more to convince himself than anything else. He knew how his father got when he'd had one too many. His mother too, though she did it for other reasons.

Swinging his legs off the side of the bed, Torsten positioned himself next to Dellbar. He felt like he'd been trampled by a wagon pulled by zhulong. A wave of dizziness rushed to his head as well, and he toppled over.

"Sir Unger, you all right?" Lucas hurried into the room and helped Torsten upright. He held his shoulders and stared straight at him.

Dellbar laughed. "Lightweight."

"I'm fine, boy," Torsten said. He shrugged him away and rubbed his temples. "Just tired."

"And alive. That wasn't part of the plan, Sir. We were ready, through the eastern gate. Didn't you see our signal?"

"I decided that this fight was my own."

"Right, ye did!" Brouben exclaimed, entering as well. "By Meungor's Axe, would I have loved to see ye work. Killing, all of them by yerself. Was a shog shuckin bloodbath!"

"I only killed one," Torsten said.

"And what a fight it must've been," Brouben said. "Yer men praise ye. Tonight, we feast in yer honor. Brought ale from the heart of Balonhearth just for such an occasion."

"Did you now?" Dellbar asked.

Torsten gritted his teeth. All their chattering made his head hurt even more. He was about to complain about the lack of privacy when he realized where he was. There was no ceiling, only a bit of charred lumber and crumbled stone. They were in one of the White Bridge's ruined towers.

As they talked, more memories of the fight returned. Mak's last words, that they'd all been deceived, and that the Buried Goddess had truly returned that day on Mount Lister, just not through Redstar. Of course, he was a twisted savage about to die. He could have been lying. One last barb to get under Torsten's skin and stick there. But if he spoke the truth?

Torsten stood, and again, the blood rushed to his head. He fell back, caught by Lucas.

"His Holiness says you took a hard blow to the head, Sir," Lucas said.

"Several," Dellbar added with a burp.

"You should lie down," Lucas continued.

"Plenty of time for that when I'm dead," Torsten bristled. "His Holiness should be out there, tending to the poor souls that savage crucified."

"You slept a full day," Dellbar said, mouth wet with his latest sip. "They're being taken care of... those who are alive. Rest have passed along to the Gate of Light." He raised his flask in acknowledgment.

"How many? This act of..." Torsten's words trailed off. He wasn't even sure if anyone answered. Suddenly, his weary mind homed in on one such victim of Mak's wanton cruelty.

"Rand," he said.

"What?" Lucas asked.

Torsten got to his feet, and this time, used the young Shieldsman. He didn't offer him a chance to resist, just started walking toward the exit, forcing him to help.

"Ye really should sit down," Brouben said. Torsten ignored him, and the dwarven prince had no choice but to step aside.

"Take me to the injured," Torsten ordered.

"Sir—" Lucas was cut off.

"Take me."

They moved outside and, where Torsten might've expected Iam's light to shine upon such a favorable day, clouds blotted the sky. A light drizzle pattered against his bald pate, though not enough to wash away the dried blood.

Blood also stained the whole of the bridge, pink puddles splashing as carts loaded with corpses rolled toward the gates—all of them, dead for nothing. And not only them—Glassmen had carts of their own, everyone who'd died from being crucified, piled high. So many that Torsten feared it was most of them. The crucifixes had been destroyed, but that sight would haunt him forever.

"Hail, Sir Unger!" Sir Marcos shouted the moment he saw him. He looked up from dragging a body… Mak's body.

"Hail the hero of White Bridge!" another yelled. Then another, until every person on the bridge was chanting his name.

Torsten froze. He had fought in many wars, countless battles, been on both the winning and losing side—he'd never been received like this. As a boy, growing up in the filth of Dockside, he'd dreamed of such a reception, of being treated like Liam the Conqueror. He shook away the thought, ashamed.

"Where are the injured?" Torsten asked softly.

"Sir, do you hear them?" Lucas said at the same time, barely able to contain his exuberance. "I heard one of them call you 'Torsten the Triumphant.'"

Torsten couldn't remember ever seeing Lucas smile like this before. Not even after Valin was slain and his family was safe from the crime lord.

The name… Torsten the Triumphant. Torsten didn't want to admit how good it felt to no longer be considered Torsten the Foolhardy Murderer of Shieldsmen, but now wasn't the time.

"The injured. Take me," he said.

Lucas' face showed his disappointment. "They're in the eastern towers. I'll help you."

Lucas took his arm like he used to when Torsten had been completely blind. Each warrior they passed proclaimed his name. Even Brouben's dwarven contingent offered him their respect. Glassmen bowed their heads, raised their swords—everything they didn't do when he'd returned from Winde Port, labeled a traitor.

Lucas led him over the spot where Torsten and Mak had battled, where Mak had told him that Nesilia wasn't gone; that they'd all been deceived. The faded circle of blood still remained, forever entrenched within the stone.

Torsten stopped again, struggling to focus through the deafening appraisal on every side of them. "Drad Mak said something, Lucas." He could barely form the words. "He said that she wasn't really defeated. That she's already returned."

"Who?" Lucas asked

"Nesilia." It felt like poison on his lips.

Lucas didn't hesitate for even a second. "He was lying."

"If I've learned anything living as long as I have, Men don't lie as death approaches. It's the one time when the truth is more terrifying."

"You've said it yourself. These weren't men. They're monsters."

Torsten shook his head solemnly. "They all took their own lives. No fear. No hesitation. It's like they wanted to die here, wanted us to think that here on this Bridge, the last shred of Drav Cra power fell. Yet they're raiding dwarven cities?"

"Sir Unger." Lucas stepped in front of Torsten, forcing him to stop. "Their Arch Warlock is dead. Their greatest chieftain is dead. It will take many years for them to be a real threat again. We won."

"Did we?"

"We must have. Why else would Iam have led us here? Mak was all that remained of Redstar's horde, and now they're all gone."

Torsten put on a frail smile and gave the boy's shoulder a shake. "When did you become so wise, Sir Danvels?"

"I had a good teacher. Come now, we're almost there."

Lucas started to lead Torsten again. He accepted the help, but his own words rang hollow. Everything Lucas had said made sense. Redstar had lost everything. The Drav Cra were probably raiding dwarves because they were scared, starving, and leaderless. They'd never been a true threat to the Glass Kingdom before, only a nuisance. They were too scattered; too wild.

Rounding a corner into one of the ravaged towers at the eastern gate, the chants of "Torsten the Triumphant" faded into memory. Here, the floor was wet. Not with blood, but from the water used to wash it away. Throughout the room, men and women lay on bedrolls. All of them had bandages tight around their hands and ankles and wore rags that could barely cover their many scrapes and bruises.

Torsten would have preferred the smell of Valin's brothel to this. It wasn't just blood, but wounds that had been left out in the sun to fester, eaten away by flesh worms. Infection had its own special stink. As monks and sisters darted around the room like flies, Torsten watched as one sister closed the eyes of a victim who'd clung to life so long yet passed on anyway.

"Everyone is doing what they can," Lucas said.

Torsten covered his mouth, turned, and leaned against the wall. Maybe it was his head, still swimming from the fight, but it was probably the fetid stench that had him teetering at the point of vomiting.

"Thanks to what you did, we were able to pull them down quicker," Lucas went on. "A proper siege could have lasted days."

"Have all of the Drav Cra bodies dumped and burned," Torsten ordered, as if Lucas wasn't in the midst of praising him.

"Sir, that's not our way."

"I will not waste precious time and resources treating them like our own. They would use fire, and so should we. I want every man we can spare focused on catering to these people—our people—not digging holes. The families of those who died here will receive a tribute from the Crown. This may have been the work of savages, but we invited them in."

"A kind gesture, Sir. I'll spread the word."

"It is not just kind," Torsten said. "It is right."

"Yes, Sir."

When Lucas didn't immediately move, Torsten said, "What are you waiting for?"

A response died on Lucas' lips before he pounded his chest in salute and departed. Steadying himself against the wall, Torsten studied each victim, searching for the face he recognized.

"Sir Unger, it is so good to see you again," a sister of Iam said, placing a hand on Torsten's arm. She then traced her eyes with her fingers, then bowed. Torsten didn't recognize her. Maybe it was the hood drawn up over her shaved head.

Torsten sloppily returned the gesture. "And you, Sister…"

"Nauriyal. My apologies, I forgot that when we met in the capital, you still had no sight. It warmed my heart to hear about the miracle which let you see again. I knew then that I had to join your march. And now, it seems Iam had a purpose for me. To help these poor people."

"Ah, yes, now I remember," Torsten lied. He'd had his mind on many other things while in Yarrington. Dealing with the absence of a High Priest while the others argued wasn't even the most pressing of those concerns.

"These people are lucky to have you," he added. "If you'll excuse me.

"Oh, of course," she said.

He squeezed by her to keep searching for Rand. He made it all the way across the ruined tower's floor before he found him. Lying on his back beside a smashed weapon's rack, was Rand Langley.

He was so skinny and ragged, not a soul would have recognized him. But even if Torsten were still blind, he'd have known this man. In the eyes of the kingdom, the truth of Rand's relationship with Valin Tehr was left buried so he could remain the Redeemer who'd stood against Redstar when nobody else had, and who'd freed Torsten from the Glass Castle dungeons to stop him.

A ratty beard now covered his chin. He was shirtless, glistening with sweat, and his ribs showed through loose skin. A redeemer… he looked anything but.

"Sir Unger…" he rasped, eyelids spreading wide as he could manage. Another sister of Iam kneeled next to him, cleaning off a stab wound on his thigh. It wasn't the only one he bore, either. By how terrible he looked, the very fact that he still breathed seemed a blessing from Iam.

"Leave us," Torsten said to the sister. She started to protest, but his glower left no room for debate. With a quick bow, she hurried off to tend to someone else. Since there were no seats available, Torsten lowered himself to the floor beside the ex-Shieldsman.

"Sir Unger," Rand repeated. Even turning his head to face Torsten seemed a struggle. "Torsten…"

"You saved my life," Torsten said. "You saved all of these peoples' lives."

"I helped put them there, too. I faced Mak and lost."

"Why were you here, Rand?"

Rand swallowed the lump in his throat, said nothing.

"I know everything," Torsten said. "I know where you really vanished to on the Dawning. I know about Valin and the Caleef."

Rand closed his eyes, tears welling in them, and turned away. His words came out in a choking gargle. "I had no choice, Torsten."

"I can't believe that."

"He helped me. I helped him. That was the vow." A moment passed in silence before he continued. "He took my sister as collateral. Threatened everything. What would you have had me do?"

A thousand different responses raced through Torsten's mind. He bit back all of them. He'd never had a family—not one worth the shog they produced, that is—and Valin knew how to use man's weaknesses. He'd done the same to Lucas, even King Pi after Oleander was murdered.

"Where is the Caleef?" Torsten asked. "The Kingdom doesn't know. It never needs to. It's just you and me here, Rand."

"He's… dead." Rand exhaled slowly. "I watched him fall over the bridge myself. Mak captured us. We nearly escaped but… but he fell. I couldn't save him."

Torsten's head fell into his palms. He rubbed his face vigorously. "They'll never forgive us for this."

"Sir Unger, I'm sorry. I'm so, so sorry." Rand grasped at Torsten's arm, but Torsten pulled it away. His hand balled, trembling, but he never struck the ex-Shieldsman.

Then Rand's tears turned to weeping. "He's going to kill her when he finds out… I… made a promise…"

"To a dead man," Torsten said.

"What?"

"The Crown knows Valin was working with the traitorous Darkings family. He's paid the ultimate price."

Rand sat up. "And Sigrid? My sister. He would've been holding her prisoner." He threw himself at Torsten. "Torsten, was she there? You can do whatever you want to me, but tell me she's alive."

Torsten felt wool in his throat, swallowed against the dryness, and held his tongue. He'd encountered Sigrid on the night Oleander died. Whatever she was to Rand, darkness had twisted her into an upyr—a deathless assassin surviving on blood and far beyond the light of Iam, a heartless monster, used by monsters to settle pacts of blood.

"She…" Torsten paused. All he could manage was to shake his head.

In Rand's situation, he knew it's what he'd want. If the person he loved had become something so terrible, it was better not to know. To hold only the good memories of her in his heart and mind forever. Like with Oleander and her husband. Better she remember the King than the whoremonger. The Sigrid Langley Rand knew *was* dead. All that remained was a creature of fallen gods and darkness.

Rand drooped back. What little color remained in his gaunt cheeks vanished. "Then, it was all for nothing." His weeping turned to uncontrollable sobs. "I left her behind to die. How could I have trusted him!"

"Everything happens for a reason, Rand," Torsten said. "Do you know what they call you in the capital? 'Rand the Redeemer.' Twice now, you've appeared from nowhere to save me from certain death. Ever since Redstar arrived in Yarrington, I should have been dead so many times, but Iam keeps placing others in front of me."

"Why would she die, yet he still lives?" Rand asked, voice distorted from crying.

"The men who led you here have paid, Rand. It's not too late to live up to your namesake."

"Is that traitor still down there in the dungeons, hiding like a stuck pig?" A pitiful chuckle slipped through his lips.

"Who?"

Rand laid back and clutched his face, lost in a mixture of crying and laughter. "Oh Iam, are you enjoying this?"

Torsten backed away slowly. He hadn't been sure what he'd say when he saw Rand again, and he still wasn't sure what to think. The poor young man wasn't making much sense. He'd endured more than anyone ever should've had to, and no matter how well-meaning he was, he always wound up knee-deep in shog.

Torsten left him there and crossed the aisle of suffering. A few people addressed him, but he was too focused to care. He'd been to White Bridge before and knew the layout, so he crossed a bit of rubble to a busted door which led outside to a staircase to the cliffside dungeons.

He descended slowly until the natural rock turned to carved stone and the air grew stale and chilly. Brushing a bit of hanging moss aside, he entered a row of barred cells. It stank. Within one cell, a Drav Cra warrior slumped against the wall, blood-soaked dagger in his hand, and his throat cut wide open.

"Hello?" a hoarse voice asked from the far cell. "Oh, by Iam, someone's here. I thought they'd leave me here forever. Please…" he coughed. "I need water, food, anything. I beg of you."

Torsten didn't lower his guard as he edged forward. A single torch flickered on the far wall, as he came around to view into the last cell. He saw ringed fingers hugging the bars first, then a chubby face. Where Rand looked starving and haggard, this man looked like an overfed noble who'd decided to see the world for the first time. Dirty, but still with an air of refinement, from manicured fingers to hair he'd clearly combed with them one too many times.

"Oh, bless Iam, you're a Glassman," he said, falling to his knees. "I heard shouting, then that one killed himself, right in front of me, for no reason. And then…" His words turned into the squeal of the rat he was as Torsten punched Bartholomew Darkings' fingers against the bars.

"I should have known he wouldn't be alone," Torsten growled.

Clutching his fingers, Darkings cowered to the back of the cell. He, who had stabbed Sir Wardric in the back alongside his father, who'd helped free the Caleef, worked with Valin, and caused so many Shieldsman to die in Winde Port with his treachery was right there. Just meters away.

Torsten didn't even need the key. He kicked the barred gate with all his might, and it flew off the hinges. His shadow engulfed the nobleman.

"Sir Unger," Darkings tittered nervously. "We can talk about this."

Torsten dragged him by the collar and lifted him off his feet. Gagging, Bartholomew tried to talk. He even kicked Torsten, all to no avail. He did, however, land with a *thud* and a grunt when Torsten flung him out of the cell. Darkings skated over the pool of Drav Cra blood in a mad scramble to stand, but Torsten grabbed him again and heaved him up the stairs.

"This is preposterous!" Bartholomew protested, holding his head which had bounced off the steps. Torsten yanked him outside. He thought about tossing him over the short railing and down into the gorge, but instead, dragged him writhing and screaming up the rickety flight of wooden steps back to the bridge. The racket he caused on the whole way upstairs had every soldier, and civilian present gathered at the top.

"Sir Unger, what's going on?" Lucas asked, hurrying over.

"This pile of dog excretion," Torsten said fuming, "is Bartholomew Darkings. First and only son of Yuri Darkings, former Master of Coin and traitor to the Crown."

"Son, exactly!" Bartholomew said. "I had nothing to do with

his betrayal. He dragged me along. Smeared my good name through the mud."

"So, you had nothing to do with the death of Sir Wardric, in your own carriage!" Torsten punched him across the jaw. With his glaruium gauntlets, the blow might have killed a weak man like him, but even with his new zhulong leather, it was still enough to knock a few teeth loose. Torsten drew *Salvation* and extended the blade to the man's heart.

Bartholomew coughed up a gob of blood and rose to his hands and knees. "I would never. I am a loyal servant of the Glass Kingdom. I was traveling west to convince my father to turn himself in when the savages caught me."

"And Caleef Sidar Rakun?" Torsten demanded.

Hearing the name made all of Bartholomew's features scrunch. "I have no idea what you're talking about."

"Rand Langley would tell me differently."

"Is that worthless sack of shog in there? Rand! Rand Langley the *Redeemer*," Bartholomew scoffed. "Come out here and tell the Shieldsman the truth."

"Rand is…" Lucas caught himself and looked to Torsten.

Torsten nodded slowly. He'd hoped to keep his presence a secret, for Rand's sake more than anything. "This has nothing to do with Sir Langley. This is between a protector of the Crown and a man who betrayed it."

"Like I said, I betrayed nothing!" Bartholomew protested. "Whatever you heard was yig and shog."

"They'll be the judge of that." Torsten shoved the man down onto the stone with his boot and looked up. Shieldsmen and soldiers were gathered before him, mostly confused. Yuri's repugnant son looked like any highborn who thought no laws could touch him, and he looked just like his father.

"This is Bartholomew Darkings!" Torsten shouted. "You know his father. You know what he did. This man conspired with

Valin Tehr, kidnapped the Caleef, started a damned war. But worse, he was there with Yuri when Sir Wardric was murdered in cold blood. Your brother!"

A wave of resentment stole over the army. Some spat. Others spat curses. Brouben shoved through them, his bushy eyebrows furrowing. Clanbreakers stood on either side of him, spiked armor looking as menacing as ever.

"Dwarf!" Bartholomew said. "Whoever you are, I've always known yours were a just people. This Shieldsman has lost his gods-damned mind. You must help me."

"This be the child of the Yuri who came begging to me father?" Brouben asked.

"The very same," Torsten answered.

"I see the resemblance," he said. "Both look like an anvil fell on them as babies. Nothing to see here, boys." He waved for his men, and they returned to their work on the bridge.

"Pitiful, tiny imp!" Bartholomew barked. "I swear to all of you. I had nothing to do with Sir Wardric's death, or the freeing of the Caleef, or anything. I'm merely a victim of the Drav Cra."

"No, you are a liar!" Torsten shoved him back down, harder this time. "Just like your father."

"I'm not! I swear it, in the name of Iam and my poor, deceased mother. On all that is holy. The one you seek is somewhere here. Sir Rand Langley. He's been working with my father the entire time. They're the traitors."

Rumbling about Rand broke out. As far as the people were concerned, Rand had already been redeemed. He'd helped save the Kingdom. Parts of the truth were left out, as now Torsten knew all too well, but it wasn't a complete lie.

"Do not dare accuse anyone but yourself," Torsten said. "Only Iam shall be your judge—sadly, for you, I am his hand. You are accused of murder and conspiracy against the Crown. The punishment for such crimes is execution."

"And what of the Shieldsman you murdered?" Bartholomew asked. "I hear everything. I know what you did. You may be a hero today, but they all know what you are, too."

A flicker of doubt passed across the faces of some of the Shieldsmen. Torsten knew that look far too well. He leaned down to Bartholomew's ear. "An accident I will spend a lifetime redeeming myself for. But I saw Sir Wardric's body, gutted like a fish. Betrayed!"

"And I. Didn't. Do it." Bartholomew snickered through a mouthful of blood. "Is this how we conduct ourselves? Condemn men based on nothing? My family resides upon the Royal Avenue —we *are* Old Yarrington. One of us may be wicked, but I deserve to stand before the Royal Council and defend my innocence!"

Torsten clenched his fists. He could see the tide of the crowd shifting. It wasn't all of them, but enough exhibited their agreement. It was what separated them from the Drav Cra who crucified anyone who didn't believe as they did.

"Then why did you send me away?" a soft voice asked. Torsten saw that same sister who'd approached him in the makeshift infirmary, now standing at the broken entry of the tower. She called herself Nauriyal, and now he remembered why she knew him. She had come to the capital, and Lord Kaviel Jolly nearly had her imprisoned just for being Bartholomew's daughter.

"Nauriyal?" Bartholomew asked. He tried to crawl toward her, but Torsten didn't let him. "Nauriyal, Daughter, I never thought I'd see you again."

"You banished me to Hornsheim!" she said. Sisters rarely allowed their emotion to show, but her pretty face was teeming with it. Betrayal, pain, loneliness—Torsten knew all the signs. He'd been like her, a child unwanted by a parent.

"To protect you because of what your grandfather did," Darkings said. "Isn't it clear? These people don't know how to separate us from him!"

"'We killed a Shieldsman,'" she said. "That's what you told me. Not him, 'we.'" The disposition of the crowd turned like a sudden storm. All those who'd shown doubt spun back to Bartholomew, eyes narrow and brimming with ire.

"Yes, I… because I was there *with* him. I had nothing to do with it. You know how we felt about each other, Daughter. Yuri hated me, and I, him. I didn't want any of this!"

"You smiled," she said like a taunt.

"What?"

"When you told me. You smiled."

"I-I. It's… I was." He made a low wailing noise as he gained his composure. "I was trying to be strong for you! As your father."

Nauriyal stepped forward, the wind catching her white dress. She looked up to the sky. "Iam is the only Father I have now," she said. "You have only yourself to thank for that."

She regarded Torsten. "Sir Unger, you are a man of honor. He is not. He never has been. I know you're angry over what happened to your friend, but don't let monsters like my father make you into one. Show the mercy only children of Iam can."

She traced her eyes in prayer, then turned to return to tending to the injured.

"Nauriyal!" Bartholomew yelled at her. "Come back here right now! Dammit. Listen to your father!"

She never turned back, not once. Bartholomew watched her go, completely dumbstruck. The very sight seemed to break him as he crawled to the bridge wall and leaned against it. It had the opposite effect on Torsten. As she spoke, he felt Iam's presence. His rage began to settle, and he could think clearly.

"Murderer!" Sir Marcos shouted, spitting at Bartholomew. A few others joined him, then more until the whole army was stirred into bloodlust. As Torsten saw them, he realized what it reminded him of: the ravenous, bloodthirsty Drav Cra desperate to watch

Mak kill him in battle. Then he saw another vision: himself after accidentally murdering Sir Havel Tralen, and the flocking Shieldsman calling for his execution.

Torsten sheathed his sword. Then he stepped forward before his eager men.

"Lord Darkings will pay for what he's done," he announced. "But sister Nauriyal is right. He will stand before the Royal Council, before the brother of the man he is accused of murdering, and under the gaze of Iam, justice will be served."

Bartholomew let out a relieved sob and wiped his snotty nose.

"Sir Unger," Sir Marcos said. "You know the sentence as well as I. Why not save the time. Do it now?"

"If we resort to spilling the blood of noblemen on the streets, we have become no better than the filth we wish to rid this world of," Torsten countered.

Then turning to Bartholomew, he said, "How it is such a wise daughter came from someone like you, I'll never understand."

"I only wish I'd shipped her away sooner," Bartholomew spat.

Torsten bit his lip and turned to Lucas. "Sir Danvels, take a horse and deliver him to the capital. Bring him before the King first, not Lord Jolly."

Lucas regarded the fat slob with disgust, then said, "Yes, sir."

"There is still a chance that his father has a heart. We will use Bartholomew in one last effort to get Yuri to turn himself over. If he agrees, his son will keep his head, and instead, live the rest of his days stripped of his name and possessions as a servant in Hornsheim."

"Well, aren't you merciful," Bartholomew bristled. "I'd rather die."

"That choice is no longer in your hands. Take him."

Lucas walked over and kicked him in the gut for good measure, playing it off as an accident. "I hope your father says no, you piece of shog," he cursed, then grabbed Bartholomew by the back of the shirt and heaved him up.

Torsten saw it happening, all too fast, but he was too far away. As Bartholomew rose, he reached underneath him. His hand emerged gripping a Drav Cra dagger that must have been left lying on the bridge, the real reason why he'd crawled after his daughter. The blade zoomed toward Lucas, who'd been too busy focusing on Bartholomew's face to notice his hands.

"Lucas!" Torsten shouted.

Before it hit, a body plummeted from the window above, knocked Lucas aside and crashed onto Bartholomew. Legs and arms thrashed as they wrestled for the blade. Lucas' savior bit Bartholomew's wrist like a rabid dog and wrenched the dagger free.

Lightning couldn't have moved quicker than Rand's hand as he drove the knife through Bartholomew's throat. "You made a deal for her!" He stabbed over and over, gashing Bartholomew's neck until blood poured from his mouth and his eyes froze open, just how Wardric's had been when Torsten found him. It took Torsten and Lucas' combined strength to pry Rand off Darkings. More soldiers arrived to help, but none of them seemed in a hurry.

"Stop!" Torsten ordered. Everyone obeyed and backed away from Darkings' corpse. Rand remained on his knees in the middle of the bridge, covered in blood.

"Some men don't deserve mercy," Rand said. He raised the dagger to his own throat, but Lucas was there to grab his arm. The others seized him again and jerked the other arm behind his back. Rand didn't fight it as they dragged him away. His entire battered body seemed to go limp, and the blade clattered harmlessly against the stone.

Torsten wasn't sure if Rand meant Bartholomew, or himself.

XVIII

THE IMMORTAL

Kazimir Mikohailov had heard of the Well of Wisdom's magic but never before had he experienced it. If he hadn't known the shift between mortality and immortality, he'd have considered entering the waters the most jarring event of his life. A life that was already centuries old.

Warm water swirled around him. It was like drinking the blood of the mystics, only it enveloped the whole of his being. Flowing over him and through him, it tickled at something on the inside that he hadn't felt in a long time. He found himself caught between a snarl and ecstasy. For the first time since he'd been turned, he felt alive. Really alive, not just living on someone else's lifeblood. It had been so long, he'd forgotten what it meant to have his own blood pumping through his heart. To feel it beating. He'd forgotten the sensation of air within his lungs.

In these waters, he had all of those things.

Shapes and colors materialized all around him. He saw things within the rush that he hadn't seen since those early days. Faces of men and women he'd just as soon have left in the past.

It was now that Kazimir's ears dialed into the screams. To his right, Whitney, the damnable thief, floated beside him, mouth open in abject horror.

Beyond him, he could see Pantego as it had once been, long before the world of men rose up around its beautiful rolling hills, mountains, lakes, and rivers. He saw Glinthaven in all its former glory. Not that it had changed much, but Kazimir remembered the emotion—the feeling of being there before the kings of Glass grew comfortable in their power.

The Pikeback Mountains reached up from the earth, stabbing into the sky like driving spears.

He saw it all—Brotlebir, the land of dwarves… but this was before the dwarves sought refuge there. Enormous winged beasts, the dreadfires, dragons, and wyverns circled the Dragon's Tail Mountains' ice-capped peaks.

Then suddenly, it all stopped, and he stood in a small dark room, Whitney by his side.

"Is that… you?" Whitney asked, out of breath.

Kazimir—a former version of himself, with golden-blonde hair and skin not so washed out, swore again and again as he pulled his britches over his hips.

"Gross," Whitney said.

A gorgeous woman lay sprawled out on the mattress. Zoya, daughter of Adrian and Sasha Bergiovek, a rival family. They were well-to-do. Kazimir could remember every detail of that night as if it had just been yesterday. The blood, his blood, burned hot as he watched her lying there.

As she'd slept, his former self climbed through an open window. That hadn't been the first time he'd slipped away in the cover of night and it sure as Elsewhere wouldn't be the last. He'd have to answer for it later, but for now, the night was young.

Kazimir followed his younger, naïve self out onto the tiled rooftops. Whitney stayed close behind, but Kazimir didn't care what the thief was doing. His mind raced with the implications of this evening. He knew what would happen all too well.

The cold darkness of night was masked by Celeste's reflection in the thick fog. Orange-hued light bounced off the snow-covered surfaces, and the other Kazimir slipped his shirt on as he carefully but quickly scurried along the rooftops. Behind them, it seemed the young woman had awoken. She stood at the window, calling for his return. Kazimir—both versions of him—ignored her.

There'd been a time when such carnal pleasures mattered. When obtaining the fairer flesh had been his only goal. Kazimir was good at achieving his goals, no matter what they were. This had been his third dalliance in as many days and Vidkaru, the capital city of Brekliodad, was in no short supply of willing partners for handsome sons of Dukes, as Kazimir had been.

They cleared a wide gap between buildings. Kazimir watched his younger self in disgust, acting as if Vidkaru was his own personal playground. But still, he remembered the exact pitch of each tiled roof even now, knew which roofs presented dangerous conditions, and knew which ones to avoid altogether.

The wind picked up, bringing biting cold and snow along with it. Young Kazimir pulled the hood of his cloak up, its tail flapping behind him as he ran. He was a shadow, a blur, barely perceptible as he leaped from place to place.

Kazimir realized that he and Whitney weren't running, but instead, floating along with the vision. They were watching as the event unfolded before their eyes. Kazimir eyed the spot upon which a silver-clasped boot came down with expert precision. Leather touched ceramic, but something happened that never again happened after this night. His younger self's ankle twisted on a loose tile, and he fell headlong, face slamming against the roof with the force of a battering ram.

Whitney let out a yelp, then asked, "What is this?"

"The night everything changed," Kazimir replied.

The young, virile man slid from the rooftop. It was almost as if Kazimir could taste the warm blood spreading across his face, the snow mingling, cold and hot, the sickening gurgling feeling entering his belly. Kazimir could feel it all happening to him. In an instant, he was weightless again, the solid roof no longer beneath him. Then, in the span of a star's twinkle, he lay broken on a snow-laden street.

"Seriously, what's going on?" Whitney asked.

"Just watch," Kazimir said.

They did, for a long time—an agonizingly long time. In the distance, wolves sang to the moons, and crickets laid a foundation for their melody. Cold Brek nights were filled with beauty, but not this night.

"So short, the life of man, no?" spoke a man on the street, shrouded in darkness. His long shadow stretched far to cover Young Kazimir's prone form. His voice was nearly as cold as Kazimir remembered the stone beneath him being that night.

"No more a man than a boy, and already your life is drawing to an abrupt end," the man went on. "Do you not wish for more?"

Young Kazimir said nothing. Kazimir remembered being unable to speak, like his tongue was tied in knots, the sharp pain in his side stealing every breath from his lungs and all hope from his heart.

"Do you not wish for more?" the voice repeated.

Young Kazimir, broken on the streets, produced a weak moan.

"Yes," the voice growled, drawing the word out. "Yes."

"Yes," the young man managed to answer.

High above, Kazimir winced, remembering what came next. Remembering how little he'd thought about the choice. How all he'd wanted in that moment was a few more days of his lavish lifestyle, seducing the daughters of nobility, using his looks and his status to do whatever he pleased.

The hooded stranger bent over Kazimir's broken form and the

young man's eyes no longer allowed light to enter into his soul. Only darkness and night were his companions. But then there had been the pain. Overwhelming agony and ecstasy, together, mingling like the salt sea into rivers of sweet water. They should not have mixed, but when they did, life was given a new habitat to conquer.

And conquer it did.

Young Kazimir's body pulsated. He unleashed a primal scream that echoed through the city, into the mountains, across rivers, streams, and even the Covenstan Depths, the sea to the south. Those wolves responded, their song turning to pained howls, stirring up Elsewhere itself.

Then as quickly as they'd arrived there on the rooftops of Vidkaru, he and Whitney were whisked away. Water rushed, beating against him like a torrent. He heard the ocean, smelled the salt. Then he stood, staring into the dark abyss, spinning, and Whitney was gone. Everyone was gone, and it was only him standing upon wet sand.

He heard a voice in his head, the same one he'd heard on the streets— Imperio Vikas Strachota, one of the first generation, born from the ashes of the Culling and the fallen mystics who'd caused it. He wasn't then, but was now one of the Sanguine Lords.

"My blood now courses through your veins," Vikas said, "but its power won't last forever. When its energy is used up, you will die just as you should have on that street."

They stood in what Kazimir recognized as the Sanctum of the Citadel—formally known as Svay Sobor iz Nohzi. It was as impressive now as ever, a vast sea encapsulated within the heart of the mountain. There was ancient magic at work, so old, Kazimir knew not its origins.

There was no Young Kazimir now, only him, and he tried to speak, to ask how he was there again after so many years, but his words wouldn't come. He had no control over his body. Instead, he felt his mouth move all on its own. "What do I do?"

Words he recalled speaking so many centuries ago—the same words he wanted to speak now.

"You must devour a piece of the ageless beast, the dark spawn of gods and goddesses; their scions of balance," Vikas replied. "Should it first devour you, your spirit, your soul will be lost to Elsewhere forever."

Kazimir, still stuck inside his own body, felt panic for the first time since he woke up in Elsewhere with Whitney. He could feel it all now and knew that if he could feel the wind against his face, he would also feel what came next, and this was not something he wished to ever experience again.

No, my Lords, he thought. *What have I done to deserve this? Please, not this.*

His eyes scanned the horizon. Dark, brooding water as far as he could see. Waves, gently lapping at his feet. A wave came to a crest, small and harmless. It was followed by another, and then another, until the waters sloshed with fury. Then, the wianu named Dakel un Ghastrin rose before him. He stared at the beast as if for the first time but with all their terrifying history as well.

Eyes, black as pitch and large as wagon wheels stared back at him as they rose like two dark moons from the depths of the waters. The underground sea cascaded off its round, lumpy head, and it opened its maw and screamed. Kazimir could feel its hot breath, the smell of death upon it. He could see a dozen rows of razor-sharp teeth and its throat, endless, like a portal into Exile.

Kazimir's heart quickened. He tried to steer his arms, but the movement was out of his control. He was doomed to experience the battle all over again, just as it had happened. He pulled a long sword from a scabbard at his waist and dug his boots into the ground.

A thick tentacle lashed out and swept Kazimir's feet from

beneath him. His face crashed hard against the sand, blinding him. He wiped his eyes as another tentacle, or maybe the same one, whipped across his back and sent him down again.

"If you do not fight back, you will surely perish," said Imperio Vikas Strachota from within Kazimir's mind.

"I'm trying!" he growled. "How am I supposed to fight this thing!"

Kazimir rolled, luckily avoiding a downward-striking tentacle. His eyes burned from the salt, and the sand, but he ran toward Dakel un Ghastrin, narrowly avoiding several more attacks, jumping, diving. One slapped him across the neck, shoving him to the side, but he kept running.

Don't do this, Kazimir thought, but if his younger self perceived it, he ignored him altogether.

He felt himself leave the ground, leaping through the air with his sword held high, poised to stab.

Fool! he cried out internally, but it didn't stop the tentacular appendages from closing around him on both sides, threatening to tear him apart.

Kazimir's eyes bulged, blood rushing to his brain. He thought he was going to pass out. Even though he knew how this ended, he still didn't want to be there. As the wianu pulled him closer to its wide-open gullet, Kazimir thrashed to no avail. His arms were pinned down, and he fought with every ounce of strength just to keep his sword in his hands.

Then he felt it. A cold, clammy tentacle wrapping itself around his ankle. Sharp, hot, blinding pain surged through him, and he felt his leg tear away from his body.

"You must fight," Vikas said.

Kazimir screamed but dug down. He could feel Vikas' gifted blood pouring from his leg. Knowing that if he did nothing, he would shrivel up and die on that beach, Kazimir bent his neck, straining against the creature, and bit hard on the tentacle closest to his mouth. It was hard and rubbery, and he nearly retched at the taste. Still, he sank his teeth in deeper and pulled away a large chunk.

Dakel un Ghastrin roared and repositioned itself just enough for Kazimir to wriggle his sword arm free. He brought the blade down in an arc that sheared off the tip of one of the appendages. As it clattered to the water below, a stream of inky blood gushed out onto Kazimir's face. He drank deeply, and as he did, he felt a tingle where his leg used to be. He didn't know it at the time, but his leg grew back like a lizard that'd lost its tail.

XIX

THE THIEF

One moment, Whitney stood next to Kazimir on a thousand-year-old rooftop, staring down onto the streets of Vidkaru, Brekliodad's ancient capital city, the next, he found himself in Yarrington. His pulse was racing from what he'd just seen.

Two Kazimirs? Yikes.

Blinking, he turned a slow circle, and then a faster one. The city was as he remembered it—exactly as he remembered it. It was as if he'd stood in that same spot once before. Continuing his examination of his surroundings, he stopped, eyes widening.

"Sora!" Whitney screamed. He ran, but as he'd experienced once before in the place Sora called Nowhere, his legs wouldn't take him anywhere.

"Not this again," he groaned. "Sora!"

She was less than ten meters away, but if she'd heard him, she showed no signs of it. She wore a nondescript, gray cloak—one Whitney had seen plenty of times before. It covered her weapons and her many scars from blooding. She talked to someone, a man, he noted, whose back was turned to Whitney. His dark green hood was drawn—in broad daylight.

What kind of vagabond, no-good dirtbag wears his hood in broad daylight?

Unbridled jealousy overwhelmed him. Then Sora smiled. That small action melted Whitney's heart like butter left outside on a hot day. With one finger, Sora tucked a wild strand of hair behind her ear. The man immediately reached up and yanked the hair back down, covering her Panpingese heritage. Her smile vanished, exchanged for bright red cheeks that Whitney knew as a mixture of anger and embarrassment. She punched the man in the arm, and Whitney instinctively clutched his bicep, knowing the feeling so well.

Whitney bit his lip and scowled. He wanted to stomp over there and drive his boot through the man's chest.

How dare he—

His internalized threat was cut off when the man peered over his shoulder, and Whitney saw familiar blue eyes staring back at him. The memory came like a rushing wind. It was so long ago in his mind—immediately after returning from the Webbed Woods. Torsten had just ennobled him, *Lord Blisslayer,* and he and Sora were making plans to travel to Panping in an effort to uncover more of Sora's abilities. Who knew she'd wind up there alone, only to find out she was King Liam's bastard, heathen daughter? Hidden away from Oleander and the world. Forgotten.

Whitney wished upon every holy and sacred thing that they'd have crossed the realm on foot, or just stayed in Yarrington, even returned to Troborough—anything but going to Winde Port.

He moved closer, hoping this vision worked as Kazimir's had and he wouldn't be seen. He was right.

"I'm telling you," the memory of Whitney said, "once we get past that guard, the wealth inside would be incredible."

"I don't care, Whit," Sora replied. "I'm not going to be party to such senseless violence."

"Sora, Sora, Sora… Oh, sweet, innocent, Sora."

"Don't do that," Sora said.

"Do what?"

"That… patronize me. Just because I don't want to lure a guard into an alley so you can knock him out doesn't mean I'm some kind of child."

"So—what then?" Whitney asked. "How do *you* propose we get in?"

"It's the Society of Nobility, isn't it?" Sora asked.

"Yes, and?"

"Aren't you a noble, *Lord Blisslayer*?"

"And freely offer them my name just before swiping every last gem hanging from their wrists and necks? No, thank you." Whitney rolled his eyes. "Besides, it isn't thieving if you get in fair and square."

"It isn't thieving if you go around beating up innocents either!" Sora protested.

"Innocents? Are you mad? That man is a city guard, not a Shieldsman like Torsten. I'm sure he's got himself elbow deep in Valin Tehr's coffers, keeping quiet about all manner of ill dealings."

"I am not *using my assets* to knock out a guard!"

"Shhhh, keep your voice down," the memory of Whitney said, patting the air. "Fine. Fine, we'll do it your way."

As he watched himself wrap his arm around Sora's back, bright light hit Whitney, and he felt himself being torn away from the vision. He thought he was going to swallow his tongue. A million colors swirled around him, rapidly. He tried to scream out, flailed his arms, desperate not to lose Sora, but that was it. She was gone. Again.

Lightning flashed around him, sizzling the very air. He felt himself swimming through water, then his body came to a halt, floating midair above a scratched and faded wooden table.

Now, he was in a dingy old restaurant. Another younger

version of himself and Sora were eating and talking. Other such tables surrounded them, but most were unoccupied. Through a dirty, grime-streaked window, he saw the Grambling Inn, still standing. They were seated at the Chowder House, and he knew this was long before the storm would sweep through Grambling and force him and all of the Pompare Troupe into hiding—but it was also mere weeks after his last vision and only days before, ultimately, he and Sora would be separated in Winde Port.

"Just follow my lead," Younger Whitney said.

"What are you going to do?" Sora asked.

"Lesson number forty-four: never pay for something you can get for free."

Before Sora could answer, he pulled a small leather pouch and a vial with a dropper from his cloak. He filled the dropper with dark red liquid from the vial and dribbled some onto his lip. It streamed down his chin and dripped onto the table.

"What are—"

One finger over his lips, Younger Whitney shushed Sora and poured the contents of the leather pouch into his chowder. Little, glinting, glass shards plopped into the white stew.

"You're kidding me," Sora said. "Whit, we have the money for this meal."

"Just play along."

Hovering above it all, Whitney laughed. He remembered the grift quite well and used it quite often.

Sora scanned the room, then Younger Whitney started coughing, loudly. His coughing turned to agonized screams, and the owner of the small restaurant rushed over.

"Sir, what is wro—oh, my!" the owner exclaimed, noticing the fake blood.

"I've cut myself on something…" He coughed. "Something in your chowder. A—a—a bone or something."

"Someone, come quick and help this man," the owner said, turning and snapped his fingers toward his servants.

Whitney quickly wiped away the "blood" with the back of his hand so it couldn't be further examined. Now that the owner had seen it, that would be enough. The owner lifted Whitney's spoon and began sifting through the bowl.

"Oh, dear, are you alright?" Sora said with believable skill. "Sir, is he going to be okay?" Whitney could see by her expression that she hated playing along, but she did it anyway.

Still coughing, Whitney said, "I'm… I'm okay. I—gracious! Is that… glass? What kind of establishment is this! You're serving me bits of glass!"

"Sir, please calm—" The whole restaurant was watching now, many whispering to one another. Some even pushed their own bowls away in disgust.

"I cannot—will not—*calm down*. You nearly killed me!"

"Oh, no! Is he dying?" Sora asked. "He's going to die, isn't he!" It was a bit melodramatic, but everyone was so focused on Whitney, it was doubtful anyone heard her at all.

"Ma'am, please. Your husband isn't going to die."

"How do you know?" she asked. "Oh, breath of Iam, it looks bad. It's bad."

The owner looked away to call over more help, and Whitney gestured for Sora to dial it down a little. She smiled weakly before her face returned to a state of shock.

"This meal is on the house," the owner told one of the others attending to Whitney. Then, he turned to address the rest of the customers. "Everything is quite alright. Please, if you ordered the chowder, stop eating immediately. There's nothing to worry about. Just give… give us a moment, and we'll make things right."

"Oh, Lord Blisslayer," Sora said.

Whitney, watching from above, had forgotten that bit. It was the smartest play he'd seen Sora make in their short time together. He remembered that moment, and the glint in her eye when she really started to have fun. That was the moment that Whitney knew—really knew—he loved her. He only wished he'd told her.

"Lord…" the owner said, breathless. "Iam's shog. Please, forgive us, my Lord." The man once again turned to an employee. "Tell Chef Regis to come right away, then quickly go across the street to the inn and speak with Mister Balleybeck. Secure a room for the Lord and his Lady. Now!"

Everyone scurried off to do their bit, but that was all Whitney would see, floating above it all.

His stomach flipped, and the scene changed once more. Red stone walls rose up on all sides. He was in the Red Tower, but not in the room with the Well of Wisdom. Instead, a moat of flowing water rushed around him. He nearly cowered at the sight of no less than five wianu within the waters until he realized they were all made of stone. They looked so real and frightful, their eyes, deep-set gems, but any fear of the wianu was entirely eclipsed by the sound of human screams.

Blood was everywhere. Had he been corporeal, he'd have slipped in a pool of it.

Sora held a knife in one hand, and her other was extended, a steady stream of flame pouring from it. The fire hit a robed man in the chest, sending him soaring across the room, blackening immediately. His crisp body splashed into the water. Without sparing a second glance, Sora twirled and sliced the throat of another man. Blood gushed out of the wound and drenched the man's yellow robes. He held up his hands—no, just one hand, and the other arm appeared to be nothing more than a nub.

Other bodies lay strewn across the room, doused in blood.

So different, this Sora was from the one Whitney had just watched. She wasn't afraid to play his games, but she hadn't even wanted to knock a guard unconscious. To see the visions so near to one another…

A bolt of lightning coruscated toward Sora, fizzling upon reaching her. Sora ducked down low, then rose quickly, her hands flat like boards. Mirroring her movement, a pillar of flames shot up in a spiral beneath the mystic woman who'd hurled the lightning bolt. The woman's screams as her skin blistered seemed to linger long after she'd fallen dead, and her now-vacant eyes stayed fixated on Sora.

"Please don't," said another woman dressed in a red robe, kneeling at Sora's feet. "Together we can start afresh!"

Whitney watched in horror, then saw deeper. This Sora looked like Sora, but her beautiful amber eyes… they were different. No longer pretty but terrifying. Then he remembered the room and the robed figures, the ones who'd torn her out of Elsewhere after their encounter with the Buried Goddess. Maybe it was the Well telling him, but he knew—it wasn't Sora committing these atrocities. The Buried Goddess had just taken over.

"Lady Sora, please don't do this," the mystic woman groveled. "I was wrong about you, your power. We can still save Panping and the Order. Together."

With a sudden explosion of power, vines burst from the walls, floor, waters, and even from Sora's hands. They covered the room, wrapping the dead bodies as well as the woman now almost prostrate before Sora, begging.

Sora's head snapped back, eyes rolling upward. Her back straight, arched, she ascended, hovering a meter from the ground. She turned slowly, and when she faced Whitney, their eyes met. It wasn't like the other visions… Whitney could see life in those eyes, and he knew, she could see him.

The Buried Goddess smiled.

This time, there was no melting butter, no warm fuzzies inside. Whitney's heart felt like it was being crushed beneath the weight of a thousand mountains. The woman in red was speaking again, but Whitney didn't care. He just watched as Nesilia watched him through the eyes of the woman he loved.

"Whitney Fierstown," she said. "Always meddling in business not your own. When will you learn?" It was definitely not Sora's voice speaking, even if it was her mouth. Every syllable made the hairs on his neck stand erect.

Whitney looked around, confused. "You… see me?"

"I see everything."

"Good, then I have a few words for you," Whitney said.

Nesilia's smile widened.

"You're not welcome here," he continued. "Why can't you just leave us alone? What did we do to you?"

"Besides killing my rotten sister, Bliss, and stealing away my opportunity at revenge? Every breath you take is an abomination. But it's no matter. Soon, you will be dead. Then, the rest of the world will bend beneath my power. Grimaurs, goblins, demons— even the wianu themselves," she motioned to the statues stationed around the room, and Whitney could have sworn one moved. "Our forsaken creations that you people call 'monsters' will want vengeance upon Iam's chosen. Soon, they will all heed my commands."

"You think that scares me? I've fought a wianu, and I live to tell the tale," Whitney bragged, although he felt no strength behind his words.

"You survived because of your little upyr pet!"

"I saved him too."

"Whitney Fierstown." Nesilia laughed, a sound like ice. "Six years forgotten below and you haven't changed. Imagine eternity."

"Sounds awful. How was it?" Whitney couldn't help himself. He knew he was playing with fire, but didn't care. "Why don't you let Sora go and come face me and my *upyr pet* yourself? I'll show you how much I've changed."

"Oh, trust me, I plan on it. Your meddling has become tiresome. I already planned to visit the Sanguine Lords and show them what a true deity looks like, now I'll really enjoying slaughtering them. Their days of toying with the delicate balance of life are through."

"We'll stop you," Whitney said.

"No—you…"

Her voice trailed off, and her eyes jerked to the ground. Whitney followed her gaze. A strange piece of jewelry lay just a meter away. It was broken, but Whitney could still make out a pendant—a golden disc surrounded by six small stones. Each stone had words written on it, though the language was nothing like Whitney had ever seen.

The Buried Goddess' eyes sprang back to Whitney. They betrayed a flicker of fear, not Sora's, but Nesilia's. Then, she was gone. It was all gone.

Whitney breathed in a lungful of water.

.

XX

THE KNIGHT

Torsten watched the cell door close, then heard the lock *click*. Rand never fought being thrown inside. He merely sat against the wall, a thousand-meter gaze aimed at nothing while Lucas checked the cell for anything Rand could use to hurt himself. Nothing was left. Not a bone, no loose stones, not even straw of hay.

The dungeons were reserved for smugglers and brigands—people brought in off the roads up to no good, thrown into a hole in the side of the Jarein Gorge. Torsten wondered if they'd ever housed a man who'd simultaneously done so much to save the kingdom, and so much to harm it.

"I'm so sorry, Rand," Torsten said, choking back his sadness. The irony wasn't lost on him. Rand had freed Torsten from a dungeon when he'd been at his lowest, had sacrificed everything to do it. Now, to save Rand from himself, Torsten had to lock him up.

"Deep down, I know you're a good man," Torsten said, stepping closer. "You have to stay here for now. Once we move on, we'll figure out how to help you. Perhaps, Hornsheim can show you the beauty of living."

Rand peered up at Torsten from within the cell, and for a moment, looked like he had something to say. Then his sad eyes went hazy, and it was like Rand was staring straight through him again.

Torsten sighed and turned, finding Lucas waiting anxiously by the dungeon entry. When Torsten reached him, Lucas said, "Sir, I saw Valin's letters about Rand and the Caleef back in Yarrington."

"He's suffered enough," Torsten said.

"He might know something."

"He did. The Caleef died here at the hands of the Drav Cra. Fell into the Walled Lake. No one could have survived that."

Lucas didn't seem surprised. "Could be lying."

"Does that man look capable of lying right now?" Torsten asked. "Besides, I trust him."

"How? He helped Valin, he—"

"He followed his heart to try and save me and his sister, and lost her for doing so," Torsten said. "A crime for a Shieldsman who must only serve the Crown, perhaps, but he threw his shield down long ago. If he says the Caleef fell to his death, then I believe it. There's nothing to gain in lying."

"Maybe you're right." Lucas sighed. "Let me take some men down below to search the shores for his remains, anyway. Best safe than surprised."

Torsten pondered for a moment, then nodded. "No men. Go alone and tell no one. Body or not, the Black Sands cannot know their Caleef is lost, not yet. As far as they know, Yuri Darkings is still smuggling him, and that friction will help us. If a new Caleef is chosen, and is braver than Sidar Rakun… I can't say what will happen."

"Yes, Sir." Lucas pounded a fist against his chest, then took a step toward the stairs. He stopped.

"What is it?" Torsten asked.

The boy turned, lips falling at the corners. "I'm sorry, Sir Unger. I know he's your friend."

"Not my friend. Just another Shieldsman I've failed."

"You haven't failed anyone."

Torsten smiled. "The light of Iam reveals only the truth. Now, go. We'll spend the rest of the night here cleaning up, then leave a few behind while we march to join Sir Nikserof, and finally put an end to this war."

Lucas saluted again, then headed out and up. Torsten glanced back at Rand's cell one last time, and his heart felt like it had been stabbed by ice picks. Anyone else would've been at the bars, banging, hollering to be freed. Torsten never could understand men who gave up on living, who'd rather take their own lives, squelch their own light, and be damned to Elsewhere. For Iam taught that to murder was to forsake the Gate of Light—whether the forfeited life be others or oneself.

That he didn't understand it made it all the more frightening.

He'd have hoped Rand would want to live a life in honor of his dead… undead sister; to do what he could to make the world a better place, so what happened to her wouldn't happen again. Torsten cared as much about Rand being 'the Redeemer' as himself being called 'Torsten the Triumphant." They were mere titles that were only a hair's breadth away from being taken away if either of them made a poor choice. The Glass Kingdom didn't need icons or heroes, it needed Iam's light alone.

Torsten had lied to Lucas. Rand wasn't just a failed Shieldsman, he was a friend, and Torsten just wanted him to find peace.

He'll recover, he told himself. *Then he can know the truth about Sigrid, and we can find a way to stop the Dom Nohzi from ever killing again.*

Torsten climbed the stairs. Each step hurt, his legs burning, back aching. The war wasn't even over yet, and he felt like he'd fought a hundred battles.

"Your accent, it's very pretty," Dellbar said from around a corner. "Where are you from?"

A young woman snickered. "Bridleton."

Torsten came around and saw the High Priest standing with Nauriyal. She held a bowl of water to be brought to the victims. Dellbar reached out and ran his thumb along her chin.

"Ah, yes, there it is," he said. "The southern dimple. You can tell a lot by a woman's chin." He turned toward Torsten as if hearing him coming, then, clearing his throat, said, "And a man's, of course."

"Leave the sister alone," Torsten said. His tone wasn't unkind, but it was a warning—something he'd never thought he'd have to do to the High Priest of the Glass Kingdom.

Times are changing, Torsten thought, and not for the first time.

Dellbar whispered something in Nauriyal's ear that got her to smirk, then he stepped aside.

"You don't need to keep working," Torsten addressed her. "I know what it's like to lose a father, even a wretched one."

"Iam is just," she said softly. "My father got what he deserved."

"Even still."

"It helps me to help them."

"You are strong beyond words," Torsten said. "We aren't our parents, Sister. You prove that."

She put on a frail grin, then hurried off. Torsten caught Dellbar taking a swig from his flask before stowing it within the folds of his holy robes.

"Haven't you had enough?" Torsten grumbled.

"Am I still breathing?" Dellbar replied. He slapped Torsten on the back. "I heard about what happened. Rand Langley. Of all the people to be here… the one I helped free you. Is that why you spared him?"

"What did you say?" Torsten asked.

Dellbar laughed and shook his head. "Bartholomew Darkings may've been a cur, but he was a prisoner of the Glass. Now, he's murdered."

"I don't know if I'd call it that."

"I may not have eyes, Master Unger, but even a blind man can see. Rand 'The Redeemer' gored the man in the throat repeatedly. If that is not murder, nothing is."

Torsten scowled and kept walking. Dellbar took a long stride and stopped him with a palm to his chest plate. "Hey, I'm not judging. Just find it curious that we three would be here on the bridge between worlds. It's almost… destiny."

"I think maybe you've had a sip too many, Holiness."

Dellbar chuckled. "Well, that's always true. Still, I've learned not to miss the signs. That poor soul who has lost so much… somehow I feel he's the key to all of this."

"All of what?"

"Now that, Sir Unger, is the right question. I think I'll go talk to him, offer him the same old rant about the light and how life is worth living. Or, maybe just a drink."

"Sir Unger!" a soldier shouted down from atop the gate. "A rider approaches. He carries the standard of the King's Shield."

"It never just rains." Torsten exhaled. "Your Holiness, if you make that man crack a smile again, it'll be more of a miracle than giving me sight."

"I'd be proud just to make you crack one." Dellbar strolled by, whistling a song mothers sang to children in Winter's Thumb about Drav Cra raiders and ice dragons. It was far too cheerful for the occasion.

Torsten climbed the watchtower to gaze over the gates that were, until now, rarely ever closed.

Another sign of the times, Torsten thought.

It was a Glassman rounding the grassy plains for sure, only, he was in as much a rush as anyone Torsten had ever seen. Mud kicked up as horse and rider slid to the ground. The horse, obviously exhausted, didn't rise again. The rider left his flag where it lay, and pressed forward on foot.

"Open the gates!" Torsten demanded as he stumbled down the stairs, still aching from his battle with Mak. He hurried to the hitches and mounted the first horse he found, then raced through as the gates were still cranking. As he drew closer, he noticed a Shesaitju barbed arrow sticking out of the man's thigh. His horse was dead, but now he wasn't sure it was exhaustion as several arrows protruded from its haunches.

Jumping down, Torsten rushed to the hobbling soldier. With a hand behind his back, Torsten lowered the man to the ground.

"Relax," Torsten offered, but even as he did, heard the absurdity of the command.

Every crevice of the man's steel armor was filled with coarse, black sand, and the metal itself suffered from countless dents and scratches as if rats had been loosed upon him. His cheeks were similarly cut, every wound filled with more sand. His hair, his eyebrows, his chapped lips, everywhere: sand.

"Soldier, can you hear me?" Torsten asked.

The man looked at him. He didn't seem like he'd gone mad, just so exhausted he could barely speak.

"The Black Sandsmen, they…" he coughed. It sounded like his throat was made of dried bark.

"Where were you posted?" Torsten asked. The man's head rolled to the side. "Have they sent out raiding parties again?" He grabbed him by the shoulders. "Speak!"

With his last breath before exhaustion took him, he said, "Nahanab… they…won."

"Uh, Sir Unger, they be with you?" Brouben said. Torsten whipped around and saw the dwarven prince atop a lonely rock, axe in both hands. A few more soldiers, dwarf and human, had followed him out.

Letting the weary soldier's head fall back, Torsten stood and what he saw stole all the breath from his lungs. Battered-looking soldiers trekked across the plains, their ranks broken. Hundreds of them, and judging by how many in the distance, maybe thousands more to come. Most were ordinary soldiers, but there were Shieldsman amongst them. Even beneath the murky sky, their glaruium armor stuck out like pearls.

"This is the Glass army," Torsten said.

"Army?" Brouben replied.

A few unmounted horses galloped toward them.

"Whoa now!" Brouben shouted to one, grabbing its reins as it slowed. He yanked it back and showed remarkable tenderness to the creature, the likes of which Torsten had never seen from a dwarf. It stopped running, but its eyes didn't lie. They spoke of pure terror.

Torsten stomped through the wet plains toward the nearest of the soldiers. All the while, on the horizon, more and more of them appeared. He didn't think black sand could coat armor like it did on some of them. The way it caked itself to their blood and sweat, it was like the very desert had come alive to fight them.

"Iam's light, what happened?" Torsten asked the first soldier he found. The man regarded him, confused, a blank look on his face. Torsten seized him by the shoulders. "I am Sir Unger, your Master of Warfare. Tell me what happened."

That finally gained the soldier's attention. "The Slayer of Redstar?" he asked, voice dry and hoarse just like the last one.

"Among other things."

The young man struck his chest in salute, though he seemed incapable of straightening his back. Like all the others filtering by, he looked scared and exhausted.

"We were camped outside Nahanab," he said. "With the help of another afhem named Babrak, who wished to see the end of the war, Sir Nikserof arranged the surrender of the rebel Muskigo. They opened the gates of the city, and he went in, but it was a trap."

"Set by this Babrak?"

The man shook his head. Torsten noticed a wobble to one of his legs and helped him stay upright.

"No," the soldier answered. Then he drew a long breath. "I don't know. Muskigo was about to take his own life in shame when reinforcements arrived under a female afhem. It all happened so fast. A fleet broke through our blockade, then flanked us both in the city and outside. We were holding our own until… until…"

"Slow down, Soldier. Speak plainly."

"A sandstorm hit. It was like... like nothing I've ever seen. The sun, the sky, all light went away. It was like ten thousand needles all around us. I can still taste it." He started hacking on the air.

"What does that mean?" Torsten asked. "Look at me, boy. What are you saying?"

"We lost Nahanab!"

Torsten nearly lost his grip on the man. "And Muskigo?"

"Alive… I think."

"And Sir Nikserof?"

The soldier's head hung, and he breathed out slowly. "Captured. That is, if the heathens even bothered to keep him alive."

Torsten's chest tightened. If he didn't have to support the soldier, he would have pounded the earth in frustration.

"I knew it was all too easy… dammit!" He cursed, his voice thundering across the countryside. He'd defeated Mak with no loss, wiping away the plague of the Buried Goddess for good. Yet, all that lingered in his head were Mak's final premonitions about her return. He'd gained the support of dwarves using the mass of gold commandeered from Valin Tehr, and in doing so, turned something wretched into a gesture for hope.

All of it was meant to provide a foundation for peace. The new king now saw with clarity. He trusted Torsten, even after all his failures, to bring the kingdom that peace. All of it made sense when the Black Sands were meant to fall. Muskigo had no support and was clinging to his rebellion. For months, Torsten had been assured of this, but it didn't take a veteran soldier to see the sting of defeat etched plainly upon the face of each man marching toward him. It didn't even take eyes. He could hear their exhaustion and their rattled breathing. He could smell the stink of blood, sweat, and tears. All of it together reeked.

And now, the one bargaining chip Torsten might have had with Yuri Darkings had just gotten himself killed.

"Look at 'em all," Brouben said, stomping over. "I thought the war in the south was almost over."

"So did I," Torsten said. He turned to the weary soldier. "What's your name, soldier?"

"Brenlin, Sir. Brenlin Coreth."

"Brenlin, start getting a camp set up outside the gates."

"With what?"

"Anything," Torsten said.

"They burned our supplies… They burned everything."

"Just do it!"

"I can go to me father and ask for materials." Brouben offered.

"No," Torsten said. "We don't have that kind of time."

"We send a galler. He'll dispatch what we need as soon as he receives the bird."

"I won't add to our debt…"

The dwarf held up one furry hand. "Won't hear nothin about it. Ye paid, we agreed. The warm hospitality of my people is just what these brave men be needing. Me cousin Hogrin'll bring an extra barrel of ale… or ten."

Torsten bowed his head. "Thank you, my Lord."

"Don't. Ye promised me a good fight and cheated me out of it with yer heroics. I ain't never fought gray men before. Always a good time to try new things." He stowed his axe and lumbered over to a few of his people, barking orders.

Torsten let the soldier march along and turned. More and more of his people flooded from White Bridge's Eastern Gates to help the battered army. Spotting Lucas in the fray, Torsten summoned the willpower to make his way to him.

"Sir Unger, there you are," Lucas said, saluting. "Have you heard what they're saying? Is it true about Nahanab?"

"Is it true? Look around," Torsten said.

"Sir… I… what do we do?"

"Sir Danvels, focus. I need you to ride east to the nearest town. Fettingborough, I believe. Ask if they'll spare their lodging and whatever supplies they have for an army."

"This region was hit hard by Mak and the raiders," Lucas said. "They might resist."

"It was, and the time to rebuild will come. But, for now, Fettingborough is all that stands between this army and the Black Sands. Convince them they'll be safer with us there than here. If Muskigo has reinforcements, it's clear that the situation in Latiapur isn't as clean as our agents might have thought. Ride fast and bring men with you."

"Yes, sir. What should I do after?"

"Return here," Torsten said as he placed a hand on Lucas' shoulder. "I need you at my side as we prepare for battle."

Lucas saluted and returned for the horses. Torsten followed behind him. The men and women of the cloth received the newcomers, filling the broken towers of White Bridge with more injured. Even Dellbar the Holy seemed to be paying less attention to his flask and more to the onslaught of refugees.

As Torsten climbed to one of the few rooms left on the ravaged upper floors of the Eastern Watchtower, he could see further.

There were too many men.

"Sir Marcos!" Torsten spotted him and called down. The young Shieldsman instantly came to attention, looking around for the voice. "Up here!"

"Sir?" he said, finding Torsten in the window.

"Start getting a headcount. I need to know how much of the Glass army remains. When you're done, return to me. I have a special assignment for you. A message that must be delivered by hand to an afhem in Latiapur named Babrak."

Even from so high up, through his blindfold, Torsten could see the Shieldsman's brow furrow. "In *their* capital?"

"They still serve the Crown. Nobody will dare touch you. It must be done."

"Yes, sir." The words passed by the lump in the soldier's throat, and he hurried off.

Torsten continued to his temporary quarters, passing several of his men, sending one to retrieve ink and parchment, and another to fetch gallers. He didn't have time to think of all the angles, but he couldn't afford to waste any either. Not after such an unexpected defeat. The most important part of losing is the recovery. Uriah Davies had taught him that.

He'd send a message to the Crown first, informing them what had happened. The people of Yarrington were hungry, but food and water would have to be found to spare. Supplies from the reconstruction efforts in Winde Port could be redirected to house soldiers.

Then, he'd send a bird to Yaolin. Now that the main route between the west and east was retaken, he'd demand more support for the war effort beyond the cohort of Panpingese archers they'd dispatched. All the soldiers hunting for the mysterious Dom Nohzi hideaway could be recalled. Ships from the eastern isles could sail south with fresh conscripts.

While the Black Sands continued fighting amongst themselves, with no Caleef to unite their vision, Torsten could move fast to establish a foothold just north of their desert. And from there, Sir Marcos would deliver a letter to the Trisps'I Afhemate which Sir Nikserof had built a relationship with. He would demand the safe return of Sir Nikserof, the handing over of Yuri Darkings, and the public submission of Afhem Muskigo. All of that, in exchange for peace talks that would forgive all offenses and offer more favorable terms to the Shesaitju than before.

He didn't have time to ask King Pi's permission. He knew the boy wanted peace more than anything. A lone rider might be able to reach Latiapur before Muskigo and his new supporters could. That would sow further discontent amongst the afhems. They'd demanded Muskigo's life before, but now, the responsibility for future death would be squarely on his shoulders.

He doubted it would stop a war. But it would give them time to recover. The Glass army had suffered a defeat, but from his window, he saw the mass of broken men spread across the horizon. By some miracle, much of the army had survived.

Torsten had hoped that, without him, the wars would've ended. He'd hoped Mak's would be the last blood he'd have to shed.

Some things weren't meant to be.

XXI

THE THIEF

Whitney emerged from the water, gasping. He coughed up the strange blue liquid from the Well of Wisdom and threw his bone-soaked torso over the ledge. The stench of mold overwhelmed his olfactory senses, and his eyes stung. Hard as he could, he tried to process what he'd just seen, but simply couldn't reconcile the thought of Sora—even if it were only her body—performing such heinous acts. It made him sick.

Fearful even the memory of it might make it all begin anew, Whitney thrust himself fully out of the Well and rolled away. Lingering there a long moment, eyes bleary, he blinked several times in an effort to drive it all away. But the mental barrage wouldn't stop. Nesilia had spoken to him. She'd all but told him her plans.

A violent splash disrupted him, and he looked over to see Kazimir rising from the Well, too. His white hair looked like a messy bird's nest atop his head.

"Kazzy," Whitney said, coughing. "Are you okay?"

Kazimir didn't respond, just stared into the dark, eyes wide, a blank expression plastered on his face. Whitney rolled over and speedily crawled to him. He reached out for the upyr, but Kazimir snapped his arm out, quick as death, and Whitney felt cold, clammy flesh against his wrist.

"Whoa!" Whitney said. "It's okay. You're back now."

Kazimir's grip let up, but only slightly. It went from bone-crushing to skin bruising as Whitney grasped onto Kazimir's shoulder and dragged him to the edge of the pool.

If Kazimir had experienced anything like Whitney had, Whitney could only imagine what it might have been. The upyr had seen centuries on Pantego, and the things he must have encountered would've made any of Whitney's memories look like a casual stroll through a peaceful meadow—perhaps even that of Nesilia.

"What else did you see?" Whitney asked.

Kazimir finally moved. His gaze shifted ever so slightly, soulless as always.

"The beginning of all things," he said softly. "The end of all things."

"Cryptic as ever," Whitney remarked.

"I saw the start of this life. You were there."

"Yeah, that part I was with you for. Actually, saw a bit more of you than I ever hoped I would," *He shuddered.* "But then, everything changed and then you were gone. It was just me… and Sora."

"You saw her?" Kazimir asked, back to grinding Whitney's wrist to a fine powder. "Where was she? Was it her, or the goddess?"

Whitney sucked in a breath through his teeth and tried to pry Kazimir's fingers loose while saying, "It was her, but not now-her. Ow. Ow. Let go, would you?"

Kazimir obliged, then rolled out of the water and laid on his back, staring up at the ceiling. "Who's being cryptic now?"

"I just mean… like yours, it was a memory of her. Of us.

Shortly after we killed Bliss in the Webbed Woods and returned Redstar." Whitney recounted what he'd seen, then went on to describe the gruesome scene in the tower and the personal message from Nesilia.

"You're sure it was really her, not a memory?" Kazimir said.

Whitney shrugged. "How could it be? I wasn't there."

"Then she knows of the pact. Nesilia…" In an altogether not-Kazimir way, the upyr sat up beside Whitney and said, "Sora's going to be okay. We will stop the Buried Goddess. Don't worry."

His hand rested on Whitney's arm—just rested, not squeezing, crushing… just… rested. For a beat, Whitney wanted to believe his friend's words… until he remembered…

"What do you care?" he said. "You said we weren't friends, remember? 'This isn't Elsewhere,' you said."

Kazimir's hand pulled away, and he stood. "You are more foolish than I first believed, Whitney Fierstown. I knew you were stupid, but I never imagined it was like this."

"What?" Whitney asked, standing as well.

"I am Kazimir Mikholov. I have seen nations rise and fall. I remember when the dwarves ruled most of what is now called the Glass Kingdom. I survived the Culling in my Motherland when all the dead rose, and all the living died only to be raised again. Did you expect that I would show any kind of weakness in front of my apprentice?"

The words hung until Kazimir muttered, "You, stupid as you might be, are the closest thing to a friend I have in this world. A millennium of living, for this… What a sad life."

A small smile spread on Whitney's face, and he started to speak, but Kazimir cut him off. "Speak of this to anyone, and I will slash your throat."

Whitney motioned locking his lips with an imaginary key. "My lips are sealed."

"Like I could ever believe that."

They chuckled together, and for a fleeting second, all the horrors of the Well of Wisdom fell away. Then, they all came rushing back.

"So, what do we do?" Whitney asked.

"She said she's going to the Sanguine Lords?"

"Yeah…"

"While I was in the Well," Kazimir started, "I said I saw the end of all things. Ghastrin de Dahkel, and my first encounter with the beast. It was the end of my days as a mortal. It gave me an idea. The upyr believe that to devour the corporeal form of the wianu grants eternal life—and by my example, we know it to be more than myth. But they also believe that to *be* devoured by one means eternal damnation in Elsewhere."

Thinking he saw where Kazimir was going, Whitney said, "Surely, not for a goddess though?"

"Why not? Your precious Iam exiled so many others there."

"Do you know me at all? I don't give two breaths and a shog about Iam, or any of these other gods. All they've done is cause havoc in my life. If this'll kill the wench, I'll be the one to throw her down the thing's gullet. But you have to be sure."

Kazimir was pacing now. "If she is going to Brekliodad… even so, it will not be easy."

"I killed Bliss—"

"For the final time: Bliss was a shell of who she'd once been. Do you think she always bore the form of that monster? That she always commanded tiny arachnid children?"

"They weren't very tiny," Whitney said.

"They were ants compared to what Nesilia will bring with her when her full power is realized."

"I saw the demons in Elsewhere." The memory of the needle-toothed beasts which had attacked him in Elsewhere crashed through Whitney's mind. The hounds… the wianu.

"You would have seen the weakest of them all," Kazimir said.

"Those who have been trapped in Elsewhere for thousands of years, unable to feed on life, cursed only to suffer alongside the dead."

"Worse than that?"

"Far worse, and far more. Nesilia might command millions of the creatures, desperate for vengeance after the God Feud. And I suspect she will seduce many of the living to her side just as she has the Drav Cra, Aihara Na, and all those worthless mortals wearing masks across the city."

"Shog, that's right," Whitney swore. "We've got to get back there. What if those cultists overran Tum Tum's pub?"

"Then your friends will already be dead," Kazimir said, his tone a bit too matter-of-fact for Whitney's liking. "You chose Sora over them. Now, you are stuck with your choice."

Whitney bit his lip. He hadn't consciously thought it was one or the other, but Kazimir was right… as always. All Whitney had was the belief that Tum Tum, Lucindur, and the others were strong enough to hold out. He hoped they were, but he'd been wrong a few times before.

"You're right." It hurt to say it, but Sora was more important to him than everyone in Panping—everyone in Pantego even. He had to get her back. "So, we somehow feed Nesilia to a wianu?"

"We may be able to reach Brek before she does… before she can summon the wianu to her cause. The Sanguine Lords will put up a fight, though I fear even they will not be a match for her, and we still must get Nesilia out of Sora if we are to have any hope of killing the goddess without betraying my pact."

"When I saw her…" Whitney swallowed. "…killing all the mystics. Nesilia looked scared of something. That necklace-thing Kai was talking about. What was it called?

"A bar guai," Kazimir offered. "You must have imagined it. Why would she care about a necklace?"

"Kai said it could store ancient magic, right? Mystic powers from their dead souls and whatnot? What if it can store more than magic?"

Kazimir's white brow furrowed. "You mean Nesilia herself?"

"Kai said things changed when Sora broke the bar guai, right? Maybe it kept Nesilia from possessing her or something. Maybe Nesilia was scared of Sora wearing it again?"

"It's possible. If we can split Sora and her mind, we may be able to separate them. One for the body, one for the stone, and contain Nesilia until she can be banished. You said you've entered Sora's mind before, so we'll need the Lightmancer."

"She won't be eager to use her powers again," Whitney argued.

"Then we'll make her. For reasons I don't understand, Sora cares for you. She is compromised around you, and, therefore, Nesilia is as well. They are still joined. If the Lightmancer sends you in, it'll give us an opening."

Whitney chewed on a fingernail, then nodded. "She'll do it. She has to. I know… it's all a long shot but—"

"But it's the best we have," Kazimir said. "The Well of Wisdom is said to give the diver the information needed to overcome the obstacles before them, if they have the wisdom to find it. It is the combined memories of every mystic who'd ever drawn on its power. Every story ever told lies within those waters. If the Well showed me the beginning of my life as an upyr, granted to me by a wianu, and to you, the beginning of Sora's captivity and the bar guai, I have to believe they are connected somehow."

"Then we need to talk to Kai. We have to get a bar guy—whatever-thing."

***

When they reached the Red Tower's main entry hall, Kai appeared mortified. Sigrid had gagged him, which was a smart move. Considering it seemed the only way the kid could cast magic was through the use of an ancient language, Whitney was surprised she hadn't just lopped his tongue off and eaten it.

Sigrid was in the corner, trying desperately to force the blood of the dead mystic acolytes past her muzzle.

"Sigrid, stop," Kazimir ordered.

Sigrid turned to them. A feral quality ravaging her features. She looked positively crazed.

"That blood is too old," Kazimir went on. "They've been dead for hours. Only fresh blood carries the stream of life. This… it is tainted by death. It will not provide what you desire."

She breathed out a mournful wail, then dashed to Kai, still tied up. He tried to scurry away, but his back found the wall.

Kazimir placed himself between Kai and his apprentice, then grabbed Sigrid by the neckline and tossed her aside. "We still need him," he said. "Any sign of Aihara Na yet?"

Sigrid shook her head but never looked away from Kai.

Kazimir then turned to the young mystic. "I will remove this gag, but at the first sign of rebellion, I will cut you down. Understood?

Kai nodded. When Kazimir untied the gag, Kai shifted his jaw around in a circle. "She's insane!"

"Quite," Kazimir admitted. "But it is not her fault. The transition to unlife is a difficult one. Many never recover the minds they knew. They can't reconcile the power."

Something in Kai's eyes told Whitney he understood that feeling.

"Can you untie him?" Whitney asked. "I don't think he's going to try to run. Besides, how far can he get with you here?"

"Do you know how long we were in the Well?" Kazimir asked Whitney.

"I don't know, a few minutes?"

"Hours." He gestured to the light filtering in through the closed front gates. "It is now dawn."

Hours, Whitney thought. He supposed he shouldn't have been surprised. Time always worked differently in Elsewhere and the realms beyond. Frustratingly so.

"All he needs to do to escape is make it outside, and he'll be beyond our reach until nightfall. No. He stays tied up."

Whitney exchanged an apologetic look with Kai.

"We will get the bar guai, and then Sigrid and I will have to last here until nightfall," Kazimir decided.

"You'll what?" Kai asked.

"What about Aihara Na?" Whitney said, ignoring Kai.

"I can't say when she'll be back. But we will need the assistance of your Lightmancer friend once more."

"Bar guai? Lightmancers?" Kai shook his head in disapproval. "You can't be serious. You're trifling with things… you can't even begin to imagine the power."

"I don't know… have you noticed the yigging upyr in front of you?" Whitney asked.

"Even the Children of the Night are babies compared to the magic of Lightmancers! And the bar guai—they were created to have dominion over Elsewhere and its power."

Kazimir let a sharp finger trace a small line on Kai's face. A trickle of blood streamed out, and Kazimir licked it. Sigrid groaned, pouting.

"Chi tse wei lo," Kai said, and immediately, the wound sealed up.

It was now Kazimir's turn to let out a deep, longing moan. "Too bad."

"Kai, we need your help," Whitney said.

"Why should I help you anymore when it's clear these two don't listen to you?"

"We think the bar guai is the only way to save Sora," Whitney offered. "She saved you once, you said. Now, it's time to finish paying her back. You said you wore one? You must have another."

When Kai didn't immediately respond, Kazimir said, "Hesitate any longer, and I'll remove my apprentice's mouthguard. We will see how long you last."

"They are sacred," Kai said. "Inhabited by the souls of the greatest of our Order. Even Sora's own mother."

"Is your life not sacred?" Kazimir asked. "Your Order can't suffer another loss."

"Kai, don't do it for us," Whitney said. "Do it for Sora. The Well worked, but she needs you."

Kai paused again, but then regarded Kazimir with a new resolve. "Okay, untie me."

Kai took them upstairs. He was reluctant, at first, to allow anyone into the Ancient One's chambers, but Kazimir and Sigrid's *unique* means of persuasion left him very little choice but to comply. They passed many floors of tiny dwellings. Most were empty, but a few more ragged-looking acolytes who weren't unlucky enough to die downstairs locked themselves behind paper doors. The last, pathetic remnants of their Order.

Aihara Na's chambers were perched at the top of the tower, and on the modest end of a queen's bedroom—not that Whitney had ever seen the insides of any. In the same way the wealth present in the entry hall could have fed an entire kingdom, the Ancient One's room could have kept Yarrington supplied with provisions for a month.

Whitney whistled and shook his head. "These are some accouterments" he said, lifting a small, but incredibly heavy broach.

"Don't touch anything," Kai said. He didn't even lift his head as he, himself, sifted through the mystic's stuff. "Defensive enchantments target the living, and Aihara never was a trusting woman."

Whitney lightly placed the broach down and turned to Kazimir, who stood in a thin stream of light which poured in through an arrowslit window.

"How are you not, you know, going explody?" He mimed an explosion with his hands and made the accompanying sound effect.

"Mystic blood," Kazimir said. "Even what little I took from Kai can do wondrous things. It won't last much longer. Allow me to enjoy the warmth, even if I cannot feel it."

"Who knew you had an imagination."

Kazimir didn't answer, but Whitney thought now he understood why the upyr had been so intent upon Sora in Winde Port. He felt pity grow inside at the thought of Kazimir being damned to live in darkness, feeding on human blood.

Thinking back to the many times he'd found himself imprisoned, and when he'd been in one such situation without hope of escape, he considered the feeling akin to being forced to murder. He'd felt it more times of late than he ever imagined he would. Killing was a thief's final resort. In all his years traveling Pantego from Crowfall and Westvale to Lilith's Mill and beyond the borders of the Glass, Whitney never once found himself in the position required to take another man's life.

War, however, had made killing a necessity to remain breathing.

"Why don't you drink something else?" Whitney asked. "Why human blood? Have you considered cow blood? Goat?"

"This doesn't seem like a good time for this discussion," Kazimir said.

"What better time? We're all probably going to die soon

anyway." Whitney meant it as a joke, though for one of the few times in his life, he feared it might be true.

"Animals don't carry with them the knowledge of good and evil," Kai answered. "They don't experience the fear that humans do. In truth, the Sons and Daughters of Night feed off fear as much as the lifeblood that carries it."

"That true?" Whitney asked.

Kazimir grunted. "You can smell fear. Taste it. It is enough to drive an upyr mad. Especially one so young as my apprentice."

Whitney turned to appraise Sigrid, alone in the darkest corner of the room, bloodlust nearly turning her eyes red after being with Kai alone so long. She squeezed the edge of a nightstand, and the wood compressed in her iron-grip. Whitney was surprised she hadn't torn him to pieces.

After a bout of funereal silence, Kai cleared his throat. "This is the only one I know of," Kai said, holding up a gaudy looking necklace, removed from a glass case. "The rest were drained training me and those you…" He cleared his throat. "…killed. It may work, but they have not been blessed by the Ancient One."

"What does that mean?" Whitney asked.

"It means nothing," Kazimir said. "Superstition and 'horse shog,' as you would say." Kazimir snatched the bar guai from Kai's hand and shoved it into the folds of his cloak. "This will do just fine."

"Hey! Careful with that," Kai protested. "We mustn't handle sacred things as though they are common. There are entire lives within those stones."

"Worthless," Kazimir said under his breath.

"What was that?" Kai hissed.

"What you consider sacred, I consider worthless. Drawing on the dead is no different than blood magic. Leaving their souls lingering in this realm. What a fine legacy you foul mystics left."

"I think you have your history messed up," Kai said.

"It's all just stories," Whitney said. "That's why I never bothered with books. Now, it sure would be nice if we could stop arguing and remember that we are in a bit of a time crunch—you know, Sora being possessed by an evil goddess and threatening to destroy life as we know it and all that."

He crossed the room. "I should take the bar guai back with me to Tum Tum's place now."

"No," Kazimir said.

"What do you mean, no?"

"It is safer with me. Such power can corrupt the minds of mortals, and Nesilia feeds on such vulnerability." Kazimir returned to the window. He winced when he reached the ray of light, and Whitney heard a sound like water boiling. When the upyr turned out of the sun, his face had become a mottled mess of blisters.

Whitney opened his mouth to argue, but Kazimir stepped out of the light and continued.

"We have all that we require," he said. "Return to the dwarf's pub, and hope they remain alive. Sigrid and I will meet you there when night falls."

"I don't feel comfortable with this at all," Whitney said, looking to Kai for support. "I really think I should take the bar guai—"

"You made this blood pact," Kazimir interrupted. His face was contorted into something halfway between pain and fury. "It is not just your life on the line. Go, and don't move until you see me at nightfall."

"Fine, then I'm taking Kai with me."

"What?" Kai said.

"Don't be a fool," Kazimir spat.

Sigrid looked like she might lose her mind at the mere mention of taking the mystic away. She charged Whitney, stopping just before entering the stream of light coming in from the window.

Whitney wished she would've continued. Maybe where Kazimir had only been scorched, she'd have burst into flames. Then he would have had one less problem.

"Mind your dog!" Whitney said.

"I'll drink yer heart," Sigrid hissed.

"The boy stays here," Kazimir said.

"With her?"

"With me."

"Are you out of your bloodsucking mind?" Whitney said. "I see how you're both looking at him. He helped Sora. Kai comes with me, or you'll have to explain to the Sanguine Lords why the job was never done."

A deep, echoing wail filled the room. At first, Whitney thought it was Sigrid, then he saw the specter in the corner, wearing robes. Aihara Na was a barely perceptible spirit, but she was returning.

"Return the soul of my daughter!" she howled. Her nebulous form soared across the room and with it, furniture upturned.

Whitney grabbed Kai by the wrist and pulled him out the door, slamming it behind them. He heard the sounds of battle ensuing as they descended the circular staircase.

"This will not end well," Kai warned.

"Nothing I ever do does," Whitney said.

It took a few minutes in the tall stairwell before reaching the first-floor entry. A few surviving inhabitants of the tower peered through the cracked doors of their dwellings along the way, but Kai shooed them to hide.

In the entry hall, Aihara Na's otherworldly moaning was even louder. Towing Kai to the doors, Whitney did his best to ignore it and threw them open. They were met with harsh sunlight that temporarily blinded Whitney after spending so long in the dim light of the tower. When he raised his arm to block the sun, he felt something sharp against his lower back. "Shog in a barrel, Kai," he cursed. "Betrayal? Is this what I get for sparing your life?"

"Don't ye move a muscle." The voice was gruff and uneducated, the very opposite of Kai. The smell that came from the man's breath was pungent, something akin to fish and ale regurgitated.

"Aye, look what we have here," another man said.

Once Whitney's eyes adjusted to the daylight, the sight before him became perfectly clear. An immense wooden ship was anchored some distance away, flying white sails, but also bearing the same gilded mermaid Whitney had seen inside of Tum Tum's pub. Two smaller rowing boats rested on the beaches around the Red Tower, just beyond the gates.

The ship, the pirates, Whitney recognized it all. Even though they were flying the false flags of traders, it all belonged to Grisham "Gold Grin" Gale, and because any ship belonging to the Glass army was moored, handling the cultist riot and helping tend to still burning buildings, nobody had stopped them. They'd just waltzed right into Panping, undeterred.

As if the notorious pirate heard Whitney's very thoughts, his heavy boots pounded across the sand. The many gold chains draped around his neck and wrists jangled like distant church bells. Worst of all, the broken half of the Glass Crown Whitney had stolen from Liam's head sat crooked atop his graying head. Two men, ugly as the day is long, flanked him with bows drawn.

"Whitney Fierstown!" Gold Grin exclaimed. "Ye godsdamned, ship-stealin rapscallion."

"Oh, hey, old friend, old buddy, old pal… listen, that was a long time ago," Whitney said with a smile on his face. And it was true. That had been years ago, and Whitney thought they were well past such absurdities. "Bygones be bygones. Water under the proverbial bridge. What do you say?"

Gold Grin returned the smile, golden like the blinding the sun. He grunted, and then said, "Aye, mayhaps. But one never does forget being stranded in the middle of the sea on a ship he ain't used to with a whole crew lookin down their noses at ye. Ye deserve to hang for it, but I ain't here for that, boy."

Gold Grin sauntered forward, swinging his gaudy boots one in front of the other, picking at his fingernails with the tip of a knife, then sucking the cuticle.

"What *are* you here for?" Whitney asked as the dagger at his back jabbed deeper. He felt his shirt getting wet with blood.

"What is the meaning of this?" Kai asked. "We will not sully the sands of this place with your ilk." He didn't wait for a response before he began muttering. He lifted his hand, laced with energy, but before anything could happen, blood spattered Whitney's face, and Kai stumbled backward. The salty taste of copper on his tongue, he spat and watched as Kai thrashed around in the Red Tower's threshold, an arrow protruding from his throat.

"Yig and shog!" Whitney yelped. "If this isn't about the bloody ship…"

"Shut up, or yer next," said the pirate on Gold Grin's left, already nocking a new arrow.

The pirate king stalked, adjusting the crown with his blade and said, "I met yer friend Sora, beautiful Sora."

Whitney lurched but felt a hand on his shoulder pulling him back.

"Next time ye do that, I'll run ye through," said the pirate behind him.

"Fortist?" Whitney asked, finally recognizing the man's voice.

"Oh, the great Whitney Fierstown remembers me, does he? Shut yer face flap." Fortist gave him another rough prod.

"Sora killed Hestor… ye remember me first mate?" Gold Grin said. "Shame she had to go do that…"

"If you hurt her!" Whitney shouted.

Gold Grin laughed, and his lackeys joined in. "Hurt her? I'm here to help her."

A minuscule speck of hope fluttered in Whitney's belly until his mind told him there wouldn't be a dagger against his back if Gold Grin truly meant to help Sora. Maybe Gold Grin helped her reach Panping like Tum Tum had said, but she'd never throw in with pirates. Thieves like him stole. Pirates killed.

But Whitney had to admit he was more than a little confused until…

Nesilia, Whitney thought. But out loud, he said, "Help her with what?"

Gold Grin stood directly before Whitney now, his thumb and forefinger squeezing the spot where Whitney's earlobe used to be. "She told me… that she wanted ye dead."

At once, Whitney heard three things: bowstrings stretching, a loud clatter behind him, and a scream. Then, Whitney was shoved aside and hit the ground in a flurry of sand. Arrows thrummed one after another. They bounced off the stone tower, *thunked* into the sand.

Gold Grin grunted and said, "Quit firing!"

When silence came, Whitney lifted his head, and turned it, blinking away sand. Fortist lay unmoving, Gold Grin had an arrow sticking out of his right shoulder, and Kazimir stood behind him, forearm wrapped around the pirate's neck just as he'd done to Kai near the Well. Sigrid, still unmuzzled, licked her blood-stained lips. She rose from Kai's punctured corpse, his cheeks now gaunt, shriveled, and colorless.

"There you two are!" Whitney exclaimed, pretending like he hadn't left them to fend for themselves against Aihara Na's whatever-she-was now.

"Thank you for our meal," Kazimir said, ignoring Whitney. "It was as if you packaged the mystic and delivered him inside just for us. His blood was just fresh enough… and delicious.

Luckily for you, after tasting him, you'd taste like rotted sewage."

"Still wouldn't mind a nibble," Sigrid said, still licking her lips. As she did, she pulled closed the doors of the Red tower, silencing Aihara Na's wailing.

"What do you think, Pirate?" Kazimir flicked his forefinger and drew blood from just under Gold Grin's eye.

The upyr might have been one of the only men Whitney had ever known who came even close to Gold Grin's stature—Torsten Unger being the only one to exceed it.

"Fierstown, I knew ye were traitorous, but I never pegged ye for a friend of bloodsucking fiends." Gold Grin said, his voice betraying a slight tremble.

"Ye know this brute?" Sigrid asked.

"Yeah," Whitney said. "He's always been a monster, but never like this."

"Says the friend of these things," Gold Grin said.

Kazimir tightened his grip on Gold Grin's neck.

"Dade, bring me the boy," Gold Grin struggled to say as Kazimir's sharp nails began to dig into his flesh.

"Wait!" Whitney said, clambering to his feet. "Boy, what boy?"

The man Gold Grin called Dade trudged down to one of their rowboats. Sigrid hissed that beastly hiss, but Kazimir kept her at bay. Dade reached into the boat and returned with a small body in his arms. Whitney had no doubt what he was looking at.

An unconscious Gentry bounced helplessly on Dade's shoulder. The pirate threw him down onto the beach. Whitney didn't know sand could sound so hard and unforgiving.

"Found him followin ye on a raft," Gold Grin said. "Told him we were old friends. Didn't think twice about tellin me yer whereabouts. Kids are so special, ain't they?"

"Is he—"

"Not yet," Gold Grin interrupted Whitney "He's livin. For how long, is yer choice. Tell this walkin nightmare to let me go, and maybe I'll suffer the boy to live."

Whitney kicked sand. He'd had enough of Nesilia messing with everyone in his life. Now he knew that's what this was "Gold Grin, this isn't you! You had one rule, remember? No children, no matter what."

Turning his attention to the pirate king's men, Whitney thought he saw a hint of agreement pass over their faces. It bolstered Whitney's resolve. "I don't know what she's done to you… but that wasn't Sora. Not my Sora."

"Yer right about that!" Gold Grin grunted, trying to free himself from Kazimir's preternatural strength. "She's mine now. Every soft inch of her."

"Shogging Exile," Whitney whispered. "Let him go. He's being manipulated by Nesilia. He has to be. Sora would never touch him."

"Oh trust me, she did," Gold Grin chortled, then licked his lips, looking as delighted as Sigrid when she tasted blood.

Kazimir yanked the pirate's neck back to stare straight into his eyes. Gold Grin cursed in protest. "There it is, the emptiness," Kazimir said. "Can you see it, Sigrid? The rage. Nesilia is nature, and nature is beauty. He has looked into her soul and has been lost to lust. There's no choice. He must die."

"But it's not even him," Whitney said, wondering why he cared if Kazimir killed this man he held no love for. But, he turned to Gold Grin's men nonetheless. "It's not, is it?"

Dade lowered his head and slowly shook it, and the other elbowed him.

"Don't prod me, ye dumb wench-lover!" Dade said. "Fierstown might've been a prig in the past, but he's right about this. Gold Grin ain't been right since we left Panping the first time, ye know it."

"Ye'll make a date with Stumpmaker Jack for that remark, ye ungrateful bastard," Gold Grin warned. "Ye let me go, and I'll kill Fierstown and each of ye as well!"

Sigrid grimaced and sucked in a breath through her teeth. Her arm started bubbling under the sun's rays.

"We've got to get to shadow," Kazimir said, "Get the boy." He took a few steps back, leading his captive and everyone else around the small island to where the tower blocked the low sun.

Whitney sprinted for Gentry, then bent and lightly slapped the boy's face. None of the pirates tried to stop him now. When Gentry didn't respond, Whitney hefted him and joined the others, then placed Gentry down nearby.

Sigrid observed the two remaining pirates carefully. Dade might have been showing signs of mutiny, but the other hadn't.

"Kill him, Gault," Gold Grin said.

The other pirate looked from Gold Grin to Dade and back again, but didn't make a move.

"Your men are no longer with you," Kazimir said before letting Gold Grin go.

The pirate king immediately started swinging.

"Ye'll never keep me from my love!" he yelled. "I'll follow ye to the ends of the map to protect her."

Kazimir ducked, Gold Grin's heavy fist soaring uselessly overhead. Then Kazimir drove his own into Gold Grin's gut, and the pirate bent at the waist. Without missing a beat, Gold Grin drove his shoulder into Kazimir and pushed him back against one of the Glass soldier statues guarding the gates. Kazimir hammered down with two joined fists, and Gold Grin cried out before collapsing and hitting his head against the base of the statue.

Whitney strolled over and kicked Gold Grin lightly. There was no movement.

"I think you knocked him out and broke his back," Whitney

said to Kazimir, then found a bit of rope in their rowboats and hog-tied Gold Grin.

"He'll live," Kazimir said.

"This wasn't him," Whitney said as he finished the knot. "She has him under some sort of spell. The only thing Gold Grin ever loved was his old ship… which I took. And gold."

"I don't care who he is. He got in the way of the mission, and he's lucky his blood smells foul enough for me to consider leaving him to breathe. The more Nesilia convinces to worship her, the more powerful she becomes."

Whitney rose and approached the other pirates who now looked far less intimidating with Sigrid sniffing their necks like they were steaks prepared by a Glass Castle chef.

"What happened?" Whitney asked.

Dade looked at Gault, who shrugged.

"It's like this," Dade started. "We was minding our business here in Yaolin. We brought yer friend, the witch… we found her in the Boiling Waters after sinking some Black Sand afhem's ship —called him al'Tariq or something. Then a storm came and stole our loot, so, we brought her and Tum Tum here. Then the Cap'n and that dwarf, they set up shop across the pond. A new fence to work through. Big place. Nice place. Everythin was dandy. The guards cleared us dockin for once, let us drink and eat. Then, next thing we know, Sora comes back like some crazed sex-demon."

Whitney's head tilted so far he strained a muscle. "A *what?*"

"Sides the point I think, ye know?" Dade continued. "Fact is, she wanted to go to Winter's Thumb and made Gold Grin all sorts of promises, so we took her. Saw her do things no one should be able to do. Flyin, killin with her mind. Then, don't get me started with the Drav Cra warlock she was with. Freydis I think was her name."

Silence followed, and Whitney let it all process until the other spoke up.

"Dade's right, though," Gault said, softly. "This wasn't our Cap. He was like a man possessed. I seen him do mad things for his love of Reba back in the day, but this was…"

Love? Whitney thought. Bile rose in his throat.

"Then she sent us back here to kill ye after some mad Drav Cra ritual," Dade interrupted. "The things we saw…" He shuddered. "She told the Cap'n to kill ye dead for her. She done the same to all the crew but us. They all refused to travel the world for yer head, so she killed them. The lot of them, though… they was right. I shoulda joined them in death. Said ye were a shog-eating son of a zhulong, but ye weren't worth killin. And that be the truth."

"Thanks?" Whitney muttered. His mind scrambled to keep up with everything.

"Ye don't get it," Dade said. "She's gonna swallow the known world or some shog."

"We know that part," Whitney said. "But we've got a plan."

"Quiet, thief. They don't need to know our plans," Kazimir warned.

"There ain't no stoppin her," Gault said.

"No, none," Dade agreed. "It's like she's a yiggin goddess. Trees obeyin her. Wind. Water. Like she owns the world itself. Truth is, we knew Gold Grin wasn't himself. Talked a mutiny the whole way west, but she…" He shuddered visibly. "The thought of her makes me squirm."

Whitney stole a glance at Kazimir.

"What's her plan?" Whitney asked, curious if what they knew would corroborate with what he'd heard in the Well of Wisdom.

"Thinkin she'd tell us?" Dade scoffed. "Alls I knows what I heard her tell the Cap'n. Kill Fierstown while she builds her forces."

"A goddess after me," Whitney said. Part of him wanted to

stick out his chest. "That means she's afraid of my connection with Sora."

"Full possession is easier without resistance," Kazimir said. "A connection to this world will pull like chains. It's why the elderly and children are more susceptible."

"She should be afraid," Whitney said.

Kazimir exhaled and stepped in front of Whitney, staring straight at the pirates. They each looked like shog was dripping down their legs. "What forces did she mention exactly. Spit it out, pirate, or I'll peel open your mind myself." Dade turned away, sputtering and unable to talk.

"Like he said," Gault chimed in, "we don't know. She set off east on land from Winter's Thumb, after gathering a whole bunch of Drav Cra… into the Dragon's Tail, maybe beyond…"

Kazimir cursed loudly in Breklian and punched the wall above Dade's shoulder. The poor man nearly fainted at the sound of crunching stone.

"Sh-sh-she has the warlocks already thanks to this lot of fools, and who knows what b-b-beasts of deep," he stammered.

"Grimaurs?" Whitney offered. He was still busy fighting back the contents of his stomach over hearing the things Nesilia had done with Sora's body. His gaze kept flicking back to Gold Grin on the floor and his hairy… everything.

"Them. Maybe worse," Kazimir said. "She's too many steps ahead. How could we miss this? If she's heading east, she's already on her way to my home. The Citadel, the wianu, she even has her eyes in the Well. If she takes the history of men, she'll take us all."

"Then forget these fools," Whitney said. "She's not that smart. Thanks to her, Gold Grin brought us the fastest ship I know of. Let's go get the others and sail north."

"What about us!" Dade demanded.

Whitney rolled his shoulders. He knew these men were just

following their captain, but still, they'd watched as Gold Grin violated Sora, knowing something was wrong with her. He felt no pity as he said, "This a nice beach out here. Or you can take your chances with the ghost."

"G-ghost?" Dade and Gault both stammered.

Whitney knew the pirates were terrified of anything supernatural. He backed up and looked toward the tower's entry. The doors were cracked, and the wraith of Aihara Na waited just inside, glaring at them but daring not go another step, as if she too couldn't touch the light. Whitney froze and stared.

"At her age, her power is bound to the Well and to the Tower," Kazimir explained, without him needing to ask. "She cannot leave, just as I cannot die."

Whitney cleared his throat. "Well then, it's about time Gold Grin got marooned on an island with a woman that suits him."

XXII

THE REBEL

Muskigo carved a chunk out of a bellot fruit, looking out over the Boiling Waters as he ate. It was the first bit of fresh food he'd had in longer than he cared to remember. It was his first time on the rough sea in longer than he cared to remember, as well. Their ship rocked side to side, and his stomach rolled with it.

Some Shesaitju I am, he thought. Sand and sea, that was where his people thrived. But he'd found himself only on land lately, losing battles. Losing allies.

Muskigo had seen the wake of his daughter's battle as they sailed out through Trader's Strait, careful to avoid the blockade of debris and battered warships. Smoke still dithered on the horizon there; bodies floated everywhere. He'd never been so proud, and yet, as he sat upon one of her few remaining ships, shame again overwhelmed him.

Only Babrak had a stronger fleet, and she'd sacrificed hers to save him and the pitiful remnant of his army. It was never a father's place to be protected by his child, let alone a daughter. Yet, there she was. A handful of Muskigo's men sat around him, skinny and exhausted, barely cognizant of what was happening, while her warriors proudly guarded her, all of them strong, and well-rested.

They never took their eyes off her, especially the young one named Bit'rudam, who seemed to have earned her trust above all others. Even Afhem Tingur didn't agree to remain behind in Nahanab with the bulk of their forces and their valuable prisoner, Nikserof Pasic until Mahraveh agreed it was the best move.

Muskigo was no fool. Hers was a victory that would ring through the ages: a sandstorm, driving the Glassmen away, the Caleef washing up on their shores as if delivered by the Current. The tides were shifting, and it was at his daughter's back.

"Impressive, isn't she?" Yuri Darkings asked, crossing the deck toward Muskigo. He brushed off the surface of a barrel, then straightened his robes before sitting. Somehow, the pink-skinned lord had found a new set of them, pristine as the day they were made.

"I barely recognize her," Muskigo said. She smirked as Bit'rudam whispered something in her ear on his way to the upper deck. Mahi watched as the young man grabbed a rope and leaned out over the water, sights set on a distant island. And Muskigo watched her watching.

"And yet the entire world will soon know her name," Yuri said. "She reminds me of my late wife. Oh, how strong she was." He shook his head. "What a formidable team we made, bending Winde Port to our will. I told her I didn't want children, that we could shape the kingdom together, but she insisted. Then he was born, Bartholomew Darkings, and my wife slowly lost her mind. He was three when she threw herself into the bay."

"Mahi was around the same age when a snake bit her mother. Not a day goes by when I don't miss her guidance. It would have helped here."

"And not a day goes by when I don't wish she'd have just tossed him in instead. Ungrateful little *pis'truda*—I'm using that right, yes?" Yuri chuckled, but Muskigo didn't. "So much for us old men getting what we want."

Instead, Muskigo turned to the pink-skin, his glare cold as the ice of Drav Cra. "You allowed Mahi to fight in the arena."

"Allowed?" Yuri replied, incredulous. "Have you met that girl? I assure you, there is nothing she does that isn't what she wants."

"Regardless. I sent you to protect her, yet now, I see her eyes. They bear the look of one who has not only lost the lives of those close to her but taken life as well."

"And I betrayed my people to join what I hope to be the side to claim victory. Now look where we are."

Muskigo sighed. "I suppose we underestimated our children for the last time. Mahraveh did what I couldn't, and above all, the Caleef is with us again right after."

"And yet my son is nowhere to be found."

"The Caleef didn't tell you what happened?"

"Your god-king has spoken as much to me as he has you, which is to say: not at all. All I know is that he washed ashore, covered in sand and surrounded by your glowing jellies. The things dried up beyond the water like they didn't even care about dying, and there he was, hacking up water like a mere man."

"The nigh'jels flow only with the Current," Muskigo said.

"Better than swimming upstream like us."

"I am sure your son is fine."

"My son?" Yuri laughed again. "I may not know many things, but if my useless slob of a son had anything to do with the Caleef's relatively safe return, I will eat my coin purse. No, no... everything changed when your daughter took to the sands. My whole life in Winde Port, I imagined the Shesaitju Sirens were a thing of legend, like so many gods. Then one came to her... in front of everyone."

Muskigo sat up. "A Siren revealed herself?"

"Revealed herself? It sucked the life out of the boy whose place she took in the fighting. Juvat, or something."

"Jumaat…" the name trailed off as he spoke it. Now Muskigo understood that look in his daughter's eyes. Jumaat had been her closest friend. Muskigo never understood why—the boy was weak, meant to be a trader and nothing more.

"Yes, him," Yuri said. "I've seen magic, Muskigo, but I've never seen anything like that. And if the Sirens are real, I fear what that means about all the other nightmares our parents scared us with." Yuri regarded the swirling, dark clouds of an impending storm. "I fear what it means for a traitor like me if Iam truly is vengeful."

"Fear not, Darkings. Your people have lost their way, following a mad child and a distraught queen. Your god must see that, as well as mine. The Sirens rarely reveal themselves except when a new Caleef rises from the sea. They are scions of the Current."

"It protected her when Babrak and all others would have cast her down for lying. I saw it then, too. For the first time in my overlong life, I believed in something beyond the power of gold."

"No afhem is to be favored," Muskigo said, unsure even of his own words.

"And yet, some are. You sent me to protect her. In the end, I advised her to let you go, Muskigo. I told her you weren't worth her life, just as that boy wasn't."

"You need not apologize. It is why I accepted your help to begin with. You see the bigger picture. Sacrificing my position to get behind the Glass was the sound strategic move."

"You want to win this war?" Yuri asked, looking off to sea.

"What is there left to win?"

"I promised to help you overthrow the pitiful lineage of our great King Liam, and now I see so clearly. The very same Caleef who surrendered to him sits in that cabin." Yuri pointed to the captain's quarters, within which the Caleef had been locked away since they'd set sail, not speaking a word to anybody. Two gold-clad Serpent Guards who'd thrown in with Muskigo stood guard outside. Many more had once stood beside Muskigo, forsaking their sacred duty for his rebellion. They, too, were now dead.

"Sidar Rakun was barely older than King Pi when he rose from the sea to be named Caleef," Muskigo said. "The God of Sand and Sea wisely saw that we couldn't resist then. We were weak. Perhaps, we can get through to him now. Show him not to be afraid."

"And how many Glassmen will die?" Yuri asked.

"As many as it takes."

"I didn't join you to destroy my people, only to free us from Liam's pitiful, dwindling lineage. We needed a new perspective. What if there were a way to end it all without another drop of blood; to earn the respect of the Glass Kingdom for generations."

"We need more than their respect," Muskigo snapped.

"I see a young woman more capable than any I've ever met—my wife included—who won the adoration of her people as you once did, and, apparently, the attention of your god. And I know of a young king in Yarrington. One they call a miracle. One who rose from the dead."

"A boy you said yourself was mad, and who displayed it when he imprisoned our Caleef!"

Yuri stood and paced. The way he strode on the deck, he looked even more comfortable on the water than Muskigo felt. "A boy all the same. And boys are nothing if not impressionable. Liam's cock led him all around Pantego. I can't imagine how many bastards are out there with no idea of what they are. King Pi comes from that same stock."

Muskigo grit his teeth. "Be very careful what you say next, Glassman."

"A marriage between Mahraveh al'Tariq and King Pi Nothhelm ends all of this. It gives the Black Sands as much stake in power as the west. No more tribute. No more bowing. Only a king and a queen, and peace across the greatest empire in the world."

"She would stand in his shadow."

"Not if she, too, were chosen by god." Yuri wound his way around Muskigo and stared at the Caleef's cabin. "I see a broken man locked in a room; a god-king who bleeds. Sidar Rakun never needs to reach Latiapur. There could be a new Caleef, one who has seen her might, or perhaps, Mahraveh herself."

Muskigo clutched Yuri by the collar and pulled him close. "What you speak is blasphemy."

"Muskigo, friend, his time has come, just as ours has. I've seen enough signs to know that."

"Then you're a fool," Muskigo said, shoving Yuri away. He sat again on a spool of rope. "The sea delivered him. I have disagreed with him much in my life, but the tides change. Now that he has seen the wickedness of greedy Glassmen, he will see reason also."

"Or perhaps he returned only so we could see how frail he is. How mortal he is."

Muskigo punched the wood beneath him. "To even speak such things invites the waves to crush us. A Caleef is not chosen by mortals. That is not our way."

"Our ways doom us, Muskigo. The Sirens came to your daughter. You said it yourself: sandstorms follow her. In the battle, I, myself, pulled her from the sea. A lesser woman might have drowned, but she didn't. The Nothhelm line has been corrupted by a heartless witch with no place in our castle; by a man who saw Iam only between the legs of a woman. But your daughter…"

"Will not be married off like some common whore!"

Muskigo didn't realize he'd sprung to his feet and had Yuri in both hands again until Mahraveh approached.

"Is everything all right, Father?" She gripped her spear tight, ready to strike. Bit'rudam waited in her shadow, no doubt prepared to do the same.

Muskigo swallowed. "Everything is fine. I was just telling our friend here that his service to me is complete. The Caleef has been returned. Yuri Darkings has earned the thanks of the greater afhemdom, and now, he can go home."

"Good," Mahraveh said. "We'll be at Latiapur shortly. From there, he can find passage to anywhere in Pantego."

Yuri's gaze darted between them, then he bowed his head. "As you all command." On his way by, he whispered in Muskigo's ear, "She made me believe in something greater than humanity. Don't hold her back like all the other men."

Muskigo held his tongue and tried not to stare. Instead, he gestured to the seat beside him and waved for Mahi to join him. All these warriors, guarding and respecting her, but the moment he gestured, she sat. She turned to him with doe eyes, expecting answers as any child would.

"No longer my little sand mouse, are you?" he said.

The corners of her lips rose slightly. "I suppose not."

"Ah, well, these things never do last forever. I am proud of you, for whatever that is worth from a washed-up rebel."

"Bravest man I know," Mahi said.

"If only these others saw things through your eyes, yes?"

Mahi nodded. "The Caleef still won't say a word," she said, changing the subject. "Is he always this quiet?"

"I've only met him a handful of times," Muskigo replied. "He never was one for many words, but he said what needed to be said."

"Father, the way he looks."

"I know. I've always had doubts about him, but the God of Sand and Sea made his decision long ago, and the Current obeyed. We have to trust in it. He has returned for a reason."

"But if we bring him to Latiapur and he sides with Babrak?" Mahi asked.

"How could he?" Bit'rudam chimed in.

Muskigo shot a glare at the young man. "This is a conversation between afhems," he said, terse.

Bit'rudam returned the glare, then looked to Mahi. She nodded, and purple-faced, he strode a few paces away.

"He means well," Mahraveh whispered. "They grow up different on the islands."

"He's loyal. That's good." Muskigo said. "But all must know their place."

A brief period of silence passed between them, and Muskigo hoped he'd find answers in it. Something to say to the girl who he'd left behind. But instead, he only heard wood creak as they pierced the waves.

"Father—" she said, but they both spoke at the same time.

"I heard about Jumaat." Muskigo took her wrist. "I'm sorry for his fate."

Her head sank. "So am I. He was meant to fight on the sands. Sometimes I wonder if he'd have won, if he'd died for no reason."

"He wouldn't have. You fought in his stead for a reason, and I know the boy would have gladly given his life for you. He would have made you his wife without a second thought."

"Like you'd ever let him." Mahi smirked. "He wanted to fight, Father. For me. For you. He was braver than you knew."

"I'm sure he was." Muskigo reached out farther and laid his hand over Mahi's heart. "Now he is in here, fighting with you. In the current of your blood. He, Shavi, your mother… all who have come before."

"I know he is."

"Then don't worry about Babrak," Muskigo said with finality. "The sea erodes slowly, but it is just. His holiness was delivered to *your* followers, not his. There is a reason for that. We will make the Black Sands see that we aren't so weak as we were." He regarded Yuri who stood peering out over the starboard rail. "And *they* aren't so strong."

"The other afhems will see you and recall their courage."

"Perhaps," Muskigo said, though he didn't believe the words himself.

Mahraveh stood to walk away. Muskigo didn't allow her to get far. He rose and embraced her, pulling her head against his chest, feeling each breath. Then he held her at arm's length and marveled at the sight of her in her new form. The scars on her face, her tattoos, her adult figure. She would eat the boy-king of Glass alive.

"You have grown so much," he said.

Mahraveh squirmed free. "You've said that enough."

"And yet still, I stand in awe of you."

"Latiapur!" a voice rang out from atop the mast. All at once, the head of every person on board snapped toward the city coming into view through fog. Mahi ran to the railing and hopped up. The Caleef's grand palace, the Boiling Keep, rose like the tip of a spear from the Golden Bluffs. Ships filled the water beneath it, some setting sail to meet them as they neared the capital.

The holy man they transported home would change everything. And as Muskigo stared at his daughter, he hoped it would be for the better.

XXIII

THE DAUGHTER

As the built-up cliffs of Latiapur came into view, it all felt like a dream. Mahi knew she'd return one day, but she didn't expect it to be like this. She'd driven the Glass army out of Nahanab, saved her father, and found the Caleef. It didn't matter that she hadn't intended upon the last part. Strange events seemed to follow her life of late. Sandstorms, Sirens… the mortal body chosen by the God of Sand and Sea to carry his presence on Pantego rolling onto shore wasn't any crazier.

Corsair ships manned by the Serpent Guard, the defenders of Latiapur which pledged allegiance to no afhem, sailed at their side, navigating them through the perilous waters which made Latiapur nearly impossible to conquer from the sea. The palace docks were carved into a fold in the sharp bluffs. Lifts affixed to cranks, which would carry them up into the city alongside fishing nets and other supplies, awaited them within.

Mahi had no idea how her people's ancestors placed aside their warring ways long enough to construct such an impressive city. To the north, the cliffs tapered to form the rear wall of Tal'du Dromesh, where she'd earned her title. It was strange, now, to see its seats empty.

Straight to port side, jagged rocks rose from beneath the massive, domed palace which extended out over the Boiling Waters. A statue of a Siren the size of a small mountain was carved into the rocks beneath it, depicted as holding the palace up. Her two arms outstretched to the rock ceiling above, and her form extended down until she was lost in a field of sharp rocks just below the Sea Door in Caleef's throne room.

There, waves met, causing an endless whirlpool. Mahi couldn't imagine how many thousands had perished in those waters, either executed and murdered like Farhan had been, or having leaped through in faith, hoping the Current would carry them to shore alive as it had the Caleef currently aboard their ship and so many before him.

"I don't know how anybody does it," she said to Bit'rudam, staring at the raging waters beneath the palace.

"What?" he asked.

"Throw themselves down there." If Caleef Sidar Rakun never showed up, the choosing of a new Caleef would begin. One by one, men would volunteer to be tossed into the depths until the God of Sand and Sea saw fit to find his new voice. Sidar was only sixteen when it had happened to him. Far from a warrior. And he wasn't the son of some afhem, just markless traders from Rakun, a small village to the northeast.

"Faith," Bit'rudam said, not a shred of doubt in his tone.

"A fight to the death seems far simpler."

"Yet, nothing about our world is simple," he said. "It stands to reason that the God who governs it wouldn't be either."

"Would you do it?" she asked. "When Sidar Rakun's body passes on."

"Will you get me killed by then, my Afhem?" he asked, grinning mischievously.

Mahi felt herself smiling back, then stopped. "I can't make any promises."

"Well, if I am alive, I suppose it depends on if I have what I want by then."

"And what is that?" Mahi turned to face him. His hair whipped in the wind, and the low-dusk night colored the black stubble on his chin in a way that made her notice it for once. He was a man. One who'd already saved her life more than once.

"I suppose I'll know when the time comes. I mean, maybe I'll be an afhem, myself,, or have many wives and children that depend on me. Who's to know?"

"Who would take you?" Mahi said. They laughed, and as they leaned against the rail, Mahi noticed their fingers touch. At the same time, she saw her father watching from behind and swiftly slid her hand away.

"I never thought about that happening with an afhem," Mahi said.

"What do you mean?" Bit'rudam asked. He was acting like he hadn't noticed her pull away. She hoped he hadn't.

"Can an afhem not leap in faith?"

Bit'rudam shrugged. "I've never heard of one who had."

"Anyone can try," Muskigo said. Mahi hadn't noticed him move around beside them. "But to earn the markings of an afhemate is to bear responsibility for your people. It is a calling. For any afhem to sacrifice their duty to become Caleef... well... I wouldn't trust such a man to guide us, and I suspect the Current wouldn't either. Warriors like us aren't built for sitting around and letting others spill the blood."

"Is that why you betrayed him?" Bit'rudam asked.

Muskigo calmly took steps toward the Bit'rudam. Mahi chewed on her cheek. Her father glowered down at the young warrior. He still favored one leg after being injured in his fight with Babrak, but he painted an intimidating picture none the less.

"I betrayed no one, boy" Muskigo growled. "I did what I had to when nobody else would. Your afhemate included."

"I meant no offense," Bit'rudam said, his voice breaking slightly. "Afhem Awn'al, my last afhem, and my father, they were angry when you left… I… I only wish to understand…"

Bit'rudam had been resistant to the legend of Mahi's father ever since they'd rescued him, combatant, even. His unwavering loyalty to this point amused her, but he'd yet to be so close to Muskigo. Now, he seemed as afraid as she knew he should be.

"All you need to understand is that I'm still alive," Muskigo said. "I believed that God was with me, that he ignored death's call. And I believe it now, as the Current has carried my fearsome daughter to me when I had come so near to forgetting what matters most: our people."

"I understand." Bit'rudam went to say something else, tripped on his words, then nodded slowly and backed away, his cheeks turning to a darker shade of gray.

"Be nice, Father," Mahi said. She chuckled as she watched Bit'rudam begin to order around a member of the crew, then her throat went dry at the memory of how afraid Jumaat used to be of her father.

"Focus, Mahraveh," he said. "We are here. Many afhems are here, the traitor Babrak amongst them. Your friend is right about one thing: I acted against foreigners without the support of the Caleef. I have paid dearly for it. But, perhaps now that he has personally seen the ways of the Glass, he'll agree with what I did. We won't know until he speaks."

"Well, I'm with you, Father."

"I know my little sand mouse—I mean, Afhem Mahraveh. First, we break Babrak's influence. Then, we deal with the fate of our people. If that means I must face judgment, so be it."

Those words silenced her. For so long, all Mahi had been focused on was saving her father, then her hatred for Sir Nikserof, and Babrak and the people he'd sided with. She hadn't even yet considered that her father had broken their laws by defying the Caleef, that he could face the very Sea Door they were approaching.

She didn't have long to think about it before the shadow of the Latiapur cliffs covered them in chilly darkness. They were led into a tall cavern, glowing green from the mob of nigh'jels following beneath their ship, drawn to the Caleef. Mahi could hear the chatter on the docks surrounding them, wondering why the creatures did so. They purposefully hadn't sent word that the Caleef had returned ahead of them. Anything to keep Babrak in the dark.

When they docked, and the Caleef emerged from his cabin, the silence made her skin crawl. Presently, he was painted black with the blood of the nigh'jels again. Only, it was obvious something was wrong. Mahi had heard stories about how it matted onto the Caleefs, inseparable from their own flesh. It was sloppy now. Applied in chunks in some places, and very clearly missing hard to reach areas like behind the ears.

It did, however, cover the myriad cuts and bruises that left her wondering why they worshipped him in the first place.

"The Boiling Keep awaits," Muskigo said as he limped by, following the Caleef at a safe distance.

The Caleef's Serpent Guards helped him onto the docks first, where dozens of dockhands were already on their knees kowtowing upon seeing him. It didn't matter their afhemate, or even if they were markless—everyone bowed.

A massive, blackwood lift carried them up through a gap in the rocks, cranking so loudly Mahi could barely think. At the top, it felt like the entire city had heard news of the Caleef's return. Hundreds amassed at the palace stairs, all bowing on every side of them. Drums pounded in celebration, but to Mahi, the beat sounded ominous.

Even in Tal'du Dromesh, Mahi had never seen a show of such adoration for someone. Robed eunuchs and sages flocked down from the palace. Servant-women as well, offering Sidar Rakun every manner of delicacy on satin pillows. Bellot fruits from Layyil Island, wine from Westvale, brandy from Brekliodad. The Caleef accepted none of it and continued in silence.

Eventually, they entered the domed palace, into the field of columns surrounding the throne room which mirrored the seventy-nine islands of the Boiling Waters. Nigh'jel lanterns hung from each one, glowing bright. Mahi's gaze darted from side to side. More servants than she ever knew inhabited the palace popped up around them, and more Serpent Guards, too. The fearsome, masked warriors encircled him, as wordless as he was, trained from birth to protect their Caleef and care for nothing else.

Many of the afhems had chosen to stay at their homes in Lati-apur during this trying time, and every one of them arrived through the open entrance of the hall. Mahi recognized some of them from the arena. Mostly, those who'd been seated with Babrak in his suite, flattering him while his wives fed him. No matter who they were, or from where, they all shared one thing in common. All of them eyed Muskigo with scorn as he entered.

Mahi's heart swelled with pride at the sight of it. She'd accomplished the impossible while they all turned their backs, while they all sucked up to Babrak—the one they perceived to be the greatest power of the Black Sands rather than seeking that power for themselves like the afhems of old.

Filth and braggarts, all of them.

She noticed her father sneering at them as they passed into the throne room. Bit'rudam and her other followers stopped before they passed the Sea Door. They didn't even need to be asked.

"Good luck, my Afhem," Bit'rudam said softly. He straight-ened his arms at his side and bowed low at the waist.

Muskigo stuck his arm out in front of Yuri to bar his entry. "Not you."

"I arranged the Caleef's freedom," Yuri replied. "And my son is nowhere to be found. He probably died to get him to the bay."

"Does that mean you'll eat your coin purse?" Muskigo asked.

Yuri sneered.

"Our laws are not mine," Muskigo added.

"My help is no longer needed," Yuri continued to argue. "I've come for my thanks and my reward, and then I'll be gone. Surely, your Caleef will not deny his savior? Besides, I expect that the riches you promised me are no longer available, considering the… condition of your home."

Lines of tension filled Muskigo's neck. Mahi took his arm in hopes of calming him. "It's fine, Father," she said. "He's entered before, and he's right, he deserves our thanks before he leaves, at the very least."

Muskigo grunted, then nodded him along.

"As usual, our lady proves the wisest of you all," Yuri said, bowing to her.

"I just cannot wait to no longer have to see your pink face," she said.

Muskigo laid down his blade, and everyone else followed his lead. All but the Serpent Guards who lined up along the gilded walls.

The Caleef was led to his coral and gold throne. Looming behind him were larger than life depictions of zhulong and sand snakes. Across the room, wind and waves sounded through the hole in the floor which plunged down into the Boiling Waters, lost behind the veil of night.

The Caleef never sat. He stared blankly at his throne, still wordless even as Afhems passed by, fell into bows, and praised the God of Sand and Sea for his safe return.

Muskigo sat on the lowest tier, his injured leg stretched out.

Mahi sat beside him. She knew the types of stares she'd earn from doing so, especially with the respected Afhem Tingur absent, but she didn't care. Yuri went to join them, but the spear of a Serpent Guard lanced out and blocked him. The silent warrior pointed to the floor.

"I think I'll stand," Yuri grumbled.

Yuri likely had no idea how long he would be standing. Minutes turned into nearly an hour. Eventually, he started pacing, probably to keep the blood in his old legs. Nobody spoke above a whisper. They all merely watched the Caleef, waiting for him to make the first move. He'd taken his seat by then, but nothing else. His stare only turned from blankly aiming at his chair to blankly aiming at the Sea Door across the room.

Mahi turned to her father after who-knows-how-long. His features remained stoic and unflinching. She opened her mouth to speak, then stopped herself. She knew he had his pride, that he refused to be the first to speak.

Finally, Yuri Darkings could maintain the silence no longer. "I suppose I'll start." He cleared his throat. "You all know who I am. Not long ago, I stood here, promising that I would deliver the Caleef from his wrongful prison. I believe a bit of gratitude is owed. I was promised land, gold—"

The throne room doors burst open while Yuri spoke.

"Promises from a traitor," Babrak said as he came stomping in. A bandage wrapped his waist, and in the short time since Mahi had seen him, he seemed to have lost weight due to the injuries.

If only I'd hit his neck, she thought.

"My Caleef." Babrak fell to his knees, unable to hide his pained wince. His left hand groped at the tightly stretched bandage. "I am so sorry I could not have been here for your arrival. I heard only as I just arrived."

In keeping with the journey, the Caleef said nothing, didn't even look at Babrak. Mahi could see the heartbreak in the fat afhem's eyes and relished it. He didn't need to know that the Caleef hadn't yet acknowledged anyone's existence.

"Why don't you tell him how you kept his throne warm?" Muskigo asked. "How you ensured that his servants wouldn't forget how to lavish and pamper him? Or, how none of his many chefs would lose a step in their art. Latiapur's protector… as if it needed one."

Babrak stood. "And how would you know, Muskigo? You were busy leading… how many to their deaths?"

"You tell me. You got plenty of them killed in Nahanab."

"Where I arranged for peace."

"You arranged for subservience!" Muskigo roared. The hairs on the back of Mahi's neck all stood erect as his voice thundered throughout the domed space. Her father reached into his belt and removed a strand of braided hair—her hair. She hadn't realized he'd found it in Nahanab before they left. He tossed it onto the floor. "You convinced me to surrender by telling me that my daughter died. By showing me that!"

Gasps sounded around the room from the other afhems.

Babrak, however, didn't seem startled in the slightest. "Oh, please," he said, looking around the room. "Don't act like you are innocent in any of this." Then he turned back to Muskigo. "Your daughter is gone, Muskigo. She is Afhem al'Tariq now. There was no lie."

"Always desperate to be clever, aren't you?" Muskigo said.

"Is any of it a surprise?" Babrak stepped in farther, spinning as he walked to address the other afhems. "How many lies must Muskigo have told to raise his rebellious army? Mahraveh learned from him after all, how to lie, how to fight in Tal'du Dromesh to steal her position."

Arguments broke out in a low rumble but were immediately squelched by Yuri Darkings laughing.

"And what is so funny, pale-skinned rat?" Babrak asked. "Whatever you have done, you have no right to stand before his holiness!"

"I just find it amusing how faithful you afhems pretend to be until it no longer benefits you," Yuri said. "And here I thought you people were different from mine."

"We are nothing like your people!"

"Then why did you side with them?" Mahi asked. She knew she spoke too softly to command respect, but it felt different addressing the crowd of afhems in this room now that her father and the Caleef were present. She glanced up at Muskigo, and he nodded for her to stand. She did, even though her legs felt a bit like nigh'jels. "Why?" she repeated.

Babrak looked flustered for once. He spun, again addressing the room. The traitor sure knew how to play a crowd. "I sought only to end this unsanctioned war, which has cost so many good lives. I made an arrangement with the Wearer of White that would spare the lives of *any* man or woman who followed Afhem Muskigo."

"A deal that would have banished my father's soul for all eternity!" Mahi shouted, surprising herself by how loudly this time. The dome made her voice carry like she wasn't used to. Muttering throughout the room buoyed her spirits. She didn't care if anyone agreed with her, only that they were willing to listen.

"Yes, that's right," Mahi went on. "He offered him a Dagger of Damikmagrin after agreeing to a deal with Sir Nikserof. Will you tell us what the arranged price was, Babrak? And I don't mean the people it spared."

"Only a Caleef can sanction exile from the Eternal Current," an afhem spoke up.

Mahi quickly whipped around to face her father, whose lips betrayed the twitch of a smirk. He hadn't told her that, and now she knew why. Her father had another play up his sleeve. Ever the strategist. A part of her was hurt by his secrecy, but the rest of her stood in admiration. She knew that her reaction, her expression, was all the proof other afhems would need to see.

"His holy personage was not here," Babrak said, looking to the listless Caleef for approval and earning none.

"It happened nonetheless," Muskigo said, now standing as well. "My brothers." He looked to Mahi. "And sister. I accepted that banishment for the sake of our people. I saw my failure, and if it were not for Afhem Mahraveh al'Tariq arriving when she did, I would be forever stripped of the Current's rest."

"And what—we should forgive everything because she saved a traitor, and nearly killed me in battle for trying to arrange peace?"

"Whoring yourself out is not peace," Yuri remarked.

Babrak became a charging zhulong, fists clenched. The blades of every Serpent Guard slid halfway from their sheathes, releasing a deafening rasp of metal that stopped him in his tracks. Violence in the throne room when the Caleef wasn't around didn't seem to matter, but he was here now.

"Is it not time for you to leave?" Babrak spat at Yuri's feet.

"Do you think I'm afraid of a man who got torn to pieces like that by a girl?" Yuri replied.

Mahi's jaw clenched at the insult, then she heard a few of the afhems behind her chuckle. Another strategist at work.

"I refused to fight her," Babrak replied dismissively. "I traveled to Nahanab for peace."

"That's true, I don't remember a good fight," Mahraveh

commented. Babrak's lips twisted, and she earned another speck-ling of laughter.

Muskigo stepped forward and faced the Caleef. "Babrak is many things, your Holiness, but in this case, he is right, I should have sought approval for my actions, but when King Liam passed, I saw a chance to change our lives forever. And I saw it in battle. The Glass Kingdom is not what it once was. If we band together, finally, all of us, we no longer have to beg for scraps."

"Have you seen Latiapur?" Babrak said. "Or Abo'Fasaniyah? Or even Nahanab before you ravaged it. We aren't begging. Just because Saujibar is filled with piss and rabble doesn't mean all of the Black Sands is. We live better lives than we ever have before. Our cities are full of life. Full of trade."

"Because we have become like Glassmen. No... not like them. Suckling at their teat. Soon, our skin will be soft and pink as theirs. Our own temples will bear Iam's symbols, as all those in Panping now do. We have lost what made us as strong as the sea."

"My father knows what he did was wrong," Mahraveh said without looking to him for approval. She was starting to under-stand that this room wasn't about permission, it was about influ-ence. She too approached the Caleef. "And if his Holiness would punish him for it, I'm certain Afhem Muskigo would accept any fate. But I have also defeated the Glass army in battle once. Their general is my prisoner. We have a chance to finish what my father started."

"Winning an ambush is far different than victory in open war, *girl*," Babrak said, allowing himself a hearty laugh as he approached. "You drove them back, but barely put a dent in their shield. And word has reached me that they've already retaken the White Bridge, dispelled the Drav Cra, and struck a new alliance with the dwarves of Balonhearth. What do you know about battling all of that after we have lost so much, thanks to your father?"

Now, Mahi knew he was desperate. He'd already played the role of diminishing her because she was a woman, and then she killed every warrior in Tal'du Dromesh.

"I know enough to know that the people who slaughtered my village can't be trusted," Mahi said. "Sir Nikserof was there, I swear it."

The afhems began to chatter.

"Your father did the same to their villages," Babrak countered. "*He* brought this upon them. We should trade their Wearer of White and use him to ease negotiations as we mend this great wound Muskigo caused."

The afhems grew louder at such a valid argument. So much so that Mahi had to shout to hear herself over them. Her blood boiled. Her hands wanted to ram her spear through Babrak's heart, and she might have if she hadn't put it down before entering. Now the custom made sense.

Then Yuri Darkings said, "Or perhaps you resent her because she refused to become one of your wives."

His voice was low, but the man always spoke with such charisma that no din could cover it, and the words got a rise out of Mahi's father. This time, she barred him with her arm, knowing full well what he might do. He and Babrak's rivalry went back to a woman—her mother—someone Mahi barely knew before the Current took her. It wasn't the first feud between afhems fought over a woman, but the children of afhems were off-limits unless offered openly.

"How dare you speak such lies!" Babrak retorted, feigning shock. He hadn't outright asked for Mahi's submission to marriage, but the implication had been made. Mahi was sure of that.

"You think there are any whispers that escape my ears? Glass or Sands, I hear everything," Yuri said.

"I will not suffer rumors from a pink-skin." On that, a majority of the afhems in the room voiced agreement.

"What about the one where you told Sir Nikserof exactly where to find the women and children of the Ayerabi Afhemate?" Yuri said. "Told him exactly when to attack your old rival."

"I would never!" Babrak protested.

Babrak didn't hold back this time. He grabbed Yuri by the throat and heaved him into the air, his feet dangling, kicking. Serpent Guards drew their weapons, but the Glassman wasn't under their protection. Mahi and her father came to Yuri's aid instead. All the afhems stood and hurried to the floor as well.

Mahi couldn't hear anything over all the shouting. Once again, the lack of weapons in the room proved to be the right move. Otherwise, many afhems might have died. Maybe all of them. They tried to tear Babrak away. One jabbed him in his wound, and he lost his grip, dropping Yuri to the floor in a breathless clump. Mahi would have joined the fray, but her father had placed himself in front of her, falling into the unbreakable stance of the black fist. Protecting her, like she was still a child.

She went to squeeze by him, and then she saw. The Caleef stood.

Her father saw next, then Babrak and one by one, all the afhems quieted down and backed away so they could look upon the Caleef.

Sidar Rakun's gaze lifted to regard his subjects. Mahi wasn't sure what she saw in his expression. The black paint made it impossible to tell, but his eyes—the whites stood out like pit lizard eggs in the desert. They were glazed over. Whether it was exhaustion or sadness, she couldn't tell.

"So much fighting…" the Caleef whispered.

"Your Holiness, I—" Babrak began before the Caleef continued on and rendered him silent for once in his life.

"The God of Sand and Sea has forsaken us." The lump in the

Caleef's throat bobbed as he swallowed. He climbed down the dais steps and crossed the room, slowly. No one spoke, no one moved except to make room for him. "Only She remains…"

In those last words, Mahi could finally feel his pain as if it were her own.

Then she saw the flex of the muscles in his shin. He stepped forward once, then again. The afhems might have noticed, but it was too late, and by the time Mahi made it past her father, she too, had missed her chance.

Caleef Sidar Rakun stepped through the Sea Door.

Mahi rushed, along with everyone else. She watched in abject horror as he plummeted down into the raging water and jagged rocks. He'd done it before, decades ago, and survived the fall as all Caleefs must, but that was in faith. This was something else altogether.

The room became a desert night, silent and cold.

"What was that?" an afhem finally spoke.

"Why would he do that?" asked another.

"Is this a test?"

Mahi couldn't match the voices, but it didn't matter, the silence the Caleef's actions inspired made each voice like a thunderclap. She and the others stood around the portal, staring into the darkness where only the greenish glow of mobbing nigh'jels and white caps could be seen. Then, the glow faded, the creatures winking away one by one until total darkness prevailed.

"If you're up there, or down there, let her be the one," Yuri Darkings said quietly, just a step behind Mahi.

Mahi turned briefly toward him, lifting a finger to her lips to shush him.

"I suppose," he said, staring directly into her eyes, "it's time to give faith a try."

Yuri's hand fell upon her shoulder, and he pushed. He was stronger than he appeared. Her sandals slipped on the polished marble floor, and then she followed the Caleef. Wind cradled her as she plummeted. She saw the green and gold glow of the chamber above and all the shocked faces framed in the opening. Yuri fell just behind her. Muskigo grabbed him by his robes in a vain attempt to slow his descent, but the old man slipped away easily.

Mahi twisted through the air, her cheeks sprayed by sand and salt. The last thing she saw clearly was Yuri smash against a cluster of sharp rocks. Then she hit the water, and from so high it felt like she too had slammed onto stone.

With all the ruckus in Yaolin, passing through the channel on the northern end of Lake Yaolin had been no trouble at all. The city guard seemed eager to get people out of the place, even. Gold Grin's ship—which he'd so thoughtfully left for them to borrow—was fully outfitted for the journey through the icy Covenstan Depths, too.

When they'd left, Whitney only cared for a moment how Gold Grin and the other pirates would get back to land after Whitney took their rowboats, too. But his concern quickly vanished. They could face Aihara Na's wrath for all Whitney cared.

Presently, Whitney and Tum Tum crossed *the Reba's* innards. Aquira lumbered along ahead of them, not bothering to fly. She'd spent the day, like every day since they hit the bitter north, soaring ahead and using her fire to clear a path through the ice to allow for a faster journey.

It had been weeks since the incident at the Red Tower, but the implications of what Whitney and Kazimir had seen inside the Well had permeated his dreams and his waking thoughts.

Nesilia had spoken to him again. She'd said, in no uncertain terms, that doom was coming, and it had arrived in the form of

Gold Grin. Luckily for him, Kazimir and Sigrid had been there to save the day, but Whitney couldn't count on that kind of luck forever. Nesilia was clearly threatened by his bond with Sora and as good as he felt knowing that his friend was still in there, it was equally terrifying. He had to take a stand. Against a goddess. A real one this time, and without Torsten.

"Crazy day when you wish Torsten Unger were around, huh, girl?" Whitney said to Aquira.

"Huh?" Tum Tum asked.

"Nothing."

Lucindur, Gentry, Talwyn, and half of what remained of their Glintish troupe awaited them in the garish galley still covered in Gold Grin's trinkets. Whitney put on a smile to try and mask his fear.

Lucindur had her salfio across her lap and fiddled with the new strings, tuning, then tuning again. The rest of the troupe were on the top deck, watching over the ship after dealing with an exasperating Tum Tum teaching them what little he knew about sailing. The dwarf deserved the break. *The Reba* was a fine vessel, but impossible to handle alone, and Kazimir and Sigrid were of no help since it was daytime.

They were headed for a dock just west of Glinthaven, with a path through the mountains. When Lucindur reluctantly agreed to help, again. Those were her terms. They'd take a short detour and bring the troupe safely to their homeland. She feared using the city docks in case Gold Grin's ship was recognized.

Gentry stood without making eye contact as soon as Whitney came around the corner. He held out his arm for Aquira to climb up and headed toward one of the crews' quarters. He'd hardly spoken to Whitney since the incident with Gold Grin. Whitney laid into him pretty good about how he could have died, could have gotten everyone killed, could have wrecked the whole plan. Whitney wasn't sure if the boy was embarrassed or angry.

"Hi," Talwyn said as Whitney approached. She patted the bench and scooted to give him room to sit, but only a bit.

"Hey," Whitney answered, not taking his eyes off Gentry as he closed the door and locked himself in.

"Just give him time," Lucindur said, frowning.

"What he did was foolish."

"Aye, and ye never done nothin stupid for someone else, have ye, Fierstown?" Tum Tum quipped, slapping Whitney on the knee. He plopped down into a seat, somehow having found a bottle of fine brandy, and took a swig.

"I don't know," Whitney said. "All my stupid deeds only affected stupid me."

"I know a Panpingese girl who'd say different," Tum Tum said. He offered the bottle to Lucindur, who politely declined.

At the mention of Sora, Talwyn lowered her eyes to the fire. "I don't understand why we're trusting those creatures," she said. "We should all be helping you."

"We aren't trusting *them*," Lucindur responded before Whitney could. "We are trusting Whitney."

"I guess." Talwyn rubbed her arms and edged closer to Whitney even though they were already touching at the elbows. "It's cold."

"Aren't ye from up here?" Tum Tum asked.

It was true, Glinthaven was just on the east side of the Covenstan Depths, but Myen Elnoir was set in a valley that received warmer winds thanks to a current coming up from the Boiling Waters, leaving it brisk, but never freezing.

"I still think Gentry should join the rest of you in Glinthaven," Whitney said, bringing the conversation back to the boy.

"You think anything you could've said would've stopped him from following you onto that lake?" Lucindur said. "He may not be your son, but he doesn't have parents. He'd have swum behind the ship. He even left Aquira with us. For you."

"Then he really is a fool," Tum Tum said. He slapped Whitney again, and they all laughed, though, there was very little mirth in it.

After that, they all remained quiet while they ate something Talwyn had thrown together. It wasn't horrible. It wasn't good either. Though, he imagined beautiful Talwyn hadn't spent much of her life needing to cook. Besides, she was kind enough to give Francesca a much-needed night off.

Dishes and silverware clanked, signaling the completion of supper, and Whitney leaned back against a thick pole, hands behind his head. One of the troupe members carried a pot up to the deck for the rest.

"This is dangerous," Whitney said after a long exhale. "For all of us going. We are literally walking into a den of bloodsucking killers to fight a goddess. I wouldn't blame anyone if they decided to stay on the ship when we get there, and I don't blame those who leave now."

"I wouldn't be here if I planned to stay on the ship," Lucindur said. "The troupe will flourish under Benon and Talwyn's lead. I kept her from the knowledge of this instrument for a reason."

Whitney could feel Talwyn staring at him, as if begging him to make her stay. He made sure not to look back. She needed to go. More than anything, so that Lucindur would be able to concentrate on Nesilia. It was the same reason he wanted Gentry to stay in Glinthaven.

"Good. There's no reason to let any more people risk death than those we need," Whitney said.

"He's right," Talywn said, terse. "I don't want to stay with Benon, but I don't want to go die either. I wouldn't stand a chance against even a man with a sword, much less an upyr or a goddess."

Before Lucindur could respond, Whitney said, "Maybe we could convince Gentry to go with you."

"He's a free person," Lucindur said. "We all are. That's what a troupe is all about."

"Tell that to the Pompares," Whitney said. "Oh, you can't."

"That's not—" Talwyn protested. Lucindur interrupted her with a tug on the arm.

"He's just frustrated."

"Aye, we all are," Tum Tum added. He pushed out from the table and backed away slowly, beard lifted from a nervous grin. "Better go check topside. Should be at the port soon."

Whitney said nothing, just merely pushed off as well and headed toward Gentry's room. He thought a full belly might help, but it only felt like a pit in his stomach. He stopped before Gentry's door and stood there awhile. Finally, he raised his fist to knock when the door opened.

"Oh, hey," Whitney said, awkwardly lowering his hand.

"What do you want?" Gentry said as he turned back into his room. "I have heard you standing there, breathing, for the last ten minutes."

"We're just about to dock."

"Great."

"Can we talk?"

"Can't stop you," Gentry said, taking a seat.

Aquira curled up next to him at the foot of the straw bed. Little swirls of steam rose from her nostrils as the heat mingled with the cold air. Clearing a path through ice had to be exhausting for a dragon, much less a wyvern her size.

"You're getting off here and going with Talwyn and the others," Whitney said. "You can't go further with us."

"Shogging Exile, I can't," Gentry snapped.

"Hey! Watch your mouth."

"You are one to talk." Gentry stood. Aquira slowly rose with him.

Whitney could see the confusion in her eyes. None of this was fair to the wyvern. She was Sora's, then Whitney's, now Gentry's, but in truth, Whitney wasn't sure she was one to be owned by anyone. *She* chose who to stay with. And one of Whitney's fears in dismissing Gentry was that she'd follow him, and they'd lose her power in the fight.

"I'm going with you," Gentry continued, "and you can't stop me."

"That's where you're wrong."

"What are you going to do—sic your upyr on me?"

"If I have to!" Whitney took a deep breath and let it out. "Let's start over."

Gentry didn't respond verbally, but he sat back down, which gave Whitney the sense that the boy might actually be willing to listen to reason.

"Gentry, what you did, following us, was reckless and dangerous," Whitney said. "You could have been killed."

"Yeah, you already made that clear back in Panping. Is there anything else?"

Whitney rubbed his eyes with his palms. "I made a promise."

"And you have probably broken a million in your lifetime based on your stories, so what? What is so different about this one?"

"To a woman on her deathbed. I told her… Modera Pompare, I'd keep you safe."

"Do you even remember her?" Gentry asked. "Do you know how many times Fadra backhanded me? Beat me with a belt? It might have been his hand, but it was her will. If she cared about me so much, why didn't she show it while she was alive?"

A tear dripped down Gentry's cheek, and he quickly wiped it away. Aquira nuzzled her snout against his neck. Gentry stroked her head, and she plopped down, chin resting on his thigh.

"I don't know," Whitney admitted. "But that wasn't me. All I know is, in my life, I've cared about exactly two people. One of them is in this room with me, and the other is being possessed by a goddess. In order to save one, I have to make sure the other doesn't get killed. I can't be worried about you in there. I can't risk losing focus."

"You mean you can't risk losing Sora…"

"Or you!" Whitney whisper-shouted. "If either of you gets hurt in there, I'll never forgive myself."

Gentry scoffed.

"What are you 'pffing' at?"

"You. Your ego is huge."

"My—my ego?" Whitney asked, incredulous.

"Not everything is your responsibility, you know," Gentry said. "Not everyone's life is yours to save. Sometimes, people have to make their own choices. My whole life… growing up under a bridge, living with a family that was mine but not mine… I didn't make any of those choices. Those choices were made for me—by my parents, by the *swinlars* when they decided I was better off traveling with a performance troupe than growing up in their precious kingdom."

"So, what—you want to exercise your right to choose now— when choosing to go with us most likely means choosing death?"

Gentry sighed. "Do you know what it's like to have no purpose?"

Whitney opened his mouth to answer, but Gentry interrupted.

"I don't think you do. You've always had a plan. 'Whitney Fierstown, World's Greatest Thief, slayer of gods and goddesses, the filcher fantastic himself.' I've heard your speech so many times, I could recite it myself. If I had a speech, you know what it would say? 'Gentry…'"

He went quiet, and Whitney didn't dare speak up.

"That's it! That's all it would say. 'Gentry…' I don't know my parents. I don't know my family name. I've never done a thing worth doing. Then I… I killed that man…"

Whitney winced.

"No, you don't get it," Gentry said. "I'm not upset. That was the only great thing I've ever done."

"There's nothing great about killing."

"Do you know that man was heading toward Talwyn when I struck him down? I saved her. *Me*."

"You did." Whitney moved forward, Gentry backed away. "But what's on its way to the Citadel isn't just some crazed group of cultists. When I was in Elsewhere, I saw things I could never unsee. I can't describe the horrors."

"That doesn't sound scary."

"The Glintish are known for art, right? I promise you, the greatest painter in Glinthaven couldn't begin to capture the likeness of those things. And that's what Nesilia has under her command. Even if she didn't, the Buried Goddess herself is going to be there. She's real. She's powerful. And from what I've seen, she cares about nothing but revenge and making Iam's children—apparently, that's you and me, regardless of whether or not we give a shog about Him—she wants to make us suffer for 'forgetting about her.'"

Outside, the ship broke through another layer of ice and slowed down. Loud as all the racket was, the silence that passed between them felt louder.

"Can I ask you something?" Gentry asked when the clamor ended.

"I can't stop you," Whitney said, smiling.

"What's worse… living, always with the potential to do something great, but never doing it, or achieving that potential and dying while doing it? Is life worth living if you don't feel alive?"

"Iam's shog," Whitney swore. "If you didn't already know my answer, I don't think you'd have asked it."

"I survived Drad Mak and the Drav Cra," Gentry said. "I survived the riots in Yarrington at the Dawning. And then, those pirates, Gold Grin and his men. I know those are nothing compared to Nesilia, but if she beats you, if she wins, I die anyway, right? We all do."

Whitney eyed the boy with a gentleness he didn't think himself capable of. He was no leader. Again, he wished Torsten were there. He'd know what to say. He'd have led this ragtag group into the finest battle ever witnessed, and he'd know how to get Gentry to make the smart move.

But the kid had a point. It was win or die. No matter where Gentry was, if Nesilia came out victorious, Elsewhere would break loose, and those left alive would be wishing for death.

"Please, Whitney?" Gentry implored.

That might have been the first time Gentry had ever called him that. Not Mr. Fierstown. Not Mr. Whitney. Just Whitney.

"I helped in Yaolin," Gentry went on. "I can help again. Lucindur's always talking about fate, what if I'm supposed to be here? Plus, Aquira will keep me safe. And then we'll keep *you* safe."

Whitney scratched at the back of his neck. *Is this how my parents felt around me every gods-damned day?*

He remembered how he reacted every time they tried to keep him from an adventure with Sora or scolded him for getting into trouble. He'd learned in Elsewhere that they cared, but it only drove him away.

"Please," Gentry said again.

"Fine," Whitney groaned. "You can come."

Gentry was midway through another reasoning, then sputtered over the rest of his words. His countenance changed abruptly. "Wait… what?"

"But! Don't get excited yet," Whitney said, sticking out a finger. "I've got conditions."

"Okay…." He wrapped his arm around Aquira and pulled her tight.

"For starters, that's enough pouting. Enough anger. What happened back in Yaolin happened. No changing that, and it brought us this ship. We don't bring it up again, deal?"

"Deal."

"When we get to the Citadel, you do as I say, even if you don't agree."

"Absolutely," Gentry agreed.

"And finally." Whitney took a second to compose himself. He couldn't believe the words about to come out of his mouth. "If it comes down to you living or me living… it's you. It's always you. Got that?"

The kid hesitated but nodded.

"All right, then." Whitney then turned to Aquira. "And you girl, we need you most of all." Her ears perked up. Whitney crouched to stare straight into her big yellow eyes. "This is Sora we're talking about. I know under those scales you care about her more than anything. Anything it takes, right?"

She lifted her snout and released a low grunt. A puff of smoke swirled up from her nostrils.

"She'll never give up," Gentry attested.

"No, she won't, will she?" Whitney reached out timidly, then scratched the billowy skin underneath her neck which inflated whenever she blew fire. She was always odd around him, but she let him do it. "She's the most important member of our group."

"That's right," Gentry said, beaming.

He squeezed her close, and Whitney regarded the two before turning to leave. "We're close. Get some rest, and then start saying your goodbyes to Talwyn and the others. Aquira, we could use your help, girl."

Gentry agreed, and Whitney closed the door behind him, Aquira on his shoulder. He drew a long, exasperated breath. He had some goodbyes of his own to handle.

The wind tore across *the Reba's* deck and slapped Whitney across the face like death's icy palm. The colorless sky went on endlessly, not a bird or cloud in sight. Just gray, gray, and a bit more gray. Scant for the wind and gentle waves, it was silent until not for the first time, a chunk of ice scraped against the hull. It was harmless to the vessel, but that didn't keep Whitney from cringing every time he heard what sounded like the hull snapping in two.

The ship was tied to a crummy old dock at a Glintish trading post while the troupe he'd helped survive debarked. Now, they could work to rebuild their reputation as entertainers without the Pompares holding them down.

Lucindur stood at the railing of the quarter-deck beside him, holding on so tight her knuckles went white. She watched as Talwyn and Gentry walked down the ramp, bidding each other farewell. Gentry carried her belongings for her as planned, Aquira perched atop his shoulder. Benon tried to hurry Talwyn along, out of the cold. Whitney had heard her sobbing when she and Lucy shared a private goodbye in the cabins, but it was part of the compromise Lucindur had made.

"You'll see her again," Whitney assured her.

"I'd be with her if I knew what was smart," Lucindur replied.

"They'll be safe here."

"Not if we fail." She turned to Whitney, her features painted by a dark brush.

"You can still go with them. It'll ruin the whole plan, but hey... free people, right?" He smiled a weak smile.

Lucindur shook her head slowly. "No. I have felt Nesilia's power, as you have. There are so few of us Lightmancers left. Perhaps, I am the only one. It is fate that I, who have carried our ancient art down through the generations, was placed before you.

The only way the upyr's plan to bind Nesilia to the bar guai will work is if I'm able to open her mind long enough that we can isolate them for you."

"*My* plan," Whitney grumbled. "But… how do we know?" The plan felt solid back in the tower, but now, all he could think about was them having no choice but to feed Sora to a monstrous wianu. If in the moment they had to, she and Nesilia couldn't be separated, he wasn't sure what he'd do.

"Did you know our art came into existence after the God-Feud and the Culling—when the boundaries between our world and those of the dead shattered? Desperate, we learned how to rip open and free the possessed minds."

"Why is Kazimir so angry with Lightmancers, then? Isn't that a good thing?"

"Even the best ideas can be twisted by the greedy," Lucindur said. "To control minds is to wield empires. We tilted the scales, and their lords re-balanced them. A shadow war long ago that we lost."

Whitney slowly released a mouthful of chilly air. "Depressing. Still, that's why I don't do books—especially history ones." He grinned, desperate to lighten the mood. Lucindur smirked, but he could tell it was forced. "I know you don't want to do this, Lucy. It means more than you know."

"You returned my people home after so much horror," she said. "I can't deny the evil I felt any longer. Even as the cultists murdered and looted, it was there. The upyr are right—something I never thought I'd say—the balance has shifted too far this time. I can't sit out."

"What if Nesilia doesn't let us back in?" Whitney asked.

"An acrobat who fears he'll fall, will fall. We can only stick to our plan. Sora's love for you drew her out from Nesilia's influence last time. It will again. We only need a second."

Whitney nodded.

Lucy glanced up at the raised sails. "The wind favors us. We should continue north soon. Are you sure about Gentry? Every league we sail, I sense her presence strengthening. It's like a weight on my heart."

"I'm not sure about anything."

"Goodbyes are over," Kazimir said from the threshold of the Captain's cabin. The door cracked open, but he dared not step outside. Though the clouds dulled the sun's power, even this small amount of daylight remained crippling to his kind.

"My thoughts exactly." Lucindur spent one more moment staring at Talwyn, who looked up from the docks. She smiled her pretty, perfect smile, then she turned.

Whitney looked at her as well, and her features tightened. Then she nodded. He glanced back at Tum Tum, who stood ready to let the mainsail drop and get them moving the moment they were unmoored.

"Your daughter deserves a king, Lucy," Whitney said. "She's an amazing girl."

Words of agreement were no sooner on Lucindur's lips than Whitney drew a dagger, and sliced one of the ropes tied to the docks. It splashed into the icy river, and he hurried to the next one to do the same.

It happened so fast, Gentry didn't realize until Whitney reached the ramp. "Mr. Fierstown, wait!" he shouted. He spun away from Talwyn, but she wrapped her arms around his chest and held tight.

Whitney kicked the ramp off, letting it plunge with the ropes. Then, he continued on his path along the port side rails, slicing the ropes. They had spare enough to dock anywhere, though, where they were going, he doubted there'd be harbors.

"Forgive me," Whitney said softly to himself.

"No, Mr. Fierstown, you promised!" Gentry yelled.

He squirmed and kicked, but couldn't break free. Talwyn was

thin, but she had the strength of a dancer. It wasn't until Aquira sprang into action that she lost her grip. The wyvern flapped up and screeched. She didn't blow fire, but even as small as she was, she painted an intimidating figure at full wingspan. Talwyn stumbled back.

Gentry sprinted and ran for the last rope still attached to the bow. By then, the wind had caught the unfurled sail, and a single boy wouldn't be able to stop it. But the force would pull him into the icy river.

"Whitney, I'm coming!" he shouted, through a mess of tears. "I need to help!"

Whitney climbed up the sterncastle as fast as he could. He knew it wouldn't be easy, but he'd gotten Lucindur and Tum Tum in on the plan right after leaving Gentry's room. It was the right thing to do, even if it made him the bad guy.

He nearly reached the last rope, when Aquira slammed down on the railing. She roared at him, a deep, buffering bellow made louder by the empty wind. Whitney stopped in his tracks. He'd seen a city burn to cinders with the wyvern's help, seen her blaze through soldiers like wheat. And he'd seen her angry, just as she was now.

"Aquira, please," Whitney begged. "This is probably a suicide mission. He should be far away from it. He deserves to live."

Aquira continued to glare, her nostrils fuming and pushing out smoke.

"Aquira, Sora needs us," he went on. "Him being there will only distract us… distract *me*. And then we'll have Sora again. Forever this time."

The wyvern glared a moment more, then spread her wings wider. The skin under her throat inflated, filling with flame. She reared back, and Whitney winced, expecting to feel the burn. He closed his eyes, but he only felt heat.

When he looked again, Aquira had turned the last rope to

ashes, leaving Gentry standing at the edge of the dock holding the other end of the line. Whitney had never seen a boy so heartbroken; maybe only his younger self in Elsewhere. Talwyn stood at his side and pulled him into an embrace.

Screeching, Aquira soared over Whitney's shoulder, and then landed on the *Reba's* prow where she could continue her job of melting ice to ease the journey. Streaks of orange painted their path ahead through the fog.

"He'll never forgive you for this," Lucindur said, waiting for Whitney on the deck.

"I'm okay with that," Whitney said. *I hope*, he didn't add. "At least he'll survive what's to come." He went to step by, but Lucindur lay a hand upon his shoulder.

"You're a good man, Whitney Fierstown. He is lucky to have you, and so is your Sora."

Whitney patted her hand but kept his head turned slightly so she wouldn't see the tears welling in the corners of his eyes. Words didn't come, so he merely nodded and continued along.

The ship started to drift faster upstream. Tum Tum stood by the mast and offered Whitney a single nod of approval.

"We'll be better off not worryin'," he said. Then he gave Whitney a slap on the side and made his way to lower the front sail, pointing and barking commands at Aquira.

Whitney found a seat on a barrel near the Captain's cabin. "Why does anyone live up here?" he said to Kazimir or Sigrid through the crack in their door. Either or neither, depending on who was listening. "It's freezing."

Kazimir pushed the door open halfway and pointed toward the gray sky. Light hit his finger, but it only steamed rather than flaking away, burning. "Where is the sun?" he asked.

"I—behind the clouds?" Whitney stammered. "I don't know... am I an astronomer?"

"Consider the benefits for one such as me, living in a place where the sun is afraid to shine in its full power. Besides, this is warm compared to Brek," Kazimir said. "The Motherland is for the strong and unbreakable."

"I must be weak and brittle then." Whitney shivered and pulled his cloak tight. "Are we there yet?"

"Have ye always been so useless?" Sigrid asked. She sat on the cartographer's table beside the bar guai, fidgeting, unable to stay still. She'd been that way since the moment she'd tasted Kai's blood. Whitney knew the signs. It's how manaroot addicts got, and there were plenty of those in the shady places he'd once frequented.

"One of my more charming attributes."

"The Citadel—Svay Sobor iz Nohzi—is a few days away," Kazimir said.

"I still think we should have raised an army," Whitney said. "I've seen what Nesilia can do. If we went to the Governor of Panping and dropped Torsten Unger's name, he'd listen."

"Your foolish people sent soldiers after us for their Queen, and they all died. The Citadel is the most secure place in all Pantego. Older than anything but the gods, and invisible to mortal eyes."

"Invisible?" Whitney scoffed.

"Why does this peasant laugh?" Sigrid asked. She scratched at her neck and shifted her jaw. Whitney wished her master would put her back in her muzzle.

"Wow," Whitney said. "Some manners. I am laughing because even with all I've seen, I'm not sure how anything you've described could be *invisible*."

"Perhaps you've not seen all there is to see," Kazimir offered. "This world is more than what can be felt by mortal hands. Nesilia may be strong… she *is* strong… but she's been buried for longer than even I have been alive. She won't be at full strength, not yet. Especially not within Sora's body. If she seeks to strike the Citadel out of vengeance against us, then let it be vengeance which undoes her. She won't be the first."

"I guess her going to the one place on Pantego filled with murderous immortals isn't smart."

"That is precisely why we must get there first to warn them. The Sanguine Lords will listen to reason. When they hear the old gods are coming, they will mount up on the backs of dragons."

"What?" Whitney said. "You mean that metaphorically, right? Dragons are extinct—"

"Aquira, there!" Tum Tum shouted from the crow's nest. A breath later, *the Reba* rumbled through a huge chunk of ice. "By Meungor and all the gods, what happened to havin a real crew?"

"They are extinct, right?" Whitney asked Kazimir, ignoring Tum Tum.

Kazimir smiled, his fangs protruding over his lower lip.

"Right?" Whitney asked again. He turned and squinted to just barely make out the distant mountains which blocked Brekliodad through the fog and the ever-darkening sky, expecting to see massive flying beasts over the peaks.

"If we make it there first," Kazimir said, "we will stand a chance of burying Nesilia once more—this time, for good. Now, go and help the others, so we don't sink before we arrive. My apprentice is in need of a lesson."

The door nearly shut, then Kazimir said, "Oh, and Whitney. Well done with the boy. We can't have distractions now."

Then the door slammed, leaving Whitney to turn and look upon the deck. *At least I have the approval of a murderous upyr,* he thought. Oddly, it didn't make him feel one bit better.

What remained without Gentry was a motley crew: a one-and-a-half-eared thief, a dwarf, two upyr, a Lightmancer bard, and a wyvern. If Whitney weren't a part of it, he'd have thought someone was setting up a particularly in-depth joke.

The truth of it was there was no joke in sight. Whitney had

spent most of his years turning life into one big festival. From the time he'd left Troborough until this very day, Whitney had no place to call home, and he liked it that way. However, now, looking at these people he'd come to think of as friends—strange as they were—he imagined there could be no greater thrill than settling down and enjoying life with loved ones.

But first, he had to get Sora back.

XXV

THE DAUGHTER

Mahi tumbled and twisted, body torn this way and that by the current. Rock and coral scraped her everywhere. They called it the Boiling Waters only because the sea was so rough it looked like the inside of a stew pot over an open flame, but as Mahi's body was punished, it felt scorching now too. Like her skin was bubbling with white-hot fire. The pain was so immeasurable she could hardly think. When she did, all she could picture was the face of the man who'd thrown her in here to die; the man who'd betrayed her, and that even if she survived this somehow, she could never have vengeance. She'd already seen his body broken on jagged rocks.

She had failed.

A dead Caleef, a betrayal by her father's own ally in the Boiling Keep—they'd nearly exposed Babrak for the bastard he was, and now, it was for nothing. Her father would never be able to regain the confidence of the greater afhemdom. Not a soul would make a move until the next Caleef was scooped out of the sea, and sometimes, that took years.

No, it's not too late, she told herself. Swinging her arms frantically to try and battle the ripping tide, kicking her legs, hoping to hit anything that might propel her upward, she strove for the surface. Though she wasn't even sure what up was. The deeper she plunged, the more darkness engulfed her…

Until the water calmed in the far depths.

Her eyelids grew heavy as the last bit of air abandoned her.

Is this really how it ends? Mahi wondered if that was what every man or woman asked before their mortal body died and their soul was cast onto the Eternal Current.

The beating of her heart slowed. She knew that soon she'd be with Shavi and her mother, Farhan, and sweet Jumaat. It'd feel closer to home than she'd felt in far too long, at least. She could stop being afraid, every single day, of the world she knew falling apart.

Her eyes closed.

Her heart stopped.

She felt it come to a halt—it didn't seem possible, but she felt it. She couldn't explain the sensation. It was like breathing, and she only missed it when it left her.

Only, she didn't die. She found herself at the bottom of deep water, surrounded by the ruins of some ancient civilization. Ruptured columns and domed buildings, all covered by coral and sea growth. She couldn't see the ancient spirits around her, but she could feel them teeming about.

"Mahraveh." She heard her name whispered all around her, each syllable drawn out like gentle waves washing ashore. "Mahraveh."

"Who is that?" she asked, shocked to find herself able to speak as if she weren't submerged. It was like she was a part of the water, and it, a part of her. She simply floated, weightless, maybe even bodiless.

"You know who I am," came the answer.

Now, Mahi could tell the voice was deep and masculine. The

water rippled in its wake. In front of her, she could almost see a face forming from the swirling wisps of black sand.

Mahi dared not speak the answer. However, she couldn't deny the truth.

"Rarely is one so worthy the first to fall," the God of Sand and Sea said.

"Is this real?" she asked.

"If you're asking if you're alive or dead, to me there is no such difference."

"Then I'm in the Eternal Current?"

"You are in between, my child. It is not your time, and yet, here you are. None of this is foretold. Her influence spreads wide now. It has destroyed my chosen vessel, and now, the Shesaitju people face darkness as well."

"I… What are you talking about?" Mahi asked, confused, and even a bit scared.

"There is no time to explain. In communing with you now, I have exposed myself to Her."

"Who?"

"Me," an equally deep, but sultry voice filled the water. It began to ripple stronger, more violent. Mahi wasn't sure why she felt afraid, only that it overwhelmed her entire being.

"Sister, how did you find me so quickly?" the God of Sand and Sea questioned. His dread, too, was palpable.

"You know we've always been connected, Caliphar."

Caliphar? It was a name for her God which Mahi had never heard before.

"I've been waiting for you to open yourself up to me," the woman continued. "Curious that this is the frail, pathetic creature who let me in." A pale woman walked by Mahi as if on land. Her head was covered in seaweed so none of her features could be seen, and as she turned, it was clear she too was formless. She was blackness that threatened to suck Mahi in.

An arm reached out and stroked her cheek like the delicate tendrils of a beautiful plant. The power—Mahi could almost taste it, if such a thing were possible.

"Not forgotten, are you?" the woman said. "No, not really. But underestimated? Yes. Yes. I could make something grand out of her."

"She is not yours," the God of Sand and Sea said with authority. The watery form of his face rushed forward and dispelled the darkness. Seaweed flaked away into nothingness.

"They will all be mine," the woman answered, her voice almost an echo.

"Our time in this realm has come to an end, sister. You must let go."

"Like you?" The seaweed creature reappeared to Mahi's left. "You remained here, hiding in the waves, playing your little games with these people. Do you remember our first game?"

"You were always playing games."

"Ah, but there was the one."

Mahi couldn't move now, but her eyes darted from side to side, trying to keep up with the ethereal voices which penetrated from all sides. The dark being formed again, swirling about within the water like a playful seal.

"Do you not recall the time when I hid for all those years, waiting for you to find me?" the woman went on.

"Yes, within the Webbed Woods," the God of Sand and Sea said. "And this land starved in your absence. All but that overgrown place which fed on your power for so long even the boundaries of Elsewhere and Pantego blurred. How could I forget?"

"But I won, didn't I?"

"You always did."

"So, you know how patient I can be," she said. "How long I've been waiting for my return."

"And you've come for me? You could have, at least, had the

decency to show up in your mortal body so I could show you what power I still wield."

The blackness expanded, filling in features on the God of Sand and Sea's amorphous form. The current shook it away, breaking him apart. Weeds filled in from every direction and coated the haven of light beneath the sea in total darkness.

"You stood against us in the feud," the woman said. "Turned the seas into our enemy."

"I stood for you, Sister!" the God of Sand and Sea bellowed. Mahi felt the seabed quake beneath her. "I stood against an old god using you to consolidate his power over this realm, like any good brother should."

"No, you were being a coward! You could have broken through, unburied me, but here in your waves, you remained, more eager to watch your gray slaves slaughter themselves in your honor than free me."

"That's a lie," his voice became soft. "I stopped feeling you in this realm. You passed on."

"I went nowhere! I was trapped in between. Stuck, voiceless. I could feel time pass as the mortals do. Ticking away slowly—so slowly—with the rise and fall of light. Eternal Current… clever name… though, you have no idea what eternity feels like."

"And where was Iam after you were sacrificed for his victory?" he asked.

"Don't worry. My beloved Iam will get his just deserts. Bliss has already seen what I am now capable of; what power true faith provides, not this game you and Iam—and even dear Meungor— play with your subjects. It's lamentable."

"What do you want, Nesilia?"

Hearing that name struck Mahi's heart. She wasn't sure why, but she knew she'd heard it before. Maybe in stories and legends from the ancient days, the kind of stories only Glassmen tell because they refuse to move on from lore and legend. All she knew, was that a second wave of fear overcame her, more pungent than before. She was terrified.

"I breathed life into the hills and the forests of this world," Nesilia said. "Without me, it would be rock and death. Dead. Yet, I was the one to be forgotten, locked in the heart of the world? I want what I deserve. Iam won because of me."

"Yes, he won… alone," the God of Sand and Sea said. "Like you said, I hid in the sand beneath the sea. Meungor in the mountains. Wherever the others you and Iam turned into those monstrous wianu couldn't find us, until they, finally, stopped looking."

"They'll be removed from the equation soon enough," Nesilia warned.

"The undying? You know they can't be. You and Iam went too far."

"We did what had to be done."

"And you weren't the only one forgotten because of it, Sister."

"The only one on the winning side."

"He used you."

"He loved me!" Nesilia spat.

The darkness frayed across Mahi's vision. Weeds were slung like knives. Mahi couldn't move, but she wanted to hunch over and grasp her unbeating heart. It felt like she'd lost Shavi and Jumaat all over again. She could see him, standing in Tal'du Dromesh, the color sucked out of him until he was shriveled on the ground like dried fruit.

"Lie to yourself, Sister," the God of Sand and Sea said. "Lie to me. But leave this world alone. The feud did enough damage. Every day, I feel myself growing weaker here. It's time for us to move on."

"No. You've had your time!" Nesilia declared. "Now it is mine." With her every word, Mahi's sense of terror augmented. "You don't have to be afraid anymore, big brother. I was lost, but now I am found. You can join me. The seas and the land as one again."

"You know I can't."

"I'm in your head, Caliphar. I can feel how weak you are. This girl will be the last to bear your essence, won't she? The last of your eyes and ears up above. You know you cannot stand against me. Don't be a fool."

"I've always been a fool when it comes to you," Caliphar, the God of Sand and Sea said. "No longer. You think you can rule all these mortals, but that's not ever what it was about. We've become whispers in the backs of their minds, Nesilia, that is all. It's time to go home."

"You disappoint me once again. I'll see you soon, big brother. But don't worry, I'll be gentle on her."

The darkness raced at Mahi, enveloping her, filling her lungs and heart. She felt hopeless—wanted to let go of everyone and everything. She would have screamed if she could have.

And then it was gone.

Her body rolled across something firm. Her fingers scooped wet sand. She coughed, and water bubbled out. Weeds, shells, and dead nigh'jels coated her arms and legs, carried by the gentle waves.

"Mahraveh." A voice, calm and sweet. Then, a gentle force lifted her from her chin to her knees. She had a body again.

Mahi found herself staring into the stark white eyes of a Siren. The sand, which comprised her being, swirled into the figure of a woman, all at once beautiful and terrifying.

"You." Mahi coughed. This was the Siren who'd taken Jumaat from her. Mahi could never forget those eyes. "What happened… I…"

The Siren hushed her. "Caliphar has chosen you to carry his essence, my daughter."

"What?" She coughed again. More water gushed out—more than should have been humanly possible to contain.

"I am the last of his will. The end of his Current. He always said that when a child of the Light sacrificed himself, I would go. I am his heart, now you will be. She comes, Daughter. Without relent. There can be no hiding any longer."

"Who?"

"The end," the Siren said. "You felt her. She's beyond reason. You must bring our people together, or we will fade into darkness. The Kingdom of Glass is not your enemy. Not anymore."

"What darkness?" Mahi pleaded. "I don't understand what you're asking of me."

"Time to come together is running out," the Siren warned. "Your union will be in life, or in death. It is in your hands now."

Before Mahi could ask anything else, the sand seized her. She was wrenched upright, gasping for air, her back arched, and the Siren rushed forward through her chest. It felt like she was being pried open. Another scream rattled forth from her lips, but it was squelched as water poured past her lips and flooded her mouth.

Mahi was drowning again. Only this time, she didn't tumble aimlessly. The water whirled around her, filled with creatures and life, glowing green with nigh' jels. At first, the coral and the shells cut her, peeling away her skin until only pink flesh remained. She could smell the blood, and not only hers. The shrill cries of nigh'-jels engulfed her. She had no idea they could even make sounds.

Then, the pain stopped. Mahi found herself on her hands and knees in the black sand, chest heaving. She looked up, and the light of Pantego's moons bathed her naked body. Then she looked down and saw her hand. Every inch of it was covered in blackness beyond her natural gray skin. Her gaze followed the blackness to her wrist, then up her arm, to her chest and legs. It was everywhere, dark as pitch, covering all the tattoos and scars she'd earned in her short time as a warrior—all the things that told the story of who she was.

Mahi's hands balled as she stood. The corpses of nigh'jels and other creatures dripped off her. She didn't just feel the sand against her bare feet, she could sense every single grain. And the air against her sodden cheeks—she knew where it came from, where it was going. The waves against her ankles, too.

She could feel all the shifting currents of her world. Now she knew why Sidar Rakun's painted skin bubbled and peeled upon his return. She knew why he was broken. The God of Sand and Sea hadn't forsaken them, he'd merely moved on. She knew in the same way all those chosen before her must have known the moment they emerged from the Boiling Waters when they should have been dead.

She was no longer Mahraveh of the Ayerabi, of the al'Tariq, or any other afhemate.

She was the Caleef.

XXVI

THE REBEL

Muskigo sat in the Boiling Keep, staring through the hole in the floor, that portal which had once seemed so blameless—a tool of dealing justice, nothing more. Now it felt like a hole pierced through his own heart.

Shavi's death struck hard, but she'd lived a long, worthy life in service to his afhemate. Farhan and Impili—they, like so many other warriors, fell with honor, knowing full well what they'd been fighting for.

But Mahraveh… his little sand mouse… It'd been days, and still, Muskigo had no idea who to ask about why Yuri Darkings would've murdered her. His God certainly wasn't answering. Yuri had been talking strangely ever since their reunion, reminiscing, but what was there to be gained by Mahi's death? Surely, he could have killed someone, anyone else to regain favor with his people, if that was his goal. Muskigo, himself, hadn't been more than another step away. If he'd plummeted, surely the petulant King of Glass would have thrown a celebration in honor of Yuri Darkings, the rebel-slayer.

All Muskigo knew for sure was that he'd been the one to put Yuri beside her. A traitor of the highest order and he'd trusted that *pis'truda* enough to let him into these chambers; to let him guide his daughter. It may have been Yuri's hand, but Muskigo had killed her.

There was a sudden pain in his hands, and he noticed he was squeezing so hard his nails drew blood, and his jaw ached from gritting his teeth. It was all he could do to keep his rage in check.

The palace sages and eunuchs stood around the gilded Sea Door which was decorated with shells and coral. One by one, they blessed men arriving from across the Black Sands as they were stripped down, doused in nigh'jel blood, and coated in sand from the seabed. They were presented a bowl to spit in; their water to mingle with all those who'd come before to take the plunge.

Only one of them would be chosen by the God of Sand and Sea. Only one of them would rise from the torrent of the Boiling Waters, carried by a Siren. The next Caleef of the Shesaitju people.

All Muskigo would wonder was if they'd see Mahi's body floating down there. Yuri's fetid corpse still remained, crushed upon the rocks below, slowly being eaten away by birds and nibbled on by fish. Muskigo spat down upon him.

All his life, Muskigo had been a warrior, but there was no war to be had against the traitor. No one to beat. Nothing to tear to pieces. There was only Muskigo "The Scythe," alone with his thoughts, worrying, hoping that his daughter's face, the one that he pictured every time he closed his eyes, would slowly be forgotten.

He cursed himself even for the thought. Like he could ever forget… that he should ever want to forget…

The latest tribute to offer his body to the waters sacrificed his spit, then was led through a prayer in an ancient dialect of Saitjuese only the scrote-less minions of the palace bothered to study and remember. One held a nigh'jel high above him. The helpless creature didn't squirm, it didn't do anything, as if mimicking Sidar Rakun in his final hours on Pantego. Their ancestors thought that meant they'd wholly given in to the Current, which somehow made them holy.

Now, Muskigo questioned if they were just senseless, that they hadn't given in to anything, only found themselves without water to breathe.

Had he once been so dense?

The sage split the creature with a serrated knife, and its iridescent green blood poured out over the tribute. Outside of the creature's translucent body, its color was quickly sapped by the air, even thickening, and morphing into a jet black paste. It ran down the tribute's neck, arms, and chest. And then, like the others before, he made the choice to step off to his likely doom. To put his faith in, well… faith.

Muskigo had little of that left. He couldn't help but chuckle. Another body given in vain, another markless man who could've served in a war against the Glass that would now never happen. Babrak had the loyalty of nearly every afhem worth his salt, and Muskigo's army remained far away… alongside the now afhemless army of al'Tariq.

The Serpent Guards at the entry lifted their fauchards and stepped aside. To speak of the betrayer…

Afhem Babrak Trisps'I strode in, still hobbling from the wounds Mahi had inflicted upon him. He left his harem of wives and servants at the door and strode toward Muskigo. His zhulong leather armor was now plated with gold on the shoulders and joints. He may as well have been wearing a crown.

"Afhem Muskigo," he said, stopping just paces away. "You're still here?"

Muskigo grunted an incoherent response. All he could think about was grabbing the traitorous liar and launching him to the same depths which claimed his daughter. But there was no honor in that, not in this sacred room, and honor was all Muskigo had left.

"This arrived today by courier." Babrak removed a scroll from his belt and presented it. "From the Glass Crown."

Muskigo didn't take the scroll. "And the courier?" he said, almost in a growl.

"Nobody of importance."

"Where is he being held?"

"He'll be on his way back across the Black Sands shortly," Babrak said, rolling the parchment between his fingers.

"You let him go? He'll know about what happened to Sidar; that we are without a leader."

"Are you so foolish?" Babrak said, looking around the room for anyone who'd laugh with him. "They already think—they know we're without a leader. Dead or lost, what does it matter?"

"You know it matters!"

"He's a courier, not a warlord. Take your rage out on somebody else, Muskigo. Only you are responsible for bringing that lech, Darkings, here. Responsible for all this mess, really. Perhaps I went beyond my allowances by giving you the Dagger of Damikmagrin, but our next Caleef will decide what will be done with you. I suspect the Ayerabi won't exist much longer and Saujibar will be left to the shifting sands."

Muskigo stood slowly, went face-to-face with Babrak. His nostrils flared. If he'd had a weapon, he wasn't sure he wouldn't have gutted the man like those poor nigh'jels.

"You'd enjoy that, wouldn't you?" he said.

"Am I really the villain in your fantasy?" Babrak asked. He pretended to brush something off Muskigo's shoulder, and both men stared each other down. Then, Babrak spoke up again. "While you made a mess of things in the west and got our Caleef killed, I was the only one who was here, holding us together." He slapped the letter into Muskigo's hand, so he had no choice but to take it. "Read this, and let me know your thoughts. It's one last chance at peace."

"Who cares what a doomed afhem thinks?"

"You are many things, and I won't be sad to see you gone, we both know that, but you've bested me many times on the battlefield." Babrak breathed in, then said through clenched teeth, "You're the best warrior we have. So, until the new Caleef decides your fate, at least put some of your knowledge about strategy to good use. They'll find out about Sidar Rakun's fate soon enough, but not that of Yuri Darkings. Only the afhems know of it, and none of us is sharing."

Babrak turned to leave. Muskigo clutched the man's wrist and spun him back around.

"What?" Babrak said, not afraid in the slightest. They were so close to revealing his true nature before Mahi was murdered. Now, Babrak seemed more confident and brazen than ever. Muskigo wanted to tear the smirk off his fat face.

"Nothing," Muskigo muttered, fighting all his baser urges. If his daughter could do so before Sir Nikserof, so could he.

Babrak grinned, nodded, then continued out of the room. The women outside fawned over him when he arrived, spreading his arms wide and receiving them. The men laughed at a joke and plied his ears with adoring whispers.

Muskigo fell back into his seat, his thumb stroking the scroll while he considered whether he even wanted to look. What could the Glassmen possibly offer at this point?

Only when another markless fool followed faith to the Boiling Keep did Muskigo give in, and slowly unfurled the letter. He counted his short breaths as he did so. Even their written language was simple and without beauty or nuance.

THE   OFFENSES   OF   YOUR   WARLORDS   AGAINST   THE

SOVEREIGNTY YOUR PEOPLE PLEDGED ALLEGIANCE TO ARE NUMEROUS. UNFORGIVABLE IN THE EYES OF IAM. HOWEVER, OUR KING IS GENEROUS. ALL HE WANTS IS PEACE. RELEASE SIR NIKSEROF PASIC, OUR WEARER OF WHITE, TURN OVER THE TRAITOR YURI DARKINGS. HERE, IN THE GLASS, HE WILL BE PUNISHED FOR HIS CRIMES. THE FATE OF MUSKIGO AYERABI WE WILL LEAVE IN THE HANDS OF THE GREATER AFHEMDOM, BUT HE MUST BE STRIPPED OF ALL POWER. THEN, AND ONLY THEN, AT WHITE BRIDGE, WE WILL RE-NEGOTIATE THE AUTHORITY OF OUR CROWN OVER THE BLACK SANDS WITH NEW TERMS. WE WILL REMEDY WHERE THIS BEAUTIFUL JOINING FOUNDED BY THE GREAT KING LIAM WENT SOUR. MAY THE LIGHT OF IAM GUIDE YOU.

Muskigo crumpled the scroll. The bottom was signed and sealed by the Master of Warfare, Sir Torsten Unger—the greatest warrior of their kingdom whom Muskigo had already bested, now with the upper hand again.

Muskigo cursed and punched the stone seat so hard his knuckles split. Then, he stormed across the room, shoved aside a helpless sage, and dropped the message down the hole.

'*Help with strategy,*' he scoffed to himself. He knew what this was: Babrak taking one last barb at him. There wasn't a part of that arrangement the man wouldn't agree upon. Renegotiation of the terms of their annexation? If Babrak handled things before the new Caleef was chosen, there would be no one to stand for the Shesaitju. No matter how many afhems sat with him and the powers of the Glass to discuss terms, Babrak had them all eating from his palms. Any new terms would be sure to favor him, the man who'd grown fatter in this palace, living like a pompous Glass lord.

One thing, however, was absolute. There was no route left in which Muskigo survived. The Current was against him. A new Caleef would look at all he'd done in violating the desires of the sniveling Sidar Rakun and know he had to be removed. No matter what, Babrak and the Glass Crown would make sure of it.

Muskigo had come here to Latiapur for the good of his people, and now, thanks to Yuri, he'd delivered his own head on a platter to all those who might want it. The meager remnants of his army would still support him, but they were in Nahanab, and while Afhem Tingur was a good man with his heart in the right place, his prime had long since passed. A bit of pressure from the regrouped Glass army, and without Muskigo or Mahraveh there, he'd fold.

Muskigo had become another pawn in Babrak's plan to become the unofficial King of the Black Sands. Maybe it would never happen by title or with a crown, but public favor was true power. Muskigo had it once, convincing so many that they could be better than handing half of everything to the pink-skinned lords they rarely saw. Then, he lost at Winde Port, and then again, at Nahanab. So many lives… lost.

Babrak would be the afhem most trusted by the Glass King and their new Caleef, the one with the largest army, the one who had reestablished peace after Muskigo forsook it.

"Afhem Muskigo," one of the sages said, his voice soft like a young woman. He bowed his head in deference.

"What?" Muskigo snapped.

"Unless you are here to pledge yourself to the will of the Current, will you please move aside so that we may continue?"

Muskigo looked around, totally forgetting that he stood before the Sea Door. For a moment, he considered tossing himself through. It would solve so many problems. The sages all stared at him, as did the ready tribute. A kid by the looks of him, barely able to grow a beard. Only, Muskigo knew this one.

He, unlike most of the others so far, was not markless. He bore the tattoos of the al'Tariq afhemate and no other. A loyal warrior.

"Bit'rudam?" Muskigo asked, blinking to make sure he was seeing clearly. The young man's head was shaved, too, making him look even more like a pup, and that youthful courage and confidence he'd had since Muskigo met him had vanished. Instead, the whites of his eyes were red from tears.

"Afhem Muskigo," Bit'rudam greeted, without regarding him. He merely stared forward, visibly struggling to contain his emotions.

One of the sages, again, requested Muskigo move, but the glare he shot back at the man would have sent his balls into his stomach if he had any.

"What are you doing?" Muskigo asked.

"What does it look like?" Bit'rudam replied.

"It looks like you're giving up."

"So, now, giving myself over to faith and Current is akin to surrender to you?"

"You've given your sword and your soul to your afhemate," Muskigo reminded the boy.

"And I'm tired of it—of giving myself and my trust over to men… women, only to lose them. I tire of wasting my life. Perhaps, if the Current wills it, I can make a difference as Caleef."

"How?" Muskigo asked. "Sitting in a chair?" He motioned toward the empty throne, nothing more than a trinket to him now. "Perhaps this holy honor once meant something, but ever since Liam ravaged us, it's meaningless." The sages gasped audibly upon hearing his blasphemy. Serpent Guards by the entry stirred and marched in, silent, deadly. Muskigo once had so much power that some of those golden masked men had forsaken their sacred oath to guard the Caleef and his home to follow the Scythe into battle. They were all dead now, too.

Muskigo slowly extended his arm over Bit'rudam's back. He didn't resist. Then, Muskigo led him off to the side, away from the door, where nobody could listen in on him.

"You would deny the Current?" one of the sages questioned. Muskigo ignored him.

"I thought she'd be the one we followed until the end," Bit'rudam said, voice quaking. "The one to change our fortune. To bring power to the islands again after the Glass trade routes forgot us in our rough seas."

"Mahraveh was unlike anyone before her," Muskigo said. Just uttering her name made his heart sting, his throat dry, and his muscles seize. "And anyone who will come after. I see that now, all too late."

"I never trusted that pink-skin from the start," Bit'rudam growled. "We should have never brought him with us. It was my job to protect her."

"No, it wasn't. It was mine. Mahi, Pazradi—Mahraveh's mother—Shavi. I've failed them all. Saujibar and all those who called it home. My entire afhemate."

"Why would the Current want this?" Bit'rudam asked. His already-red eyes were beginning to tear up again.

"I don't know, but you won't find out down there." Muskigo pointed at the hole and the disgruntled sages. "The al'Tariq Afhemate remains strong. Soon, blood and water will be spilled in its name. I've seen you fight. You can win."

"Or I could lose. What does it matter? A new alliance is coming. Haven't you seen? There're more markless than ever. More traders and merchants. The age of the Shesaitju warriors is passing. My father told me it was coming long ago, that he didn't want this life for me. I didn't listen."

"Then listen to me, boy." Muskigo clutched Bit'rudam's jaw and forced him to stare into his eyes. There was resistance, but Muskigo only squeezed harder and pulled him closer. "I have seen every horror this world has to offer. I found victory snatched from me by flame and wicked magic. I have won, and now I have lost. But the one thing I know for certain is that no matter who rules us, the Black Sands needs strong men like you. Grieve the life of my daughter as if you loved her. For perhaps you did, or still do, and her father wouldn't blame you, but whatever you choose, don't throw your life away on a prayer to a god whose voice remains absent after so much death."

Bit'rudam swallowed hard. "Maybe, he'll offer me the power to change things."

"If he has that power, I have not seen it. Only we can change things. Wise men who follow the Current, float with it. Embrace it. However, the sharks cut through it to find their prey. They make their own survival, and maybe their lives burn short, but they burn bright. And boy, you have the heart of a shark. You're not meant to sit and listen. You've been called to hunt."

Muskigo cupped the back of the boy's neck, pulled him in, and leaned forward. Their foreheads met. He said nothing else, just walked away. But Muskigo knew, deep within, that Bit'rudam wouldn't leap. He was a young man willing to stand up against the legend of the Scythe. Whether it was out of bravery, brazenness, or lust, it didn't matter. He was an afhem in the making. A true warrior.

That was Muksigo's people's greatest export. Not carpets, or gold, or fish, or anything else they traded with the Glass Kingdom and beyond. Warriors. For centuries, kings around Pantego would hire afhemates like mercenaries, would back some, ally against others—watch in awe as they killed each other with relentless passion and unparalleled skill.

The Shesaitju's finest were trained from birth. They survived the great desert on their own as children, hunting their own food, learning the land. At least, Muskigo's generation had, and all those before. Things weren't so simple once all the trading started.

Yet, in rebelling alone, with only his allies and not the backing of all the Shesaitju, Muskigo knew now that he'd merely fed the stereotype that his people were fractured warrior tribes which could never expand beyond their desert. When even the Drav Cra could find a common leader, the Shesaitju were just tools to be played with and traded by rich lords.

In trying to undo that, Muskigo had made it worse. He'd allowed false afhems like Babrak to rise.

No more.

Sweeping out of the throne room, retrieving his weapon, he burst out onto the palace courtyard. His long strides quickly brought him to the bluffs overlooking the Intsti Reef to the south and Latiapur to the east. Ships docked, and men and women flocked to their great city on the coast, all in the name of a new Caleef. There were traders everywhere, peddling wares from every corner of the world. No Glassmen were foolish enough to show their faces in these times, but there were dwarves, Panpingese, Breklians, anyone who thought they could take advantage of the loss of the Caleef and make an autla or three.

Sellouts and whores.

While Muskigo was out trying to claim a crown for themselves, they'd festered in his home like a virus—a sickness fed by Babrak and the greedy afhems at his side.

No more.

Muskigo delved down through the markets. His ears were assailed from every direction by Shesaitju who'd forsaken their ways. Soft men. Women who couldn't even stand in Mahraveh's shadow. It didn't even feel like the city he knew. A city built on respect and honor. Now, it felt like Winde Port, a place the gods saw burned down for good reason.

No more.

He pushed through all of it until he reached the outer arches of Tal'du Dromesh where his legacy began. That hallowed concourse was like an extension of the markets now, filled with stands and traveling carts, selling luxuries that weren't necessities, selling weapons made in faraway lands, nowhere near as sharp or sturdy as the one hanging at Muskigo's hip.

A wave of sickness blended with his rage. He wanted to tear the place down. Instead, he kept moving into the aisle of afhemates. Surrounded by a flood of seawater, the place was home to the palaces erected long ago to house afhems upon visiting the capital. A needless luxury. Muskigo could count on one hand how many times he'd visited that which belonged to the Ayerabi. The dust and webs covering its portico displayed that well enough.

Many homes were presently occupied with so much happening in Latiapur, zhulong rolling about in the stable's mud pits, children playing in the streets. Muskigo wondered if perhaps he should have spent more time here over the years, shaking hands and making friends. More time playing these modern political games the Glass Kingdom plagued his kind with.

Too late now.

Rage carried him like a storm right up to the Trisps'I palace's blackwood doors. Babrak's door. One guard bearing the marks of the Trisps'I Afhemate stood along with two Serpent Guards being used as Babrak's own personal protection.

Within, drums pounded, lutes strummed, people caroused. While the Black Sands mourned the loss of afhems and a Caleef, Babrak was throwing a feast. Dozens of dignitaries and women filled the place, gorging themselves on his riches.

"Afhem Muskigo," one of Babrak's guards addressed him. "I'm so sorry, but you must leave. Babrak hosts a private gathering of the most trusted members of his afhemate and beyond."

"Gathering?" Muskigo said, seething. "I must have missed my invite."

Each palace was identical on the outside—equal—but Muskigo could see through the man's windows at the rooms illuminated by both nigh'jels and torches—something no Shesaitju would consider using. Wood was scarce in the Black Sands, and to waste it in such a way… it sickened Muskigo how Babrak displayed his fineries with no care in the world.

If that wasn't enough, one sight sent Muskigo's ire bubbling over. A Glassman sat on a silk couch being *attended to* by a Shesaitju woman. Maybe one of Babrak's own wives. This was the Glass courier, being shown the night of his life courtesy of the afhem who would *bring peace*. And, judging by his physique and the exquisite clothes lying at his feet, he was more than a messenger, maybe even a Shieldsman.

"Do you have a message to convey to my afhem?" the guard asked.

Muskigo snickered. "Must I hire a courier to bring him messages, too? Step aside, boy. Now."

"I'm under orders."

Muskigo sighed and cracked out his neck. He'd remained calm, collected even, but…

No more.

"At least his men are loyal," he muttered to himself. Then he unsheathed his sickle-blade. The Serpent Guards drew their weapons in response.

"Step aside," Muskigo demanded.

"How dare you draw your weapon here?" the guard said. "There are to be no feuds between afhems within these sacred walls."

"Nothing is sacred anymore."

"Go home, Afhem Muskigo," the guard ordered. "Do not make things worse."

Muskigo raised his blade to the moonlight. He studied the curve, the engravings along the side made in their ancient tongue. It was perfectly balanced, forged from black iron. "You've heard how I got my name, yes? All my life, I thought the Current was at my back," he said. "I wonder how long I can swim against it."

The guard drew a scimitar. "Muskigo, turn away."

"He wanted my wife, but couldn't have her," he said, still more to himself than anyone listening. "So, he took my world instead. Babrak!"

Muskigo flounced forward, and one of the Serpent Guards thrust a polearm at him. He twisted out of the way, snapped the shaft in half, and used it to deflect the strike of the other. Sliding back, low, under the slash of Babrak's guard, his sickle-blade caught one leg and swiped the man from his feet. A spear split a gash in his shoulder but missed the rest of him as he flipped back off a column.

He landed behind a Serpent Guard, then jammed the broken edge of the spear through the base of the man's skull, and it burst through his mouth.

Muskigo let the spear go as the guard collapsed. The other Serpent Guard's fauchard rushed at Muskigo, but he deftly ducked behind the body, then flung it forward at the guard. Two things happened next: Muskigo's knee came up, and his scythe went out in a smooth arch. A second later, the Serpent Guard's head was crushed against the stone by Muskigo's knee, and Babrak's guard's chest was split open, throat to navel.

Muskigo staggered back against the door, blood pooling in his mouth. It'd never felt so good to kill. It was almost like he was drunk.

He spit and bellowed, "Babrak!" then kicked the fallen warrior as hard as he could, sending the body into the front door and it splintered off its hinges. Shrieks filled the room as the bloody corpse skidded across the marble floor. Naked men and women fled in every direction. The moment Muskigo was inside, he knew what the torches were for. They burned incense, masking the putrid stink of this unholy orgy celebrating Babrak's glory.

"Babrak!" Muskigo shouted again.

One of Babrak's men charged him from a room on the left, wearing only a loincloth. Muskigo hopped back, caught him by the throat, and snapped his neck. Another charged from the front. Muskigo parried high, then punched out and shattered his windpipe.

Muskigo caught a glimpse of pale skin in his peripherals. The Glassman scrambled for a window, naked as the day he was born. Muskigo kicked one of the fallen men's sword up to his hand and threw it. It spun end over end three times before sinking straight into his back. He tumbled forward, already dead, and his body slumped against the sill.

Muskigo turned back and saw Babrak hurrying down the main stairs, struggling to put on his robe. What must have been ten naked women ran down with him, more than just his wives. This was the life he would have had for the one woman Muskigo chose to love—to be a tool of pleasure and nothing more. Everything and everyone was a tool to him.

"Babrak, it's over," Muskigo snarled.

"Kill him, you fools!" Babrak yelled. "He's finally lost it."

Muskigo heard more attackers before he saw them. Warriors flooded through the living area. He whipped around, slashing open a nigh'jel lantern, sending the water spilling out, mixing with blood, and making the floor slick. He stepped out of the way of a wild swing, sliced a warrior across the chest, and threw him into the opening to block the others.

"You can't run from me, Babrak," Muskigo said as he came around the corner and saw the man, still tying his robe. He was in a dining hall. The walls were covered in tapestries and paintings —luxuries from places far away.

"Are you insane, Muskigo?" he asked. "You'll die for this."

"I'm already dead. Isn't that why you showed me those demands?"

Babrak grabbed a vase and threw it at Muskigo. It shattered against his raised bracer, then he tracked Babrak's eyes, and saw that they focused behind him. Muskigo twirled his sickle-blade and thrust it back, gutting a warrior trying to sneak up on him.

"Muskigo, think about what you'll be doing to the good name of your afhemate," Babrak said.

"You've already destroyed that name."

"It's not too late."

Muskigo made a move toward Babrak around the table, and the big man edged in the other direction, flinging more antiques, more for effect than anything. Shards of clay slashed Muskigo's skin, but nothing deep enough to stop him.

"It's all too late!" Muskigo shouted. "You've sold us out, one by one."

"She died because of you!" Babrak yelled.

"Every word out of your mouth is poison. Why did you show me that letter—to taunt me? Yuri was loyal until he got around you. I wonder what you offered to make him murder my daughter. Perhaps to get the Glass to spare the life of his son?"

"I don't know what you're talking about."

Muskigo grunted and shoved the table aside. He lunged forward and slashed, catching the big man across his gut. Babrak howled, but he was too massive to go down from the graze. He reached beneath the wooden table and flung it with only one hand. Muskigo drove his blade down, splitting the wood, but not before it shoved him back into one of Babrak's men who'd been trying to take him from behind.

The man grabbed Muskigo, but Muskigo kicked back, cracking the man's shin. His elbow rose to the man's nose, and blood gushed as he collapsed.

"No more!" Muskigo shouted as he lurched forward and

kicked Babrak in the gut. Still, he didn't go down. Babrak slapped one of the fire basins, and hot embers peppered Muskigo's face. It caught him off guard and sent him staggering.

"Out of my way!" Babrak roared, clearly determined to take advantage of the distraction.

But Muskigo recovered fast and swiped wildly with his scythe. Babrak grabbed one of his wives and flung her at him. Any lesser warrior would have decapitated her out of sheer instinct, but Muskigo's discipline allowed him to pull back just in time and shave only a thin cut across her neck. His foot caught debris and the ankle-injury he'd received in the battle of Nahanab flared up.

He fell, rolled out of the way of a thrusting spear, then kicked up to his feet and shouldered his attacker back. Pain didn't matter any longer. It couldn't.

The spear came at him again, and Muskigo pushed off with his bad foot, then used his other to spring off the attacker's shoulder. He soared across the main hall, grabbed hold of the nigh'jel lantern hanging from the domed ceiling, and swung over Babrak's men.

Portions of the ceiling rained down, cracking under his weight. He let go and landed at the front entry and nearly toppled from his ankle pain. He didn't let it stop him. With wounded back and belly, Babrak did what passed for running for the stables, and was now mounting a zhulong. A sword slashed at Muskigo's head on his way through the front door, but he ducked in time and raked his blade across the warrior's hip.

By then, horns and alarm drums sounded throughout the afhem district. It wouldn't be long before they spread across the whole city.

Serpent Guards marched in while Muskigo hopped down from the portico and limped to the stable. A young stablehand wielding a small dagger stood before the gate, trembling. Muskigo took one more step, and the boy tossed the weapon and forsook his post.

Muskigo hopped on the first beast he could find. Zhulong were notoriously stubborn, but it was as if the creature could feel his wrath. It lowered its back in trepidation, and with one kick to its hide, it barreled forward through the fence. A few of Babrak's men tried to stop it, only to be trampled.

"Babrak!" Muskigo's scream pierced the night. The big man was up the street, rounding a large fountain. He glanced back, uncharacteristic terror filling his eyes.

Muskigo chased after him, swerving around a group of Serpent Guards come to put an end to the feud. Muskigo batted aside one of their polearms and swiped down. Another with a bow fired. The barbed arrow just missed, but still left a deep but non-fatal gash on Muskigo's thigh.

They raced beneath an archway sculpted to depict two clashing zhulong, and Muskigo spotted Babrak tearing down the streets toward the markets. Muskigo's mount was faster with his lighter weight atop it. He took a better angle and cut Babrak off before he could disappear into the crowded dusk-time markets.

"Stop running from the inevitable!" Muskigo yelled. "Our age is finished."

"You're a lunatic!" Babrak said. He grimaced and clutched his side. Mahraveh had started the job of killing him in Nahanab, and now Muskigo would finish it.

Babrak yanked on his zhulong's mane and turned it back toward the afhem district where the guards and his men were grouping. Muskigo snatched a fishing spear from a tradesman's barrel and gave chase. He launched it in front of Babrak's mount, frightening the beast and causing it to veer right toward Tal'du Dromesh. Traders cleaning their wares dove out of the way as it barreled through a stand and onto the concourse. Its hooves slid, and it squealed just before slamming into a column and hurling Babrak off and down through the open gate.

Muskigo watched as Babrak rolled down the stands and out of sight. Then, peering left, he noted a group of Shesaitju warriors charging toward him. He hated how they'd view him. Like a traitor. Like a madman. But he'd never cared when people bowed to him. He only wanted his people to be strong again; to build a world for his daughter that belonged to them.

He gripped tight to his zhulong's mane and directed it toward the same column that Babrak's had struck. It hit at full speed, and Muskigo used the momentum to launch himself down across the stands. The column cracked. A portion of the ceiling loosened and down came an area of the concourse, blocking off the entrance. Dust and sand smothered the area in a thick fog.

Muskigo landed hard, but he knew how to ignore the pain. He rose to his feet and saw Babrak in the sands of the arena staggering for the rock wall which retained the sea. A trail of blood coated the ground behind him. Muskigo rolled over the low bulwark separating the stands and limped after him.

Babrak reached the southern rock wall and started to climb, groaning so loudly Muskigo could hear him from across the battlefield. He struggled for longer than he had to spare, and when he rolled over, Muskigo, eyes raging like two great storms set to devour the world, stood before him.

"Muskigo Ayerabi, step away from him!" a voice shouted from the upper stands.

"Please... please... don't," Babrak whimpered.

Muskigo took another step at him, and Babrak cowered further. Muskigo then looked from side to side, empty stands all around him but for those at his back where the guards were amassing. He remembered, all those years ago, when he'd fought in this arena with honor, when he'd stood defiantly before King Liam, and promised that the Shesaitju would rise again. He remembered how the great conqueror smiled and laughed as if it were all a game. Maybe to men like Liam and Babrak, it was.

Muskigo was done playing.

"You think this changes anything?" Babrak rasped. He tried to crawl back again, but pain wracked his features and made the veins on his neck bulge.

"I remember fighting here like it was yesterday," Muskigo said.

"How grand for you. The great Scythe, reminding me at the end that not every afhemate was handed to a worthy, male heir like my father."

"None of us was worthy. Our feuds and hatred. King Liam's conquest was inevitable, and we were our own undoing."

"At least I can keep us alive," Babrak said.

"To a life not worth living."

"Life, nonetheless." Babrak held his side as he struggled to stand, patting the rocks to find purchase. "Use your head, Muskigo. All the fighting you complain about. I can bring peace. The greater afhemdom will follow my lead now. Thanks to your war, it can happen."

"My war." Muskigo chuckled. "There will always be another like me who refuses to bow to unworthy men."

"There will never be another like you," Babrak said. He vocalized the agony he felt with a grunt. "The old ways are dying."

"And we go with them!"

Muskigo swung at him and saw the glint in Babrak's hand an instant too late. A small blade not unlike the one the stable boy had wielded slid out while Babrak rose. He rammed it once, and then again into Muskigo's rib cage. Any other man would have been sent to his knees, but Muskigo drew on his black fist training, channeling energy to his fists in attack, and legs in defense.

Babrak skewered him again, but Muskigo squeezed the grip of

his own blade tight. He stabbed down with two hands, the top, curved portion of the scythe crashed through Babrak's upper chest and shoulder. Both afhems buckled to their knees, pierced by the other.

"Stop this madness," a soft, but stern voice spoke above.

As Muskigo flopped over alongside Babrak, each refusing to release their weapon, he saw the speaker standing atop the rocks. Her figure was lean but had the grace of a warrior. Her skin was black as the night sky. But her eyes… Muskigo could never forget those.

"Sand mouse?"

XXVII

THE IMMORTAL

It felt like home. Cold. Harsh. Unforgiving. A place without life.

They'd left the ship as far north as it could reach, and now, before Kazimir, there was nothing but white. Not even the Pikebacks, the massive mountain range that ran east and west across the Northern reaches of Pantego, showed stone. What few trees survived this high up groaned and creaked under a heavy wind that whistled like the gentle whispers of the dead.

Kazimir pulled his hood forward. The entirety of his face was shrouded in shadow, as was Sigrid's. Heavy cloaks covered their bodies, and their hands were gloved. However, unlike the rest of their companions, it wasn't for warmth. Even as a thin ray of light broke through the clouds, the protection provided by their clothing would allow them to last until the clouds swallowed up the daylight once more.

The Motherland was kind to the upyr, never allowing the sun to fully break through the clouds for more than minutes at a time. It was said to be her blessing upon them for putting an end to the Culling, for stopping the mindless undead from ravaging the land, for slaying Mamon the Mad Mystic, who'd raised the dead and brought ruin to Kazimir's home and everyone in it.

Kazimir took a breath, though he had no need for it. His lungs had stopped inflating centuries ago when his heart had stopped beating. Now, the only thing keeping him alive was the fear of mankind and the lifeblood pulsing through their veins. He did, however, enjoy the feeling of the cold, crisp air against the back of his throat, in his chest. He closed his eyes but didn't see darkness. Instead, he saw the crimson-stained landscape that was Elsewhere. But there was something different. He'd been seeing it for days. He kept telling himself he'd have to circle back around to it later. It troubled him greatly, but he couldn't afford to lose focus. Not now. Not with the old gods threatening to feud once more.

Kazimir heard Whitney and the others behind him, snow crunching beneath their boots. He could hear the beating wings of the wyvern which, without the Glintish boy, followed Whitney around like a pet. It'd kept its distance since Gentry left, like an angry teenager. He knew it should be terrified, not bitter.

Mortals... their eyes were always open, but they didn't see. Like infants, they were, seeing only that which was splayed out before them in the natural realms. They'd need to see far more than that if any of them were to survive.

If the Sanguine Lords were willing to enact a blood pact upon Nesilia, that meant they were all preparing a return—all the gods, even Iam, and none was more vile than he.

With the Covenstan Depths at his back, Kazimir could see the many pillars, walls, and ruins that once made up the great city of Vidkaru. This, where they stood, had long ago been the seat of kings, the most powerful to ever live, kings that made Liam the Conqueror look like Liam the Meek. Compared to the god-kings-and-queens, those mere men would be like insects.

Now, all of Pantego faced a threat far greater than any

Culling. This wasn't some necromancer or sorcerer at work. It wasn't just the dead they'd have to worry about now.

"This is it?" Whitney asked, brow furrowed as he scanned the ruins.

The thief always knew the exact wrong time to speak. It was a skill.

Kazimir looked to the gray sky. "As I said, *Svay Sobor iz Nohzi* is not something you will see with your naked eye."

"It's a shame. I left all my eye clothing back on the ship."

"Why can't we just kill him?" Sigrid groaned.

"I've considered it many times," Kazimir said. He pointed. "There, through the pass. Come."

He led the group down a snow-laden escarpment. The Lightmancer slid a short distance before Whitney reached out and steadied her. Only the dwarf managed to make it to the bottom without looking foolish.

"I'll help you," Whitney offered.

"I'm not a child." Lucindur swatted.

"No, but if you slip and break that instrument of yours, we're doomed."

Lucindur muttered under her breath before accepting his proffered hand.

Such weakness in mortality. Like babies thrust into the deep, hopeful to survive by sheer luck. Kazimir thought.

He ignored the rest and scanned the landscape. Not long ago, in the shallow valley between the Pikebacks and the hillocks which acted like a dike around the Covenstan Depths, Kazimir and Sigrid caught a contingent of soldiers prodding around in vain efforts to find the Dom Nohzi and the Citadel. Not everyone knew how to call upon the Sanguine Lords, and it was obvious that with Yuri Darkings no longer on their Royal Council, that knowledge had escaped them all.

More fools. All they need do was ask and then prepare to face the consequence of rejection.

Crossing the valley plane where their feet now fell would have been littered with corpses if the snows hadn't piled up. But now, they were waist-deep in the stuff, trudging forward, stepping over what would only feel like rocks and roots, not skulls and bones. The dwarf barely kept his head above the powder, but he'd have been used to such things.

Kazimir kept moving briskly and forcing them to keep pace. Just as it had been in Elsewhere, something was off here, too. To anyone else, it would have only been another stark landscape, quiet and unassuming. But to Kazimir, who'd spent generations in this valley, he could hear the subtle sound of footsteps echoing off the mountain pass; small rocks clattering across the snowy rock face; miniature avalanches slowly cascading down.

He hadn't even realized he'd stopped until the dwarf spoke up.

"What are ye doing?" Tum Tum asked. "Legs froze?"

"We are being watched," Kazimir said.

"Your Lords more upset with you than you thought, huh?" Whitney said.

"Not by them." Kazimir shifted, just one foot back, then the other forward. His hands fell to a pair of small throwing daggers on a bandolier across his chest. In a swift and sure movement, he crossed his arms, then threw the blades. One *thud* sounded after another, and two winged beasts dropped.

"Grimaurs, again?" Whitney asked.

"Where there's one…" before Kazimir could complete his sentence, a loud screech sounded above, and a shadow moved over the party. Another grimaur dove down, and this time, Sigrid dispatched it with a bolt through its throat.

"With all the Glassmen up this way lately… it must have attracted scavengers," Kazimir said.

"Are you sure that's all it is?" Lucindur asked.

Kazimir made a noncommittal grunt and waved them on.

The pass narrowed up ahead, and they climbed single-file for some time before Whitney started complaining. He'd broken some kind of record, Kazimir was sure.

"I hope there's a fire when we get there," the thief said.

"And mead," Tum Tum said. "Hot mead."

"There will be hard wood and blood," Kazimir said. "Do not expect the comforts of your southern homes."

"Aye, ye arrogant prig," Tum Tum spat. "I be from the Dragon's Tail themselves."

"And you've lived a human lifespan near the sea, serving ale to sailors and wenches. You've forgotten what the Far North is like."

"Say it to me face," Tum Tum shouted.

Kazimir only saw him for a second longer until his attention was drawn to the road ahead. The dwarf continued muttering curses, but he too soon fell silent.

The soft sound of flesh tearing, beaks clacking, wings flapping, and angry grunts echoed from a group of grimaurs. Blood flew into the air, and the snow around them was stained red.

"Weapons ready," Kazimir whispered.

The dwarf pulled his warhammer.

Movement from behind them drew Kazimir's eye. Down the mountainside, goblins in the dozens flooded the pass. It disturbed the feasting grimaurs, and the bird-beasts looked up and back, spotting the party. The lead one shook its head, sending a spray of blood and gore, then flapped its wings, slowly at first, making a beeline for Kazimir.

"Starting already, are we?" the Lightmacer asked, pulling a short sword they'd pilfered from the pirate ship from a scabbard on her side. Kazimir eyed her suspiciously, wondering if she knew how to use it.

"Now they are working together?" Whitney said. "Never even seen grimaurs flying outdoors, and now this?"

"That buried witch is already workin hard, I suspect," the dwarf added.

As the next of the grimaurs swooped in, Kazimir launched a dagger, and it sliced through the beast's chest and into its heart, then landed in a puff of snow. At the same time, Aquira swooped down from her higher position and scorched the lead grimaur, causing their formation to spread.

"These creatures are not unheard of here," Kazimir said, fending off a goblin who'd made it down. "If they are with her, these are her scouts. Expendable. Weak. Follow me. Keep them off your back. The entrance is not far off."

When they reached the spot where the grimaurs had been eating, they saw the remains of a Glass soldier.

Kazimir swore. *Meddling mortals.*

Just before he and Sigrid had been summoned to Panping by Whitney and the Lightmancer, they'd been hunting Glassmen who were desperately trying to locate the Citadel—dispatched to bring the Dom Nohzi to justice for murdering their queen, who deserved death more than most who earn the wrong end of a blood pact. It appeared they'd gotten closer than Kazimir would have liked to admit.

A grunt interrupted Kazimir's musings as the dwarf swatted up at one grimaur with his hammer and missed, but at least he drove it back. Aquira raced by and dug her talons into its back, tearing it farther away,

Whitney engaged with two goblins at the mouth of the pass, and the Glintish woman did her best to help. Goblins leaped at her weapon, unafraid of her weak strikes. They grabbed the blade and struggled to pry it free.

A volley of small dart-like arrows suddenly filled the sky above. Kazimir rolled away from one, and another caught his cloak. On a thin ridge to the east of the pass, a line of goblins, faces masked with bone and feathers, had squeezed out of a fissure in the rock and had their blow-guns ready for another salvo. Further proof that these weak beings born of darkness now had a master to guide them. Groups were rarely so organized.

"Don't let the darts touch you!" Kazimir shouted. "They will poison your mortal blood, same as the grimaur talons."

Two more grimaurs dropped to the ground dead, though Kazimir couldn't see what had killed them. He turned, looking for Sigrid, but she had already begun taking glee in chopping through goblins to the north.

Something slammed into Kazimir's side. He spun, ready to strike but found the dwarf climbing to his feet.

"Aye, watch it!" the dwarf screamed as he rose and returned to the battle.

In quick succession, three thrums sounded, and the same number of the flying creatures rained down from above. In life, Sigrid had become a near-expert with ranged weapons, now, in the afterlife, she'd become a master of the crossbow. The Lords had given Kazimir's kind unique eyesight, the ability to track and anticipate movement as if the world around them had been slowed to a crawl.

"Lucy!" The cry came from across the field to the north. Then again, "Lucy!"

Kazimir left his post and tore through the snow to Whitney.

"I can't find Lucindur," Whitney said.

It was good to see the thief wasn't totally unaware of his surroundings. He dodged a dart, then one of his fists connected with a goblin's mouth. Whitney pulled his hand away quickly, its sharp teeth drawing blood from more than one knuckle.

Aquira zoomed by, and carved a fiery circle around them, so they had clearance.

"There!" Kazimir shouted. He threw a dagger, and it found the eye of a grimaur, which had been flapping its wings wildly. Just visible above the snow line was a dark hand slapping at the beast until it fell dead.

Kazimir and Whitney reached the scene, pulled the grimaur off, and located a tattered Lucindur.

"Lucy!" Whitney yelped. He fell to his knees and lightly slapped her face. She moaned and squeezed her eyelids, but she was alive.

"She's still breathing," Kazimir said, yanking his knife from the grimaur's eye. "Take her. Those talons scratched her deep, and she will not be able to move without treatment."

"And where do we get her that?"

"Just take her," Kazimir demanded.

"My salfio..." she whispered.

"Shog!" Whitney rolled her slightly to check and breathed a big sigh of relief to find that the snow had softly cradled it beneath her. He then dug his arms in and heaved her up onto his shoulder. She didn't weigh much, but he was glad Elsewhere had made him more than the scrawny man he'd once been.

"This way," Kazimir said.

He turned ahead, toward Sigrid who picked grimaurs out of the sky with remarkable ease. Aquira flew a line in front of them, scorching the earth and any goblins who dared get too bold.

As Kazimir ran toward the opening at the top of a steady climb, he noticed Tum Tum off on his own, pummeling goblins. "Everyone, to me. Now!" Kazimir ordered. "Dwarf!"

From this vantage, he could see the battle as it truly was. Lost in the thick fog were hundreds of grimaurs and double that of the goblins, though many didn't attack. However, if they chose to, the mortals would be dead in minutes. Aquira zipped overhead and immolated them with lines of fire, but the swirling haze and smoke made aiming difficult.

When they reached the clearing, Kazimir shouted the Breklian words of entry and a glamour shimmered to reveal the Citadel in all its splendor. Two tall upyr statues made an archway, hands grasping in the middle. A thin line of stone came down in the center in the form of a rivulet of blood.

As soon as the last of them passed under the archway, Kazimir spoke the words again, and the glamour returned. A few of the beasts filtered through and met their immediate deaths, but Kazimir knew, by and large, the creatures were too stupid to pass through en masse. They'd be afraid, having seen things disappear, that it would be destruction waiting for them.

To be fair… it was.

The sounds of the grimaurs and goblins still pressed on beyond the veil, but soon, it became silent again.

Sigrid stood at their rear, keeping an eye on the hellish creatures, panting like starved wolves. Aquira perched on Tum Tum's shoulder, her breaths rattling, exhausted.

"Ye done good, bird," Tum Tum said. "I got ye."

Kazimir approached a set of tall doors. They were stone and cold. On each side, flush against the mountain, a pair of towers rose into the sky like daggers, tapering into sharp points.

A head poked through the glamour, a curious goblin. Then it disappeared. When it returned, it brought friends with it.

"Hurry up," Whitney said.

Kazimir spoke the words of entry, sliced his hand, and placed the bloody palm against the doors. Symbols carved into the wood —an ancient version of Breklian that pre-dated even Kazimir—lit up red like life-fluid flowing downward. Rock ground against rock and the doors opened slowly.

"Everyone in," Kazimir said. He spun and loosed three knives from his bandolier at once, taking out a cluster of goblins. They slid dead to Whitney's feet, who stared, dumbstruck. Kazimir heard the *ping* of the goblin darts against the Citadel. He grabbed Whitney by the back of the shirt and yanked him inside.

Once everyone was in, Kazimir and Sigrid followed. The doors slammed shut and utter darkness surrounded them.

"What do we do? What do we do?" Whitney said. He was frantic over the Lightmancer's condition.

"What happened?" the dwarf asked.

"Grimaur got her across the chest," Whitney answered. "She's completely paralyzed."

The dwarf swore. "There a torch? Anything?"

"No," Kazimir said without compassion. "This place was not designed for mortals—even mountain-dwellers such as yourself. The darkness is magical. Just stick close."

"Kazimir," Whitney said, "She's going to die if we don't do something."

"Apart from giving her my own blood, there's nothing I can do."

"Then do it!" Whitney shouted. "The plan doesn't work without her."

"That would begin a process I am sure neither you nor she would desire. She will survive until we get to the main hall. There, we will be able to treat her. The Lords may not be mortal, but they've been alive long enough to know how to cure any and all ailments."

"Then what are we waiting for?" Whitney asked.

Kazimir's gifts allowed him to see everything, even in the darkness, including Whitney lurching forward, and his foot hovered over a near-bottomless pit.

"Stop," Kazimir said. "You don't understand the dangers within."

Whitney shrugged off his hand. "We have to go."

"Whit... boy, I think it's time we listen to him," the dwarf said. "We're in his realm now."

The thief stopped.

"One more step," Kazimir warned, "and you will be dead along with the woman you carry."

"Good riddance," Sigrid remarked. She remained at the exit, crossbow loaded, ready to fight anyone or anything. She had a long way to go to sate her bloodlust.

"If you want to live, stay right behind me," Kazimir said. "Sigrid make sure none gets lost."

She snarled a response. Kazimir would have to work hard to tame this one.

Leading them through a labyrinth filled with fatal drops like the one which almost claimed Whitney, Kazimir said, "This maze zigzags throughout the whole of the mountain. There are one-hundred-forty-three dead ends, and only one way leads to the Citadel."

"And you're sure you know the right one?" Whitney asked.

"Indeed."

It was only a few minutes, but the thief couldn't help himself. At every turn, he asked if they'd arrived yet, or told Lucindur to hang on, or begged Kazimir to hurry. In all his centuries, Kazimir never imagined he'd bring strangers to the Citadel, let alone the likes of him. The thief was lucky his presence was necessary to weaken Nesilia's control over her host.

Kazimir knew enough about demonic possessions. Even when the host's personality and will seem to vanish, they are never fully gone. He had to hope being possessed by a goddess was no different.

Eventually, the maze opened into a spacious antechamber. Kazimir knew only he and Sigrid would be able to see it.

The room was simple, but elegant—like everything Dom Nohzi. The walls were ancient but were smooth and inlaid with simple, geometric design—every shape perfectly symmetrical and balanced. Red velvet couches sat upon intricately designed rugs. However, this was just the entry to the true Citadel.

"Why'd we stop?" Tum Tum asked.

"Kazimir, we can't take our time with her like this," Whitney added.

"Who's there?" came a woman's voice.

"Skryabin," Kazimir said and broke free from the human chain he was leading.

He clasped forearms with the upyr, another like him. She wasn't one of the first generation, but she'd earned the right to dwell within the Citadel.

"We have a mortal with a fatal wound," he said. "She needs aid."

"I'm more concerned about why you would dare bring mortals here?" she spat. "Their kings hunt us. Their fear blinds them to balance."

"Skryabin, you know me," Kazimir said. "These beings are no danger to us. I need them."

"Since when do we need the help of… *mortals*?" The very word seemed to sicken her. It had once had the same effect on Kazimir until the Lords cursed him to Elsewhere for his failure and trapped him with one.

"I will not ask again, Skryabin. They are the key to our salvation—all of us. I will explain once they are safe. Now, lift the darkness and get the Glintish one help."

Skryabin groaned, then whispered in Breklian.

Kazimir barely perceived it, but he knew the mortals would be glad for the shift and the ability to see as a roaring blue flame sparked to life in the room's stone hearth.

"A grimaur slash," Skryabin said, moving toward Lucindur and identifying the wound without having to look for more than a second.

"A grimaur slash," Kazimir confirmed. "There are hundreds of them filling the pass beyond the veil, hidden by fog, and goblins, too."

"Prishka," Skryabin called, snapping her fingers twice. "Get this woman treated."

"Will she be okay?" Whitney asked the woman called Prishka, a younger upyr with hair like silver who rushed over.

"If you give her here," she said. Then she grabbed for Lucindur, easily hefting her with supernatural strength.

Whitney grabbed the Lightmancer's hand as she was pulled free. "You'll be fine, Lucy," he promised. Then he turned to Kazimir and asked, "Right?"

"She will," he said.

"I'll make sure of it," the dwarf declared. With Aquira still recuperating atop his shoulder, he followed behind Prishka, who carried Lucindur into a room to the right of the hearth and closed the door. When they were gone, Skryabin motioned for Kazimir to be seated on one of the couches.

"We have much to discuss," Kazimir said.

"That we do." Skryabin snapped again, and a shirtless man with a cuff around his throat hurried in from behind Whitney.

"Iam's ghost!" Whitney blurted, startled.

The man's body was covered in scars, most concentrated at his neck. He looked emaciated, his eyes bulging from within rings of exhaustion.

He held a tray with two ruby-encrusted goblets filled with blood. He passed one to Kazimir and another to Sigrid, then quickly shuffled out of the room. Sigrid's goblet was drained, and she was licking the rim before Kazimir had even taken a sip.

"This fresh?" Kazimir asked as he took a sip. He moaned. "Ah, yes. I've needed this."

Whitney gagged. "Really?"

In addition to housing the upyr, the Citadel stocked many *hopefuls*—upyr-worshiping mortals who would do anything for the chance to become one of the Sons or Daughters of Night, including frequent drainings which left them weak and helpless but kept the upyr well-nourished. They were like the cattle men milked for sustenance.

"What game are you playing at this time, Kazimir?" Skryabin asked. "This mortal is worthless." She nodded toward Whitney. "But I know the instrument on the Glintish one's back. Do not think me a fool."

"That is the least of our worries, Sister," Kazimir said. "Have you not seen?"

Skryabin bit her lip. It was a nervous habit, but one Kazimir quite enjoyed watching. His carnal desires were mostly for blood. Mostly.

"You have seen it then…" he uttered.

Skryabin nodded. "It means nothing, though. The gods play their games. It isn't for us to meddle there."

"Shog in a barrel, what are you two on about?" Whitney asked.

Kazimir looked over to the thief. He didn't answer him, but addressed Skryabin, eyes never leaving Whitney. "We have to gather everyone. All the Children. Every ally we have. We must call them in immediately."

"You know they'll need a good reason," Skryabin said. "They aren't all so eager to bend our purpose as you."

"You've seen. When you close your eyes. You know what this means."

"Come now, you're not—"

"I have seen what's coming," Kazimir interrupted. "I have seen it with my eyes, and it is unlike anything we've faced before. This will make the Culling look like a rose garden."

"Seen what?" Whitney insisted.

"There's a war coming," Kazimir replied.

"Yes, we all know that," Skryabin said, unimpressed. "There always is. The foolish ways of men will never stop just because one king dies."

"I don't mean war the way men war," Kazimir said. "I closed my eyes."

"And?"

"Do it," Kazimir said. "Do it now, all the way."

Skryabin hesitated. It was a high request. For mortals, blinking was such a habit they scarcely even notice it. A sane upyr, however, rarely did so. Even then, to allow both lids to touch until there was only darkness was to invite horrors.

After a deep sigh, Skryabin slid her eyelids shut.

As she did, Kazimir whispered, "The old gods are coming."

Skryabin sucked in another unneeded breath.

"What is it? What's wrong?" Whitney asked for the third time. He grabbed Kazimir by the arm. Sigrid snapped forward and bore her fangs in his face.

Kazimir regarded him, and Whitney removed his hand slowly, releasing a nervous chuckle. "You've got to give me something," he said.

"Elsewhere is… empty," Kazimir said, barely able to get the last word out. It could mean the end. It could mean nothing. He wasn't sure, because he'd never seen it like that.

"Empty?" Whitney said. "What does 'empty' mean?"

"Has that word ever meant something different to you?" Kazimir retorted. "It is empty. As in, nothing is there except the wianu."

XXVIII

THE DAUGHTER

Mahi watched her father and Babrak wrestling on the ground, spilling blood on the sand of an arena that had seen more than its fair share. Mahi's own blood even, as she fought against nearly one hundred others to claim the al'Tariq Afhemate. And yet, now that she'd drowned and been one with the Current, what a waste it all seemed to be.

One by one, the bravest of her people threw themselves into Tal'du Dromesh for glory and honor, and one by one, all the best Shesaitju died.

She scaled down the barrier of rocks. Bare feet sliding across the jagged surfaces, she wondered what she was capable of now. Her body felt different… the sting of sharp stone against her soles, the wind against her skin. It was there, the sensation, but… different. She still needed to breathe. Yet, there was a sense of all-encompassing calm pervading her being ever since the Siren plunged into her heart. She knew she should be afraid of the scene before her. There was the father who'd created her, bloodied and dying in the sand, and next to him, the monster who'd caused so much pain.

Underwater, in that strange haven of ruins, filled with strange voices which she could now only remember in fractured segments, it'd almost felt like an eternity had passed.

Before, she'd been constantly reminded that she was just a young woman.

Too female to fight.

Too young to lead.

It all felt silly now, as if she'd lived many lives before. The memories of every Caleef dating back millenniums to the God Feud hovered in her mind, just outside of reach. She couldn't see their pasts; it was only a feeling, like she'd experienced indescribable loss, and more than just that of her village, Shavi, and Jumaat. Her entire people, they were hurting so much. They had been for a very long time, even before Liam. All they'd ever known was blood.

"It can't be…" Babrak said, more blood bubbling on his sand-covered lips, red saliva dripping to the ground.

"Stop this," she said. She kneeled beside her father and Babrak and peeled them apart. They were in too much of a state of shock to do anything about it. Both rolled onto their backs, deep wounds oozing from their respective torsos.

"My daughter…" Muskigo rasped. He reached out and stroked her cheek. His touch usually brought with it a sensation of warmth and safety. Now, there was nothing. She could still *feel* the touch, but it was different. Everything was different.

Armor and weapons clanked. When she looked up, a legion of warriors and Serpent Guards stopped at once. The tongueless guards were the first to fall to their knees and kowtow. Mahi rose to her full, impressive height, her bare skin coated in black, the nature of the nigh'jel blood making her shimmer in the moonlight. It was faint, but they all seemed to notice. A second later, the warriors bowed to her as well.

"Mahraveh…" Muskigo whispered weakly. He crawled for her. "My daughter…" She'd known her father as many things, but weak or dishonorable were never any of them. She had no idea how long she'd been underwater, but already, it seemed he'd forsaken everything he believed in. The old ways and the new. He'd attacked Babrak in Latiapur and was about to be killed by the warriors in front of her.

She walked away from him, and he collapsed while grasping for her ankles. The warriors parted for her, Serpent Guards rising without requiring orders, surrounding her on all sides, weapons armed.

"My Caleef, you return to us," one of the warriors said. "What should we do with them?"

Mahi glanced back. Both her father and Babrak clung to life, barely. Clutching at their wounds, watching her—the two greatest military powers in the Black Sands, looking pathetic, letting an old grudge drive them to horrific ends.

Is this all over me? she wondered. So much remained foggy.

"Clean them up, and keep them alive if you can," she said.

The man looked nervously to a few of the others. "But Muskigo, he—"

"Is a fool. We all are." Mahi turned away and crossed the arena. The Serpent Guards followed her, helping her over the rubble of a collapsed portion of the arena's arcade, no doubt more of a mess caused by her vengeful father.

It was night, but it didn't take long for people to crowd the streets. One woman dressed in a bright purple sarong noticed her, then another. Shesaitju poured forth from their homes and fell to their knees, offering prayers. Mahi studied each of them, genuine adoration written on all their faces. These were the same people who may have shirked her for being a female warrior, or for siding with her father in the rebellion against the Glass Kingdom. Men who would have seen her naked body and felt only lust, didn't show it, not now.

Blooming green light drew her focus upward. Nigh'jels were

being spilled down the grand steps up to the Caleef's palace, lighting her path. 'A river of the old souls,' the sages would call it —of Caleefs past inviting her into their shared home.

As she ascended, step by golden step, they all flocked her. Sages offered words of prayer so quickly she couldn't even keep up with what they were saying. Afhems' and warriors' faces touched the earth before her. All the way up the stairs, into the sparse forest of blackwoods in the courtyard, thousands worshipped her for nothing which she did on her own.

Suddenly, she understood why Caleefs could wind up scared and diffident like Sidar Rakun. She understood how young kings like Pi Nothhelm could make drastic mistakes and invite monsters into their home. Nobody knew how to wake up one day, worshipped by all.

Why me? she wondered as she stopped in the grand entrance to a magnificent home she'd never wanted.

Everything felt like a blur until she stood in the palace. Why would the God of Sand and Sea choose her to carry his essence when she thought such things?

"Mahi!" Bit'rudam ran over, his feet pounding the gravel. No sooner had he thrown his arms around her, his slender fingers grazing her back than a Serpent Guard shoved him. He hit the ground hard, and nearly a dozen spears angled up against his throat. He raised his chin, not daring to even take a breath.

It took her a few moments regarding his pleading expression to remember who he was to her. "Release him."

At once, the Serpent Guards returned their blades to their sides. Mahi had only been an afhem for a short time, and it was nothing like this. It wasn't that they listened, it was how quickly they did so. Not a moment's hesitation, as if they knew her desires before they even escaped her lips.

"It can't be," Bit'rudam said, a tremor in his voice. Murmurs filled the grand chamber. Mahi ignored them all. She extended a hand to help him up, but he didn't dare move. She stood, waiting until he finally found the nerve to accept her aid. As he reached his feet, he studied his hand as if expecting black paint to rub off.

"A woman has never—" he began.

"Done a lot of things," Mahi interrupted. She scoured all the columns, engraved and painted with legends of old. A thousand years of warrior afhems and conflict. "Man, Woman, afhem, markless, Caleef... all of these titles. I think I finally understand." She started walking again. Serpent Guards spread the doors to the throne auditorium wide. Beings of the sea, small and large, had already been sacrificed around the hole she'd fallen through.

Mahi couldn't keep track of how many markless servants came at her on approach. She was only grateful that the guards were there to keep them at bay. Seeing that portal in the floor made her whole world feel crowded. Falling, knowing she was going to die, slamming into the sea.

Not falling... pushed.

It felt like so long ago, but the wound was still fresh.

Mahi stopped before the Sea Door, and the moment she did, she could hear the feet of the guards shifting behind her, and the stifled gasps of everyone else. Tension was thick in the air. She stared down into the darkness, saw the dark stain where Yuri Darkings had landed.

Did he know this would happen? she thought, but she knew he couldn't have.

She listened to the wind howling like starving wolves and the crashing waves.

"I'll be gentle on her..." a sinister voice suddenly echoed. Then came a cackle that made every hair on her body raise. The very night seemed to reach through the Sea Door, grasping, ready to devour her. She fell to one knee and hid her face. There was a time when she thought that evil was just something men invented, but not anymore, not as she recalled that dark presence under the

sea. The Buried Goddess named Nesilia. How the very water rippled in fear from her. How her voice made Mahi's heart turn to ice, then like it might wither and die. She recalled feeling hopeless…

"Mahi… my Caleef. Are you all right?"

A strong hand fell upon her shoulder. Mahi snapped to focus, grasped the man's wrist and thrust it away. For a long moment, she only saw that dark figure and heard that menacing laugh. Then, Bit'rudam's features became clear again. She backed off, leaving him stunned and speechless.

"I'm sorry…" she stammered. "I'm sorry." She crawled along the floor, taking a wide arc around the Sea Door. She reached the dais leading to the Caleef's throne—her throne. She patted the first step, then the next, climbing without even realizing it. Then, her hand fell up on the polished, black sandstone seat.

"Let me help you, my Caleef." One of the eunuchs grabbed for her.

"No!" she snapped, then pulled herself up. She slid back into the seat only to find that even smoothed stone wasn't comfortable. And it was cold. The fact that she was utterly naked had evaded her until then. Looking out across the room at dozens of servants, mostly male, ogling her, she felt shame.

She crossed her legs and covered her chest.

"My eternal forgiveness," the same eunuch said. "You must be freezing." Without waiting for a response, he stepped out of his heavy robe, revealing only a soft stomach and loincloth that covered far too little. He went to hand the robe over to her himself, but she quickly snatched it and covered her lap.

"Everyone out," she muttered.

"My Caleef." Bit'rudam coughed. "Mahraveh. Are you all right?"

"Out!" she bellowed. The domed ceiling carried her voice like that of a Siren.

The eunuchs and servants fled like a frightened flock of gallers, like a startled pit lizard, like a peasant at the command of the master. Only the Serpent Guards remained.

"All of you, as well. Leave me." She shooed them, and they filed into the center of the room, then marched out together.

When the room was empty but for her and her thoughts, she heard a cough. Bit'rudam stood, hand pressed against his mouth. Where earlier there had been reverence in his expression, now there was only concern.

"You don't seem yourself," he said. He took a step toward her, but her glower stopped him from getting any closer.

"Do I look like myself?" she replied.

"No… you… what happened down there?"

"I lived."

"Mahi."

Her gaze shifted toward the Sea Door. Even looking at it, she could feel the sensation of falling again; of her body, limbs slapping against the water. The fear of knowing that she was going to die, thanks to a traitor. But she didn't.

"Please, leave me, Bit'rudam," she said softly. "I need to think."

"Maybe I can—"

"You no longer need stay by my side. I'm not your afhem."

He kept his head raised. "Maybe not. Even still, if you need me, I'll stay close." He stared at her for a few long seconds, and just before she finally gave in and looked back, he turned to obey her commands. She barely knew the young warrior, but she'd never met anyone so fiercely devoted. Even Jumaat split his heart with care for his family. For Bit'rudam, there was only his afhemate.

Only his *afhemate,* Mahi thought. *Not the rest of her people.*

"Bit'rudam," she said.

He whipped around to face her in a heartbeat.

"Yes?"

"Keep an eye on my father and Babrak. No more fighting in this city. Enough of us have died here over nothing. Enough of us have died everywhere."

He bowed at the waist, deep and teeming with respect. "I'll do my best, my af… my Caleef." At that, he stepped out of the chamber. The Serpent Guards closed the doors with a resounding *gong,* and now, Mahi was indeed left alone with her thoughts.

Slumping back, head pressed against her palm, she let her eyelids close, but the darkness behind them was met by Nesilia's sinister cackle. Her eyes shot open, and she found herself short of breath.

So, instead, she watched the floor and dug through her memories. What had happened down there wasn't clear, but she recalled some of the things she'd heard, and then from the Siren beyond.

"Time is running out to come together."

"Your union will be in life, or in death."

"It is in your hands now."

She wasn't the only one terrified by Nesilia. Caliphar, the all-powerful God her people thought protected them was even more so. His sister, as he said, another goddess.

Mahi wasn't sure if this is what it meant to be Caleef—to hear the conversations caught in the Eternal Current between eternal beings. However, she knew what she'd heard. What had been asked of her.

Only, she wasn't sure where to start, or why she should listen to that same Siren who had so mercilessly stolen Jumaat from her —murdered him right before her eyes. Just as she wasn't sure why her God would choose her, a woman foolish enough to be assassinated by a traitorous Glassmen.

Why me?

XXIX

THE REBEL

Muskigo awoke to a splitting headache. He'd been trampled by stampeding zhulong—or at least, that's how it felt. He tried to move, but something on his wrist resisted. Realizing his eyes were still clenched shut, he opened them and blinked. Manacles.

Imprisoned again?

He pulled, only his arms were restrained in a way that kept him on his knees. His mind went to the worst-case scenario: the Glass had attacked while he was too busy chasing Babrak through the streets like he was nothing more than a common thug.

Then Muskigo noticed the one window in the room, narrow, with a pointed arch. He was in a Shesaitju building, for certain. A guard stood at the door, one of Muskigo's own people, a Serpent Guard, staring silently forward through the eye-slits of his intimidating, golden mask.

Muskigo's last memory before going under hit him like a tidal wave. His daughter, Mahraveh, emerging from the sea wearing the color of a Caleef.

"Don't worry, Muskigo," a voice rattled. "She's keeping us fresh."

He strained to look right. There, chained to the other corner of the room, he saw Afhem Babrak. Long strands of seaweed stretched across his belly. The stuff had healing properties and grew around the shores of Latiapur. That meant Babrak's wounds weren't enough to kill him.

Too bad.

"*Pis'truda*," Muskigo growled. He pulled in the direction of the damnable afhem, stretching his chains until the metal threatened to tear his flesh. The pain in his side burned like fire. His own torso was coated with healing weeds, and he recalled Babrak's hidden knife ramming into him again and again.

"You should have killed me," Muskigo said.

"If it wasn't evident, I tried."

"When I get free—"

"Don't waste your breath," Babrak said.

"Whatever it takes to end you."

Babrak chortled, then groaned in pain. "The real question is: Why I am locked in here with you when only one of us went rampaging through the streets of this protected city?"

"You deserve far worse."

"Just because we don't agree on the best path toward peace, doesn't mean my way is wrong. That's always been your problem, Muskigo. Too stubborn for your own good. You think every problem can be solved with a sword."

"And you've always been a jealous hog," Muskigo spat. "All this… is it really because Pazradi decided to love me? Aren't there enough women in the world?"

"You really think it's that? Fool. I barely remember her face. All I cared about was you thinking everyone should worship and love you because you stood before King Liam in Tal'du Dromesh and proved that—what—you're entertaining? He laughed at you, right after he slaughtered our fathers and brothers in open battle."

"Exactly why we should be free of them!" Muskigo roared.

That brought the sound of steel upon the dungeon door. A warning.

"Why? So, we can go back to killing each other over women?" Babrak said, lower. "Maybe I should have let you have her."

Muskigo scoffed.

"Maybe I shouldn't have cared," Babrak continued, ignoring the interruption, "but then my afhemate would have seen me as weak. I'd be dead already, throat cut in my sleep. Those are our old ways you so revere."

"And we'd all be better off." Muskigo offered his chains another futile tug, then gave up.

Babrak started to laugh, but it turned into a pained groan. He seemed to be enjoying the struggle far too much for Muskigo to indulge him.

"I came to you before I sailed west," Muskigo said softly. "I stepped into your home and shared a meal, and I put it all aside, practically begging for your support."

"What did you expect? Our Caleef already refused to break the alliance he'd agreed to."

"*Alliance*," Muskigo sneered. "You said you'd consider it. You said it was time to put our pasts behind us. When Liam died, and the time came to make our move, you never showed."

"After you left, I walked out into the sea to reflect." Babrak shook his head. "The Current wasn't with you, I felt it."

"Lies. Me... the others, we were just obstacles out of your way so you could flirt with the Glass Crown, and earn their favor. If you'd sailed with us, they'd already be on their knees."

"I am flattered, but you overestimate my power."

"More lies!" Muskigo barked.

"I defend the lives of my afhemate. What can you say for yours?"

"At least they died with honor."

Babrak sighed. "Dead, nonetheless."

"And that's such a bad thing? To ride the Current? To be free of this… suffering?" Muskigo slouched back, and watched gulls soar by the window; listened to the din of the city, traders in the markets squawking louder than the birds. Here they were, the two most powerful and renowned afhems in the Black Sands, locked up, and the world seemed to go on fine without them.

"How does this end, Babrak?" Muskigo asked, not taking his eyes off the gray-blue sky.

"I think it already has for me. You saw what your daughter has become. Unlike you, I follow the will of our Caleef—the will of our God. It won't matter that I violated no sacred oaths. It won't matter that *you* murdered men in this city." A fit of coughing overtook him before he finished. "Nothing matters in the end."

"The way we live our lives resounds upon the ocean's tides."

"Beautiful words, perhaps, but we all wind up in the same sea. She won't let me rob you of that, even if you deserve it."

"And you don't?" Muskigo pushed his injured side enough to turn all the way and face him. "You did it, didn't you?"

Babrak blew out through his teeth. "And what am I accused of this time?"

"You went behind my back to convince Yuri Darkings to murder my daughter. Take her army out of the equation. What did you offer him?"

"You of all people must know the consequences of dealing with Glass Lords."

"That doesn't answer my question!" Muskigo snapped.

"And I never will. How dare you accuse me of that?"

"How dare me? You lied about my daughter. You murdered Farhan right above us."

"Farhan tripped," Babrak said with a little laugh.

"You lie about everything! You are the worst kind of snake, Babrak Trisps'I."

"If I lie, it is because you are a plague to the Black Sands which needs removing. A relic of an old way that believed in nothing but blood and death when diplomacy is the way of the future. We fought them. We lost miserably, now again. How could it be any clearer?"

Muskigo wanted to curse him. However, nothing came out. He could only sigh. "Perhaps we should have put an end to each other in the arena."

"And miss all this fun?"

Footsteps sounded at the door. Orders came in Saitjuese, then Serpent Guards slithered in. Two for each of them. They unlocked Muskigo's wrists, and his arms fell to his sides, unbelievably sore from being held up for gods-knew-how-long. Gripping him, one on each shoulder, they dragged him. He resisted at first, but his battered body made it too difficult.

"What is this?" he asked, knowing full well the tongueless guards couldn't answer. "I have to speak with my daughter. I have to speak with the… Caleef." It was difficult to say out loud. Of all the futures he could ever have wanted for Mahraveh, this was never one of them. It wasn't even a fate he could've dreamed up.

"You're being brought to her," Bit'rudam said, waiting just outside. Now, Muskigo recognized where they were: far beneath the Caleef's throne room, in the palace dungeons.

"Tell me what's going on, boy!" Muskigo demanded of Bit'rudam.

Behind them, Babrak grunted with every step. It appeared that between the two of them, Muskigo had dealt the greater damage. At least he could take some semblance of delight in that.

"What's going on is that you should never be allowed in this palace again," Bit'rudam said. "I don't care who you are. I'm ashamed that as a boy, all I wanted was to grow up to be like the great Muskigo Ayerabi. The Scythe."

"Some dream," Babrak laughed.

Muskigo ignored him. "You will come to find the world is not so simple. What's done, is done. I only want to know if my daughter is all right."

"She's been locked in the throne room, alone for two days," Bit'rudam said as the guards led them up a switchback stairwell. "Hasn't said a word to anybody since the doors closed, but I hear her muttering. I've spent much of the time anchored offshore, watching just to make sure she didn't throw herself into the Boiling Waters."

"Why would she do that?" Muskigo asked.

"Why did Sidar Rakun?" Bit'rudam retorted.

"Bit'rudam, she seems to trust you. I know she must be angry over what I've done, but I did it for her."

"For her?" Babrak laughed again.

"It's the truth," Muskigo said. "Ask her to speak with me. I… I have to talk with her."

"You will," Bit'rudam said. "She's summoned every afhem."

"All of them?" Babrak asked.

"No one knows why," Bit'rudam continued, "but she says she's come to her first decision as Caleef."

"I need to talk with her alone." Muskigo fought the clutch of the Serpent Guards to take the young warrior by the shoulders. They promptly tore him away. "Please, I have no idea what she's going through, but I'm her father. I need to talk to her."

"A Caleef has no family," Bit'rudam quoted from the texts. "Has no afhemate."

Muskigo could hear the bitter disappointment in Bit'rudam's tone, but the young warrior was right. The blood of the nigh'jels erased all former affiliations—made the Caleef exist only in the image of the God of Sand and Sea. All former loyalties were meant to be forgotten.

"She still knows who I am," Muskigo said, more trying to convince himself than anything. He'd never spent much time around Sidar Rakun, but every time he had, he'd always gotten the sense of the man's detachment.

"She's different," Bit'rudam said. "I don't know how, but she is."

"She needs her father," Muskigo said.

"Nobody needs you anymore. The blood you spilled here, that's all they'll remember."

"I like this one," Babrak said.

"Harsh words from an afhem-less child," Muskigo responded. "I see how you look at her. How you lust. It'll never happen now, you know that, don't you? You can win her old afhemate, become the greatest warrior we've ever known, and still, she'll never be yours."

Bit'rudam stopped in front of him at the landing. He turned, eyes rife with fury. He set his jaw and whispered, "All because the pink-skin you brought here pushed her off a ledge." With that, he turned with a flourish of his robe, and left.

Muskigo's heart sank. He wasn't sure why he'd treated the boy that way. The only man who deserved such spite stood behind him. He was just so angry at everything and everyone. Babrak, Yuri Darkings, The God of Sand and Sea, Himself, who stole his daughter's chance for a normal life. However, more than anything, he was angry at himself.

The Serpent Guards gave his arms a yank, drawing him toward the throne room's open doors. More afhems entered around them, regarding Muskigo and Babrak as if they carried the blight. The closer they got to the coral throne, the more Muskigo realized that the last person on Pantego he wanted to see was Mahraveh.

She'd stood by him through everything, saved him when all hope was lost. Now, he brought shame to their ancestral family—a family that would die with him in disgrace.

Afhems backed away as Muskigo entered the room, glowering, the sages, too. They did the same to Babrak, who cursed them, claiming he had nothing to do with what happened. It seemed that Muskigo's wounds made Babrak appear guilty enough. Or, maybe, perhaps everyone now saw him for the gold-monger he was.

At least I accomplished some good…

Muskigo's thoughts were stolen when his gaze fell upon his daughter seated high above on the Caleef's throne. She looked so small in the seat, it was almost like she was a child again. A dress of golden lace was draped over her thin body. More skin showed than any father would approve of, and every inch of her was black as the midnight sky. A flat crown sat atop her half-shaved head, beads hanging down over her face.

The look in her eyes made Muskigo want to shrivel to a husk. Thankfully, the guards helped him to a spot on the stands across the room from Babrak. They did, however, remain posted beside each of them.

Muskigo cared about none of it. Suddenly, his rivalry and hatred of Babrak or any other afhems who'd abandoned him melted away. There was only Mahraveh, and the struggle contorting her features. No matter what color her skin, Muskigo knew when she was distressed, and more than anything, she seemed afraid. A deep sort of fear, like when her mother had died. Mahraveh probably didn't even remember, but he did. He could never forget when her small face turned to him, and she asked if she would ever see her again.

What are you afraid of, my little sand mouse?

"Mahraveh, please," he said out loud. His voice cracked. "I have to talk to you. What you saw—"

She looked up at him and stunned him into silence. All the afhems joined her, muttering, judging. He could hear a few, and they didn't only adjudge him to be guilty of breaking their laws and attacking Babrak in Latiapur, or him starting a war, but they whispered about the nerve he had to address the Caleef by her name. The very name *his* wife had given her so long ago.

"You know me," he said, leaving out his claim to being her father, but also refusing to back down. "I did what I thought necessary. For us. For all of us."

"You murdered an envoy of the Crown. A Shieldsman under a white flag!" Afhem Usef yelled. "Not all of us asked for this rebellion. When they find out… Who can say what they'll do?" Others voiced their agreement. Babrak sat, quietly grinning.

A response died on the tip of Muskigo's tongue. Of all the things he'd expected his peers to be angry with him about, that fact never entered his mind. But he couldn't deny it. He'd killed a Shieldsman on neutral ground.

"They'll do nothing," Mahraveh said. All heads turned back to her. Even her voice sounded different. Maybe it was the room, but it was firmer, more commanding, and it gave Muskigo goosebumps all over.

"My Caleef, why have you summoned us here if not to discuss the fate of this traitor?" another afhem asked.

"Surely, he must be stripped of his afhemate," added Babrak, purposely holding his side like he was still in excruciating pain. "Hasn't there been enough blood spilled because of him?"

"Only you remain before I'm done," Muskigo bristled.

"Will you two tear apart this sacred chamber as well?" Afhem Usef asked.

More arguing broke out. Muskigo couldn't stay out of it. He shouted, Babrak shouted, and all the afhems with them. He wasn't even sure who he was angry at or what the sides were. Just the sight of Babrak back in his element, manipulating and twisting words—it had him seeing red again.

And then Mahraveh stood. A hush fell like a thick blanket over the gathering. She sauntered slowly down from her throne, across the room, and around the Sea Door. Muskigo's muscles tightened as she did, and the whole room held their collective breath. Only days had passed since they'd watched Caleef Sidar Rakun leap to his death.

After a lap around the hole, Mahraveh turned and walked straight toward Muskigo. Not since the day Sidar Rakun surrendered to King Liam had Muskigo respected the Caleef as the true voice of their God. He'd never seen Sidar Rakun fall, then emerge from the sea upon the sands of a Siren, after all. A part of him had started to believe it was all games played by the palace servants.

Then his daughter fell. She died because of him, and yet, here she was, skin like polished obsidian.

"Daughter," he said softly. There were murmurs, of course. "You have to talk to me. I had no idea Yuri would do that."

No answer.

"You have to talk to me," he insisted.

She stopped before him, seeming taller than ever. Her brows lifted, offering him a pitiable look that broke his heart. Then, she lay her hand upon his shoulder. Her skin was warm as freshly spilled blood.

"And we wonder why the Glass cut right through us," she said, then she turned her neck to regard the entire room. "Always bickering. Darkings saw it all. This is what he meant by the shore that day. This is why he pushed me."

"Darkings tried to murder you," Muskigo said. He grasped her hand and pulled it to his cheek. The entire room gasped as if he'd stabbed her. "You've been alone in here too long. Whatever happened, we need to talk about it."

Mahraveh clutched him by both sides of the face. Her forehead touched his like they used to do when she was little, and he was proud or she was frightened. It was so different then. Now, he barely felt like the elder between them.

"He set me free," she said. She turned and addressed the rest of the afhems before he could respond. "For centuries, the faithful have trekked up our steps and thrown themselves through. A few were chosen as Caleef, and unshakeable as they were in their faith, they were not strong men. Not like all of you, sitting around this room."

"My Caleef, surely you do not mean to spare Muskigo of all consequence?" Babrak said, then forced a pitiful groan.

"I agree," Usef said. "It should not matter who he was before."

"That's not what I'm saying," Mahraveh went on. "I've sat in here, wondering why it's come to this. My father—despite what any of you think of him—is right, we should not bow and beg for scraps from the Glass Crown." Mumblings of disapproval greeted her, but her glare silenced them.

"Nor should we be forced to fight them over what is rightfully ours," Mahraveh went on. "Over these Black Sands. They want us to follow them into Iam's light, but his gate is not for us. Has anyone in this room hoped to die and see the Gate of Light? No. Of course not. So why the games? The sand and the sea… that is where we belong. That is our fate unless we allow darkness to swallow it."

"And we should fight for it!" Muskigo proclaimed.

"With what army?" Babrak replied. "You've already lost so many."

"Stop," Mahi demanded. She squeezed her eyelids shut as if warding off a horrible headache. "Our God… so much strength in this room, but none of us knows him. Are you even aware that He has a name?"

She looked directly at Babrak, who didn't respond. Then she

turned to the rest of them. "A name that has been lost for so long, just as we have been. He speaks in riddles. I'm… trying to understand them all. What I do know, is that a power greater than the Glass Kingdom is coming."

"Another conqueror?" Afhem Usef asked.

"Worse. Something that will drown us all and stop the Current if we don't stop it. Everyone, Shesaitju, the Glass—everything that breathes."

Afhem Usef stood proud. "Then we should hand Muskigo over to them as they demanded, and fortify our own cities!"

"You mean their cities?" Muskigo said, a harsh edge to his tone. "We'll be their vassals again. Pink missionaries will trample our streets like so many mice, desperate to convert us in greater numbers than ever. Their taxes and tariffs will bury us. Again."

"At least there will be enough of us alive for any of it to matter," Babrak said.

"So, fear should keep crippling us?" Muskigo asked.

"We'll all die," Mahi said. Again, silence came. "Us against the Glass. Us against each other. We're all going to die because we can't stop fighting."

Babrak struggled to stand, and the guard beside him helped. "We've had our differences in your past life, my Caleef. But command us, give us guidance, and we will follow."

"Thank you for your permission," Mahi said.

Babrak deflated noticeably. "I—I'm sorry—"

"Try as you might to follow my command, you'll fail," she went on. "As you always have. And not just you. I can see it, every moment where we went wrong. Caleefs displaced over disagreements. Ignored by warlords. Your ancestors wanted so intensely to be faithful, but you're all only men in the end."

"My Caleef, Babrak is right," Afhem Usef said. "You need only tell us your desire, and so the Current flows."

Mahraveh glanced at Muskigo. The fear in her returned, and

he wished to go to her, hold her tight, to tell her that she no longer needed his or anyone else's approval.

But the moment was fleeting.

"The cycle of this war amongst ourselves must end if we hope to fight what's coming," Mahraveh said.

"And what is coming, my Caleef?" Babrak asked.

Muskigo could tell how hard it was for him to stifle a smug grin, knowing he'd get everything he wanted.

"The end," she muttered. "I've never felt such terror."

The way she said it, with such certainty, there wasn't much that could send a shiver up Muskigo's spine, but that did. And he wasn't alone. All around the room, warrior afhems regarded each other with panicked expressions. Even Babrak sat right back down.

"And we'll never be able to face it like this," Mahraveh said. "Fractured. No matter what any of you promises. No matter what any of you believes. There's too much bad blood and too much history. I fought to earn the same marks as all of you, and still, nothing changed. We must march as one—as Shesaitju and nothing else. Yet to do so, there can be no more afhemates."

Silence like a winter storm fell upon them. They stared, not even blinking until finally, Muskigo summoned the nerve to break it. "How can there be no more afhemates?"

"Each of you wears the mark of an ancient clan," Mahraveh answered. "That mark gives you power, but as the power of one clan rises, our combined strength wanes. It is time we unite. Truly unite as one people."

"The afhemates are our strength, my Caleef," Babrak insisted. "The strong rise to guide our ways, the weak fade into the sands."

"And yet, to survive—to make the Black Sands our own again —we must *all* be strong." Mahraveh stared through the Sea Door, gazing at it, longingly. The more she spoke, the less Muskigo recognized her.

"Mahraveh, what are you thinking?" Muskigo asked. There'd been a time when he wouldn't have had to ask that question, when he could tell—a father's intuition. The descent into the sea had changed her. She appeared exhausted, like a world-weary old warrior ready to lay down his sword and die in his sleep.

She slowly returned to her throne and sank into the seat. Then, she looked up at the Serpent Guards standing by the closed doors into the room and nodded. And that was all she needed to do.

The doors opened and in flowed dozens of Serpent Guards. More than Muskigo had ever seen in one place. Maybe all of them. They were men with sad origins, made purposeful. Unwanted children left at brothels or abandoned on the streets, found and trained by black fist masters into fearless, mindless warriors. Extensions of the Caleef's will.

They seized Afhem Usef first, and without weapons, neither he nor the others could fight back. One held him down, while another dragged the curved blade across the man's tattoo which marked him as an afhem.

Then they took another afhem, then another, until all of them bled from their necks and heads. Some fought it, but it was no use. All his life, Muskigo had never known the purpose of the Serpent Guards when any Shesaitju warrior would die to protect the Caleef. Now, he knew that he'd simply never known a Caleef fierce enough to use them to their fullest potential.

They came for Muskigo and he knew, of any of the afhems, that maybe he could resist. He knew their art of war, was trained in the same manner, but he let them push down his head and scrape away the mark he'd fought so hard to earn. Babrak squealed like a stuck boar across the room as the same happened to him.

It would have given Muskigo at least an ounce of satisfaction as he tried to ignore the horrible pain of being skinned, if not for Mahraveh. She didn't look away. She watched as all the warlords, the most powerful men in the Black Sands, were robbed of their power; their authority.

On the other side of the Boiling Keep's threshold, Bit'rudam watched as well, seeing the work of the young woman he admired so. And in that moment, Muskigo had never been prouder of her. Mahraveh saw what he never had—that one afhem couldn't unite them all, and she didn't allow herself to worry what anybody she cared about might think. Only the Caleef could rise and become a proper king or queen of the Black Sands. In mere minutes, the afhemate markings on hundreds of thousands of Shesaitju would become meaningless, leaving them to follow her without question.

If they followed her. Kings of Glass had been turned on and murdered for doing far less.

She knelt by Muskigo's side as he sat, hunched over. Blood trickled from his head onto the polished stone, but he turned to face her and smiled. Now he recognized her fully. She was resolute, but even through the strange darkness coating her skin, he could see the regret.

He reached out and ran his hand over her ear, finally able to touch her.

"Don't," he said. "I understand."

She nodded slowly.

"Get off me!" Babrak barked, suddenly. He shoved a sage away who tried to pour water over his fresh wound. He rose and stomped toward the exit, then stopped long enough to glare at Mahraveh and Muskigo. His eyes twitched with rage... Then he left.

"He won't be alone," Muskigo said.

"No, he won't," she replied.

Her gaze was aimed at Muskigo, but it wavered. She wasn't focused on anything. So he dropped his hand down to her jaw and forced her to look at him. To actually look.

"I haven't always made it easy, daughter," he said. "I've made so many mistakes that I don't deserve my markings anymore anyway. But worse than any, was ever underestimating you."

"I'm glad you did," she said. "I am me, only because of you."

"And so much more."

She lifted away and looked around the room. More afhems struggled or received care, the Serpent Guards keeping most in line. Bit'rudam joined the sages in fetching water, his eyes flitting toward Mahi more than a few times.

"This is only the beginning," she said to Muskigo.

"Better than the end," Muskigo replied.

She bit her lip, swallowed hard. "I have to ask something of you. Something I know you will hate. Something *I* hate."

"Anything, my little sand mouse." He said it so quickly he didn't have a chance to consider the gravity of her words. And yet, he was unafraid. This calculated bit of ruthlessness was precisely what the leader of armies and men needed to be capable of. It was what made Liam the Conqueror great. Muskigo thought he had it within him, but he was wrong.

"These men, I've taken so much from them," she said. "I must lose as well."

XXX

THE KNIGHT

Once again, Torsten found himself sitting outside the bars of Rand's cell. This time, he was shoveling a bit of stew down his gullet. He was starved, and sister Nauriyal was a wonderful cook. Even Brouben couldn't get enough, and dwarves among many things were known for their savory cuisine. Torsten was glad she'd learned something growing up in her father's lavish mansion.

"You should try some," Torsten said, mouth full as he gestured to the bowl in front of Rand. The fallen Shieldsman was as haggard as ever. It'd been weeks since Torsten found him and locked him up to protect him from himself. He'd barely had food or water except when his body grew so desperate his rather impressive willpower caved.

He'd barely spoken either.

Nauriyal tended to his wounds, and sister or not, she was a pretty girl around his age.

Nothing.

Lucas would try to get the man to play gems.

Nothing.

Dellbar even attempted to offer him some of that sweet,

honeyed wine after Torsten reminded him how Rand had turned to the bottle after his short spell as Wearer of White. He shoved it away.

"This is good," Torsten said, taking another long slurp on his stew. "Really good."

"Don't you have a battle to prepare for?" Rand asked.

"Not sure," Torsten said, bolting upright, shocked that his friend had spoken. "The Shesaitju sent word back that Caleef Sidar Rakun was found dead in Trader's Bay, and that a new one has already been chosen. She has an emissary marching here as we speak to discuss terms for ending this rebellion."

"A woman?"

Torsten shrugged and lifted the bowl to his lips to down the rest of his meal. "I've seen stranger things."

"I suppose," Rand agreed, then moved a bit closer.

Torsten offered Rand the stew. He acted disinterested, but Torsten could practically see the saliva forming in the Shieldsman's mouth.

Stubborn.

Considering that Lucas hadn't had luck finding Sidar Rakun's body, and Sir Marcos hadn't yet returned from Latiapur with word about the situation there, it was either true, or the Shesaitju had decided to move on and prove they were as hypocritical as the Glass lords they so despised. From what Torsten knew, it could take months for a new Caleef to be 'chosen by the sea,' not days. This seemed more like a selection of someone popular with their people.

Torsten wiped his mouth. "She's some hero from their arena, who then led a fleet to break our blockade and free Nahanab. A few of the soldiers who were there say they saw her, like a warrior-goddess from above."

Rand leaned back against the wall and tilted his head to stare at the stone. "Then we're all doomed."

"Why do you say that?"

"Gods, goddesses… we're just toys to them." He ran his finger in a circle around a bit of broken stone. "Pieces on a game board."

"The last Caleef saw reason," Torsten said. "Maybe this one will, too. Or maybe the army she leads will be our greatest test. Either way, we'll be ready."

Rand grunted something indiscernible in response, then let his head fall back and closed his eyes.

Torsten's heart broke at the sight of him. He had no idea what to do for him besides pray. Even watching him destroy his body with alcohol was preferable to this forlorn state. He considered telling Rand about Sigrid, that she was still out there somewhere, but false hope was worse than none at all. He'd waste a lifetime thinking he could find and save her when she was beyond salvation. Beyond life even. Worst of all, from everything she'd said to Torsten, she blamed Rand for her condition. By leaving her in Yarrington, she believed he'd damned her to the fate she'd received.

To Rand, she'd just be another person he'd failed.

If Torsten had learned anything since the day Redstar came to Yarrington, it was that sometimes the full truth brought nothing but pain. Rand's own story was a lie to inspire the Kingdom. If Torsten could just help Rand wait out the storm of pain, he knew that the young warrior could find a way to become worthy of his title: The Redeemer.

Picking up his bowl, Torsten stood to leave.

"Why do you keep coming down here?" Rand asked softly. "Why can't you just let me go?"

Torsten stopped. He leaned on the wall just beside the bars, letting the stone cool his face. "No man in the Glass has sacrificed more than you. For it never to be known…"

"'A Shieldsman must be selfless.' I've heard it enough times."

"Yet, no man truly is," Torsten said. "I don't have a family, Rand. Not even some distant cousin in Glinthaven. I thought, perhaps, the Crown was for a while, but… it took you to show me that this Order is my only family. You were a part of it once. You were my brother, and I didn't do enough to help you, but I won't stop trying."

"Then let me go."

Words caught in Torsten's throat. Silence pervaded, and he watched the way the firelight of the nearby torch played across the imperfections in the stone.

"Just rest," he said finally, as he slapped the wall. Then, without even glancing back, he made his way to the surface of the bridge where his horse and Lucas awaited him.

"Sir," Lucas saluted.

Torsten acknowledged him, then mounted his horse. White Bridge itself remained in shambles, but the whole region was bustling with activity. The injured civilians had been transferred to Fettingborough so they'd be out of the way. The ruptured structures along the bridge were now being used to support the army.

Makeshift weapons and armor smiths, cooking pots, bunks— it was shoddy, but on short notice, it would do. White Bridge was essentially a fortress, after all. Though, without any doors or locks, keeping goblins out of their growing stores at night was proving difficult. Torsten suspected that the dwarven aggression against them was causing them to scavenge further south.

"Galler arrived with word from Governor Nantby," Lucas said.

"And?" Torsten asked.

"He apologizes for the delay, but Panping can't spare any men. It seems…" Lucas cleared his throat.

"Spit it out."

"It seems the Buried Goddess' cultists we rooted out of Yarrington decided to turn their terror upon Yaolin City. They caused quite a commotion, looting, and burning with blood magic, and he had to recall all available troops."

"Why would cultists care about Yaolin?" Torsten inquired. "Was it a Panpingese holiday?"

"Didn't say."

Memory of what Mak had said about Nesilia already having returned flashed through Torsten's mind. He quickly shook it away. She was defeated. The Drav Cra had now grown completely silent. The Shesaitju were the last problem caused by King Liam's descent into madness left to be cleansed. Then, there could be peace.

"Their only aim is terror," Torsten decided. "They probably think the Panpingese will more easily succumb to their temptations. When we're done, return word that hunting down and eradicating any cults in Panping should remain top priority."

"Yes, Sir. Governor Nantby did send a shipment of arrows, both for us, and to pass through White Bridge to Yarrington."

"That should help."

Together, their horses galloped through the Eastern Gate. White Bridge wasn't large enough to serve the entire army, so the past weeks had been spent fortifying their position. They passed dozens of tents housing men, helping those from Sir Nikserof's army rest and get healthy.

Amongst the losses, Torsten counted Sir Porthcombe—a loud-mouth, but a Shieldsman nonetheless. If they survived these wars, Taskmaster Lars would have his hands full training new men.

"Defenses are coming along well, thanks mostly to Brouben," Lucas said.

Torsten had forgotten the value of dwarves. Even with as few of them as King Cragrock spared, they had trenched entirely across their position, blocking the main pass out of the northern Black Sands. Glassmen set up stakes along it using the broken posts leftover from Winde Port's palisade wall. That city could wait to be protected, considering it barely remained intact anyway.

"When it comes to dwarves, you get what you pay for," Torsten remarked.

"Thank you, Valin Tehr."

Torsten glared at the young Shieldsman and wiped the smirk from his face.

"What about food?" Torsten asked.

"We're running low, and rationing like you asked, but a new shipment from Yarrington should be arriving soon. It'll hold us until this new Caleef and the Shesaitju arrive."

Torsten pulled on his reins, and they slowed to a trot, skirting along the trench. It really was impressive, though, he supposed Balonhearth, the city he'd visited months ago was far more so. Even as the stout men continued to dig it out, they didn't appear exhausted or bored with the monotony of the work. They were having fun, humming tunes, drinking, playing pranks on each other.

What a way to live, Torsten mused to himself.

"Do you really think they'll hand over Sir Nikserof and exile Muskigo?" Lucas asked.

"Honestly, I'm not sure," Torsten replied. "That's always been the problem with fighting the Shesaitju. Nearly one hundred generals who all want something different, pulling and tugging. They're unpredictable. It left our people scared for centuries, but King Liam saw the weakness in it."

"What about the Caleef?"

"They had one when this all started, and Muskigo didn't seem to care. He'll be with them again now if our terms are met. I don't see him going quietly."

"Exile is a mercy for all he's done," Lucas said.

Torsten thought about drowning. About the ice-cold water flooding his lungs when he and Muskigo plunged into the canal in the battle of Winde Port. He'd had his chance to kill the rebel and Iam saw differently. It was time to change.

"Mercy is the will of our king," Torsten said. "And God."

"Yes, sir."

A moment passed. Lucas was probably waiting just long enough for the talk of Iam to settle before saying, "The forward scouts say the entire army in Nahanab left to march here. A man fitting Sir Nikserof's description was seen in bonds. Hardly a show of peace."

"They're just making a spectacle in the name of a new Caleef. We have the defensive position. They'll need more than the army of a few angry afhems to win." A hawk soaring overhead caught his attention. He turned back to Lucas. "Any word on Sir Marcos?"

"No sign of him," Lucas said, shaking his head. "The heathens probably killed him."

"The Shesaitju are an honorable people. They wouldn't kill a messenger. But you know Sir Marcos… There are certain… delights in Latiapur."

"I should have gone…" Lucas said. "Oh, no. That came out wrong. I only mean that—"

Torsten chuckled. Joy, happiness… it had been an emotion he hadn't experienced in quite some time. It felt good, which made him feel bad.

Clearing his throat, he said, "You read all the tomes I showed you in Yarrington. Studied everything from the war of the Black Sands to the upyr scourge of the second age. I need Shieldsmen with brains here."

"I'm honored, Sir. Truly."

"Hold strong, Sir Danvels. The Shesaitju will see things our way, or we will defeat them once again, right here."

"Let's hope the latter, eh!" Brouben shouted over. Torsten wasn't even sure how he'd heard from so far away, barking orders at his diggers. "What? Ye promised us a battle and me boys are gettin antsy. Fun as it is, I be sick of choppin up goblins."

"You have a lot less at stake here than we do, my Lord Brouben," Torsten said as they trotted over to him.

"Aye, that be true. Maybe I'll head back to Cragrock and get more men to make things even?"

"If you're offering..."

Brouben chortled. "Don't get greedy now, Glassman. Two hunerd of us be worth a thousand of ye fair flower-pickers. 'Sides, I've got ten clanbreakers. Set them loose on the gray men and watch them squirm."

Brouben flopped around to demonstrate, and he and his men fell into hysterics.

"I'm sure that's true," Torsten said once they'd calmed down. "This is incredible work."

"It's no trouble. They needed the exercise." Brouben hopped up onto a small boulder. "Put yer backs into it, ye wee runts. Big enough to trip a zhulong, I said, not a doe!" He turned back to Torsten. "If the Shesaitju agree to negotiate instead, ye owe me a duel."

"A duel?" Torsten said.

"Aye! I be needin to feel the power of he who slew that monster, Mak."

"I don't fight allies, my Lord."

"No killin! Just a good old-fashioned brawl. For the men." He gestured from side to side. "Who wouldn't wanna see two titans clash!" His nearest men cheered in support. A few Glassmen filled in around them, as well, to see what was going on.

"Ye win, I'll promise me axe to the Glass in yer next war, gold or not," Brouben went on. "And if I win, ye'll..." His words trailed off, and his features tightened, like he was desperate to think of the best idea ever.

"Then he has to chug a flagon!" a Glassman shouted.

Torsten whipped around to see who'd said it, but more of his people had gathered. They all wore smiles. Some laughed. Torsten's irritation immediately dissipated. It'd been a long time since he'd posted defensively in camp. Since the rebellion started, they were constantly on the move, racing to stop a slaughter like in Winde Port. He could barely remember the last time they'd dug in. The camaraderie of soldiers forced into the same tents for weeks—men who believed as he did. Far from the politics of lords and crowns. Strangely, he missed it. It made him ache for Sir Uriah Davies, King Liam, Sir Wardric Jolly… If Nikserof was truly dead, Torsten was the last of the old guard remaining.

"Please," Lucas said, joining in. "Sir Unger will show you how many of you he's worth in seconds."

"How bout we settle in now, then!" Brouben scooped his axe from its position leaning against the rock. "Ye win, ye get me support for good. I win, we all watch ye chug ale like a true dwarf. None of yer prissy cups."

"I don't think now is the right time." Torsten studied all the eager faces around him and couldn't help but crack a smirk. "Besides, I don't think those are fair terms... nor do I think it's a fair fight."

"Oh, ho, ho!" Brouben stuck his empty hand out and snapped his fingers. In a mere instant, one of his men placed a flagon in it, and he chugged, the ale dribbling down his dirty beard. "Is it a fair fight now?"

"C'mon, Sir Unger, show these dwarves why they should stay hidden in the mountains!" a Glass soldier hollered.

"Beat him down!" Lucas shouted, turning away and cupping hand in a failed attempt to make it seem like someone else had said it. Torsten's scowl did nothing to scare him this time. They both laughed.

"The people spoke, Sir Unger," Brouben said. "We can't be disappointin them."

Before he knew it, Torsten was down off his horse, boots in the mud with the rest of his men. He recalled in his long-ago past, when he was but a squire, how the men would grapple and argue, him amongst them. They'd distract themselves from the simple fact that death was coming. He used to join in then, at least until Sir Uriah came around. The general of the army never partook of the fun.

But times were changing.

"All right, all right," Torsten said. "I'll fight him, but only—"

Brouben leaped from the rock on which he stood, axe racing at Torsten's head. Torsten jumped back.

"Don't worry, Unger, she ain't sharpened yet," Brouben said. He swung at Torsten a few more times, sending him weaving back across a stretch of trampled grass.

"Let him get a sword out!" Lucas shouted.

"What's he compensatin for with that thing on his back?" Brouben argued. "Wouldn't be fair."

Brouben kept pushing, keeping Torsten from having a chance to draw *Salvation*. Torsten thought he'd be angry by the lack of courtesy, but he heard the dwarves and all his men cheering and found only excitement. It was like Valin Tehr's underground arena, only none of the bloodlust.

Rolling out of the way of another strike, Torsten came up with a rock in hand and lashed around to parry Brouben's next attack. The furry dwarf grinned impishly.

"A rock?" Brouben laughed. "I eat rocks for breakfast!"

He pressed his advance, leaving Torsten on the defensive. Their duel took them back toward the tents, where more soldiers joined into the crowd. Torsten swatted the axehead down. The dwarf used the momentum to whip around, but Lucas rode by and tossed his sword down.

Torsten snatched it out of the air, and when Brouben came around, Torsten's sword stopped close enough to Brouben's neck to shave his beard. Simultaneously, the dwarf's axe halted at Torsten's neck.

The soldiers went quiet.

"A tie, what's that mean?" one asked.

"A tie? He cheated!" Brouben griped.

"You refused me my weapon," Torsten said, winded. "You're the one who cheated."

"Being smart ain't cheatin."

"You'd discount him because he has the support of his men?" Lucas asked.

The dwarf grimaced.

Torsten watched him carefully, noting his mistake. These were allies, but they were new ones. Dwarves were known for their hot tempers and big egos. Even a friendly bout might cause issues they couldn't afford.

Then, taking Torsten by complete surprise, Brouben broke into a fit of laughter. He threw his axe down, then embraced Torsten. "The slayer of both Redstar and Mak the Mountainous doesn't disappoint! Did ye see that boys? Two times my height and only equal to my strength."

Torsten joined in the merriment. He stabbed the sword down into the dirt and wiped his hands. "I went easy on you."

"Next time, I'll go harder for yer weakness."

"What's his weakness?" Lucas asked.

"Like I'd tell? We be friends now, but if ever we weren't? It'd take Brouben the Bear to take ye down!" His men raised their shovels and chanted their prince's name.

Chants of "Brouben the Bear" clashed with "Torsten the Triumphant."

"Thank you, Lord Brouben," Torsten said softly, only between them. "I think they all needed that. Losing a battle isn't easy."

"Aye, but don't think yer out of it that easy," Brouben said. "A tie's a tie. I swear to fight at yer side in a future war, and I get to watch ye chug a flagon of ale. And not ye southerners' piss. Real, mountain stuff."

"My Lord, I don't think it's wise—"

"None of this be wise!" Brouben shouted. Then he climbed back up the rock. "War ain't for thinkin, it's for doin. He fights like the best of us, now let's see if he drinks like the best!"

Brouben put his arm on Torsten's back and guided him toward the nearest tent. Torsten so desperately wanted to resist, but the duel had left him tired, and the way his men encouraged it made resistance impossible. He looked back at Lucas, who smirked and said nothing. Brouben forced him down onto the bench at the soldiers' slop table.

"I really shouldn't," Torsten said. "There's work to be done."

"It'll be done," Brouben said. "Look around ye, Sir Unger. These men, they worship ye for what ye've done. Now, I ain't fought in many wars, but me father always told me that dwarves most respect leaders who are dwarves like them. I s'pose it's the same with men."

"Not King Liam," Torsten remarked. He couldn't remember the great king even leaving his own tent often. He'd take a stroll through their war camps on the eve of battle, and join the men in prayer, that was about it. Upon return to Yarrington, after his many great victories, parades would ensue. The people would revel, but he would just stay atop his horse, receiving praises.

"King Liam be dead, Shieldsman," Brouben said. "And so we'll drink to ghosts and the warriors who replace 'em. An ale, over here!" He slammed on the table. A dwarf with a gray beard down to his waist and big, bushy eyebrows waddled over.

"One of Balonhearth's finest," he said. "Dragon's Draught. Them brewers down deep say the secret ingredient is a bit of dragon blood."

Torsten covered his mouth to hide a gag.

"It's really just a bit of dye," Brouben leaned over and whispered. "Gives it that rich color. But nothing makes for drinking like a good story!" He snatched the flagon and *clanked* it down.

Torsten stared at the frothy, gold-red liquid. It really did look like ale stained with blood. Torsten felt his throat begin to close. He knew it was all in his head. He'd seen the liquid of Elsewhere do horrible things. From his worthless parents to Oleander, and then Rand after what her drunkenness pushed him to do.

Torsten lifted his gaze and took in all the men around him. Hundreds of eager eyes watched, more engrossed for this spectacle than the duel. Torsten had entered the Glass army as a squire for Sir Uriah, then became a Shieldsman himself. Never in his entire life had he the chance to be amongst the rabble—with the farmers and tanners forced to pick up a sword and serve the will of their king.

In the madness of it all, Torsten forgot that those were always the people who war hurt most: common-born men and women like him. They were the ones whose farms and homes were burned down when Muskigo started his rebellion. Many were probably still here, ready to fight against injustice. Torsten was just glad Dellbar the Holy was nowhere in sight, waiting to say "I told you so."

"All right then, a deal's a deal," Torsten said, then swallowed the lump forming in his throat as he grabbed the flagon. This received an eruption of cheers. Lucas squeezed Torsten's shoulders with jubilation, then backed away slowly, probably thinking he'd crossed a line. He probably had, but in that moment, Torsten couldn't find it in him to care.

"Wait!" Brouben said. He banged the table again, and his server brought him an ale. The flagon looked massive in his small hands. "No good friend of a dwarf should ever drink alone." He raised the cup. "Rock below, rock above, a drink too many and I'll join ye with love." He tapped the pint on the table, then brought it back to his lips and started chugging.

Torsten tried his best to follow him. It's not like he hadn't had ale before, but never dwarven stuff. The first swallow was like hot coals down his throat—Dragon's Draught, indeed. But once he started, it went down easy, and the raucous cheers didn't hurt. Before he knew it, the flagon was empty, and he slammed it down.

Brouben had already long since finished, at least, if the ale covering his beard didn't count. Torsten opened his mouth to say something, and a loud burp snuck out. He couldn't believe himself. Sure, he grew up on the streets, but it'd been decades since he was anything but a proper Shieldsman.

Only he seemed to care. The celebration amplified, and dozens of soldiers came by to show their support. He'd been victorious in many battles, but never anything like this. Shieldsmen had always remained above all this, and he was more than that now. The Glass Kingdom's Master of Warfare, but wars were won by these grimy-faced people who'd helped dig holes around campsites, and Torsten wasn't above any of that.

Dusk hit, and Torsten didn't leave. He, Lucas, and Brouben all stayed in the camps, drinking and reveling. He even ate the same slop the others did. By the time exhaustion set in, and he'd had his fill, Pantego's moons were already sinking, and dawn approached.

"The gray men will shake at the sight of Torsten the Triumphant!" a soldier cheered as Lucas helped Torsten to his feet.

"I had too much, didn't I, Lucas?" Torsten asked, slurring his words slightly. The feeling was made even stranger by being stuck without his true vision. It was less dizzy and more lost. Through his blindfold, he saw through the presence and absence of pure light, but now it merged together, making his entire world appear spilled across itself.

"Only a bit, sir," Lucas replied. He got under Torsten's

shoulder to help walk him back to his makeshift quarters at the bridge.

"You shouldn't see me like this."

"Nonsense," Lucas said. "Glad to. The men… they loved that. You're a good leader, Sir. Best I've ever known."

"I've known better." Torsten slipped out of his grip and had to lean against the wall of the bridge's gateway. He looked up. The light still swirled, but he noticed that a large shipment of food had arrived by carriage.

"Not me, Sir. Not me." Lucas helped him back upright and toward the broken tower.

"Wait," Torsten said.

"What is it?"

"Rand. I need to tell him something."

"Sir, I—"

Torsten pushed free and moved to stagger down the wooden stairs leading to the dungeon. He couldn't voice it, but he was grateful Lucas followed close behind, a hand on his arm to steady him.

Darkness hit them, and they pressed deeper. Finally, a small, flickering torch brought a meek illumination to the space.

"Sir Unger!" Dellbar said, seated across from Rand's cell. "Look at you, finally enjoying life a little. I'm so proud."

"Sir, you really should go to bed," Lucas whispered.

Torsten strode in farther until he could see that Rand was seated right in front of the bars, actually paying attention to whatever it was Dellbar was saying.

"What are you doing down here?" Torsten asked. He stumbled, then caught himself on the wall.

"If I'm being honest, I'm not used to having to keep up with soldiers. I needed a slow night. Though, now I see what I've missed." He looked up, smiling. "Oh, Iam, why have you led me astray?"

"Lord Brouben challenged him," Lucas said, excitedly.

"Don't listen to the priest, Rand," Torsten said. "He's insane." Torsten made it a few more steps, then plopped down near the cell, though it was hard to know if he was sitting or lying down.

"That might be," Dellbar admitted. "But Rand here was just telling me about his lovely sister. I believe I met her at her tavern or in the Vineyard once or twice, but I wasn't so practiced at holding my alcohol then. A lot like you now, Sir Unger."

Torsten half-grunted, a sorry excuse for a laugh. Then his head bobbed. Lucas shook his shoulder to try and get him to stand and leave again, but Torsten didn't have the energy.

"I'm sorry, Rand," he said softly.

"For what?" Rand asked.

"For what happened to your sister."

"It was my fault," Rand whispered. "I should've never trusted those men and left her behind."

"It was nobody's fault," Dellbar said. "Nobody still living at least. Even Iam cannot hold back all the darkness in our world. Sometimes, it seeps through. Trust me, I know."

"The moment I met her at the Maiden's Mugs—"

"Thoughtful title," Dellbar said with a snicker.

Torsten went on. "When she would keep me, the very Wearer of White, from seeing you… I knew she was special."

"She sounds it," Dellbar agreed.

"Aye, she does," Lucas added.

"Not special enough…" Rand lamented.

Torsten ignored him and allowed his head to tilt back against the wall. Anything to stop the spinning. "No wonder the upyr turned her."

Bars rattled, and Rand was on his feet, face shoved his face between them. "What do you mean turned?"

"Okay, Sir, let's get you back," Lucas said.

"Yes… I uh… I think maybe that's smart," Dellbar added.

"What do you mean?" Rand said. "Torsten, you tell me what you meant."

"I'm sure it's nothing, Sir Langley," Lucas said, still tugging at Torsten. "He's very drunk."

"Upyr—you mean like the bloodsucking undead assassins from the old stories?" Rand asked. "I overheard some men saying they were what killed Oleander."

"Not they." Torsten hiccuped. "Her."

"What?"

"Okay, here we go." Lucas forced his arm around Torsten and started lifting. Dellbar joined him. They got Torsten to his feet, where exhaustion set in.

"Sigrid's not dead?" Rand asked, voice hopeful.

"Worse than dead…"

"Ignore him," Lucas strained to say, now bearing Torsten's full weight. "He's speaking nonsense."

"Wait, come back here!" Rand shouted. He shook the bars again. "Bring him back here!" His screaming echoed up the stairwell as Lucas and the blind High Priest helped Torsten ascend. By then, his vision was speckled blackness, swirling like a vortex. He fought to reach up and pull the enchanted blindfold from over his eyes.

"How do you function like this, Morningweg?" Torsten asked, feeling himself being shoved upstairs, feet barely operating. By the time they'd reached the top, Rand's yelling seemed as if it came from across a canyon. Torsten couldn't even understand what he was saying.

"Practice, my friend," Dellbar said. He groaned as he raised one of Torsten's massive arms a bit higher to re-adjust its position on his shoulder. "And staying away from drunken dwarves…"

XXXI

THE IMMORTAL

Kazimir had endured many things for many centuries, but none were more insufferable than the thief, Whitney Fierstown. He was sure of that now.

"Why isn't she better yet?" Whitney asked for the thousandth time in the day since the attack that had left the Lightmancer, Lucindur, paralyzed. She lay on a table covered in rags used for makeshift blankets. The Dom Nohzi had no use for those or beds. The wyvern kept her warm, curled up between her legs.

The deep, chestnut color was returning to her cheeks. A bandage covered Lucindur's chest, stained red. Kazimir had caught Sigrid eyeing it a few times, and Sigrid had caught Kazimir catching her. Now, he didn't allow her even near the bedside.

Prishka had been a healer in her old life, and the auits—the nearly microscopic insects native to Brekliodad—she had cleaning out the wound were fast-actors.

Lucindur was, in fact, getting better. Quickly, considering the depth of the scratch, but nothing was ever fast enough for the thief. He was becoming more and more belligerent as the hours passed. If it wasn't Lucindur, it was griping about Sora, or even how dry the air was.

"She is healing," the upyr Prishka said. "These things take time."

Prishka's words seemed to do very little to comfort Whitney, who had returned to pacing the room.

Skryabin had gone off to gather the rest of the Dom Nohzi upyr throughout the vast Citadel, and contact those beyond. They'd need all of them if Kazimir's worst fears were true.

"We are running out of time," Whitney said.

Tum Tum agreed.

"You mortals are always so concerned about time," Kazimir said. His fists were clenched. Being in a room, waiting with Whitney, reminded him of his failures, of the lost years. But he had to oversee everything. Lucindur's ability to use her powers would be crucial. If it came to it, he'd even offer her his blood, allowing her the strength to last until the job was done, or she could devour the flesh of a wianu and become like him. Nesilia was coming to destroy everyone and everything—a problem for everyone involved and those not involved as well.

"But in this case, you may be right," Kazimir added. "Skryabin can't be much longer."

Whitney paced again. "Couldn't she have just sent a galler to your friends like everyone else in the world?"

"There are formalities one must adhere to when dealing with the intricacies of—"

"Oh, don't give me that shog!" Whitney interrupted. Tum Tum placed a hand on Whitney's arm, but he yanked it away. "I've had just about enough of these Dom Nohzi, better-than-everyone—"

Sigrid hissed a curse, and Kazimir shifted his weight. If there were any mortal on Pantego he'd call a friend, sadly enough it was

Whitney, but even still, Kazimir's long fingernails were on their way to slicing a neat line across the thief's face when he stopped. Kazimir's eyes bored into Whitney's like a dwarven pickaxe. "We will make believe that didn't happen. Come with me."

Kazimir watched Whitney's narrowed eyes flicker toward Lucindur's unconscious body, and then to the dwarf. Tum Tum acknowledged the unspoken request and Kazimir led Whitney out into the antechamber.

Prishka was right outside, leading a sallow slave who carried a bowl of water for the mortals. She looked to Kazimir.

"You brought mortals in here, and now you let them talk to you like that?" she whispered, shaking her head. "The Lords will not be pleased."

"The Lords won't matter if we can't stop what's coming," Kazimir replied.

"So you say," Prishka said. "You'd better be right."

"I wish that I were not." Without another word, Kazimir pushed by her. "Come," he addressed Whitney.

"This better be important," Whitney griped.

Kazimir kept walking, giving him no choice but to follow. They moved into a hall leading deeper into the Citadel. The same smooth walls drew deep lines into the mountain.

"This place has stood longer than any other stronghold built by man," Kazimir said. "The combined ages of the upyr living within these walls out-age cities… kingdoms even."

"What's your point?" Whitney asked.

"My point is that the preservation of this world means far more to us than to any of you."

Whitney stopped. "That's a mighty big claim."

Kazimir kept walking and wasn't surprised when Whitney followed. They moved through chambers lined with thick columns, down a set of marble stairs.

"Think this place is big enough for all what… three of you?" Whitney remarked.

Kazimir took a sharp left through a passage behind an opulent-looking chair set at the back of the great hall they'd crossed, once used by the Lords when their bodies remained corporeal. There were no candles or torches, but Kazimir held a small blue orb to cast a bit of light for Whitney to see.

"A man is dwelling in another man's home when a fire breaks out and devours the walls, furniture, and the thatch of the roof," Kazimir said. "When the flame has done its wicked deed, all that remains is ash. Who has lost more—the landlord, who built the home with the sweat of his brow, or the tenant?"

There was silence for a moment before, voice fraught with irritation, Whitney answered, "The landlord, I suppose."

"Wrong," Kazimir said. "They have both lost equally, for one is without a home, and the other has watched his creation destroyed."

"And we are back to the question, 'What is the point?'"

Kazimir sighed. He'd lived as an upyr so long, but simply couldn't let go of certain humanisms—sighing, swallowing, even breathing.

Kazimir looked around the room, at the large tapestries covering the walls, telling the stories of the Sanguine Lords, the first upyr who gave their bodies to end the Culling an age ago. He knew his superior eyes could perceive what Whitney couldn't. It was so representative of the truth. Mortals would never see things the way the upyr did.

"Darkness is coming," Kazimir whispered, "like none we've seen." He looked to Whitney, who despite his attempts at being calm, looked terrified. "They call us Children of the Night… true night is on its way, and even I am afraid."

"You? Scared? I don't believe it." Whitney smiled. It was an uncomfortable, awkward expression that Kazimir had seen many times in their years imprisoned together. The thief covered up his true emotions with humor.

"Many things can be made light of," Kazimir said. "But, sadly, Whitney Fierstown, this is not one of them. I'd rather be trapped in Elsewhere."

"It wouldn't be very fun, there, without me."

Kazimir ignored him. "Nesilia is powerful. Apart from Iam, she is the most powerful being ever to walk the face of Pantego."

"She's not unbeatable."

"How would you possibly know what she is or isn't? Now, here, in the face of such ancient power, is where we must accept our truths. The Sanguine Lords humbled me in condemnation to Elsewhere with you, but you, Whitney, are a thief. A good one or a bad one, it's irrelevant. You know nothing of gods. You can't."

Whitney stuck a finger into Kazimir's chest. "For one, I *was* a thief—and a damn, yigging great one. And, I'm not saying that because of me. I spoke to Sora. She was resisting Nesilia, and maybe she's got magic, but she's mortal, too."

"Her bloodline is strong. It drove me to act blindly. It helps her to resist the goddess, but in the end, everyone breaks in the face of such supremacy. It is inevitable."

"So, what do we do?" Whitney asked. His voice betrayed it all now. Every doubt, every fear, every sadness. "We can't kill Sora."

From somewhere behind them, a woman cleared her throat. They turned as one. Skryabin stood, hand on her hip.

"Kazimir, they are here," she said.

Kazimir went to follow her when a hand turned him around.

"We can't, Kazimir," Whitney said. "We can't kill her. No matter what. You promised."

Again, Kazimir wondered how life had led him here, making a deal with a mortal. Most insane of all was that he meant it. Those six years in Elsewhere with Whitney were the purest form of exile. They felt longer than a century on Pantego. Yet, as much as Whitney challenged his nerves, he'd also done what was necessary to free them, when even the Sanguine Lords turned their backs on Kazimir for how he'd strayed.

"We won't," Kazimir agreed.

Back through the halls and chambers of the immense Citadel, they went, Skryabin leading the way. They kept quiet, passing old relics on pedestals—reminders of the deep, rich history of the Dom Nohzi, reminders of all that would be lost if it all came to a cold, bitter end.

"Thank you, Skryabin," Kazimir said, once they were back to the cool blue light of the antechamber. "Get the cattle and prepare."

"Of course, Imperio," she nodded, then hurried away.

Kazimir hadn't noticed, no upyr would, but Whitney brought attention to the sudden shift. His teeth started to chatter. "It's s-s-so c-cold." He shuffled toward the fire blazing in the hearth, the only source of light in the room—a courtesy for their mortal guests and the few servants that milled around.

"Weak mortal," Sigrid hissed from the shadows. She leaned on the wall outside the room where Lucindur recovered, no doubt needing a break from those inside. Kazimir couldn't blame her.

"They are here," Kazimir said.

"Who?" Whitney said.

Kazimir shushed Whitney and looked to a set of oaken doors, which opened without being touched.

"Where are they?" Whitney said. He then leaped a meter vertically when the air around them popped, sizzling like lightning.

Ten men and women appeared, the Imperios comprising the Dom Nohzi. Kazimir was another, and by the look of it, the twelfth, Imperio Vikas, hadn't yet arrived. Each was ancient, though few as much as Kazimir. They all wore clothing far better suited for an earlier era, modest in appearance, but high quality, and very expensive. Kazimir refused to play dress-up, much preferring practical armor and cloak to blend in.

Whitney's eyes went wide. "How did they? Were they invisible?" he asked Kazimir who ignored the question.

"Kazimir, this better be worth it," said Imperio Teryngal, just as brazen as always.

He belonged exiled to Elsewhere for failing balance. Not me, Kazimir thought.

"Teryngal, brother, in more than a thousand years, have I ever called upon you for help?" Kazimir asked.

Teryngal tilted his head in response. Then, with thoughtful calculation said, "No. But now, all ten of us have been beckoned to your side like children?"

"Trust me, I'd just as soon never see any of you again."

The other Imperios' faces scrunched into rage, and they showed their teeth. Sigrid took a defensive step forward, but Kazimir stuck a hand out to quell her anger.

"The feeling is mutual," Teryngal said.

"Where is Imperio Vikas?" Kazimir asked, looking around.

"He was not in his wing of the Citadel," Skryabin said from behind.

Each Imperio had their own wing in the expansive complex that incorporated the entire Pikeback range. Even at Skryabin's supernatural speed, it had taken the better part of a day to reach all of them.

"What do you want, Kazimir?" Teryngal asked.

"Have you not seen?" Kazimir replied.

"What we have seen has happened before, and none of us believes it was worth this upheaval."

"Upheaval? Did I interrupt something more pressing? You sound like a mortal, Teryngal. Elsewhere is empty."

"Yes, we know," Teryngal said. "Skryabin told us as much."

"You know? It is not just sparse," Kazimir said as if speaking to a child. "It is bare. Upon some of you, I have hundreds of years, and in all of them, I've never seen this. Only the wianu fill the dead seas."

There were murmurs from the gathered upyr.

"That means nothing," Teryngal offered. Then he turned to the others to quiet them. "It means nothing."

"The last time we saw this, the old gods were stirring, and you know it, Imperio Teryngal," Kazimir said. "They are stirring again. The Goddess of the Material Plane is with us once more, unburied, and she threatens to bring all of Iam's creation against his children."

"This does not concern us, Kazimir," Teryngal said. "The gods will play their games just as they always have. It is not our place to involve ourselves."

Kazimir opened his mouth to argue when Whitney cleared his throat, stepped forward, and bowed his head. "Oh, great and holy Sanguine Lords, I beseech you…"

The whole room burst into a paroxysm of laughter. Whitney stopped talking, head on a swivel. Kazimir even smirked.

"What…" He turned to Kazimir. "What are they laughing at?"

"Settle down," Kazimir ordered. He turned to Whitney. "These are not the Lords. Together, plus one who is not with us, we are the twelve Imperios of the Dom Nohzi."

"And now this?" Teryngal said with obvious disgust. "Skryabin said you brought mortals, but seeing it is so… different. I've heard of playing with one's food…" He moved toward Whitney, sniffing the air. Sigrid took a hard step in his path. And while Kazimir hoped it was for the right reasons, serving her maker, he knew it was more likely her defending a feast she hoped she'd get to enjoy herself one day.

"Who is this fool you dare bring here?" Teryngal asked. "To our home!"

The other Imperios joined in.

Whitney made a small sound of protest.

"This is Whitney Fierstown…" Kazimir started.

"Interesting," Teryngal said, scratching his chin. He looked around at the other Imperios who quieted. "The same Whitney Fierstown who killed the beast?"

"Ah-ha, even they know I killed Bliss!" Whitney declared. "See Kazzy?"

"Yes," Teryngal said. He leered at Imperio Zlata. "Our servants in the Webbed Woods said that it had upset the balance of things." He glared down his sharp nose at the thief. "Frankly, I'm surprised you've not yet been killed."

"Perhaps we will mend that oversight," Zlata said, licking her lips.

Whitney gulped. "It… it was really a sort of a group effort?" he added, the last word sounding like a question.

"Nevertheless…" Teryngal brought the conversation back around. "Why is he here in the Citadel? Why are the mortals not in chains with the rest of the cattle?"

"The old gods stir once more," Kazimir said. "I fear it is already too late, but we cannot sit back and allow another God Feud."

"And how do you expect to stop it?" Zlata asked.

"We must separate Nesilia from her host and destroy her once and for all."

Teryngal chuckled. "There is no way to separate a goddess from her chosen vessel."

"There is." Kazimir grew timid for breath, then said, "We have, with us, a Lightmancer."

Instantly, the features of every upyr in the room changed. Each of them went from being pale, mostly attractive, and docile to feral, beastly, furious. Once again, Sigrid dropped into a fighting stance, ready to pounce at a moment's notice.

"Now I know you've lost it, brother," Zlata said.

"Let me finish," Kazimir said, pushing the air with his palms. He gestured to Whitney. "The Lords saw fit to accept this *fool's* blood pact against the goddess herself, and so, I do what must be done. We looked into the Well of Wisdom, and this is the way."

"That is preposterous!" Teryngal interrupted.

"You communed with mystics?" Zlata asked.

"Commune's not really the *best* word…" Whitney chimed in, quietly.

"Traitor," Teryngal hissed.

"Do not dare accuse me of twisting our Lords' will," Kazimir snarled at Teryngal.

"Like you did to get yourself banished to Elsewhere?" Zlata asked.

"A mistake for which I have dearly paid, and which has swollen our ranks." He nodded toward Sigrid. "Pantego remembers the Dom Nohzi now because of the queen *she* killed. We're out of the shadows. Perhaps, just in time to keep light in the sky. Or would you rather question the Lords?"

Teryngal's lip curled, but he nodded.

"This will go much faster if I'm not interrupted again." Kazimir walked toward the cask of blood set on a mahogany cart in the center of the room, twelve crimson roses rising from a vase in the center. He hadn't seen one of the cattle roll it in, but they were adept at keeping out of sight. Kazimir slowly poured a goblet only for himself and sipped it before continuing. "Now… where was I?"

Kazimir told the others of all that had occurred, of how the Lightmancer had breached the mind of the goddess, how the thief's presence had allowed her to do so, and how, within the Well of Wisdom, Nesilia had said she was coming to the Citadel. He told of her threat to bring ruin upon the Sanguine Lords and all those who could face her.

"She dares threaten us?" Teryngal said. "We exist only

because of the depths she and her love descended to in order to win the feud."

"She dares do whatever she wishes," Kazimir said. "It seems you've gone unopposed for far too long, Teryngal. She is no Imperio. She is a goddess, and her power is almost fully realized once more."

"So what—we somehow force her into the bar guai and throw her to the wianu?" Zlata asked. "You think to stop Nesilia using the very beings she and Iam cursed with half-life?"

"I believe Elsewhere is on the cusp of eruption, and we are all in grave peril for the first time in many centuries. We must do whatever it takes to stop her. If she destroys us and frees the wianu again... it will be the end of Pantego, and we will cease to exist in either realm. Erased."

"The Citadel is unbreachable," Teryngal attested.

"Which is why this is where we stand," Kazimir said. "Hubris and revenge drive her here. She's susceptible so long as her host loves this man." He pointed to Whitney, who swallowed hard in response even as he forced a nervous grin. It was nice to see him scared into silence.

"Imperio Kazimir," Teryngal said. His voice was soft and lilting, as if he was in negotiations. "You are how-many-centuries old, and you wish to die upon the hill called love?" He looked around the room. "Love! Oh, how powerful it must be to harness the strength to destroy a goddess!"

"Love destroyed her once before, Teryngal!" Kazimir said, slamming his goblet down.

The other Imperios had been smiling, but no longer.

"It was love that ended the God Feud," he went on. "It was love which has ended a thousand wars. Love, whether real or contrived, holds a power all its own."

"He's telling the truth," Whitney added, earning every Imperio's glower. For what it was worth, he didn't cringe in fright of them this time.

"Love," Teryngal said again, dismissively, but almost a whisper this time.

"If you don't trust me, trust the Lords," Kazimir said. "They accepted the pact, but this will take more of us than a king or queen."

A prolonged bout of silence passed as the threat sunk in.

"Have you spoken with the Lords?" Teryngal asked.

"I had hoped we would all do so together." Kazimir lowered his head. "But we are not all here, are we?"

"Vikas will have to answer for his absence," Teryngal said. "But the Lords cannot wait. If this is true, we must move quickly."

"We are safe here in the Citadel," Zlata said, her voice commanding. "We should wait it out, and pick up the remnants of this world. Help them rebuild again in balance."

Some agreed.

"The glamour will not work on Nesilia," Kazimir said.

"What would possess you to make such a claim?" Zlata asked.

"When we arrived, the valley was alive with goblins and grimaurs. Even the Glassmen were heading up the path before the beasts took them to their graves. Goblins, grimaurs, they are weak, but they'll be drawn to her power."

Frenzied voices whispered and argued, and finally, Teryngal spoke up again. "What does this mean?"

"I don't know," Kazimir admitted, "but it cannot be good."

Kazimir took another sip of the blood. Once he finished, he put the goblet down and raised the cask toward the other Imperios. Several of them broke rank to pour their own.

Teryngal, however, didn't move. "You really think this the work of the goddess Nesilia?"

"I do not think," Kazimir said. "I know. Brothers and sisters, the end of all things is upon us. If we do not stand against her, we will fall before her. She will break the balance."

"There is another option," Teryngal said.

"Not one worth voicing," Kazimir warned.

"Brother—"

"I am not your brother if you speak another word of it!" Kazimir roared.

Teryngal didn't back down. "I am only saying that if we join her—"

"Whoa, whoa, whoa," Whitney interrupted.

"Not now, thief," Kazimir snapped. "Be quiet."

Whitney took a step forward anyway. Kazimir had to admit, he was either brave or stupid. Probably both.

"No way am I just going to sit around while you people… or whatever you are… debate about whether or not to join forces with that evil witch," he said. "We made a pact."

"This is none of your concern, mortal," Teryngal spat.

"This is all of my concern!"

"Back off, Whitney," Kazimir warned.

Sigrid eyed Kazimir. She'd been busy sharpening the broadhead of a bolt, listening with one ear. But now, she was practically begging for the chance to gut the thief, or Teryngal, or anyone.

"No, no," Whitney said, staring right into Teryngal's soulless, black eyes. If he was afraid, now he didn't show it. "You said it yourself: I killed a goddess. I upset the balance. You think I did that by luck? Kazimir said we have a Lightmancer. We do. And we have a plan. Now, for once in your privileged, far-too-long life, shut up and listen."

Teryngal turned to Kazimir, biting his upper lip, rage etched all over his smooth face. He was ready to tear open Whitney's throat, which the foolish thief probably didn't even realize. "If you think we are going to let your pet speak to us like this—"

If Kazimir's heart could beat, it wouldn't have pulsed twice before his fingers were entwined with Teryngal's hair, wrenching his neck back to expose his throat. Kazimir's silver-coated knife rested against the upyr's soft, pale flesh. He kept the blade buried at the bottom of his bandolier, out of sight, insurance for if Sigrid got out of control again like she had with Oleander.

"You know what this is?" Kazimir asked as Teryngal's skin blistered from the touch of the blade.

Teryngal nodded vigorously. Upyr had few weaknesses, but silver had been conjured long ago by mystics keen on fighting them—a fact few knew, and fewer who found out stayed alive long enough to talk about. This blade had been made by them hundreds of years ago, and Kazimir had killed its owner.

"Then you know I am serious," Kazimir said. "The goddess will not spare us—she will spare no one. We have tasted of the wianu—and anything born of her and Iam's former love is now her sworn enemy. Now, are you prepared to listen to the will of our Lords, or shall I kill you all right here, and save her the trouble? I imagine none of you has fought so much as a fly in centuries."

"You presume much, Kazimir," Teryngal said through clenched fangs.

"I felt her," a frail voice spoke. All eyes snapped toward the Lightmancer. She leaned against the dwarf in the entry of her room. Though she was on her feet, she looked anything but refreshed. An inch deeper, and that talon would have stopped her heart. Then, unlife would have been the only option.

Even in her weakened state, she showed fortitude.

"Lucy!" Whitney exclaimed and ran to her. "You're all right?"

"These old bones have experienced far worse than a little grimaur toxin," she said weakly. The dwarf handed her salfio over, and she strummed a chord. The fire in the hearth waved in response, and behind her, the wyvern's ears perked up, and it soared to the dwarf's shoulder.

Teryngal didn't seem impressed. "And here I thought all of your kind were wiped out."

"A Lightmancer should not be here," said another Imperio. "Are we to forget all they've done?"

"She's really the one on trial here?" Whitney scoffed.

The dwarf muttered something about the undead. His ever-vigilant gaze darted from side to side, ready to fight all of them if he needed to, like the fool he was.

"I play music, and am cursed for it," the Lightmancer said. She gripped her side and grimaced. "And it dies with me. But I've seen into the mind of the goddess, and I fear nothing in this room in comparison."

"You would dare—"

"Enough, Teryngal!" Kazimir bellowed. "If I'm wrong, then I will walk into the mouth of Dakel un Ghastrin myself, and you can feast on the mortals to your black heart's delight."

"Yeah," Whitney said with undue confidence, then paused. "Wait, what?"

Teryngal's jaw set, eyes thinning to narrow slits. "What would you have us do, then?"

Kazimir lowered the silver knife. He knew he could get them to listen. He'd been banished, but at least he was out in the world fulfilling blood pacts while the rest of them ignored the call, delighting in the decadence of immortality, acting as if balance had already been achieved. They feared him, as they should.

He met the eyes of each Imperio present, raised his cask of blood. "This place—it has been the home to our Lords for longer than any mortal lives. Only the gods remember its founding. And now, our very walls are threatened because of the millenniums-old spat between lovers. It's time she tastes Elsewhere as we all have."

One at a time, seven of the Imperios stood and drank from Kazimir's cask, nodding their agreement. The others didn't drink but stood nonetheless. They'd do what they had to, for without the Lords and the wianu, the immortality the upyr had grown so accustomed to, would cease to be.

"I can feel it," Kazimir said. "She is close. Let us go and speak with the Lords."

XXXII

THE DAUGHTER

Mahi closed her eyes and tried to feel the wind on her cheeks, screeching through the sea door. She fought to remember the way loose sand would brush against the exposed parts of her body. The way it found its way under clothing and got entangled in her hair—became a part of her. The chill when a breeze touched sweat on the back of her neck.

Ever since the nigh'jel blood coated her, she couldn't—not the way she used to, at least. The more time passed since her rebirth, the more she forgot how things used to feel. Her mind stopped filling in the blanks.

"My Caleef, are you ready?" Bit'rudam asked.

She regarded him and the nearly one hundred Serpent Guards around the throne room. She had no idea how they weren't sweating to death in their cumbersome, gilded armor and masked-helmets. As a young girl, she'd been terrified of them—the way all their heads seemed to move in unison, like snakes lost in a melody.

A part of her was afraid of them still. She knew she shouldn't be, but it was hard when around them, all the former afhems left in Latiapur rode with dried blood crusting their heads over patches of peeled skin. The idea of removing the marks came while trying to piece together the fragments of memories, her own and ancestors beyond. The Serpent Guards had agreed before she could even second guess herself.

Not one voiced opposition to wiping away generations of historical significance. They couldn't. The afhemate tattoos were works of art, added to for centuries and recorded nowhere. They could never be perfectly reproduced. Yet, not one Serpent Guard showed the slightest hesitation in sawing skin away, nor remorse after having done so. And when they were finished, nobody dared stand against them.

Their work still stained the floors. No matter how the sages tried to scrub it away, it was too substantial. Blood found its way into even the slightest seams and cracks in the stone surfaces.

"Do you think I did the right thing?" Mahi asked, staring at the Sea Door. Blood even stained its rim, slowly dripping into the Boiling Waters.

"It's not my duty to think," Bit'rudam said.

A diplomatic answer. He was learning quickly from being in the capital. Mahi knew he was more than a trader or a warrior. She leered at him, remaining silent until he cleared his throat and tried to elucidate.

"I understand, my Caleef," he said. "But some are saying that you only did it because you lost your own markings. They aren't pleased."

"You think I am?" Mahi said. "I asked for none of this. I just woke up. But I had to do something. Three times I stepped into that chamber, and every time, the same arguing. All their voices, flowing over each other like angry waves. We were doomed."

"They were, and are scared. They don't know what will happen to their cities and their followers."

"They won't be burned down by war, like mine," Mahi said. "That's all that matters."

"Do you think your father can…" He couldn't finish. His gaze turned to the floor, feet shifting uncomfortably.

"He can. It was for the best. He can't be here, not right now." She started walking toward the exit. The Serpent Guards shadowed her, never daring to be seen.

"And word has been spread, for all our armies to gather here?" she asked, without bothering to glance back and ensure Bit'rudam was following as well.

"Every rider we can spare has been sent with the message that the Caleef requests their presence at the capital," he said. "To every corner of the Black Sands."

"Good," she said. "We'll need them all."

"Mahraveh." Bit'rudam tugged on her wrist. She could hear the armor of the guards shifting. "You have been vague ever since you returned to us. Then that violence in the palace."

She set her jaw, stopped walking. "You don't trust me now?"

"I do. I know that you are not, but to me, you are still my afhem, and I swore an oath. And the common people? To them, you are still a mighty champion. Stealing the marks of afhems won't erase their followings."

"Would you have me throw them into Tal'du Dromesh, then? Have them all executed?"

"No… I…"

"There is more than fighting," Mahi said. "There must be. Babrak was right about that. And yet, so is my father. We shouldn't be second-class citizens of our own nation. We shouldn't forget everything that makes us who we are."

"But what if the Glass Kingdom rejects peace?" Bit'rudam said. "We've spilled enough of their blood already in this war. What if they can't forgive?"

"They have to." Mahraveh continued toward the exit. "Do you know how amazing it would feel to watch Sir Nikserof on his knees and carry out the sentence he so deserves? I remember so much now… too much… but also his face when he destroyed my home. His life is my gesture. My father will be theirs."

"And here?" Bit'rudam said. He hurried ahead of her and pushed open the grand doors of the Boiling Keep. The din of Lati-apur immediately assaulted their ears like she'd never heard it before. The brightness of the beating sun blinded her temporarily, its heat was more apparent than ever. That was the one thing she could feel more vividly. Perhaps it was the new darkness of her skin.

She stared down the steep steps. The nigh'jel blood spilled in her honor had dried, now like swirling black veins in marble all the way down to the palace square. This time, no crowd awaited to cheer, but they were there, filling the city, every street, every market.

The district of afhems bustled as well. She couldn't take their honorary homes, though, their armies did. Shesaitju travelers flowed through the gates, these from the nearest settlements. Lines of them extended across the dunes like marching ants. More arrived every day to give blessings to their new Caleef. Or perhaps, they imagined the arena would be filled with tournaments. Many afhemates were now without leaders, though none of them yet realized how many.

They'd all be baffled when they arrived. She could hear it already. The murmurs of confusion. What could she possibly tell them? That she'd encountered a mad goddess set on devouring all the world? She'd been unconscious, drowning.

What if it was all a dream?

"Mahi, did you hear that?" Bit'rudam asked.

She looked up. Another formerly al' Tariq warrior kneeled before them and had apparently spoken, but she was too lost in her mind to hear him.

"What is it?" she asked.

"Babrak, he—" Bit'rudam paused. "Come this way."

He waved her along and led her down a branching stairwell that cut through the bluffs. The Serpent Guards kept pace. An arch of moss-covered rock led them to a circular promontory. Mahi knew it had to be manmade—a place for Caleef's to reflect.

Bit'rudam pointed across the Boiling waters, past Tal'du Dromesh to where the water calmed slightly, enough for a series of blackwood jetties to drift, held firm by thick lines anchored into the rocky coast.

There, a row of warships shoved off, filled with warriors. But the docks were bustling as well with others being left behind. Though they were a great distance off, Mahi could see the size of the man at the lead ship's helm, and the glean of his armor.

Babrak.

His ship sailed away, but he faced back toward the Boiling Keep, toward her. She could only imagine his glare from so far away, but it set her blood boiling.

And he wasn't the only former afhem aboard the fleeing vessels. They were easy to spot by the opulence of their armor and weapons, by the way they held themselves. Proud, always. Too much so to surrender their titles and their followings so easily.

"That fat *pis'truda*," Bit'rudam cursed. "My Caleef, allow me to lead ships after them."

Mahi stared back at him. Like Nikserof, it would bring her great joy to see Babrak and his ship lying at the bottom of the sea like rocks. He deserved it.

"Let him run," she said. Even only a few days ago, she never would have. But so much had changed beyond only her appearance. "All he's doing is proving that all he ever cared about was his own power. Not the Shesaitju."

"Others join him," Bit'rudam said. "Others still might. Rebellion is like a sickness in the way it spreads. I've seen it in other afhemates, my Caleef. A commander turns, kills their leader, thinking he is strong enough to win the charge. If we don't—"

"If he won't join us, he'll die," Mahraveh said. "I need you to focus only on the people within our walls, Bit'rudam. They are who matter now."

She didn't wait for an answer before turning on her heels and setting off back toward the city.

Mahraveh was getting used to the way people looked at her. She told herself they were just scared of the Serpent Guards surrounding her, but she knew it was her they stared at. She almost wanted to request the Serpent Guards stay behind, so she could be like one of the people again, though she knew that was foolish.

For every expression of reverence aimed at her, there were those who were equal parts livid. Older folk, mostly—staunch followers of the old ways. The changes were too quick and drastic for her not to be protected at all times. To do so would be to deny a very simple fact—she was not one of them any longer.

She didn't want this, yet here she was. She could stare at the way Bit'rudam's back-muscles creased as he pushed through the gathered throng ahead, at the sweat glistening on his smooth skin. She could dream and fantasize, but she'd never have anything so simple as a lover again—not that she'd ever had one before. She'd never again walk into a room and be ignored or go unnoticed.

Former afhems and their entourages roamed by. Some eyed her like they wanted to tear open her throat. Others offered a simple nod, a gesture of respect. They were commanders after all, and a good leader recognizes good strategy. Her father taught her that, long ago, when she asked why he studied texts about Liam the Conqueror's many victories.

Markless and traders and warriors kowtowed as she passed. That level of adoration, she hoped she'd never grow accustomed to—yet, she already was. She didn't like it, but she couldn't hate it. She had to portray strength every moment her people looked upon her, or she'd lose more followers like those who'd gone with Babrak.

She had to be more than a young woman from a desert town whose father had gone off to meet with their enemies, and might never return. She might never see him again. And worse, if he did return with the peace she offered, her world would change even more.

"My Caleef!" a haggard old man shouted. He pushed through the gathering of onlookers and fell to his knees just behind the feet of the Serpent Guards. "My Caleef, please accept this humble offering." The guards lowered their fauchards and pushed him back.

"Stop," Mahi ordered.

They immediately parted enough for the man to show through. He lowered his head, his ratty beard scratching the sand, and on two open palms, presented a small figurine carved out of blackwood. It was a Siren. The detail was impeccable, from the way her face was there but not there to the wisps of sand she had for legs.

Mahi kneeled and took in from him. Then she reached out and lifted his chin. A man of such talents, she knew he shouldn't look like a homeless beggar. But in the Black Sands, for so long, swordsmanship was the only art form that truly mattered.

"Thank you." She smiled. It was slight, her lips raising just a hair, but he looked like he might faint.

Then she stood, and the guards closed him out again.

"I'll hold that," Bit'rudam offered. She handed it over, and he studied it from every angle, like he was worried it might be some sort of trap. "It's beautiful," he said, satisfied. "It looks just like the one from the arena that… well, you know."

"It does," she said. She breathed in deep, taking the Siren figurine back. He couldn't know that, like Jumaat, who she'd killed, she was gone now, too—her life essence given to Mahraveh. Or that she was the last Siren. Mahi looked up, and over the row of Serpent Guards, she saw Tal'du Dromesh standing proudly on the horizon.

The damage caused by her father was still being repaired, but throughout the other colonnades, trading stands were packed. With so many arriving at Latiapur, there was barely enough food and goods to go around.

Her gaze lifted toward the zhulong statues lining the arena's upper tier, their tusks clashing. She recalled how far away they looked from down in the sands. It was as if she could hear the roar of the crowd as they watched her, could imagine the rumble and the thrill experienced by the thousands of afhems who'd come before. From her father, who won while Liam watched, to the first tournament held by the first Caleef, centuries ago.

She'd taken that thrill away from her people, but looking down at the Siren in her hands, knowing that craftsmen like this should be respected, she also knew that she couldn't take away the essence of her people. Her father sought unification in the north, but here, in Latiapur, it was her job to win over her people.

"Bit'rudam, summon the former afhems to the Tal'du Dromesh."

He turned to her, brow furrowing. "My Caleef?"

"We must evolve, but we cannot forget who we are… or from where we come," she said. "There will be a tournament for all afhems. They will fight. Not to the death, but for honor. The winner will serve as the commander of the Serpent Guard. The people need a distraction before the darkness to come."

Bit'rudam's eyes lit up. "A brilliant idea, my Caleef! A tournament in your honor is exactly what this city needs until your father returns with news."

"Not in my honor." She pointed to two afhems walking past. Seaweed wrappings covered their skinned necks and heads. "In theirs. They have given so much for their future. I think a bit of the old ways is exactly what we need now."

Bit'rudam bowed. He took one step away, then froze, looking back at her. She couldn't say for sure what she saw in his expression. Love, respect, envy, maybe all three.

"I hope you do not take offense, Caleef Mahraveh," he started. "But I was wondering… can I have your permission to stand for the al'Tariq Afhemate?"

"You weren't an afhem," Mahi said.

"And you are Caleef." He took her hand, fell to one knee, and lowered his head. "If not for the honor of the name I dedicated my life to, then in the name of Mahraveh al'Tariq, whose life was cut too short."

All Mahi wanted to do was pull his hand to her cheek, to feel his warmth, and feel safe. She'd loved Jumaat, but it was never meant to be. Then, this fiercely loyal warrior found her, helped her find new purpose and feel full again, like she belonged. If she were luckier, she might have found happiness with him, like her own father and mother had known.

But she wasn't lucky.

She was Caleef.

"You can fight," she said. He looked up at her, with the same level of adoration as the old woodcarver had. A man, ready to put his chosen art on display in the name of his ruler. "But only if you win."

XXXIII

THE THIEF

Together, Whitney, Tum Tum, Sigrid, Lucindur, Aquira, and all the upyr rushed down into the lower Sanctum. Most of the upyr straggled behind, likely speaking ill words of the *mortals* Kazimir dared bring into their *oh-so-special* place.

Lucindur hobbled along behind them, refusing help from anyone. She was surprisingly strong for an older lady. Aquira flew with her, making quite a racket.

"I fear this is the end of the Dom Nohzi," Kazimir said to Teryngal.

"A shame," Whitney muttered. "Now who will murder all the innocent people?"

"We do not murder innocents," Kazimir said.

"Potato, potahto," Whitney said. "Murder is murder, I think."

"And thievery is thievery."

Whitney smirked at that. If they all weren't about to die, and Sora wasn't in even more danger, he'd have to admit, he was enjoying seeing the Dom Nohzi Citadel. Even if these awful, dank walls reminded him of every dungeon he'd ever been in, there was a certain elegance to the design.

The thought of dungeons made him wonder where his old friend Torsten was. If the Buried Goddess were on her way to Brekliodad, Sir Torsten Unger would have been a great help in defeating her.

"If she got to the wianu already, we might be walking right into Elsewhere," Teryngal replied.

"I've been there," Whitney said. "I survived. We'll be fine."

"Aye, and if these wianu taste anything like regular squid, we'll be in store for some good eatin," Tum Tum agreed.

As if neither of them had spoken, Teryngal continued. "She will have restored them." He turned and grabbed Kazimir by the cloak, stopping them all. He looked the upyr in the eye and said, "You know what they are capable of. If the curse is lifted…"

"That's the second time you've mentioned a curse," Whitney said. Then he turned to Kazimir. "We deserve to know what he's talking about. I don't like curses."

"We don't have time for this," Kazimir said.

Whitney crossed his arms and said, "Elsewhere or not, I'm not moving until I know what we're walking into."

"Mmmmhmmm," Tum Tum agreed.

Kazimir punched the wall and cracked the rock. "Fine. Listen carefully, I will not repeat myself." He glanced over Whitney's shoulder, presumably to check the position of his fellow upyr. When seemingly satisfied, he continued. "Bliss was not the only one banished into obscurity. Although, arguably, she suffered the worst fate. The wianu are more than mere beasts of the sea."

"Yeah, they live between realms, right?" Whitney commented.

"You said you were in the Red Tower, in the vision when you visited the Well of Wisdom. Do you recall seeing their likenesses?" Kazimir asked.

"Yeah, huge statues, glowing eyes. Evil-looking things."

"You've heard stories of the God Feud," Kazimir said, "but

not all stories are the truth. Especially when it comes to the affairs of gods and goddesses."

"Tell me about it," Whitney said.

Whitney had heard every story there was about the origins of the world and the gods who'd hated each other. He'd just as soon ignore them and hope they paid him no mind either.

They quieted momentarily as the upyr who'd been lingering behind caught up. After they'd passed, Lucindur stopped to rest, and Aquira landed on Tum Tum's shoulder.

"The Panpingese worship many gods," Teryngal started where Kazimir left off. "They call them *Pinyun*—the Many and the Few. Those gods are the fallen, the rebels cast down by both Iam and Nesilia in the early battles of the Feud. But the war endured for thousands of years until she and Iam did the unthinkable. They cursed the gods they'd already defeated to become the wianu, beasts trapped between Pantego and Elsewhere. Made children out of their foes. Then, they used them to hunt their remaining enemies until the One Who Remained, Bliss, destroyed Nesilia, and damned her to the space between realms. Iam then cast Bliss out and stood alone as the god of this world."

"The... wait. You're telling me that those ugly things are gods? Well, Iam's golden shog, people worshiping seafood." Whitney laughed, but then his face grew deadly serious. "But you... you do eat them. That's what makes you like you are..." He turned to Kazimir. "Are you a yigging god?"

"What is a god if not immortal?" Kazimir said.

"Shog in a barrel. This whole time I've been standing before divinity." Whitney exaggerated a low bow.

"And we are walking right into their lair?" Lucindur asked, shifting her weight.

"Ye sure I can't help ye?" Tum Tum said.

"Chivalrous, but no," Lucindur said dryly.

"This is the safest place in the Citadel," Kazimir assured them. "Perhaps in all the north."

"We are hiding?" Whitney asked, then added, "Not that I'm complaining."

"The Dom Nohzi do not hide," Teryngal said.

"Mmmmm, this looks and sounds a lot like hiding," Whitney said.

"We must seek the Lords' wisdom on this matter," Kazimir said. "I have put off this visit only long enough to allow my brothers and sisters to be present. I warn you, however, they will not be happy for the presence of mortals." Then he looked at Lucindur. "Especially you, Lightmancer."

"It won't be the first time I'm unwanted at a party," she said.

"The question still remains," Teryngal said. "What if Nesilia already got to them? What if we get down there and the wianu have already been won to her side?"

"It is always a risk we take that we are on the wrong side of time," Kazimir said, pointing back in the general direction from which they'd come. "But this place is a fortress protected by the Lords themselves. Even I would be surprised if she'd breached its walls without us knowing."

Aquira flapped her wings hard and shrieked.

"Can you quiet that thing?" Sigrid hissed.

"That *thing* has a name," Whitney said. "What is it, Aquira?"

She screeched again.

"We should be moving," Kazimir said, and then followed his own advice.

Each step was slippery, wet with condensation and mildew. Making it more difficult was the lack of lighting. Kazimir carried that same small, glowing orb which gave off just enough blue light for Whitney and the others to see, but still, Whitney slipped or stumbled more times than he could count.

Finally, the staircase leveled out to flat stone. Somewhere

ahead, there was the slow rumble, echoing off the damp tunnel walls.

"Is that… an ocean? Inside a mountain?" Whitney asked.

"The Citadel has many wonders," Kazimir responded. "Now, keep up. We are running out of time."

"Who is it now that sounds like a mortal?" Teryngal jested.

They reached the end of the tunnels. Stepping through metal doors which the other upyr had already opened, out into what Kazimir called the lower Sanctum, the place where his Lords supposedly dwelled in their ethereal form, cold air hit them like a giant's fist. Wind… wind inside the mountain… burned his face like hot coals.

Just as it had outside in the snow-laden mountain pass, here stood an archway, hewn from the natural rock. On either side, as if guarding the place, two mammoths of creation stood. They looked vaguely human, but in the same way Whitney looked vaguely female. They held hands above, meeting above the arch. Hanging from the curvature where their hands met, also carved from stone, was a thin line of what must have represented blood. A blood pact being made. Whitney had done it before, twice, and he knew what that looked like. And felt like. Without a thought, he rubbed his hands together as if to ward off the pain of it.

Kazimir extended his hand, and the orb of light floated out to reveal an endless cavern. In front of them, down a sharp cliff, was, indeed, an expansive ocean that stretched without limits—a sea of gray as far as the eye could see. It was impossible. Whitney knew he was within a mountain, but he saw… sky—faint clouds even.

Steady muttering in a language that sounded vaguely like Breklian came from within. If Whitney heard it, the upyr surely had too. That fact was confirmed as he was shoved aside by Teryngal, finding himself out in the open cavern.

"Imperio Vikas!" someone shouted, to which another responded, "Hush! He is praying!"

If that indeed was what he was doing, Whitney had never seen prayer anything like it. His body, hair, clothes… they were all sopping wet with blood, and he lay on his back, face to the air. His arms and legs were splayed out in a way that reminded Whitney of all those years ago with Torsten in Oxgate. They'd happened upon a man, crucified to a post just before being abducted by Nesilia's cultists.

So many things had come full-circle. That had been the day that Sora and Whitney had been reunited after so many years. Now, history was set to repeat itself, only Whitney wasn't sure he wanted to see what Sora had become.

The upyr called Skryabin was already beside the man. She was beautiful like a polished stone statue—flawless, but cold and lifeless. One of their enslaved men lay near her, puncture marks in his neck, dead.

"Kazimir," she said, rushing to them. "I found him like this. He won't feed."

Kazimir pushed by her, kneeling next to Vikas, one hand upon his shoulder. Unsure what else to do, Whitney and the others watched from a distance.

There was a word Whitney strove for to describe the scene before him, yet for lack of finding it, he settled on *demonic*.

Blood everywhere.

Unnatural underground oceans.

Mass murdering monsters.

The threat of death or worse.

It was a lot for anyone to bear, much less the person upon whose shoulders rested the fate of the entire world.

Whitney moved closer, even daring to push past the Imperios. He stopped only when he stood close enough to Kazimir to hear his conversation.

"Vikas," he said, lightly shaking the man.

Vikas looked crazed—although, Whitney had never seen the upyr before and that could very well have been his natural state. He'd overheard Kazimir say Vikas was older than all of them. How old must he have been?

His stringy, thin hair was disheveled. It was white, like Kazimir's, Sigrid's, and every other upyr present, but while they were all breathtakingly beautiful, Vikas was gaunt and skeletal. His cheekbones protruded like knives from his face, a shelf for his soulless eyes. His mouth was wide open, unmoving, using only his throat to utter the words to his prayer.

"Vikas," Kazimir said again. "We've been searching for you."

As if drawn out of a trance, the upyr called Vikas closed his mouth, teeth smashing together. His head whipped toward Kazimir but he still said nothing.

"Vikas, are you alright?" Kazimir asked.

The other Imperios were whispering now, words like, 'madness,' and 'lunatic.'

"Imperio Vikas, the old gods are stirring," Kazimir said. "Nesilia is coming. She's coming soon, and we must be prepared." Kazimir tried to help Vikas to a sitting position, but the older man swiped his hand away.

"Foolish children," Vikas said. His voice came out like a wagon wheel on a gravel road. It sounded like it hurt. "She is already here."

If it was possible for the room to become colder, Whitney was sure it had. The air about the platform began shimmering. Greens, purples, dark blues, all these colors and more swirled above them.

The Imperios all dropped to their faces, together as one. Whitney and the other humans remained standing, but he soon wished he hadn't.

A deep voice like thunder spoke in that same language Vikas

had been using and sent half the mountainside bouncing down from above, rocks slamming into the water.

Whitney couldn't understand it, but the other upyr repeated the words.

Then, a sound so horrible it could have been death in auditory form assaulted Whitney's ears. It was followed by a high-pitched whine, and then he heard the rumbling voice in the common tongue.

"A Lightmancer?" it said. "A Lightmancer and an insecure child."

Whitney looked around, wondering who the voice was speaking of when he realized it was him.

For, perhaps, the first time in his life, Whitney couldn't speak. He'd stood before kings and queens, and the Wearer of White himself—both of them—but he'd never heard a voice with such a commanding timber, Bliss and Nesilia included.

"The gods have a sense of humor, do they not?" the voice said. "Balance has not just been threatened, it has been undone. The thief was right in making the pact, yet, Kazimir... you've not yet fulfilled it?"

Kazimir's head shifted, but he didn't look up. "Lord Thian, there were complications."

"Yes," the Lord Thian said, slowly. "A blood pact made in Elsewhere whilst you were banished. One that we did not sanction, might I add."

Another voice spoke, this one dignified, female. It came from another spot in the misty, multi-colored fog. "But one that was made for honor, with a mind for balance."

"But now, both marks are here—and the one spared is also the one who's death has been called for," she said. "You, Kazimir, have made things very difficult. Was your time in Elsewhere not enough for you to understand?"

"All due respect, Lady Anavink," Kazimir said, bowing his

head lower, "but if we do not handle this delicate matter… delicately, we will all suffer a far worse fate than Elsewhere."

"You presume to tell me of our fate?" Lady Anavink asked. Her voice echoed throughout the Sanctum, quaking the stone, and Whitney promptly understood the power of the presence before him.

"It does not matter," Vikas said, his eyes returning to that of a crazed man. "She is here. This all ends. She is here." He turned to the vapor in the air, the Sanguine Lords, and said again, "She's here."

Then, turning to Kazimir, he said, "My son—for that is what you are to me. My child. My first, only, and most precious. I am so sorry for all these years. I became complacent in my old age. I am weak, you see me now. I've tasted no blood for ages, and what is left in me, you see here." He raised his hands, tugged at his garments. "I should have been there."

"It's fine, Maker," Kazimir said. His voice was soft, softer than Whitney had ever known it to be.

"Not for me, child. I will not let her have me. If she wins me, she wins far too much power." He was standing now, backing away slowly.

"Vikas," Teryngal said, "what are you doing?"

"As long as I live, I am a threat to us all. I am the eldest," Vikas continued, still backpedaling. "I'm sorry."

The Imperios all moved toward him, but they were too slow. He turned and, with agility his frail form didn't seem capable of, ran for the cliff, then dove off.

Whitney wasn't sure what the big deal was. The upyr couldn't drown. But then he saw it: tentacles slashing to and fro, the waves sloshing with their rage. Wianu in vast numbers screamed down below, and Whitney remembered those sounds from Elsewhere when he'd met Dakel un Ghastrin. One of them was horrifying—this was paralyzing.

"No!" Kazimir shouted, grasping at air but pulling back as the sharp tip of a wianu's tentacle reached for him.

"Maker!" Sigrid raced to him and pulled him to safety. From his knees, Kazimir let out a primal roar.

"She has stirred them all to madness," Teryngal said.

"You fools!" the Sanguine Lords said, all their voices booming at once. It wasn't just the two, Whitney realized, but so many voices, he couldn't even keep track. Whitney's flesh exploded in little bumps. "Are you so blind?"

Kazimir looked to the mist. "Lords, just tell us what to do."

"She has felt the mind of the Lightmancer," they answered as one. "You've doomed us all bringing her, Kazimir…"

The mist slowly dissipated, and their voices trailed off. The chill that had been running through Whitney's entire body since the swirling colors had manifested was replaced by warmth. No, not just warmth—overwhelming heat. Sweat beaded on his forehead, and already, his shirt was soaked through.

Kazimir didn't have time to respond before a portion of the wall across the plateau burst open. Rock fell loose, cracking the ledge and knocking more into the subterranean sea. Two of the Imperios happened to be standing there and were cast into the deep, immediately swallowed up by the wianu.

Dust, filling Whitney's lungs, sent him into a coughing fit.

"The Sanctum has been breached," Kazimir whispered, incredulous.

"She's found us…" Zlata said, and she and all the other upyr who hadn't drunk with Kazimir back in the antechamber seemed frightened for once.

From the shadows beyond the miasma of debris, figures emerged, a horde of beings clambering nearer. Aquira must have seen it too because she flapped a frenzy, and blew little puffs of smoke from her nostrils.

"She followed me…" Lucindur said, voice faint as Whitney had ever heard it.

"She knew I'd bring you here after the Well," Kazimir added, he, too, seeming scared.

"The Lightmancer has unveiled the realm of the Sanctum," Teryngal said. "What have we done?"

A plume of flames shot through the breach, gobbling up the air, surely the cause of the immense heat. Vines extended from the rock, grabbing chunks and spreading them out further.

Whitney wiped sweat from his brow and looked to Kazimir. "What now?"

"Lord Thian!" Kazimir shouted, like something had just come to mind. He turned back to the place where they'd been. The multi-colored mist comprising the Sanguine Lords was now completely gone.

"What are you doing?" Teryngal asked.

Kazimir ignored the question and shouted again. "Lady Anavink!" Neither answered.

"They've left us!" Teryngal said.

"The Lady said Nesilia was coming for them," Kazimir said, "and they run?"

"We're next," Skryabin warned.

A portion of the plateau the size of the house Whitney had grown up in slid off and landed in the ocean, sending a tidal wave slamming against the cliffside and spraying water against Whitney's hot face.

"If they have abandoned us, then it is true… the blood pacts are no more," Teryngal whispered, though not soft enough to keep from Whitney's ears.

"Nuh, uh," he said, shaking his head. "A deal is a deal. We are not killing Sora, no matter what."

"Sanguine Lords or no, we will continue with the plan,"

Kazimir said, rising from his knees with Sigrid's help. It was the most exhausted the upyr had ever looked.

"This is madness!" Teryngal declared.

"If you would like to leave, you can find your way," Kazimir snapped. "I choose to believe the Lords yet remain. Their power is sealed here in this realm, but *here* has been ruptured. The blood pact is intact. Leave, or cease arguing."

A soft skittering sound drew their attention to the breach.

Through the hole, the shadows had finally become clearer. Goblins crawled into the Sanctum in pairs, many of them too stupid to avoid the nearby ledge, and falling dead to the waters below where thrashing wianu fed. Grimaurs soared in as well, screeching, and swirling the dust clouds.

"If we are going to do this, it's now or never," Lucindur said. She moved to beneath the archway at the Sanctum's entrance, as far from the attacking beasts as possible.

Whitney dabbed at the sweat pooling beneath his eyes with his cloak, then turned his attention to Lucindur, pulling the salfio from her back.

Kazimir barked orders in his ancient language. He and all the other upyr formed a line in front of them, between the breach and the arch. Tum Tum got the hint and joined them, patting his hammer. Aquira also, somehow, understood and unleashed a blaze in a wider, protective circle around them.

"We will keep them away," Kazimir said.

"Aye," Tum Tum added.

Whitney's gaze moved between Lucindur and their impending doom. Another section of the cavern's wall crumbled away, revealing more beasts.

"I can feel her presence already. We must hurry." Lucindur tugged Whitney and pulled him down, so they were seated across from each other under the arch. The exertion made her grimace.

"We've done this before," Lucindur said. "It should be easier now. Clear your mind. Focus on me."

"Okay. Yeah. You're right. All clear."

"No, it's not," Lucindur said.

"There are goblins and demons attacking us!" Whitney argued.

"If you cannot ignore them, we have lost already," Lucindur said.

"Then give me some of that manaroot," Whitney said.

"We don't have any," Lucindur said. "If I can still manage after what happened, Whitney Fierstown, you can do it, too."

Whitney's brow was pouring sweat now. He continued to look over his shoulder at the descending foes. "Okay, Okay. Clearing my mind. Clearing my mind…"

"Good," Lucindur said. "Focus and be fast. I do not know how long I can go now."

"Oh, great."

"Focus."

He thought about Sora, and then about Gentry, alone in Glinthaven, probably cursing Whitney's name. That wasn't clearing his mind. He took a deep breath, exhaled, and his shoulders dropped. Took another breath. All the sounds around him became distant, and there was nothing but the darkness of his closed eyelids.

The enchanted strings of her salfio vibrated under her fingertips, echoing throughout the cavern. As always, she started slow, playing a smooth and soothing melody. Then she sang the song Whitney had heard enough that he wanted to sing along, but he fought the urge and just listened, letting the music bathe him in sweet serenity.

> *Let your mind be opened,*
> *eyes be opened.*

> *Let the winds of eternity*
> *bring upon them clarity.*
> *Your eyes can't see*
> *but your mind is free*
> *to travel Pantego*
> *wherever she may be.*
> *Darkness engulfs her*
> *brimstone and sulfur*
> *Love lost but found*
> *hear only this sound*
> *Upon song and light*
> *give us sight.*

Embers danced. He could see them even with his eyes clenched shut. Then, blinding and severe light overwhelmed Whitney, and he felt the pull.

> *See what you came to see.*
> *See with your soul, not with your eyes.*

He slipped completely now, white light zoomed past him at an incredible rate. His stomach lurched, and he saw various landscapes rush by. Finally, he landed upon stone with such force that he felt it throughout his whole body. This wasn't Elsewhere, it wasn't Troborough, and it wasn't even Nowhere.

He stood and dusted himself off, grasping his side where it felt as if he might have bruised a rib.

"Sora," he said softly, not only due to his lost breath but also afraid to awaken anything that might be listening.

The room looked similar to the Sanctum they'd just been in, but there were no monsters, no ocean, and no one but him. Only a soft dripping sound coming from the other side of the room. Following it, Whitney found that the archway now dripped crimson—blood hitting the ground and going nowhere as if vanishing. The altar upon which the upyr named Vikas had been praying was now just a tall pile of bones.

"Hello?" Whitney called, his voice trembling almost as much as his knees.

His voice called back, but there was no Sora.

He chanced a few steps, and then a few more. After a minute of walking, he entered through an oppressively dark tunnel, again, not unlike the one they'd used to enter the Sanctum.

Am I going back to the Citadel?

Lichen grew, mold festered, and soon, the darkness closed in around him like death itself. He was shaking, breathing heavy, sweating.

"Hello!" He screamed the word, but it was immediately swallowed up as if he'd shouted into a thick blanket.

Hands outstretched, feeling for the walls, he pressed on, not knowing what else to do. His heart was pounding at a rapid pace, mouth dry.

"Sora," he whispered. "Is this the exile you've been in?"

The wall met his fingertips, and he jumped back when he touched something soft and squishy. His back hit the wall behind him, where something popped. The sound of a thousand little feet berated him. He thought he felt chills running up his spine until he realized...

If he could see, he knew he'd have seen hundreds of translucent little spiders crawling all over the walls and now, all over him. Swatting and yelling, he felt them in his hair, on his skin, in his mouth. He gagged, spit, nearly vomited, but they kept coming. Deciding to run, he took off as fast as he could while still being careful not to slam into the walls.

Whitney brushed frantically, feeling their little pointy legs. There was some light now, and although he felt them, he saw nothing.

"Gods and yigging monsters," he swore. "Sora!"

And then, the ground fell out beneath him, and he plummeted.

He didn't know if he could die in this place, but he was sure he was about to find out. His arms and legs spasmed through the air as he twisted, trying in silent desperation to face the direction in which he plunged. Then, just as he managed to do it, he felt the ground, and all sense of direction escaped him.

The ground was wet... or was that blood?

The ground was cold... or was that death?

The ground... was water, and he was sinking.

He swam, but then stopped, worried he might be taking himself even deeper. Floating there, eyes open and seeing only darkness, he heard a high, shrill cry. His heart threatened to leave his chest altogether, battling with vomit for the position at the back of his throat. He had to breathe but couldn't. He needed air...

Something slippery brushed against his hand. Whitney yanked it back, but then something bumped his leg. He kicked and pumped his arms, but it didn't feel like he was moving at all. Then, any air stored in his lungs was forced out as that same something constricted around his midsection. He still couldn't see, but he felt the water pulling at him as whatever held on propelled him forward.

Bubbles tickled his nose as they slipped past his lips. He was lightheaded, and he thought, screaming. Then, he experienced euphoria as oxygen entered his lungs, and his ears popped, but he was underwater again just as quickly. He was too disoriented to even consider the implications, trying with strained effort to not drown—which only made drowning all the more likely.

His eyes met two bright globes like the one Kazimir was holding, only much larger. He thought maybe his salvation had arrived, but hope fled his heart when the orbs blinked.

Crippling fear pierced Whitney's heart at the sight of the

wianu. He'd faced them before—twice—but never had he been at one's mercy like this.

Together, Whitney and the wianu broke the surface. Whitney gasped, slapping at the tentacle that wrapped him. It was no use. Teeth like longswords protruded from bloody gums, strings of sticky saliva stretching between them. He was close—so close to experiencing precisely what they'd planned to do to Nesilia; to being devoured by the otherworldly beast which he now knew to be a cursed god turned into a god-killing weapon.

Whitney kicked it, which was akin to kicking a brick wall, and whip-fast, he was in the air again, thrust from the thing's grasp. He heaved even as he landed on the sand, having been hurled all the way to the coast. Salty water filled his lungs, making him wheeze and cough until a bucket of water came out and drenched the sand. As soon as he could, he spun around and crab-walked from the shore, unwilling to be caught up in the wianu's tentacles again.

"Help!" a woman's voice said from still a great distance. "Someone help!"

"Sora!" Whitney shouted back, scrabbling to his feet, kicking and clawing sand. He couldn't hear the voice clearly, but he hoped against hope it was her.

He ran toward the sound. His legs, however, wouldn't keep up with his heart. He slipped a few times before finally regaining his footing. It was still dark, but soon, he could feel that the sand had given way to the undergrowth of forested area. Tall trees with trunks thick as a giant's torso rose all around him, pine needles prickling against his face. He tripped on a knot of roots and landed in mud.

Swearing, he rose and pressed on.

Whispers bounced back and forth from every direction. Yellow eyes glinted from the bushes, reminding Whitney of the satyrs in the Webbed Woods. Red blisters that he recalled to be spider-egg sacs dotted the bark in all directions. Those same little specks undulated in the canopy above—human eyeballs hanging from silken string. Beyond that, he couldn't even see the sky.

"Help!" the woman shrieked.

"Sora, I'm coming!"

From the bushes, spindly appendages swiped out at Whitney as he ran, cutting him deeply across the neck and chest. He swatted at them, and kept on, the forest growing denser with webbing until at last, the tree line broke.

Whitney skidded to a stop. He tried to whisper Sora's name, but his mouth felt as if it were filled with cotton. But she was there, tied to a post—no, not tied—wrapped by silky webs, not ten meters away. She thrashed violently, but she was secure.

"Whitney!" she yelled.

"Yigging Exile, Sora!" Whitney shouted as he began toward her.

"No! Don't come any closer!"

He tried to listen, knowing she probably had good reason to warn him, but his feet just kept going, unable to stand another second apart from her.

"Please, stop," she pled. "Please."

"Fear is such a funny thing, isn't it?" the voice came, sweet as venom-laced honey.

Whitney knew who it belonged to by now, and knew that everything she said would be a lie.

"It's over, Nesilia," he said. "You've lost."

Whitney moved closer.

"Stop! Whitney, stop!" Sora shouted through tears.

"What is it?" he said.

"Don't you see her?" Sora asked.

"Who? Nesilia?" Whitney looked around. "There's only you and me here."

"Bliss!" Sora shouted.

Whitney spun a tight circle. He reached for his daggers but found that here, he didn't have them. "Where?"

"Right in front of you," Sora said. "She's right in front of you."

"Sora, none of this is real. She's not really there." Whitney kept moving toward Sora but kept his hands raised and ready for a fight just in case.

A moment later, he was upon her, tearing at the webbing. It was sticky, and as he removed it, it clung to him just as it had in Bliss' lair when he was wrapped up like a finger treat.

"We'll get you out of there," he said as he furiously worked at unwrapping.

Glancing up at her, he saw the overwhelming sadness in her eyes.

"It's no use, Whit," she wept. "It's no use. I'm—she's... She's me now. I'm her. I..."

"Shhhhh. Shhh. Shhh. Shhh. It's going to be okay. We have a plan."

"Ohhh, I do love plans," Nesilia purred. "Was revealing this unholy Sanctum to me one of them? My creations will help me retake the world that should be mine!"

"Shut up!" Whitney shouted.

Sora fell free and landed, boneless in Whitney's arms.

"I'm too weak," she said. "I can't go on."

"You've got to try," Whitney said, lowering her to her own feet. He held her there long enough for her to find her legs, staring straight into her eyes and never breaking contact. They took a few steps, cautious at first, but then she began to gain confidence.

"Can you?" Whitney said.

"I-I think so," she said, then stumbled. "Whitney, there's so much I want to—"

"Whitney caught her and brought her up again. "Tell me after we're out of here. C'mon, we'll take it slow."

"Slow isn't going to work for me," Nesilia said.

The world around them shook, and the rocks above them fell, landing with deadly force.

"We've got to move," Whitney said. "Let's go!"

He led her, one hand at her hip, the other keeping her arm tight over his shoulder. Through the trees, spiders crawling up and down the trunks reached out for them. Out of the corner of his eye, Whitney saw something to their right—a large silhouette running alongside them. When he turned his head, it was gone. When he turned his head back, they nearly collided with Bliss herself.

The Spider Queen Goddess was taller than he remembered—nearly twice his height. She wore her carapace like a gown and horn-like growths like a crown. Those dazzling purple eyes drove steel through him, pinning Whitney. She was gorgeous, and she was deadly.

"You're dead," Whitney said, but he didn't sound sure. "I—we killed you."

"You cannot kill… a goddess!" she shouted and launched herself with powerful back legs.

Sora yanked Whitney down beneath the attack, and they kept moving. He could feel her, hot on their heels. The trees snapped, careening to the earth, kicking up dirt. The many egg sacs burst, and the baby spiders carpeted the forest. Bliss hissed and drove a sharp claw into the soil beside them.

Sora yelped in fright.

"It's okay," Whitney said. "She can't hurt us—"

Something slammed into them… and it hurt, badly.

Whitney swore as he slid across the forest floor, feeling every bump of the root systems against his already throbbing ribs. He smashed into a tree and reached out to stop Sora from sliding too far from him.

He kept telling himself that none of this was real, but it felt real. It hurt. He hurt. Sora was crying, and he felt his own tears tickling his cheeks. But he bit back, determined to fight his way out. He reached for daggers that weren't there as Bliss edged toward them, each of her eight legs rising and falling in hypnotic sequence. Beyond and above, her children descended on silk, twisting until they landed and skittered to stand beside their mother and queen.

"I've waited a long time for this," she said. One of her legs stroked Whitney's cheek, little prickling hairs scratching him and even drawing blood.

"You're not real!" Whitney shouted as if saying it would make it true.

"I'm more real than you've ever been. I am eternal. I am—"

"Leave him alone!" Sora screamed.

The earth quaked again and more trees toppled. Fear passed over Bliss' face for an instant, but it only took that long before a chasm in the earth opened and consumed her and her minions.

Whitney grabbed Sora and rose, pounding dirt as they ran from the ever-growing fissure. Boulders hurtled down, creating craters everywhere they landed. The quaking intensified, tossing them around like dice in a cup. Sora fell to her knees.

"I can't go anymore…" she panted.

Whitney grabbed her around the waist, but she wouldn't budge. "You've gotta run. Sora, you've got to—"

"I can't…"

Whitney looked down at her, then at the world breaking apart behind them. Such a delicate poem being composed all around them—the story of their life. Together, just to be torn apart once more by insane, supernatural causes; by the affairs of angry gods and demons.

He knew this could be his last chance to say it. To make sure she knew—really knew—how he felt before there was no more time.

"I've always said I knew how I'd die... and this is it. Right here with you. Sure, I wished it would have been more peaceful..." They both laughed. "But Sora, you're all that matters. You're everything, and I love you."

She looked up at him, and him down at her.

"I know," she said. "So do—"

He couldn't even wait for her to finish before he kissed her. Deeply. Passionately.

His head swirled, darkness enveloped them, and the world went black.

XXXIV

THE IMMORTAL

Goblin and grimaur bodies littered the landscape, though their numbers only seemed to swell with every passing minute. Nesilia had bated him, used a threat to draw him here. The protective enchantments of the Citadel were strong, but here in the Sanctum, it was almost a realm between, shielded by the Sanguine Lords' ancient power. It was supposed to be impossible to find for those who hadn't been there, even if they'd found the Citadel, it'd stay hidden.

Something had failed.

That something came in the form of the Lightmancer, Lucindur, who had felt Nesilia's mind, and vice versa. She'd led her right to the heart of their order, but it was Kazimir's fault.

"Still only beasts of the mountains," Teryngal mocked, slashing a grimaur in two. "We can clean them out in minutes. This is what you were worried about?"

Sigrid was behind him, firing her crossbow while Aquira battled grimaurs in the air.

The ground groaned, and sizable chunks of the mountain broke free and slid, kicking up puffs of dust and rock debris, killing so many of the goblins along with it. At this rate, the whole of the mountain would soon cave in on them.

"Have you always been such a fool, Teryngal?" Kazimir asked.

He rushed to Sigrid and had to yank her by her shoulder, to get her attention away from fighting. She snarled at him before realizing who it was.

"Sigrid, don't let anyone touch them!" Kazimir shouted, pointing to Whitney and the Lightmancer who were now wholly absent this world, their eyes rolled back to reveal only white as Lucindur's fingers absent-mindedly plucked her magical instrument. The dwarf stood guard on one side of them, and Sigrid joined him on the other.

Kazimir knew they'd need time.

"Yes, Master."

Now that the feral beasts had cleared the breach, new shadows marched forth through the swirling haze. The first to emerge were Drav Cra warriors in their furs and painted skin, a horde of muscle-bound warriors with axes and spears, led by towering chieftains. They were followed by a warlock, a female with the top half of her face painted completely black, and the bottom, red down to the curvature of her neck.

Packs of dire wolves moved in after her, bearing razor-sharp fangs, long as daggers, each of them standing as tall as Kazimir's chest. More goblins and grimaurs flooded in with them as well.

Kazimir's Dom Nohzi brothers and sisters had repelled the first tide of creatures and sent them scampering back to gain reinforcements.

"Where did they come from?" Teryngal asked. The tremor in his voice finally matching the gravity of the situation.

"From within the earth," Kazimir said, "which she's learned so well over eternity."

"What do we do?" Zlata asked.

"They've come to the wrong place," spoke Skryabin. "We'll slaughter them, and feast for a year."

With that, the other Imperios charged to battle. Kazimir stayed behind as a mass of goblins, emboldened by the reinforcements, rumbled toward him and the Lightmancing ceremony behind him.

Goblins were hideous creatures, with their reptilian skin, yellow eyes, and long, protruding lizard-like mouths. They wore jagged bone masks, showing no preference for any particular animal or creature. Sharp teeth, which would have drawn their own blood if their skin wasn't strong as hardened steel, overlapped black lips. Even so, it wouldn't stop Kazimir's blades—a fact proven by the sound of one slicing through flesh as he rent a goblin across the neck. It dropped at his feet, and he used it as a step to vault him toward the next. Landing in a roll, Kazimir came up slashing. Blood gushed out onto his arm as it sputtered from a goblin throat.

The female warlock shouted in Drav Crava. Her voice carried across the Sanctum, the sheer power of it sending a few grimaur soaring. Then, she drew a serrated dagger and sliced her palm. The warriors hollered in glee, watching as fire wreathed its way up the warlock's arms.

The woman stared straight at Kazimir, grinning as if challenging him to leave the Lightmancer exposed. The hate in her eyes was palpable. He'd once felt hunger like that, capable of destroying everything in its path, but the centuries had tempered Kazimir's passions.

He heard a war cry and turned in time to see one of the reptilian pests careening toward him. Kazimir fell backward into a reverse summersault, and kicked out with one foot, catching the goblin in the chest.

Then, he pivoted and shot two daggers from his spring-loaded wrist bracers. One sliced the thing at the ear, and the other was a direct hit. The blade exploded through its eye, sending black and yellow ichor spraying out the back of its head, and it fell dead a foot away.

Across the plateau, Sigrid and Tum Tum guarded Whitney and the Lightmancer as she played her preternatural tune. Light motes floated all around them, and a line of blood leaked from one of the Lightmancer's nostrils.

Kazimir had to hope the thief was finding success—and soon, or there might be nothing left to return to. Beside them, Aquira was doing a fine job dispatching any enemy that appeared to even think about touching Whitney. Fire streamed from its maw with an intensity beyond the wyvern's meager size. But it cut through ranks of goblins just fine.

A snarl was Kazimir's only warning before a dire wolf bit down hard on his arm. The leather armor he wore curbed the brunt of the bite, but the pressure was intense. He punched once, then snatched a small dagger designed to fit between his knuckles and punched again. This time, the blade pieced fur, skin, and bone, and sent a steady stream of blood pouring from the already dead wolf's forehead.

Vines, summoned by the warlock, rose from the rock and entangled Skryabin. They were not able to harm her but held her still. Even with all the Dom Nohzi Imperios working together, they were overwhelmed by mystics and Drav Cra, but Kazimir couldn't afford to offer his assistance.

He fought his own war against goblins and wolves throwing themselves at him from every direction. Sigrid could fend off any immediate attack on Whitney, but she wouldn't be able to hold her ground alone for long. So, Kazimir had to do his part quickly.

He was fast—all upyr were—but there were so many beasts, even his speed didn't account for it. It had to be every wicked creature throughout Pantego here thanks to Nesilia's power. He thrust one knife while throwing another. Both hit their marks, but a goblin landed on Kazimir's back, wrapping an arm loosely around his neck and punching with the other.

Goblin blood tasted awful—like maggot-infested, rotting corpse—but Kazimir bit down hard and cringed as the goblin screeched in his ear. It afforded him the opportunity to reach back and remove it from its perch. It screeched again when he tossed it aside and into another approaching beast. He spat, careful not to drink any of the putrid ichor.

Poison-laced darts zoomed through the air all around him, but their toxin would have no effect on any of the upyr since there was no blood flowing through their veins. That didn't mean Kazimir wouldn't feel the sting, though, and if one hit Whitney, or the Lightmancer, it would spell disaster.

Sigrid stowed her crossbow and now had her short swords out, cutting down a pack of dire wolves with speed and precision.

Wings flapped, and Kazimir looked up to see a murder of grimaurs sweeping in, staying high to dive-bomb Whitney, being strategic—something Kazimir knew they were incapable of on their own. Nesilia had a deep hold on these creatures.

"Sigrid! Focus on the grimaurs!" Kazimir shouted.

She did, dropping her swords and drawing her crossbow again. As she made short work of the flock, Kazimir filled the gap she'd left in the ranks of land beasts. A goblin charged him, a female this time. Her sagging, shriveled breasts flapped as she ran, mouth wide to reveal jagged and crooked teeth. Pulling one of his longer blades, he took the first blow with the flat of it and rolled the goblin's spear away with ease.

Normally, goblins and grimaurs offered very little thought behind their raids, and dire wolves only hunted for food. They were senseless, unthinking beasts, but as two more goblins came at his front, and then another wolf came at him from behind, Kazimir wondered just how manipulated these creatures were by Nesilia to act with such strategy.

He didn't have time to concern himself with the thought. With upyr reflexes, Kazimir took out the wolf first, then took seconds to turn the goblin blades against their owners, and finally, brought up his own weapon and cleaved the first one through the jaw and the second in the gut.

Moving forward with ruthless efficiency, he cut through the throngs, hacking at spines, daggers eating through their armor-like skin. Aquira swooped down, protecting his right side with a blast of fire. Soon, after retrieving several of his thrown blades, he was by Sigrid's side, gutting a row of Drav Cra warriors before they killed Tum Tum.

"I owe ye..." the dwarf huffed, struggling to keep his hammer up.

Whitney and the Lightmancer were behind them. Bodies, strewn haplessly throughout the cavern poured out rivers of blood and ichor which coalesced to form a pool in the center, then streamed out toward the sea.

The tips of wianu tentacles continually stretched over the cliff's edge, grasping like they themselves were bloodthirsty upyr.

A sound like thunder reverberated the Sanctum and fire erupted from the warlock, who'd now drawn a great deal of her own blood. The pillar of flame torched a few of the upyr. Kazimir saw Skryabin within the inferno, unable to escape thanks to the warlock's restraining vines. Her body wasn't given the chance to heal as the magical blaze burned without fuel, searing through the layers of her flesh all the way to her cursed heart, which was left charred.

More vines trapped an upyr, though Kazimir couldn't tell who. The vision was too obscured by the dire wolves feasting on their ancient flesh. Drav Cra warriors surrounded another, giving their lives to his quick strikes before grimaurs held him in place, talons tearing into his chest, aiming for the heart.

It was not a normal thing to see an upyr meet eternity in such a way. Their bodies were eternal, but none of them knew where their spirits would wind up. The mystics—so closely related to the upyr, were spirits by choice, still roaming Pantego. The humans, regardless of race, each had their own belief as to what happened to them. From the Gate of Light to the Eternal Current, everyone believed in some grand adventure after this life fled them. But Kazimir knew different.

It was said that the eyes were the window into the soul, and upyr windows were nothing more than darkness and the void.

Kazimir spoke a few words in near silence for his fallen brothers and sisters while he continued his assault on Nesilia's vile forces. Then, he looked up to the remaining Imperios.

Teryngal, who was still holding his own, used a short sword and a simple staff for blocking. It was a masterful dance in a forgotten style of fighting, as he swiped and stabbed, putting down Drav Cra attackers.

"This is still just the beginning," Kazimir said to himself more than to Sigrid.

"Let them come," she said, still firing bolts. Of all the upyr, only she appeared to be having fun.

"Just hold on a little longer," Tum Tum said to Whitney, wheezing in exhaustion.

As if in response to Kazimir, another legion of Drav Cra charged through the breach in the Sanctum's walls. They were shirtless, Drav Cra berserkers, on enough manaroot to punch through a wall and feel nothing. The tips of their weapons shined, though, Kazimir wasn't sure why.

"Aquira, stay with Whitney," Kazimir looked up and said. "Nothing gets near."

The wyvern screeched in response, then burned a cluster of grimaurs to ashes.

By now, the beasts and Drav Cra swarmed the Imperios, who'd fanned out into their ranks, each a one-man army. There were still plenty for Kazimir to kill. A dire wolf came at him, straight on. He couldn't believe how stupid the thing could be until he realized two goblins were closing in on him from either side and a grimaur was in mid-dive above.

Reaching for his bandolier, Kazimir pulled four daggers, two with each hand. He dropped low, spun once, and then rolled forward, releasing all four blades. Each one found their target.

Kazimir then weaved through the battle. Slice. Cut. Stab. Cut. Stab. His muscles didn't tire. He'd fight for eternity if he had to.

One of the Drav Cra berserkers bum-rushed him, whirling his great axe like a tornado. The man's eyes were red from manaroot. The drug had him raging with relentless power.

Kazimir sidestepped, but the warrior recovered and wheeled back around, swinging his weapon in a wide arc. Kazimir took a slice to his arm and expected it to heal, but his skin bubbled as the blade made contact. A thin cut that should have been nothing more burned like sunlight.

Silver, Kazimir realized. The blades of the berserkers were coated in silver dust. Meant to defeat the upyr, the metal was long ago imbued with sunlight and summoned by ancient mystics into veins of iron ore around Pantego. And now that the initial wave of attackers had the upyr spread out, they were all exposed to it.

"She thought of everything, dead man," the Drav Cra taunted. "We will purge this world!"

Kazimir heard the whizzing, saw the bolt sticking out of the warrior's eye before he went down. Kazimir turned to thank Sigrid, but she was already firing in the opposite direction. Metal *clanged.* Grimaurs screeched as the last of them fell to Sigrid's bolts.

The dwarf was caught up in a battle with another Drav Cra warrior at least two times his height. For what it was worth, he held his own.

The female warlock battled Zlata, dodging her attacks, and using vines to pull back her arms and slow her. Teryngal engaged another group of Drav Cra berserkers, mowing through them with masterful grace, but occasionally a silver-tipped weapon sliced him, earning a wince, weakening him. Other upyr weren't so lucky.

Kazimir turned aside, ignoring the roars of rage, and the dying being done all around him. His focus was singular—the beautiful Panpingese woman now standing in the breach and looking out over the battlefield.

She looked momentarily distracted, which meant Lucindur's spell was working. She barely seemed like the young woman Kazimir had captured in Winde Port. Even from such a distance, Kazimir could see her eyes, so bright yellow they were almost white, and he feared that for her to look upon him would be no different from standing naked in daylight.

The scorn of centuries was etched fully upon a face that was not hers, and an overbearing sense of terror washed over him.

"Fear is such a funny thing, isn't it?" she said, her voice carrying across the cavern.

Kazimir fingered the bar guai in his pocket. "She's here!" he shouted.

Turning, Kazimir saw Aquira staring at her master… her friend, Sora, and he hoped the wyvern was bright enough to know this wasn't truly her.

"Aquira!" Kazimir called, and drawing out the word, soft but stern.

"Come to me, pretty bird," Nesilia countered, but Aquira heeded neither call. She landed on a stalagmite, frilled head low and growling.

"Thief, if you can hear me," Kazimir whispered, "it is now or never. Do something."

Kazimir took a step forward, hoping Sigrid and the dwarf

could keep their companions safe without the wyvern, but he hadn't expected Nesilia so soon—he had to draw her attention.

Nesilia strode forward into the chaos, or rather, floated, studying it all. Mountain crumbling—the whole place was forever compromised. Imperio Urlar came at her from the side, but she didn't even panic. A warrior flung his axe in front of her, the blade sinking into his chest, destroying his heart. Urlar burst into ash.

"What a disappointment," Nesilia said, her voice carrying. "This place holds such a revered position in all of creation, and it falls like a poorly stacked house of cards."

"Ye'll do the same, witch!" the dwarf shouted across the plateau. He downed a dire wolf, then hefted his warhammer, as if it'd do anything against the goddess, and charged like a crazed zhulong.

Nesilia stretched out her hand, showing him how little he mattered. The ground erupted beneath the dwarf, sending up a thick column of rock, and tossing him high. He landed with a resounding *thud* beside the entry statues towering over Whitney and Lucindur and didn't move.

"I must thank you for leading me here so easily," Nesilia said. "I suppose Aihara Na's failure in protecting the Well wasn't a total loss."

Nesilia strode forward. Her monstrous horde still vastly outnumbered them but had suffered a great deal of loss. Kazimir took stock of his own forces. Many of the upyr had fallen, dispelled by both magic and silver, so they couldn't heal.

"You will pay for this!" Zlata shouted. She charged Nesilia next, unafraid, cutting through every beast and Drav Cra warrior in her path.

"Freydis, be a doll, and take care of her, would you?" Nesilia asked, a playful edge to her tone.

"With pleasure, my Lady," the female warlock said, hopping

in front of the Buried Goddess. She flung her hand forward, and droplets of blood sprayed out from the wound on her palm. Where they hit the rocky ground, huge vines burst up. With violent force, they gripped Zlata's body, heaved her into the air, and pierced through her heart. Her mouth opened to scream, but the vines constricted her throat so tight, her head no longer communed with her neck, and her body burst into a puff of ash.

Kazimir had never seen masters of blood magic so skilled. It was as if Nesilia's presence fueled them, or maybe with so many mystics and warlocks dead around the world, there was more magic available to them.

The remaining foes all withdrew to Nesilia's side—dozens of Drav Cra, with who-knows-how-many armed with silver. Dire wolves stalked around them, growling low. Kazimir couldn't believe how many there still were. It was beginning to feel pointless with all the goblins and grimaurs squealing and swooping in from every direction, many falling off the cliff to feed the wianu, but they'd only been a distraction used to isolate and weaken the Imperios.

The remaining upyr formed a semi-circle to guard Whitney and Lucindur, along with Kazimir and Sigrid. Teryngal was among them, half his body bubbling from the touch of silver.

Nesilia stopped by a crooked column at the Sanguine Lord's altar and casually leaned against it, checking her nails.

She sighed and looked up, directed at Kazimir. "Upyr..." She didn't shout, but her voice carried as if the air itself were beholden to her. "I believe you may know this body? Have desired this body? Do what your fellows have failed to do, and you can have as much of it as you please. In whatever manner you wish."

Kazimir stepped forward. "Come up here, and I'll show you what I'd like to do to you," he snarled.

"A pity. You're so strong. So powerful. So... willful. You

could be a god yourself, but instead, you squander it for that pesky Fierstown."

"It's time for ye to die!" Sigrid broke their plan and loosed a flurry of bolts at Nesilia. With but a wave of her hand, Nesilia turned each to fizzling ash before hitting her.

Nesilia's attention snapped to Sigrid, and Kazimir cringed.

The Goddess stretched out a hand, and as if caught upon wind, Sigrid soared through the air and slammed into the smooth but unforgiving stone wall behind her. Two other upyr were stirred to anger and charged her as well. They were impossibly fast, and Kazimir's calls for them to stop fell on deaf ears. None of Nesilia's followers moved to help her.

They knew she needed none.

The Goddess dodged their strikes, as fast as they were. Then, she cut the air with her open palm and a portion of the ground split. The upyr didn't even register the action before they were falling, gone to the darkness. With Sigrid incapacitated, that left only Kazimir and Teryngal.

"Kazimir," Nesilia said, striding toward him, ahead of her forces, somehow knowing his name. "Where are your Lords? Did they run?"

Kazimir swallowed, though he had no need to. He set his feet, clenching his fists tight.

"I can't feel them at all" Nesilia taunted. "Maybe they've finally decided to move on. A pity. I'll have to find a new use for my creations." She nodded toward the wianu-filled sea.

"You lie!" Kazimir shouted, pulling a longer blade from the sheath at his waist.

Teryngal stepped forward. He whispered, "If she tells the truth, the blood pact you made no longer matters… neither of them. Let us kill her now, and this will all end."

"He is right, you know," Nesilia said. "Why not destroy this beautiful host for me. I tire of her resistance."

"No," Kazimir growled.

"You are treating food like friends, Kazimir," Teryngal said. "We are the eldest. The Dom Nohzi is ours now. We can shape it how we like."

"Can't you see? We are the only!" Kazimir screamed, wanting to snatch the man by the throat and tear him apart. "Stick to the plan."

"Ohhh, I do love plans," Nesilia purred. "Was revealing this unholy Sanctum to me one of them?"

"Let me slaughter them," the female warlock said. "These abominations deserve their end."

"No, not yet," Nesilia said. She looked to Kazimir and said, "Do it."

Kazimir gritted his teeth, his free hand still close to the bar guai in his pocket.

"Do it," she repeated, moving toward Whitney. She staggered a bit.

Keep going thief. She's growing weaker, Kazimir thought to himself, willing it.

"You think I won't destroy him?" she asked.

"I think you would have if you could," Kazimir said. "But you're not completely in control, are you? Her heart holds you back."

Nesilia smiled and turned to the wyvern, now flapping in front of her.

"Aquira," she cooed. "Come see me. You remember me—don't you?"

Aquira edged forward, head tilted. Then, she struck out to bite, and Nesilia swatted her away like nothing more than a pesky fly. She hit the wall hard and dropped down near Sigrid.

There was swift movement at Kazimir's side, and he felt a hand in his hair, jerking his head back. Then, something sharp pressed against his throat.

"How does it feel, Imperio Kazimir," Teryngal said. "To be betrayed by your own kind. To be offered up as a sacrifice?"

"Teryngal, what are you doing?" Kazimir growled. He reached for the silver blade he'd always kept hidden, but it wasn't there, now in Teryngal's hand. "You fool."

"Traitor!" Sigrid roared, as she fought to rise, still recovering from the Goddess' attack. She fired her crossbow. Teryngal's speed allowed him to easily avoid the bolt.

Vines burst forth from the cracks in the earth, enveloping Sigrid tight like chains. She continued to curse and spit until the vines forced themselves down her throat, and her words turned to gurgles. Nesilia didn't even look at her.

"You chose mortals over your brethren!" Teryngal barked, letting the dagger sear Kazimir's flesh "Over us all! Now, we are all that remains of thousands of years of history."

"I wondered where the wisdom of the Dom Nohzi disappeared to," Nesilia said. She approached the upyr, hips swaying, yellow eyes blazing. Again, she staggered ever so slightly. "Finally, someone with brains as well as brawn."

"Allow the Dom Nohzi to endure, and I, along with every remaining upyr across Pantego, are yours," Teryngal said.

"You will regret this, traitor," Kazimir whispered.

"Kazimir Mikohailov… you are infamous in Elsewhere, do you know that?" Nesilia asked. "My former kin—the ones you call wianu—they tremble at the thought of you. Whatever did you do to make the gods tremble?"

Kazimir knew better than to look into her eyes, and Nesilia noticed.

"Look at me!" she bellowed. She rushed forward and gripped his jaw, strength like a lion's maw. Teryngal's silver blade slid closer.

Kazimir's fear was realized when beams of sunlight from Nesilia's eyes burned into his. He fought it, as she drew ever closer. She was now so near he could taste her mystic blood even as he smelled it. But now, it was so much more than it had been in Winde Port—the blood of kings and gods and mystics.

"I can make you a god," she said.

"We don't need him," Teryngal said.

"You've lived a long time, Kazimir," she said. "Longer than most. Do you not wish for more?"

She spoke the very words Vikas had said to Kazimir when he'd met him all those years ago on the streets of Vidkaru. The words Kazimir had said to Sigrid and the words heard by every other Dom Nohzi recruit. And in that moment, he knew the answer. He noticed the twitch of her pupils, glancing once over his shoulder in Whitney's direction. That oh-so slight tell.

"End this," Teryngal whispered in his ear.

Kazimir grinned. "I wish for you to die!"

His hand thrust outward, and Nesilia gasped. Her eyes followed his arm to her chest, and when she looked away, Kazimir could see again. He saw her face, confused, looking up as Teryngal removed the blade from Kazimir's throat. She looked down again at the bar guai drilling itself into her chest at the heart.

"Impossible," she muttered. "I am eternal. I am—"

Blood poured out as the bar guai went deeper into Sora's chest, and Nesilia collapsed.

The warlock, Freydis, howled like she'd been the one stabbed through the heart. She was already weak from losing blood, but she cut herself once more, screaming as she hurled a stream of flame and ice from her fingertips.

The elements shot across the cavern, when from the altar of the Sanguine Lords, rose a multi-colored mist.

"Suffer not a witch to live!" Lord Thain's voice resonated.

The mist rose like a wall in front of Nesilia's forces, catching Freydis' flame and ice in the cloud and blocking their sight. The elements coruscated from it, slashing across walls and loosening more rock, turning the stone into molten slag. Nesilia's forces retreated to where they'd come lest they be crushed. The cavern quaked. More stalactites shook over the sea, some breaking off and plunging like spears hurled from a giant's fist.

The vines fell away from Sigrid, and she crumpled to a heap, unmoving.

"The Dom Nohzi may die today because of you, Kazimir," the voices of the Lords echoed around them. "But balance is preserved. We cannot hold for long. Finish her."

"I knew it," Kazimir said. "They're still with us."

"Hiding in the shadows, waiting to strike. Same as ever," Teryngal said.

"Good work. For a moment, I thought she'd gotten to you," Kazimir said.

"For a moment, she had…"

XXXV

THE KNIGHT

Torsten's head still pounded. He wasn't used to a sip of ale, let alone a few flagons. It was well past mid-day by the time he woke to the sound of horns signaling the Shesaitju army's arrival.

He knew his men needed the distraction after seeing poor souls crucified, others losing a battle and being choked by whipping sand. Morale was everything, and Torsten wasn't sure when exactly it'd happened, but he'd become a hero to the common soldier. The way they regarded him that morning—he'd never experienced anything like it. It wasn't only respect, it was adoration. He recalled the same look in his own eyes when King Liam would ride by on his white horse.

There was a lesson he couldn't wait to impart to young King Pi. Killing Redstar, winning battles, defeating Mak—to the people he was just a commander atop a horse wearing armor. It was only when he stepped down in the dirt with them, became one of them, that the respect blossomed into something more. He knew that no matter what happened, if talks with the Shesaitju army broke, and continuing war was inevitable, these soldiers of his wouldn't be bested. Iam was with them.

"Your light shines bright upon us this day," Dellbar the Holy said to Iam. He and Torsten were alone together, off wedged into one of the many alcoves along the White Bridge, Torsten kneeling before the old priest in one last prayer.

"Our little kingdom has been through so much," Dellbar went on. "Today, by your grace, we hope we'll see an end to the struggle. Let it be that the peace which dwells within this man, dedicated to your love and light, will hold it until he reaches the Gate of Light. May your Vigilant Eye guide our paths."

Dellbar circled his eyes in prayer, and Torsten did the same. Then, he stood. Dellbar cleared his throat and cracked his neck. A small exhale followed the *pop, pop, pops*. His breath reeked, though Torsten imagined his smelled far worse.

"Thank you, Your Holiness," Torsten said.

"All in the job," Dellbar replied. His hands fell to his side, and Torsten noticed that he wasn't holding his flask. A rare sight.

"No drinking this morning?" Torsten asked. "Dare I say, I'm proud of you."

"Even I am only human. Breaks are required." He wrapped a feather-light arm around Torsten, and they started off toward the gate. "I had no idea you had it in you. Perhaps, I should have asked Iam to ease the pain in your head."

Though his hangover was severe, Torsten smirked. "I prefer the reminder."

"Suit yourself."

"How do you live this way?" Torsten asked. "I can barely recall falling asleep. Or… no, I don't remember it at all."

Dellbar stopped. "Do you remember your late-night visit with Rand Langley."

Torsten shook his head. "Not a second of it."

"I see…"

"Is he—"

"He's fine, don't worry," Dellbar said. He ran fingers through thin, dirty hair. "However, you may have revealed some… unsettling truths about his sister being an upyr."

"I didn't."

"You did."

Torsten's face fell into his palm. "Oh, Iam's Light, what a fool I am. I should speak with him."

"I wouldn't. Sir Danvels is hard at work trying to explain things; make things right. He's a good man, that one. A bit nosey, but solid as a zhulong in a mud bath. I do believe you have more important things to handle." The echo of Shesaitju zhulong-tusk horns echoed, as if to emphasize his point.

Torsten wasn't sure what to say. Embarrassed was too soft a term.

Dellbar patted Torsten's shoulder. "Everything will be fine, Torsten. I'll pray for him. I may not be able to see, but I have a sense for men who've been hurt far more than they deserve. He will feel the light again."

Torsten blew out a mouthful of air. "Thank you, Your Holiness. I promise you, that's the last time I'll be drinking."

"And Pantego will be a lesser place for it."

"I should know better. My parents—"

"Were not heroes," Dellbar assured him. "You are. Stay strong, my friend. War has robbed us of so much. My home. My friends. End it today, and perhaps we can finally start the arduous process of rebuilding. I know a few towns in desperate need of a new church."

"Your mouth to Iam's ears."

Dellbar smile, then angled his head, as if listening to the sky. "Do you hear that? It appears my time of restfulness is over. I find myself incredibly thirsty."

"You're a peculiar man."

"So, I've been told." Dellbar released Torsten and drew his cane from his belt. He tapped along, back into the watchtower where he and the other members of the Church of Iam had made their temporary residence.

Torsten watched him leave, hoping with all his heart that the High Priest was right, that the warring could finally end. Leaning out over the gorge, his gaze jumped to the dark portal leading down to the dungeons where Rand now likely stewed. Torsten's heart sank. He'd lost his composure just for a moment and made the poor man's life even more miserable.

Sigrid was gone. At least, the version Rand knew. In the realm of Iam, unlife was equal to death. She was a cursed, murderous being, closer to a monster than human. Rand would see that in time. But Torsten also understood, more than anyone, how being close to somebody could make it so impossible to see the truth about what they'd become.

He'd been so preoccupied with battle, and blood, and death that he hadn't thought much about Oleander lately. A Shesaitju horn sounded again ensuring it would be a bit longer before he would. Turning toward the gates, Torsten gave his temples a squeeze to combat his throbbing head and pressed onward.

Peace.

That was what was needed.

Then, and only then, would Rand and all the others scarred by battle be able to heal, find their happiness.

Sir Hystad waited, holding Torsten's chestnut mare by the reins. Their defenses were ready, their army, prepared. The infantry stood at attention behind the first spiked trench dug by Brouben's people. The formation of thousands, men and dwarves alike, extended across the horizon, each legion under the command of a Shieldsman. Behind them were lines of archers, consisting of both Glassmen and Panpingese conscripts. And Torsten himself led them all, a man of Glintish descent.

"Find your place, Sir Hystad," Torsten told the Shieldsman as he took the reins and mounted his horse.

All these peoples fighting together. It reminded Torsten of days under King Liam. He'd made sure they were all visible, presenting a unified front for the arrival of the Black Sandsmen. Not just to show their strength, but to show that it was possible— that men and women of all races and all colors could stand together for a purpose.

For all his faults, Liam had crafted an empire worthy of lore.

The ranks parted as Torsten trotted through. They nodded, raised their spears; honored him. He'd been Wearer of White, then Master of Warfare. He'd commanded the battle of Winde Port and Fort Marimount before it, but for the first time, he felt like a true general, like he belonged at their head.

"Sir Unger, ye finally woke," Brouben called, looking up at the sun which was already beginning its descent. He stood out in front of the army, a spike-armored clanbreaker on either side of him. "Look at 'em all. By Meungor, I hope they fight."

As Torsten broke through the ranks, he saw it: across the plains, so muddled by foot-traffic there was no more grass to be found, awaited the Shesaitju army. They'd begun to set up camp, but the bulk of them had lined up for battle, mirroring Torsten's men.

Their force was smaller, but it was by no means small. It, too, stretched out like the sands of the M'stafu, and boasted a full complement of zhulong cavalry at the core. He knew how they operated. Charge the heart of the enemy formation like a wedge, and crack them open like a nut. It was why he'd had two layers of spikes built-up on the center of the trenches and a horde of clanbreakers to meet the charge.

Torsten imagined it all unfolding. Arrows from both sides would blot out the low-hanging sun. Their ranks would rush one another, warriors screaming like banshees. They'd crash like an avalanche. He was confident his army would prove victorious, but countless men would die. Torsten may have had the numbers and the better position, but as he scanned the faces of the Shesaitju, he knew what advantage they did have. Experience.

These savages weren't conscripts or young soldiers who'd enlisted in the Glass Army to find their place in life. Not men who'd mostly trained in fighting, but had seen few battles. These Black Sandsmen had been fighting each other since they were kids, born and bred under heat and iron.

Torsten knew he'd win. But the cost… would be unbearable.

"No, Brouben, I hope our duel is the last fight I ever see," Torsten said.

The dwarf frowned. "I been hopin that when ye saw them, ye might change yer mind. But I get it, me Lord. Ye do what ye must."

Torsten stared across the prospective battleground. Surprisingly, he didn't recognize the leader of their army. It wasn't Muskigo, but an older afhem who barely looked in good enough shape to make the trek across the field.

Torsten considered having Lucas summoned to him, and a handful other Shieldsmen. Together, they could ride out with Brouben and a clanbreaker as well. Really show them how outmarched they were. Instead, he pulled on the reins and held his horse in place.

"Well?" Brouben said.

"They're our visitors," Torsten said. "They ride out first."

"Men," Brouben scoffed.

An hour passed, maybe longer. Torsten's headache was gone, and he was as clear-headed as ever. Armor rattled at his back as the men started to grow weary and lax. They muttered, wondering what was going on. Torsten never moved a hair, just stared straight ahead at the enemy commander. The expanse of dirt and flattened grass had turned a hue of pink as the sun began its retreat into the night. He knew how these sorts of negotiations worked. He'd seen enough men surrender to Liam. It was only when neither side desired a fight that armies lined up to present themselves like whores in one of Valin's old brothels.

"I'm about to charge," Brouben murmured. He was seated now, tirelessly sharpening the blade of his axe with a whetstone.

"Be patient," Torsten said.

"Me axe'll be nothin but dust soon."

Another minute went by, and then, finally, the enemy commander stirred, hopping down from his zhulong. His hand flourished, and more men shuffled behind him. Then, he started a slow waddle across the field. A strange, long-shafted, two-faced hammer was latched onto his back.

"See?" Torsten said. "War is an art, my Lord Dwarf."

"I s'pose things be more simpler in the mountains," Brouben replied.

Torsten dismounted as well. It was a show of faith when commanders met, ensuring the other that there was no means of a quick escape, betraying an honorable parlay wasn't possible.

"You," he said, pointing at a mounted Shieldsman. "Please, go and retrieve Sir Danvels. He should be here for this." The man pounded his chest, then rode off as Torsten turned back to the field and started walking, all by himself.

"Shall I accompany ye?" Brouben asked.

"No," Torsten said, without looking back.

Showing no fear would earn him the upper hand. He did, however, ensure that his back scabbard was arranged so that the razor-sharp blade of *Salvation* was displayed for all his enemies to see.

The walk was long. Lonely. He kept his gaze fixed straight ahead on the rival afhem. If he allowed it to wander; to steal a glance of the thousands of Shesaitju warriors arrayed before him, then he'd already be at a disadvantage. The afhem remained similarly disciplined. The closer they got, the more Torsten noticed the man's gray gut bouncing with each step. However, even with the belly, Torsten could tell by his composure that the afhem clearly had experience in war.

Neither spoke until they were only a few paces apart. Torsten stood straight, shifting his right arm ever so slightly to show more of *Salvation*. The afhem stretched his back, a few of his vertebrae popping. A few more seconds tittered on in silence.

Torsten's eyes betrayed him only momentarily, and he eyed the army. The fearsome warriors may not have wanted to fight, but they were ready. Their dark, gray faces spoke of decades of imagined abuses. They may as well have been snarling.

"Perhaps, we should have lined up closer," the afhem said, finally. Shaking out his legs, his gaze flitted to Torsten's blindfold, but he said nothing about it. "This old body isn't what it used to be." He drew a deep breath. "Where are my manners. I am Tingur Jalurahbak, acting commander of Caleef Mahraveh's armed forces. You must be Sir Torsten Unger. They were right," he said, with a gentle laugh, "you are tall."

"It is an honor to meet you, Lord Tingur, under the light of Iam this day." Torsten circled his eye in prayer and wasn't surprised when Tingur didn't return the gesture. The Shesaitju had been more difficult to convert to the one true faith than almost any other—save the Drav Cra. "Your name is familiar to me."

"I fought in the war, the last one, at least. You'd have been a much younger man then." He spread his arms. "Now, here we are."

"Here we are."

Tingur cleared his throat.

"I was sad to learn of the fate of the late Sidar Rakun," Torsten said. "I hope you know that none of what happened was our intent."

"Our new Caleef wishes only to look forward," Tingur said. "That starts today. Before we begin, I will warn in advance that affairs in Latiapur following the death of Sidar Rakun were tense. The Shieldsman you sent with word of your offer was killed, as was the man who betrayed your king, Yuri Darkings."

Torsten bit his lip. He couldn't believe how matter-of-fact the man was about news like this. Sir Marcos was just another Shieldsman Torsten had sent to his death. All the good feelings about leading a unified army fell to the wayside.

"You're only bringing this news now?" Torsten asked, though it was closer to a growl.

"The transition has not been an easy one," Tingur said. "Outsiders became easy targets. Many afhems were loyal to Sidar Rakun. When he was lost, many refused to kneel before a new Essence of the Current, a woman no less. Mahraveh a'Tariq of Sauijbar decided that the time of the afhems was at an end. I am the last. Our markings have been erased from history. When I return to Latiapur, mine will join them in the sand."

"No afhems?" Torsten said. He wasn't exactly sure what that meant. All his life, throughout history, the warlords of the Black Sands had been infamous. Men taking names, stealing armies, competing for the adoration of the masses in their great arena.

Tingur clasped his hands. "Only one Black Sands," he said. "United under the grand vision of our Caleef—but there is expected resistance. We hope our respective peoples can move beyond these losses. Yuri Darkings helped our people, your Shieldsman served yours."

"He has a name," Torsten snapped.

"A name, we promise, will be inscribed on the walls of the Tal'du Dromesh, with your blessing. If that is agreeable, we may continue."

Torsten grimaced. *Agreeable...* He was glad he'd grown older and wiser over the last few years. A younger him might have called things off then and there with a slash of *Salvation*. But Tingur was right. Someone had been lost on each side, and more death wouldn't bring them back. Only peace between their peoples could ensure it wouldn't happen again.

"I must request both bodies be returned to us for proper rights," Torsten said. "Even a traitor like Yuri Darkings deserves to be buried beside his son."

Tingur nodded. "The Shieldsman—"

"Sir Marcos," Torsten offered.

"Yes. Sir Marcos, has been preserved and will be transported to Yarrington. Yuri Darkings, unfortunately, cannot be. His body has been lost to the Boiling Waters."

Torsten sighed and scratched at his chin where thick stubble had grown. He tried to do the proper, pious thing, but he couldn't deny the tinge of satisfaction in knowing Yuri's soul would never be at peace. If his son had earned his own fate, Yuri had earned it two-fold.

"What of our Wearer of White and the rebel, Muskigo?" Torsten asked.

Tingur turned to the side and gestured to his army with two fingers. Two men strode forward. Torsten recognized both. One was Sir Nikserof, stripped of armor and wearing a fine, white tunic marked with the Eye of Iam. At least, it once had been fine, and once had been white. Now, it was stained by black sand, dust, and dried blood. In addition to the collar and hem, the embroidered seams were torn. The only armor he still wore was the gleaming white helm signifying his position.

A gag pulled at the sides of his mouth, hemp rope at his wrists. His face was adorned with all manner of open cuts and bruises. Blood caked his bare feet, wounds filled with sand and dirt. So muddied was his lower half that it appeared to belong to a Glintish man.

None of it surprised Torsten. He was a prisoner of war, after all, and whether he deserved it or not, he'd lost the battle.

What was unexpected, was that walking beside Sir Nikserof, was Muskigo Ayerabi. He looked no different from when Torsten had faced him in Winde Port. A bit thinner from the trappings of war, perhaps, but he still wore his zhulong-leather armor, its scales interplaying with that of the spiky, white tattoos coating his entire body. His sickle-blade dangled at his side.

He appeared nothing like a man about to be traded for prosecution. Torsten's mind flashed back to Winde Port, to the headless bodies Muskigo had slung over the walls to taunt him. He imagined his sneer before he let loose a barrage of arrows that claimed the lives of many Shieldsmen.

Out of pure instinct, Torsten set his feet, tightened his jaw. Muskigo stopped to the right of Tingur, Sir Nikserof to his left. Like Torsten, messy stubble hugged Nikserof Pasic's chin. Purple bags hung from tired eyes—or were they bruised? It was impossible to tell. He stared at the ground, a broken man if ever there was one.

Muskigo, on the other hand, Torsten could see straight into his rage-filled eyes. He recalled their fight on the streets, when he plunged into the icy depths of the Grand Canal, broken and defeated for the first time in his life.

"I understand," Tingur said before Torsten could speak. He raised an open palm. "Please, just listen to what he has to say."

"I am here in good faith," Torsten said, seething. "But I will not speak openly with that man. The things he has done, he deserves worse than chains."

Muskigo didn't speak, only continued to glare.

"The situation is complicated," Tingur said. "Your letter was sent to Afhem Babrak, who has abandoned his people, addressed to a Caleef who is… dead. And so, Muskigo is here, not as a warlord, but as the father of our new Caleef."

Torsten felt like he'd been punched in the gut. Now he really wished he hadn't drunk the night before. "The... father?" he managed to say.

"Yes," Tingur answered. "His daughter is Mahraveh al'Tariq of Sauijbar, victor in the battle of Trader's Strait, and then the Battle of Nahanab. Champion of Tal'du Dromesh, and former afhem of the al'Tariq. She was thrown into the Boiling Waters, and by the blessings of the God of Sand and Sea, and the will of the Eternal Current, she was chosen to carry his essence."

Torsten looked between Tingur and Muskigo. Then he snickered. He wasn't sure why, he just couldn't help it. "You expect me to believe that this was an accident? That your god chose her, and that it wasn't him trying to secure more power." He gestured to Muskigo.

Until then, Muskigo had been staunch and silent. But now, he snapped. "I would never disrespect my daughter in such a way. I am no man of Glass. I do not use my children as pawns like your kings and queens."

Torsten's fists clenched. He'd forgotten the power in the man's voice, the way it boomed and hung on the air like acrid smoke.

"The birth of a Caleef is sacred," Tingur said. "I don't expect you to understand, but it's not something to be counterfeited. To do so, would invite only death."

"You seem like a decent man, Tingur," Torsten said. "But trust me, there are no depths Muskigo wouldn't go to if it meant destroying us. He burned innocent villages to the ground, hung civilians from walls like butcher's meat."

Muskigo stepped forward. Torsten's hand itched to reach for his sword. Only then did he notice that portion of the skin at the base of Muskigo's skull and neck was mottled, like a specific cluster of tattoos has been gruesomely cut off him.

"And your beloved Liam didn't do similar in his campaigns?"

Muskigo said. "Oh, I could tell you stories, Torsten Unger. The things I saw that you holy men refused to. They'd make you squeal."

"Our eyes are open," Torsten said.

"Then you must know what Nikserof Pasic did to my home. How he burned it and slaughtered the civilians, women, and children. The caretaker I knew for my entire life, who was like a mother to me."

Torsten's breath caught. He looked to Nikserof, and the man finally lifted his gaze. Torsten hoped, begged for him to show some sign of denial. It never came. And just as quickly as he glanced up, his attention returned to the dirt. Torsten recognized a feeling he knew well after Muskigo defeated him and Redstar turned him into a killer. Unbridled shame.

"Our king would never endorse the killing of innocents," Torsten said, fighting a sensation in his mouth like paste.

"Do you believe he fell so far from the tree?" Muskigo asked. "Did his mother, the Mad Queen, not sling her own people over the parapets?"

"She is dead," Torsten said, trying to bite back emotion. "And her son stands on his own."

"But this was war," Muskigo said. "We make the moves we need to, when we need to, for the desired effect. Even if they're difficult. Especially when they're difficult. Otherwise, we lose."

"Sometimes, having integrity means doing the right thing and losing."

"Said every general who's ever lost." Muskigo stepped forward again, and Tingur bowed off to the side. It was no longer a question of who was in charge between them.

Torsten grunted in agreement.

"I promise you, it is not an easy thing for me to stand here with the man who destroyed my home," Muskigo said. "As I know it is not easy for you to stand here with me, for all I have done to you, and your people."

"Don't presume to know anything about me *or* my people."

Muskigo scoffed. "The Glassman wants peace but refuses understanding. Are you all such hypocrites?"

"You—"

"Please, friends, enough," Tingur declared, stepping between them with his arms raised. He didn't shout, but he was stern enough to earn both their attention. Torsten and Muskigo both wore the physiques of battle-trained warriors, but despite his physical appearance, Tingur spoke with the authority of a commander. "We all have much to gain here, and much to lose. Petty rivalries must be put aside." He turned to Muskigo. "Hasn't your daughter taught us that?"

Muskigo released a low growl, then took a step back. Torsten imagined he did the same, himself. He was so heated, he couldn't quite be sure.

"You made a worthy foe, Sir Unger," Muskigo said. "I'm grateful for that. A warrior must always be challenged if he wishes to grow."

"A fair fight, and things might have turned out differently," Torsten replied.

"Perhaps... I have to ask, why willingly hamper yourself now?" He tapped at his eyes.

"Faith."

Muskigo released a noise that resembled a chuckle. "Of course."

This time it was Torsten's turn to take a step forward. "This is a matter of war between the Glass Crown and a vassal under its sovereign rule. As the Master of Warfare, I have been granted full authority to deal with this negotiation. So please, say what you came here to say, and let us hope that these two, great armies, can go home to their families and rest."

Muskigo opened his mouth to speak, then bit his lip, and finally, bobbed his head. "You're right. Agree with that or not, enough blood has been spilled."

Tingur dusted off his armored skirt. "Agreed."

Another bout of silence passed between them. A galler squawked above, making its last move before nightfall, no doubt hoping the foolish nature of men would provide a feast of flesh for the ages.

Torsten nodded Muskigo along.

"It is our Caleef's feeling that the wounds between our people are too deep," Muskigo said. "They can't be healed by simple measures. It is no different than between afhems, but Mahraveh has shown us a path. Not all agree with abandoning so many of our ways. However, it is clear, one grand afhemdom is mightier than seventy-nine pulling in different directions. If it comes to open war, we wouldn't lose."

"Did you really come here to threaten us?" Torsten questioned.

"Quite the opposite. The people would lose. With so many warriors arrayed against each other, their homes would burn, their children would be trampled. The world we know now might cease to exist. But when my daughter communed with the God of Sand and Sea, he showed her a vision. That a darkness is coming."

"A vision? You're here because of a vision?"

"My daughter is the most honest woman I know. She said our God warned her that another of his kind had returned. That one called Nesilia threatened them. Now, for my people, that name would mean nothing, but I have fought the Drav Cra, as you well know."

Torsten felt faint. Sweat beaded on the back of his neck. He willed his body not to show it, but his legs were so weak they almost gave out.

"The Buried Goddess," he whispered.

"I'm not versed in the legends of your God Feud. Barely believed such a thing ever happened. But I also looked into my daughter's eyes. She believes if we do not stand together, this Nesilia will return and destroy us all."

"She can't," Torsten said. He could hardly breathe. "She's gone."

"According to my daughter, she's already returned," Muskigo said, pointedly.

"That's impossible." Even as he said it, Drad Mak's last words bounced around in his skull, stabbing at his psyche. *'She... she's returned already. You failed... You're all just... too... blind.'*

"Maybe. Perhaps, she's shrewder than I ever imagined, and she invented all of this to force us into peace. And perhaps, I do not know my daughter anymore at all. Either way, we're here, and her offer is this: Sir Nikserof will be pardoned of his crimes against my village, and returned to his people. He will be stripped of his title as Wearer, and a Shieldsman, and live out the rest of his days as a civilian."

Torsten was still too taken-aback by what Muskigo had claimed about the Buried Goddess to react regarding Nikserof. The status of man seemed pointless when held up against the return of a scorned goddess. Nikserof winced but showed no signs of protest.

"My fate will be the same. I will take sole responsibility for instigating rebellion and after whatever darkness coming is turned away, I will dedicate my life to rebuilding Saujibar, and reme-dying the scars caused by my actions."

"Yet, you'll live," Torsten said. It sounded like an accusation, and that's how he'd intended it.

"In so much of a life as that is for a warrior. Until the Current takes me. Know that I would gladly give my life for my daugh-ter's future, and this is what she wants."

Torsten forced back the foul taste building in his throat. He had to focus.

She's returned already, the voices in his head echoed. *You failed.*

"Both of you live, ostracized," Torsten said, "and your daughter will renew her allegiance to the Glass Crown. And together, we will face Nesilia, if any of this is even true."

You failed.

Muskigo and Tingur exchanged a look.

"Not exactly," Tingur said.

"Are you really prepared to lay out *more* terms?" Torsten said, his tone as sharp as *Salvation's* blade.

"We won't capitulate any longer," Muskigo said. "My daughter has one last... *proposal.*" He paused. His lip started to twitch. His features darkened. He couldn't make eye contact. "She offers her hand in marriage to King Pi. Two young souls resurrected by their gods. Their union will bring our peoples together in a way that war never could."

Just when Torsten imagined he could hear nothing more shocking than Mahraveh's vision, her father offered this. He wondered if, perhaps, he was still drunk, that he lay face down in some gutter, mind painting horrible, vivid nightmares. That had to be it.

However, Muskigo looked sick, just offering it.

"You're serious?" Torsten said, barely above a whisper. "What happened to not treating your children like pawns?"

"Trust me, she only does what she wants to these days," Muskigo said. "I don't have to like it to see the wisdom in it. If my dream of a new Kingdom of the Black Sands can't come true without us turning those sands red, then what better outcome? If our two nations truly came together, not only through promises and easily broken contracts... no enemy could stand against us."

Torsten ran a hand over his bald pate, wiping off a thick layer of sweat. His thumb absent-mindedly pulled at the side of his blindfold, reminding him of an itch he thought he'd forgotten.

"I'm only the Master of Warfare," he said. "I can't agree to that without speaking with King Pi."

"We understand," Tingur said.

"We don't expect an answer here," Muskigo added. "Return to your camp. Write to your king, and as a show of our confidence, take your Wearer back with you."

Muskigo approached Nikserof, grabbed his wrist, and gave him a shove toward Torsten. He staggered before finding his balance. Then Nikserof glanced back at Muskigo, as if needing his approval.

"Go on," Muskigo said. "I can't stand to look at you another second."

"We swear upon the Eternal Current, upon the sand and the sea, we will not violate this armistice, or may our God drown us." Tingur spat in both hands, then kneeled to press his wet hands against the dirt, groaning all the way from the effort.

Torsten approached Nikserof. He untied the rope on his wrists. Then he lifted the man's chin and yanked the gag out of his mouth.

"Are you all right, old friend?" Torsten asked. Nikserof was too busy coughing to answer, so he nodded instead.

"Torsten," Muskigo said.

Torsten looked up at the rebel warlord. He appeared calm, collected as always. He opened his mouth to speak. At the same time, a spray of dark liquid spattered onto Torsten's blindfold, some hitting his cheek with such force it made his head turn away. When he looked back, Nikserof had his hand to the side of his neck. Planted firmly in his neck was a bolt from a crossbow.

He gagged, blood bubbling at the corner of his lips. His eyes were spread wide in shock. He pawed at Torsten with his other hand, and Torsten caught him by the arm as he dropped to a knee.

Metal rasped as Tingur and Muskigo drew their weapons.

Torsten's big hand cradled the back of Nikserof's head while blood poured down his neck, coating his chest. All the energy seemed to flee his body, and it was all Torsten could do to lower his head to the earth. He didn't die. Not fast. His eyes stayed glued open, darting from side to side, brimming with fear. His lips trembled over words, and the muscles of his throat convulsed as his body clung to life.

XXXVI

THE THIEF

Colors of every hue and shade whipped past Whitney. It was as if he were caught in a whirlwind, fragments of time itself berating him, slicing his flesh, bruising him. His eyelids fluttered, and his eyes watered.

"Sora!" he shouted.

"Whitney!" came the reply. Far off, distant.

Whitney tried to swim through the air as he fell, tumbling but with no end in sight. He figured that was for the best because if he were to hit anything at this speed, he'd be dead without question.

He didn't know what had happened. One moment he and Sora were face-to-face with Bliss, then they were kissing, then they were here, wherever 'here' was.

He called her name again and heard her response. He started swimming again, not knowing what else to do. The wind fought him at every stroke, driving him farther and farther from Sora. He reached out, and something batted his outstretched hand aside. He pulled it back with a wince.

"Sora!" he shouted again.

This time, he gave into the wind, let it drag him backward until he was on the other side of the massive funnel. They were close now, and as she turned, he could see her… truly see her—long black hair whipping her face. Those almond-shaped, amber eyes were hopeful.

Then it all stopped—the fury of the wind, the constant barrage. The colors faded to dark grays and cool blues. All he could hear were gentle waves lapping against rocks.

He was confused and felt lost.

His eyes slid open, and Lucindur was slumped over before him, salfio in her lap, eyes still closed. Her shoulders rose and fell, telling Whitney she was still alive—whatever else might be wrong, they'd have to deal with later. Behind her, Aquira was in a heap, and Sigrid was in a similar state next to her.

Tum Tum appeared in front of him, snapping his fingers to get his attention. Whitney felt paralyzed. Which worried him, making him think he'd been scratched by a grimaur while he was under Lucindur's spell.

Soon, however, a tingling heat coursed through his limbs, and his body began to respond to his will again. Remembering where he'd been, and realizing where he was, he forced himself to his feet, then spun a quick half-circle, and spotted Sora lying in the middle of the room.

"We… we did it?" he asked.

"Almost," Tum Tum said.

Kazimir was on his knees next to Sora's prone form, manipulating the bar guai in what looked like an attempt to remove it.

Whitney pushed Tum Tum aside and rushed to Kazimir, sliding on his knees and cradling Sora's head. He bent low and whispered in her ear, telling her it was going to be okay, telling her to wake up.

"Ye were faking!" Sigrid shouted. She rushed toward Kazimir, but she was looking at Teryngal. "Ye shog-eating—Why didn't ye tell me?"

"Watch how you speak to me," Kazimir warned.

"Sigrid, I have been a part of the Dom Nohzi longer than you can trace your lineage," Teryngal said. "I would never betray this place, not for Iam himself."

"Ye could have told me!" she snapped.

"He didn't tell me either," Kazimir said. "But it worked."

"I hate to interrupt this little love spat, but what about Sora," Whitney said.

Kazimir returned his attention to Sora's chest where the pendant bearing six large discs had driven itself in. Small prongs dug into reddened flesh.

"I believe I can remove it," he said. "But it drives in deeper than I'd expected. It will injure her, if it doesn't kill her."

Whitney shook his head. "We just got her back. Find another way."

"There's no other way," Kazimir said. "Not without one of the mystics."

"Then we go back to the tower," Whitney said matter-of-factly. "We take her back there, and make one of the mystics help."

"There's no time for that," Teryngal said. "Look around you!"

The place was a war zone. Dead bodies were piled everywhere, upyr scattered among them, bodies steaming, headless, or hearts cut out. Grimaurs, goblins, dire wolves, Drav Cra, it was as if all of Pantego's most horrifying things had accompanied Nesilia. In confirmation of this notion, on the far end of the plateau, the air crackled with violent energy, tearing fragments of rock from the walls. Whitney thought he could see the shadows of people on the other side of it.

"The Lords give their essence so we can end this," Teryngal said. "Surely, the life of one woman cannot compare. I will rip it out."

He bent over her, and Whitney pushed him away. Teryngal

swore and went to retaliate, but surprisingly, Sigrid held him back before even Kazimir had to act.

"Whit?" Her voice was weak, but it was Sora.

"Sora! Sora, Sora, Sora." As her eyes slowly flitted open Whitney kept repeating her name like it was the only word he knew. Whether or not he knew other words didn't matter. He'd waited long enough to be able to speak to her, her name was as good a word as any.

"Whit, what's going on?" she asked.

"Iam's shog, Sora. Iam's yigging shog." He grabbed her and pulled her against his chest. She winced, and he lowered her.

"Sora," Kazimir said.

She looked to him, and terror painted her features. She pushed herself away.

"Sora, it's okay," Whitney said.

"Like Elsewhere it is," she spat. "What is he doing here? This is all his fault."

Kazimir lifted a placating hand. "And it's a crime I've been punished for more times than I can count," he said. "Now, we're here to help."

Sora looked to Whitney.

"It's true," he said. "Please, trust me."

Tum Tum appeared at his side, Lucindur's unconscious body slung over his broad shoulder. "I didn't believe it at first either, deary," he said. "By Meungor, it's really you."

"Tum Tum?" she said, but her eyes were drawn downward, following everyone's gaze. They widened as she regarded her blood-soaked chest. "This thing?" She tugged at the bar guai.

"It's okay," Whitney said. "It's all okay. We put that on you. I'll explain later. I know this is a lot to take in, but I need you to trust me, and I need you to cooperate."

Sora continued to study the room, dumbfounded. Then, she spotted Aquira on the ground.

"Aquira," she said. She tried to move but couldn't.

Whitney rose and trotted to where the wyvern was knocked. He scooped her up, feeling her soft breath and warm scales, and returned to Sora.

"Is she…"

"No, she's breathing," Whitney said. "She—we all went through a lot to get you back." He placed Aquira down next to Sora, then turned to Kazimir and said, "Let's get that thing off."

"We are trying," Kazimir assured him, busy studying it from every angle. Sigrid had now joined him in doing so.

"Do you remember what happened to you?" Whitney asked Sora.

She stammered. "I—Nesilia… she."

"We can reminisce when there isn't a horde ready to slaughter us," Teryngal said.

Whitney rose and collared the upyr. "You have no idea what we've been through, you dead, heartless piece of shog. *Six years!*"

"Unhand me, mortal filth," Teryngal spat.

"Whitney," Kazimir said, giving his pant leg a tug. "Whitney, just calm down, and help me."

Whitney released Teryngal with a light shove that seemed to do nothing to the immortal being, then rejoined Kazimir on the stone floor.

"Do you know how to remove the bar guai without destroying it?" Kazimir asked Sora.

She shook her head.

"We have to remove it," Whitney told her, "but it can—" He stopped talking, a thought striking him like hot iron. "Healing… Sora, can you heal yourself? Like that farmer in Bridleton, can you?"

She grimaced but fought through the pain. "Yes, but—"

Whitney jostled her a bit, placing his hands beneath her shoulders. "We need to take it out. Kazimir can do it, but it'll leave you bleeding. Bad. You can use that to heal yourself, right? Blood magic. Sacrifice power to get power, just like you told me."

"You listened?" she said, her smirk quickly fading. "I don't know how much I can manage like this. I can feel her. She's still there, pushing back. My head… it…" She squeezed her eyelids and groaned.

"Sora, please," Whitney said. "Please, you've got to try." He was begging her now, desperate to stop this madness and possibly have a normal life… with her.

"I don't know."

"Nesilia is trapped in there. We plan to—"

"She's in here?" Sora said, clawing at it again. Fear overcame her in full force. "Get it off. Now. I'll do it. I'll do anything. Get her away from me."

Kazimir leaned in closer. Whitney knew how intimidating the upyr must have looked to Sora who'd just spent so long cooped up in her own mind. His long, thin fingers and knife-like fingernails edged beneath the bar guai.

"This is going to hurt," he said. "A lot."

Sora took a shuddering breath. "Just do it."

Whitney grasped her hand and squeezed, more for him than her, he knew. She was always the brave one. Then, Tum Tum grabbed both their hands and held steady.

"Ye'll be okay," he promised.

"One," Kazimir started. "Two…"

"Wait!" Whitney said.

"What is it, thief," Kazimir said, eyeing him with concern.

"Are you going to pull on three? Or after three?"

Kazimir growled, looked knowingly at Sora and yanked. The bar guai tore from her chest, blood literally gushing out. She screamed, and the sound made Whitney's eyes water.

Kazimir wasted no time with it in hand, standing and moving

toward the cliff. Sigrid and Teryngal followed. The cavern shuddered, and some of the lightning crackled overhead. The veil of mist was breaking.

Sora covered the wound with her hand, and her screams turned to muttering. Blue smoke rose from her chest and hand while flesh stretched, veins mended, and slowly, the wound began to close from her blood magic. Then she pulled her other hand from Whitney's grip and set it atop the injury as well.

Whitney didn't know where to look. To see Sora in so much pain, it was almost unbearable for him to watch, but she needed him. However, Kazimir was about to banish Nesilia forever, using the very beings she'd apparently cursed long ago. A fitting end.

Whitney decided to compromise, moving behind Sora's head, holding her while watching Kazimir and Sigrid.

Kazimir raised his hand to toss the bar guai into the wianu-infested waters when Whitney heard a *zip-thunk* followed by another. Kazimir faltered, swaying twice before turning. His face screwed up, and as he turned, Whitney saw an arrow piercing his back, the sharp blade poking through the center of his chest. Whitney followed his gaze to the Sanctum's entrance leading to the Citadel.

Another arrow soared by in the confusion, gashing Teryngal through the eye. The upyr dropped, his face boiling and bubbling. Steam rose, and he let out a moan that rivaled that of any beast in Pantego.

"Ye didn't think I'd just die, did ye?"

Grisham "Gold Grin" Gale stood in the entryway nocking another arrow into his bow. His clothes were in tatters, his face gaunt and unshaven. He looked like he'd been through Elsewhere and back.

It all happened so fast. Kazimir stumbled back, an arrow in his chest. His foot met the edge of the cliff, and rocks broke beneath his boot. He fell, but caught himself on the ledge with his elbows, still clutching the bar guai.

"Kazzy!" Whitney shouted.

"Maker!" Sigrid yelled. She grasped Kazimir by the wrist. They seemed to lock eyes for a moment. She grabbed his forearm, trying to lift him.

"No," Kazimir said. "Let me go."

"Maker, I can't—"

Just then a wianu breached the depths, and its tentacle lashed up, wrapping Kazimir's midsection. Sigrid resisted its pull for a moment, but the beast was exceptionally powerful. Kazimir's eyes showed a hint of sadness that morphed to shock as the tentacle tore Kazimir in half and Sigrid lost her grip.

"No!" someone screamed. It might have been Whitney, he didn't know. He was overwhelmed by it all.

The bar guai arched upward. Aquira let out a cry, conscious again, and darted for it, but she was too slow. The discs hit the ground, exploded and emitted a shockwave of force that sent Aquira skidding back toward Whitney.

The wave of energy sent Sigrid staggering to the ground. She looked up toward Gold Grin and snarled, "I should have devoured ye when I had the chance." She crawled forward, her hands scraping through the bar guai's broken shards without care. Raw energy swirled all around them and through her. Her eyes flickered, and she stopped moving.

"Silver-tipped arrows," Gold Grin said, showing off the gilded teeth for which he was named. "Took 'em from me own ship you lot left floatin alone to be picked clean by any brigand. *The Reba* is always prepared! Ye never know when ye'll need to slay an upyr."

Whitney looked back to the pirate king, stunned.

Tum Tum laid Lucindur down. He glanced back and forth between Gold Grin and Kazimir, then cracked his knuckles.

"Ye traitorous, no-good, rotten…" He continued like this as he stomped toward Gold Grin.

"Ye know," Gold Grin said, "I liked ye, dwarf. But our business is concluded." Then he fired another arrow, and it caught Tum Tum in the shoulder.

Tum Tum looked down in disbelief, swearing as blood seeped from the wound.

Whitney was too confused and flustered to even process it all. They'd left Gold Grin to die, but for all his being a braggart, he truly was a pirate deserving of his renown.

"Get away from the love of me life," Gold Grin demanded. "Ye thought ye could leave and I wouldn't find her? I'll always find her. Stole a Panpingese fisherman's ship after me traitorous crew untied me and followed ye right here. They didn't get to come for the ride, but ye fools made it too easy."

Stepping down into the cavern, Gold Grin beheld Sora. Her chest still bled, but she'd managed to stem the worst of it and now clung to consciousness while Whitney held her tight.

"By all the gods, me love. What have they done to ye?" Gold Grin asked. "Ye couldn't handle her lovin me and decided to take her out, did ye Fierstown?"

Tum Tum, still swearing, snapped off the arrow.

"Aye, that's it, ye big, ugly fruitcake," Tum Tum said. He raised his warhammer overhead with both hands. He grimaced and groaned from the pain in his shoulder, but didn't stop. Bringing the hammer back all the way, he launched it forward with all his dwarven strength.

Gold Grin was too focused on Sora to see it coming. The weapon smashed into his chest and crushed the pirate king against the wall.

Tum Tum then collapsed to one knee, clutching his wound.

"Well, I didn't expect that." The voice was feminine and came from the general direction of where Kazimir had just been gruesomely murdered.

Whitney turned toward Sigrid and the broken bar guai. The voice came from Sigrid's lips but didn't belong to Sigrid.

"Nesilia," Whitney whispered.

The bar guai's energy continued to swirl around her as she stood, gaze moving from side to side like she wasn't sure how she'd gotten there.

Licking blood from her lips, moaning sensually, she turned to Sora and said, "You foolish mortal. You could have been a goddess."

She stalked toward them, and Sora cringed. Whitney drew a dagger and held it toward the upyr, though, he knew it was no longer Sigrid. Her black, soulless eyes were no more, now they were something else altogether..

"Get away from her!" he yelled, thrusting the dagger forward. Sigrid grabbed it, letting it slice through her flesh. Then, she pulled her hand away and watched as it healed. A grin straight out of Elsewhere spread across her face.

"I think I'm going to like this," she said. "Don't resist, girl. I'll show you exactly what you want. It starts with them." She took one more step, and Whitney stabbed again, but the blade met only air as Sigrid suddenly vanished. He searched from side to side and saw her nowhere. He knew how fast the upyr could move, but he hadn't even seen a blur.

"Where'd she go?" Sora asked.

"I… I don't know," Whitney answered, still looking around the room.

"Whitney, we got to get out of here!" Tum Tum yelled.

He rushed over and hefted Lucindur with one arm, fighting through the pain. He nodded toward the Sanguine Lords' magical veil that had been protecting them, which was now gone. Nesilia's followers were still slowly trickling out, as confused as anyone and without the will to fight any longer.

The cavern continued to crumble, rocks smashing on the plateau and into the sea. The wianu remained in a frenzy, likely feeding on an upyr they'd despised for so long.

"Nesilia, she—" Whitney began.

The warlock, Freydis, called out, "Stop retreating, cowards!"

"It doesn't matter!" Tum Tum said. "We gotta go."

Whitney realized how right he was when a rock shattered only a few feet away. "Sora, get up!" He helped her to her feet, then scooped up Aquira and they limped toward the entry back into the Citadel.

Whitney glanced down at Gold Grin, who was slumped against the wall with the hammer on top of him. He looked confused and scared, like he'd just woken from a nightmare.

"What'd I do…?" he muttered.

Whitney thought about stopping, helping him, making the pirate king join them. Gold Grin had been manipulated by Nesilia, after all. It wasn't all his fault, was it? But Tum Tum shouted for Whitney to hurry, not even bothering to take his beloved hammer. With all their injuries, they had no spare arms to help the mad pirate king.

"I'll destroy all of you!" Freydis screamed behind them.

Whitney left Gold Grin and helped Sora through the threshold and into the long tunnels toward the Citadel. A vine broke through the floor, grabbing his ankle. A moment of panic overcame him, and he saw and heard dire wolves snarling as they raced for the door. Sora bit her lip, then pushed free of Whitney and turned. Stretching her arms, she cracked her neck, then screamed. Fire leaped off her shaky fingers in a steady stream, melting the very stone around the door. It collapsed, closing them in and severing Freydis's magic The vine shriveled and relinquished its grip on

Whitney. The dire wolves barked and scratched at the other side, but for now, they were safe.

Despite everything, Whitney couldn't help but marvel at Sora's abilities. "You're back," he said softly.

"And we need to go," she said.

This time, she took his hand and pulled him along, seeming reenergized. He still needed to help her after a few strides, but he was certain: Sora was back.

With Aquira cradled in his left arm, Sora holding his right, and Tum Tum just ahead of them with Lucindur over one shoulder, they fled back through the Citadel as fast as they could. Wianu cries echoed like mournful thunder, stone broke, and thousands of years of history crumbled all around them.

Nesilia had survived due to Whitney's mercy in not killing Gold Grin at the Red Tower. And the pirate king arrived just in time to end Kazimir for good, all because of Whitney's decision to drop off Gentry and the others in Glinthaven. Because of him, the Dom Nohzi and their eternal lords were eternal no longer.

But Sora was back.

Sora was alive.

XXXVII

THE REDEEMER

The inside of Rand's mouth bled. As he listened to this Sir Lucas Danvels try and explain everything that had happened, he couldn't help but chew at his gums and lips. All the lies and deception. He'd trusted Torsten more than anyone, and he'd lied straight to his face. Said his sister was dead. He'd lied, like Valin Tehr lied. Now, he had this young whelp of a Shieldsman lying, too.

It seemed that in the exile his life had become, only the witch, Oleander, had been truthful. At least she'd been honest about what she was.

"Sir Langley, are you listening to me?" Lucas asked.

Rand bit deeper, the taste of iron fresh on his tongue. "I'm tired of listening."

"I was there. I saw her, or what Torsten said was her. I'm still not sure if he heard clearly. There was so much chaos when the upyr attacked. But her hair was white as snow. Her eyes were black. She looked Breklian, if anything."

"It doesn't matter," Rand said. "Torsten lied."

"Not to him. If that really was her. If she's an upyr now… then you must know, that to the Vigilant Eye, she is dead."

"She's not dead if she's walking!" Rand snapped.

"Not alive either. I didn't know your sister, but the woman I watched that day was a ruthless, savage killer. She took blood to her lips. I thought the stories told by soldiers around campfires were just that... stories. They're not."

"I don't care what either of you thinks she is. If she's alive, then I must find her. I'll get through to her."

Lucas slid closer to the bars. "Sir Langley, I studied all the texts on the upyr and Dom Nohzi in the Glass Castle, and even beyond. They place those tomes beside entries from ancient priests on demonic possessions, next to writings on the Culling and necromancy. Every single one of them says that once a person is kept from the afterlife and transformed into an upyr, they lose who they once were. Bloodlust overwhelms them."

"How?"

"How what?"

"How are they transformed?" Rand demanded.

"Nobody knows."

"Then how do you know that's what she was?" With every ragged breath, Rand's lungs stung. He wondered if that pain from his crucifixion would ever leave him. Hoped it wouldn't. It felt like a fine reminder of all those who'd met similar fates. First Tessa at his own hand, now Sigrid by lack of it. "Maybe she escaped Valin and disguised herself as a Breklian."

Lucas shook his head. "Valin called a blood pact. It took a great deal of studying to find out exactly what that was, but it appears that, long ago, the Dom Nohzi organization found use for the upyr lust. A blood pact targets their hunger when accepted."

"Get to the point."

"The point is," Lucas said with a bit more authority than he'd shown thus far, "Valin's follower asked them to kill Queen Oleander. The Dom Nohzi accepted, and your sister, along with another upyr Torsten recalled encountering in Winde Port, arrived to carry out the sentence."

"You think my sister is with them because she went after Oleander? Did you ever think to ask yourself if, maybe, she went after that shog of a queen because of all the awful things she did?"

"Like I told you, I saw her. Is it possible that she was merely accompanying the male upyr on behalf of the Dom Nohzi after having her skin and hair died white?Maybe. But that seems far-fetched."

"And her being a murderous, bloodsucking monster from myth and legend doesn't!" Rand shouted.

Lucas sat quietly for a moment. "Rand, the way she moved, and talked, it was… unnatural. Faster than anyone I'd ever seen, and powerful enough to bend metal with a fist. Furthermore, they attacked at night. It lines up with all of the respected texts."

"I don't care what the books say." Now Rand was kneeling at the bars, hands gripping them tight. "I need to see her."

Lucas backed away. He stood, straightened his breastplate. "I can't let you out. I'm sorry you had to find out this way, but I have orders."

Rand scoffed. "Orders. I've had those too. By Iam, do I wish I broke them."

"I promise you, Sir Unger only has your best interests at heart. Don't ask me why he cares so much about a deserter, but he does."

"Torsten only cares about the kingdom," Rand spat. "Haven't you realized that? I thought there was more to him, but that's Iam's ugly truth. The only reason he wants me locked up in here isn't because of Sigrid. It's because he doesn't want anybody to see the truth of what I am. Because the truth doesn't fit the pretty little story of 'Rand the Redeemer.'"

"I don't believe that. He took a risk to help me protect my family."

"Well, aren't you special?" Rand pulled himself to his feet using the bars. "I saved him twice. Saved everyone from the savages. And this is how he repays me!" He rattled the bars, shouting. His raspy voice echoed across the cold, empty dungeon. "Let. Me. Out!"

"I'm sorry, Sir Langley," Lucas said. "I can't."

He actually looked like he meant it. *Pathetic.*

"She's all that I have," Rand said. "She's my world, and I left her with rotten men. Please. I have to tell her I'm sorry. I don't care what she is to you, she's my sister. And she needs me."

"I watched her slice through Shieldsmen like hot wax," Lucas said. "She doesn't need anybody anymore."

"You can't know that!" Rand slapped the rough stone and sliced his palm. He sucked in a breath and swore before a sob escaped. Raising his hand to his mouth, smearing blood in his beard, he let the sound die there. Lucas was busy saying something, but it was all white noise to him.

Pulling his hand down, Rand stared at the red covering it. "How exactly does a blood pact work?" he said.

Lucas stopped whatever he was talking about and asked, "What?"

"A blood pact. How does it work?"

"Rand, if you keep dwelling on all of this, you'll drive yourself mad. Isn't it enough to know that somehow, by some miracle, you have a second chance at life? To do some good for this world. Isn't that what being a Shieldsman is all about?"

Rand couldn't help but picture the sallow corpses Oleander had him hang from the castle walls. How they swayed in the wind to be picked at by gallers, the woman he loved amongst them. Betrayed by their kingdom.

"Not for me," he said unequivocally. "You're all claiming that my sister is an undead killer now. I need to know what that means." He turned back and stared straight into Lucas' eyes. "Please... you said you read all the texts."

Lucas exhaled through his teeth. "Information varies. But, think of it as a writ of assassination granted by the Dom Nohzi leadership. Some say they're Breklian Dukes, others that they're mystics of the necromancy arts—a sect that went dark long ago. I've read that they call themselves the Sanguine Lords. All that's clear is that when they're beseeched, if they reject the target, he who offers it is then killed instead. History is vague. They're listed as responsible for deaths of merchants, warlords, even farmers—and now Queens—all random. I can't say why one would be accepted or rejected, I only know that they came for Oleander, and they showed no mercy."

"She didn't deserve any," Rand said, the creaking of the ropes still filling his head.

"Trust me, she didn't deserve what they did. Rand, your sister didn't just taste her blood. She tore into her neck like a feral wolf." He lay his hand against the bar and peered in farther, deep remorse painting his features. "I really am sorry. About everything."

"Then let me out. Let me leave. Nothing that you, or Torsten, or a High Priest, or anybody can do will change anything. Thieves, knights, kings and queens... they're all rotten. Only my sister wasn't." Tears welled in the corners of his eyes. His throat felt jammed. "I'm so sick of this world and everyone in it. I don't want this anymore."

"Iam's Ligh—"

"No!" Rand screamed. "Iam can eat His own shog. I'm ready to move on. I'd split my head apart on those bars right now, but I can't do anything until I see Sigrid again. I won't let you, or Torsten, or the entire Glass army stand in my way."

"A Shesaitju army is at our doorstep, and Sir Unger has me

here trying to ease your concerns," Lucas said. "That should tell you enough about how he views you. Please, just try and relax until this negotiation is finished. Then I'm sure Sir Unger will do the right thing. He always does."

Rand bit his lower lip again, let out a low, simmering growl. "Have it your way." He looked down at his bloody hand. "Sigrid. Sister. If you're out there, then please answer. I don't know how to do this, but I offer my blood and my life." He spread his fingers wider, opening the gash.

"Rand, what are you doing?" Lucas questioned. His hand fell to the grip of his longsword.

"To you, or the Sanguine Lords or whoever in the Dom Nohzi might hear, I summon a blood pact upon Sir Lucas Danvels of Yarrington," Rand continued. "Whatever it takes, I will do. Whatever sacrifice. Just get me out of here." He was fuming by the end, chest heaving with each heavy breath.

"Rand, are you insane?" Lucas said. "That's not how it works."

"But nobody knows how it works, do they?" He squeezed his palms as tight as he could, causing a steady trickle of blood. He spit blood from his mouth, each splatter against the stone sounding like an explosion.

"Exactly."

Rand grinned wickedly, closed his eyes. "Dom Nohzi, hear me. I call for this blood pact!"

"Rand, stop…" his words trailed off as he fumbled for his keys. They slipped through his fingers and hit the stone.

When Rand opened his eyes, he saw Lucas gawking into the cell. All the color had left his cheeks like he was petrified. Rand soon saw why. In the corner stood a woman, her hair wild and pure white. A crossbow was slung over her shoulder, and she wielded two daggers like she was ready to fight. Her chin slowly lifted, and she studied the room, a look of confusion upon her pale face. Her eyes were black, but color didn't matter. Rand would recognize them anywhere—and her freckled cheeks, the subtle cleft of her chin.

"Sigrid?" he whispered, reaching out for her cheek.

At the same time, Lucas abandoned the keys. "No," he repeated over and over while scrambling for the exit. He tripped on something, a rock, a bump, his own fear. It didn't matter because, in a flash, Sigrid zipped through the bars, bending two apart as if they were paper, and she was on him.

Her dagger drove deep into his calf, sending him sprawling to the floor. He yelped, and a guard by the stairs ran down. She flung one of her daggers backhanded, straight through the newcomer's neck. She admired her arm as it remained extended.

"I like this new body," she said.

Lucas tried to draw his sword, but her boot hit his side and flipped him short ways across the corridor. Then, she tore his sheath from his belt, snapped it and the blade in two with a single hand.

Rand had never seen such raw strength. Such power. His sister was fit from years of serving tables, holding trays, but her muscles were lean and thin. Her body lithe and desirable—at least, that's the way the grubby men she'd served treated her. But what Rand was witnessing was the strength of a giant.

"P... please... I don't..." Lucas stammered. He turned his face and closed his eyes.

Rand slowly stepped through the bent cell bars, mesmerized. His sister hunched over Lucas, then ran one of her long nails across his cheek, drawing a thin line of blood.

"I'm supposed to kill you, aren't I?" she said. She looked from side to side. "I can hear the ancient voices whispering. Begging me to do it. And you, girl." She raised her blood-covered finger toward her mouth, it started to shake. "How badly do you want to taste this? Yes. I can feel your hunger, your rage. All the awful things men like this have done to you. You're afraid. Don't be. I will make you stronger than you can imagine… if you don't resist."

Her finger slowly stopped shaking, lowered away.

"Good, that's right," Sigrid said. "We're more than the base needs these people give us. You won't resist like the last one, will you? You want this. Nobody to hurt you anymore. No man to boss you around."

As she spoke, Lucas reached for his sword. His fingertips brushed the hilt.

"Sigrid!" Rand warned.

She stomped down on Lucas' chest and lowered the dagger to his throat. "I could squash you like an insect, Shieldsman," she said. "Pathetic servant of a lying god." Then she looked up. "But that would just make her old Lords happy. You sad, pathetic, broken mystics. You brought me here to kill him, yes… I feel the draw. Elsewhere, begging. But you can't do anything to *me*." She punched Lucas in the face, knocking him unconscious. Then she slowly rose.

"But you didn't summon me on your own, no," she said. "It doesn't work like that, does it. Blood was offered, for blood given. Balance." She snickered. "Perhaps, I'll kill the other just to show you how little that means."

Rand was behind her now. Close enough to touch her. But she whipped around, and her arm lashed out to his throat. In an impossibly fast motion, she had him lifted against the wall back on the other end of the dungeon. In her other hand, a dagger was raised, the needle-sharp point hovering right in front of his eye. It quaked like her bloody finger had.

"Why did you bring me here?" she growled. "I had them cornered!"

As Rand saw her up close, there was no more doubt in his mind, it was her. Every freckle was in the right place. Only, her voice wasn't hers. It sounded like her on the surface, but the Sigrid he knew, spoke with a heavy, docksider twang. Now, her speech was refined, noble, like his had become after years training in the Glass Castle.

"To get to you…" he replied, throat compressing.

"Why would you…" A smile spread across her face. "Brother. This is him, isn't it?"

"Who are you talking to?" Rand asked.

"The one who left you behind to be murdered," Sigrid said. "To be left, bleeding on the street."

"That's not true!" Rand said, but it mostly came out as a gurgle.

The blade lowered closer to Rand's eye, but only started to shake more. Sigrid's own glare softened, only momentarily, but Rand couldn't miss it. He noticed the sorrow; that same glint his sister would wear when she caught him drinking.

"Why do you resist?" Sigrid said. "He deserves to die for leaving you."

"I wasn't…" Rand protested.

"Quiet!" She pressed her forearm tighter, closing off his air so he couldn't speak. "He allowed you to be turned into a lifeless, blood-craving monster! He forgot about you. He abandoned you!"

Sigrid's head flinched to the side. Her face scrunched, pain filling black, lifeless eyes. Then she let off of Rand and allowed him to drop to the stone, coughing and gasping for air.

"I suppose you're right," she said, still looking away, talking to herself. "He left, but he didn't forget. I suppose he'll say all of this was for you? They lie, my dear. My brother did, so will yours. They lie, and they cheat and then smother you in darkness." She raised her dagger, ran her tongue up the flat of the blade. "Let me break this bond for you. Let me set you free!"

She swung down again. Rand didn't flinch, not even as the blade stopped a finger-length away from his heart, then shook again. He welcomed it. Thanks to him, this is what had become of his sister. He could have left Torsten locked up, let the Drav Cra take over, and at least she'd still be the woman he'd once known, loved.

"It's true, isn't it?" Rand said. "You're what they say." He leaned up, allowed the tip of the blade to poke into his flesh. He brushed his fingertips across Sigrid's face. His touch seemed to disgust her as much as it did him. She was ice-cold, like Tessa's corpse.

"Is that pity?" Sigrid asked, speaking through her teeth. Her muscles were tensed all over. Her hand, turned somehow paler around the grip of her dagger, shivering uncontrollably. "This is the brother you wish to spare? He's even less deserving of mercy than mine. I promise you, the relief will be like nothing you can imagine."

The blade pushed a hair closer, then Sigrid's hand flew out to the side. The dagger clattered across the floor.

Sigrid clicked her tongue, appearing repulsed. Standing tall, she said, "So be it. I spent too long arguing with my last host. He can live but open your soul to me, and together, this whole world will finally know true balance. My balance." She closed her eyes, breathed in through her nose, and clutched her hand into a fist.

"Oh, Sigrid," Rand sniveled. "What did I let happen to you?"

She regarded him, sneered. "So much like a man, to take credit even for this... Gideon Trapp, Valin Tehr, The Sanguine Lords, God of Sand and Sea, not even Iam can touch us now. This union is exactly what was fated. Not the forgotten daughter of a dead king and mystic, but she who truly lost everything. A daughter of nobody, from nowhere—to make Pantego tremble."

Rand's heart skipped a beat. He had no idea what she was talking about, only that this was not the sister he knew. And yet, it was her. For all the difference in appearance and behavior, there she was, right in front of him. She'd found a way to become strong after he'd left her with the monsters. She always was the stronger of them.

He rose and threw his arms around her, squeezing with all his might. "Sigrid, I'll do whatever you need. I'll never leave your side again. I just don't understand…"

The strength in just her hands as she sent him hard into the wall, stone crumbling off onto his head and shoulders, was enough to kill a man. Air fled his lungs, and he felt bone crack.

"You will." She cackled. "They all will."

Spinning on her heels, she strode toward the exit. There was something playful in each step, even as she knelt to tear one of her daggers out of the soldier's throat. She licked the blood off, and her back rolled in response like she was being pleasured.

"I like this new body," she said again before skipping along, up the stairs, and Rand couldn't help but follow. He glanced down at Lucas as he passed. The young Shieldsman was conscious but didn't move. His eyes tracked him from side to side, flush with terror.

"Don't…" he groaned.

Rand stopped, frowned. "I'm sorry."

As he climbed the steps, he heard a few muted yelps, and when he reached the top, two more guards were slumped against the wall, their throats gaping. One was a clean slice, as if from a blade. The other was a gruesome tear, and Sigrid had blood covering her mouth and chin.

Backed against the wall in the shadow of the doorway, her foot was right on the edge of reddish light being cast by the low, dusk sun. She extended her bare hand slowly, and her pale skin began to crack and simmer as the light touched it. The awful stench of burning hairs assailed Rand's senses.

"In all things, balance," she said. "The makers of the undead did so have a twisted sense of humor. But don't worry, my dear. Soon, Iam's light will be extinguished."

She cracked her neck, then took a step out. Her skin steamed as more light struck her, but she didn't stop. Rand trailed behind in the wake of suffocating heat and ash. His eyes stung, and his throat scratched.

Glassmen marched by on the bridge not far above, workers carrying water, and supplies, but nobody seemed to notice his sister as she sauntered around the corner, still roasting. A young woman waited, bearing a bowl of water. She was a sister of Iam, the same who'd been present when Rand killed Bartholomew Darkings.

She dropped the bowl, the clay splitting on the stone, water splashing into puddles. Sigrid grinned at her, lips cracking like molten rock, skin flaking away in the light. Just the sight of it made the woman faint. Her head hit the stone, and blood seeped out. Beyond her unconscious, perhaps dead body, the room where Rand had been treated for his wounds was less full. But those who'd been crucified, who were in the worst shape, remained in constant care.

"You did well Mak, my child," she said. "The fear you instilled will go on to break them."

"Child?" Rand whispered. Then louder, he asked, "You know Mak?"

Sigrid didn't answer. She continued up the tower stairs, one landing until they were broken and covered in loose stone from the battle with the Drav Cra. It didn't stop her. She clawed her way up the collapsed floors, to all that was left of the perch.

Rand followed after her, far less gracefully. He couldn't help himself. Her new aura it was… magnetizing. He slipped, gashed a knee on a sharp bit of stone, but kept going. Only a sliver of the top floor remained under a broken arch of the decimated roof that provided her cover from the fading sun.

Sigrid's skin was now bubbling as it healed in patches. Her face was already back to normal save for exposed sinew on her left temple. Soon, that was healed, too, and she was good as new —like a Breklian, alabaster doll.

Rand got his torso onto the treacherous ledge. Another bit of it crumbled off, and he almost fell. Sigrid, too busy staring off at something in the distance, didn't help him.

"Sigrid, please..." Rand groaned, heaving his body to safety where he could catch his breath. Every pull on his lungs was agonizing. "You have to explain what's going on."

"Look at them all," she said. "They have no idea what's coming."

Rand grabbed the sill of a window that no longer existed, and drew himself to his feet. He leaned and followed her gaze. Across a vast war camp, the entirety of the Glass army was arrayed. He'd never seen anything like it. Tens of thousands of armored men, standing at attention, their armor reflecting the sunset like countless diamonds.

It was romantic and beautiful in the way stories of grand wars always are. Rand had trained to be a Shieldsman, but he'd never seen an army or battle on such a scale—and they weren't alone. Across the field stood a rival, lesser only in number. The Shesaitju warriors were menacing, their zhulong beasts even more so. They were a dark wave in a raging ocean, ready to wipe out anything in their path.

Between both armies stood four men. Two of the Shesaitju, and two Glassmen. Rand recognized one of them by their armor and bald head. Torsten Unger, the man who'd told him his sister was gone after all Rand had done for him. The man who'd lied.

"Torsten..." Rand grumbled.

"You know him, too?" Sigrid said, peering back, eyebrow raised, a fleck of dead skin above it.

"Too well."

"I should despise him for ruining so much, but if he never interceded that day on the mountain, I never would have found the perfection that is your sister." Again, she lifted and marveled at her arm. She dragged the blunt side of her dagger over the curves of her lean muscle.

"Sigrid, *you're* my sister."

Turning back to him, she ran her fingers through his hair. They felt like icicles. Her gaze seemed to puncture his very soul; made him want to cringe, and at the same time, embrace her again.

"You have so much to learn," she said. "We are so much more than you could possibly imagine. We are all the forsaken: your sister, their wives, and mothers who were left behind while vile men march out here to create widows."

"Torsten says they're here to negotiate for peace."

"Are they? Perhaps my coward of a brother actually did pass along my message to his people. The fools. They think it's that easy? I'll show you how weak they are. One snap of my fingers and their dream of peace will be buried as I was."

Rand swallowed. "Buried?" His head was swimming, but there was something about that word that struck him. It sent a cold chill, like Sigrid's icy fingertips tracing up his spine.

"But not dead," Sigrid said, drawing her crossbow. She aimed it toward the armies, then angled up toward the sky. There wasn't a person in the world who could hit anything from so far away.

"What are you doing?" Rand asked.

No answer came. She merely smirked, then fired. The bolt sailed out into the graying sky. She stepped forward into the fading light to see clearer, letting the little sun that remained sear her flesh. Rand lost sight of the bolt in the glare, but, when it hit, he had no trouble locating it. The Glassman with Torsten clutched at his throat, then fell headlong into Torsten's arms.

"Wrong one," Sigrid said, lowering her weapon. Then she shrugged. "Oh well. Now watch as they prove how little they deserve this world."

XXXVIII

THE KNIGHT

"Sir Unger, that was not—" Torsten didn't hear the rest of what Tingur had to say. Rising to his full, impressive height, Torsten's glower set upon the Shesaitju warriors like iron. He reached back, grasped the *Salvation's* leather grip, and drew the claymore in front of him.

"You honorless bastards," he said, a low rumble. He set his feet and dropped into a battle stance. Every breath was a snarl.

"Sir Unger, please, we wouldn't," Tingur protested. He threw down his weapon.

Muskigo did not. Instead, he advanced with a few careful steps, his blade angled downward but his muscles tensed, ready to strike like the snake he was.

"Lower your weapon, Torsten," he hissed. "Use your reason. Why kill him now?"

Torsten glanced down at Nikserof. He was a ghost, pale, sickly, eyelids twitching. Studying the bolt, Torsten was unsure what to make of it. Then, even without proper sight, Torsten saw the sky go completely dark. It had been dusk, but this was like midnight.

Two waves of arrows soared above, one from his army,

another from the Shesaitju. They buzzed like thousands of angry hornets, and the ground started to shake. Both armies charged, their enraged screams becoming the only sound.

"Torsten, stop this!" Muskigo yelled. "We came here for peace! I swear it!"

Torsten's gaze moved from him to the armies to Nikserof. At the sight of the man, now clearly dead, Torsten's grip tightened. He was now all that remained of Liam's old guard trained by Sir Uriah Davies.

The arrows plunged, driving down into both forces as they charged. Screams of pain and rent metal pierced the din of thundering footsteps.

"Torsten!" Muskigo shouted.

Then Torsten noticed the feathers on the back of the bolt. Sometimes, perceiving color with his new way of seeing was difficult, but they were similar to those used by the goblins up north. Which meant, they'd come from grimaurs, like those used by the Dom Nohzi when they came for Oleander. Having been shot by a Shesaitju barbed arrow himself, Torsten knew well enough to be sure this wasn't their doing.

Senses returned, he whipped around and waved his arms, sword high in the air.

"Pull back!" he bellowed. "Hold!"

Muskigo and Tingur did the same. But it was all too late. Their voices were drowned out by the avalanche of footsteps, and another volley of arrows racing across the sky, only to drop and tear through more flesh and armor.

All at once, more than a generation of hate festering between the two kingdoms came to a head. There was no stopping it. They'd burned each others' homes, killed each others' families, won and lost in battles.

Torsten spun back and lowered his sword to face the wave of Shesaitju warriors. Zhulong bounded in his direction, his own horse-riding cavalry charging opposite them. Tingur had no choice but to grab his pole-hammer. Muskigo prepared for battle but stared at Torsten. Calm as always, he seemed at a complete loss for what to do.

For once, he and Torsten had something in common.

It had been a long time since Torsten experienced the clashing of two charging, bloodthirsty armies. With blindness having honed his sense of hearing, now, it was infinitely louder. He perceived each spear shaft cracking in two, the clang of iron sword upon shield, the cry of men and their blood-gargled final words—mostly curses. It sounded as if the very world was unraveling.

Dust swirled up all around him, drowning him in a ruddy fog that only added to the chaos. A Shesaitju warrior came screaming at him, and Torsten sliced down with his long claymore, gashing him across the chest.

"Fall back!" he screamed, then coughed. The air was too muddied, there at the front. He could hardly breathe, let alone yell.

Another scream. He spun and blocked a flailing swing of a scimitar. As he did, he saw Muskigo being attacked from every direction. He parried, punched, did everything he could to not kill unless it was absolutely necessary. Brouben arrived, his war cry like a fearsome dragon and his mighty axe blew back the warrior Torsten was tangled with.

"Die ye gray bastards!"

Sir Hystad raced by, decapitating another warrior coming after Torsten.

"Sir!" he shouted to Torsten, then swung down at another. "Fall to the backline, we can't lose you!"

Torsten's chest burned as he drew in a sharp breath of the musty air. Then, charging the horse, he grabbed the man by his leg and tore him off. He hopped up, himself, and raised *Salvation* high. Even that small bit above the fray, breathing was infinitely easier.

"Fall back!" he shouted and set his horse to spin and carry his orders in every direction. "Fall back!"

Another wave of arrows from archers on either side soared overhead, blotting out the dying bit of sunlight as night approached. They stabbed down into the rear ranks, causing them to push forward, pressing the front. Their frantic footsteps and screaming made it impossible to hear.

"Fall back!" Torsten yelled again, refusing to give up.

A war cry sounded. He turned his head in time, but not his horse. A zhulong crashed into its flank, sharp tusks tearing open its haunches. Torsten toppled off. He managed to hold onto his sword, at least until he slammed into the ground and it rattled loose.

Quickly rolling onto his other side, he avoided the swipe of the zhulong tail as it stamped over the writhing, squealing horse. The Shesaitju rider raised a scimitar high and pulled the beast's mane to coax it forward.

Torsten got to his knees, but he was completely disoriented. All he could manage was to raise his bracers and attempt to deflect the attack. Only, he didn't have to. The Shesaitju swung his weapon, but a sickle-blade met it in midair. In one smooth motion, Torsten's savior locked the other blade in the curve of his, and wrenched it out of the warrior's grasp, pulling him off the zhulong as well.

"Get up!" Muskigo said. He helped Torsten to his feet, then placed *Salvation* back in his hand. "This is not how we die." He pulled Torsten to the side of the now riderless zhulong. "I remember when you raided my camp in the swamp. You can ride one?"

"More like go along for the ride," Torsten replied.

"Good enough."

Muskigo helped him up halfway, and Torsten heaved his aching torso the rest of the way. The zhulong bucked, but he was big enough to get it to obey. He grabbed a clump of its rust-colored mane with one hand, wielded *Salvation* in the other.

Then, Muskigo leaped up and stood on its back, managing to maintain his balance even after the zhulong started barreling forward. Torsten didn't know much Saitjuese, but, enough to know that Muskigo was calling for retreat in the old language of his people. The greatest warrior of their generation, ruthless and calculating with his every move, was willing to lose.

"Retreat!" Torsten screamed, twirling his sword as they rode. He yelled it again and again until his voice was hoarse, the muscles of his throat feeling like they might tear from the relentless dust of war.

But it worked. Shieldsmen finally heard Torsten's orders and started echoing them. Muskigo's lieutenants joined him in their language. Afhem Tingur had commandeered another zhulong and rode opposite them, calling for the same.

While Torsten pulled the zhulong back the other way, he heard Muskigo's foot slip from the sudden change in direction, yet, somehow, he remained upright. Torsten was no longer surprised that the man had been his equal in battle.

Brouben lay ahead, clanbreakers spinning around him in their spike-laden armor, wielding oversized axes, and mowing through Black Sandsmen like tornados. The pure joy on Brouben's blood-drenched face was unmistakable.

"Fall back, Brouben!" Torsten called, pulling his zhulong to a stop nearby.

"Are ye crazy?" he said, bashing another enemy on the head. "We have 'em on the run."

Torsten gritted his teeth. "Sound the retreat, or consider our alliance finished. I won't ask again. This battle is over!"

Brouben's grip on his axe tightened, then a flurry of curses filtered through his lips. He waved his axe to signal a retreat, and the rest of the dwarves joined him.

Torsten looked from side to side. Both armies fell back to their respective camps at the same time, trampling over all the fallen bodies. He'd never seen anything like it. Kicked-up dust and dirt mixed with the darkness of the sun sinking below the horizon made it impossible to tell if their enemies were in pursuit.

Clashes among the frontlines still raged—those who hadn't heard the orders or had been too lost in battle to obey them. They'd need daylight to see clearly, but thousands were already dead.

"What now?" Muskigo asked, hopping down from the zhulong. Tingur was nearby, hands on his knees, wheezing.

It was a good question. Their peoples hated each other enough already, and this was only sure to make things worse. It really would take a miracle to bring them together. And what was more miraculous than a king and queen, who'd both were said to have risen from the dead by the will of their gods?

Torsten gathered his breath. "We have a ceremony to plan."

"I was trying to make a point, and again, you ruin everything." A deep, melodious voice hung on the air. It was all at once matronly, seductive, and highly intimidating, like Oleander, only it wasn't her.

Torsten turned and watched as, in an instant, a cluster of warriors still locked in battle collapsed, blood pouring from their necks. One remained lifted, hanging slack in the arms of a woman. She raised her head from his neck, then dropped the body.

Through the enchanted blindfold, masked in the palette of light that was Torsten's vision, he could make out no details. The woman was pure shadow, and nothing more. Even blacker than the night, like the glow of Pantego's moons couldn't even touch her.

"Who is this?" Muskigo asked.

Torsten struggled to muster the word. The bolt, the drinking of necks—he knew. This was the sister he'd never wanted Rand to find. There was no doubt about it. The upyr, Sigrid Langley, who'd murdered Oleander right in front of him, had returned.

"Sigrid," Torsten bellowed across the field, "why are you here?" It took every ounce of willpower not to charge at her for what she'd done. She was lucky he was so exhausted from the brief battle.

"Oh, Torsten, can't you see beyond that name?" she said, taking long strides forward. A few more stragglers charged her, only to drop in an instant, cut open sternum to stem. She moved so fast, he didn't even register the strikes.

"Torsten," Muskigo said. "What is that?"

"The cause of all of this," Torsten replied, fuming. His knuckles went pale from squeezing the grip of his sword. She vanished momentarily, and his pulse quickened. Then she re-appeared, within only a few paces of them now.

"This new body," Sigrid said. "I can feel the realms of Else-where closing the distances all around me. I can feel the others, forgotten, abandoned, clawing to be free. To escape where Iam and I put them. Perhaps, unlike the wianu, I'll set them free."

"What in Iam's good name are you talking about?" Torsten spat.

She sneered. "I'm disappointed in such a holy man. Gifted sight, and still so blind. Can you not see?"

Muskigo brandished his sickle-blade. "If you caused this, you will not leave this field alive."

"What do the Dom Nohzi want, Sigrid?" Torsten asked. "Oleander, now this? Who are you here for!"

"Everyone," she said. The word lingered on the air like the smell of rotting flesh, coating Torsten's arm in goosebumps. It seemed to echo from all directions, the syllables like hissing snakes. This was Sigrid, but he didn't remember her voice resonating like that in their last encounter.

"I wanted to take my time," she went on. "To enjoy seeing this world fall, one blade of grass at a time. But fate pulled me here through Elsewhere. The love of family to undo you all."

"Torsten, who is this?" Muskigo asked again. Tingur was beside him now as well. He could barely raise his unique polearm he was so exhausted.

"Yes, tell them, Torsten," she said. "You can feel it, I know you can. My loyal Mak warned you I was coming. My brother was meant to be first, but you'll have to do."

"You're a monster, that's all," Torsten spat.

"Look closer!" she hissed. His stomach turned over as her voice penetrated his every pore. "I was buried... but not dead. Now, look upon me with the sight of he who forgot me!"

Torsten's throat clenched. His chest constricted. "Nesilia..." he said, softly, daring the world to hear it and make it so. Desperate for it not to be.

"In the flesh," she said. "Or, rather, her flesh."

"Nesilia?" Muskigo said, his eyes going wide. "Mahraveh was right."

"My brother's last mistake, yes?" Sigrid said. "You were all supposed to kill each other, but I suppose I can handle it for you. I deserve to enjoy your end."

"Only you shall end!" Muskigo charged at her. He swung high, then low, with speed that would have ravaged any other opponent. Not her. This new form set Nesilia's feet, and parried every attack with impossible ease, using only a single dagger.

She was toying with him, the greatest warrior in all Pantego, proven by the fact that he'd bested Torsten one on one. Tingur joined in and swung mightily at her head. She ducked, then flowed this way and that in avoidance of his attacks, all while parrying each of Muskigo's, as well.

Torsten saw an opening at her flank and made his move. His blade hummed, then met only air, swirling up the dust that made their battle invisible to both retreated armies.

"Over here," she taunted.

They spun to find her waiting behind them, not even panting. Her nightmare grin spread wider, causing the dried blood beneath to crack and flake off.

Tingur, the closest, charged first. He swung once, and she arched her back to avoid the blow. His full weight made him stumble, while she rose up, and slashed him across his gut. A sideways kick to his chest sent him soaring across the battlefield. She held his polearm in her free hand and snapped the shaft. That should not have been possible—not by any creature living or dead.

Torsten and Muskigo looked to each other, then came at her side-by-side. They'd battled, and so, they had intimate knowledge of each others' fighting styles that could only be gleaned from a duel—an unspoken thing filled with mutual respect.

They attacked her in perfect unison, him high, Torsten low. Weaving in and out of each others' motions. Torsten focused on power, attacks meant to kill, while Muskigo distracted her with quick strikes like a stinging snake.

Nothing hit. Not even one.

Her speed was immeasurable. It was like she wasn't even there. Torsten's arms and chest ached with soreness from swinging with such might only to hit nothing, not even a parrying blade. He caught Muskigo's intent for a last-ditch effort at landing a strike, stabbing for her hip as she took a wide step, Torsten thrust above. They had her. But she leaped and twisted sideways through the air, her thin torso passing right between their blades.

One of her boots caught Muskigo on the chin and sent him skidding across the dirt. Torsten ducked under another. It was a guess because she moved so fast, but the gamble worked. He gripped one half of Tingur's polearm—now a normal warhammer —and whipped it, catching Nesilia across the cheek.

Backing away, and grabbing at her skin, she stared down at the freshly drawn blood. And then Torsten watched as the shallow, superficial wound healed all on its own. He'd been blind last he'd faced any upyr, so he hadn't been able to see their true capabilities. There were only legends. In some, their undead bodies healed rapidly. Now, he wasn't sure if that was Sigrid's power or Nesilia who now inhabited it.

Torsten gripped *Salvation* with both hands, checked his footing. "You'll never win, Nesilia," he said. "Iam's children will strike you down. I've done it already. I will again."

"All you did was delay the inevitable," she said. "Can't you see? Iam has forgotten you as he forgot me." She lowered her dagger to her side. "I could crush you like an insect. All of you. Or you can see the truth, Torsten Unger."

"I see through His eyes, and I see only darkness and death before me," Torsten said.

"You see his lies. You're fighting for a world he doesn't want. I can make it so much better. Stop struggling over nothing. Embrace me. Love me. And you'll be free of him."

Torsten decided to change his tack. "Sigrid, if you're in there... I don't know what happened to make you this way, and I don't know how Nesilia has corrupted you, but fight it. You don't want this."

"I've promised her everything she could ever want." Nesilia rolled her fingers. "And I keep my promises."

"Think of your brother!" Torsten yelled. "He wouldn't want this. I know what Oleander did to your family. Look at all of this!" Torsten gestured to the thousands of bodies around them. Many still clung to life, bleeding out in the dirt. "We can end the violence. You can fight her."

"There's nothing to fight," Nesilia said. "She understands how men like you forsake people like her. Abandon them in the street once they've lost their usefulness."

"Do you think that makes you special? That Iam didn't love you back? I've been scorned, and I've been abandoned by my own parents to the street. You aren't the cure, Nesilia. You're the poison. Sigrid, fight this!"

Torsten saw her eyes flit toward the death around them. It was momentary, but it was there. The glimmer of regret.

"He lies!" Nesilia screamed.

She pounced at Torsten, closing the difference between them in less than a second. He barely got his blade up in time to parry, but the force of her attack was enough to send him to one knee and make the bones of his hand chatter so hard, he thought his fingers might break.

He raised his blade, but she grinned.

"Glaruium, from the mountain I was buried beneath," she said. "You should know better." She raised her hand and closed it into a fist. *Salvation* was specifically redesigned by Hovom Nitebrittle, the castle Blacksmith to not contain the enchanted metal she mentioned, but his armor still did. It began to constrict, pinning him in place so he couldn't move. Crushing him.

Salvation clattered to the earth.

He couldn't even speak as his throat was closed in by the collar of his chest plate.

This can't be how it ends, he thought.

He didn't close his eyes. He watched in complete disbelief as Nesilia hefted *Salvation* and stalked toward him.

Just then, Muskigo barreled into her side, knocking her to the earth. He plunged his sickle-blade toward her chest. She was pinned, no way out. Yet, still, his blade merely buried itself in dirt. He gawked down, and she was already behind him, her long, thin fingers spreading over his scalp, her nails pressing into the skin.

"Protect, Mahra—" Before he could finish, Nesilia yanked Muskigo's head back and slit his throat.

"Damn you, Nesilia!" Torsten shouted.

She shoved Muskigo's face down into the dirt with her knee. "The best Pantego has to offer?" she sneered. "Oh, Iam, how did you let our world come to this?"

Torsten stared as blood pooled out from Muskigo's neck. Within arm's reach—*Salvation.*

"I won't let you leave," Torsten said, breathless. Fighting against the strain of his crumpled armor, he reached out and grabbed the sword. Stabbed it into the ground, he used it to rise, like a cane. Memories of his weakness flooded him—blindness created by the hand of one of Nesilia's followers.

"Oh Torsten, can't you see?" she said. "You can't stop me."

With her tongue, she cleaned the dagger she'd used to kill Muskigo, then crept toward him. He shifted back and almost fell. He could hardly stay upright, his legs were so exhausted. Squeezing the handle of the claymore was a chore. His eyes teared from dust, and utter fear gripped him, refusing to let go.

"I can't watch any longer, my love," a powerful, basso voice echoed.

He wasn't sure if he was seeing clearly through his blindfold, but he thought he saw Dellbar the Holy standing a short distance away. His hands rested atop his cane, clutching the Eye of Iam there. What was strange was the light radiating off him in the same way shadow clung to Sigrid's body. Stranger still, was that the High Priest's eyes were open, revealing slits of bright, white energy staring down at them.

While Nesilia turned to face him, Torsten's muscles finally surrendered, and he fell to both knees, leaning on his sword.

"After all this time, now is when you choose to show your-self?" Nesilia asked. "For him!" Her playful tone was gone. Her every word dripped with rancor.

"We weren't meant to rule them, only be their guide," Dellbar said. "Until eventually, they forgot us entirely. You know that. It's why the feud happened and tore us all apart."

"Then why is your name still on their lips! Iam, Iam, Iam everywhere. While mine is spoken only in the shadows or the bitter cold."

Iam, Torsten thought.

"It's what they chose," Iam said through Dellbar's lips. "We left it in their hands."

"You left it!" Nesilia's roar hit the air like a thunderclap. Torsten's very rib cage vibrated. "I gave everything to protect you from Bliss. Chose you over my own brother. Over all of them. And you left me buried!"

"I couldn't reach you," Iam said.

"You were the strongest of us. Anything you imagined would have come to pass."

"Reach *you*, Nesilia. Darkness swallowed your heart. I saw it in the feud. When I hated every moment, you delighted in the fighting. I lost you in it." Dellbar's body stepped forward, his white robe fluttering in an unfelt breeze. "I should have seen it sooner."

"No, I should have," Nesilia snarled. "Should have seen that the only thing you were capable of loving was yourself. You don't care about these people. All these bodies... you could bring them all back to life with a snap of your fingers, but you won't."

"Because it's their world now. You never understood that."

"No, Iam, that's where you're wrong. It is mine."

She bolted at him. He raised his cane to greet her attack, and the ripple of energy blew Torsten onto his back. All he could see was distortion, whipping around them. He had to hold his ears just to drown out the sound.

The energy erupted, and Nesilia's body wheeled back. She scrambled to her knees and glared at Dellbar. Finally displaying weakness, she wheezed, her chest heaving. She tried to use her daggers, as Torsten had, to steady herself, but the blade slipped, and she lurched forward.

"Stop this now," Iam spoke through his host. He stood amidst the swirling ribbons of light, leaning on his cane, catching his breath. He, too, seemed weakened.

Nesilia started up with that familiar cackle, rising once more to her knees, back arched. "You have so little left, don't you?" she said. "I can feel it. I may be constrained to this mortal shell… but your essence is fading in this realm just like my brother's."

"Don't make me do this," Iam said. His voice was soft, but light began to accumulate in the Eye of the cane. The air itself hummed from the raw energy. The hairs all over Torsten's body stood on end.

"You made a mistake wasting your energy this early, my love," Nesilia said. "Now, you will watch as I destroy your beloved creations. And when I'm done, there will be no whispers of your name. Not in the dark. Not in freezing air. You will be forgotten for eternity until even I won't spare you a second thought."

Dellbar breathed in, then bellowed.

Coruscating light lashed out from the cane, but before it struck, Nesilia vanished in a wisp of dust. The earth where she'd been cracked, splitting open across the field like a web. One ran right under Torsten's foot and nearly swallowed him, but he crawled away and toward Dellbar, moving between his feet and knees. The light enveloping the High Priest and filling his blind eyes blinked away, and Dellbar collapsed.

"Where am I?" he asked weakly, grasping blindly at the air, scared like Torsten had been when he awoke without sight. "Hello, where am I?"

"I'm here, Dellbar," Torsten rasped. He fell beside him, then fought his battered muscles to help him upright. "You're fine."

"What happened?"

Torsten looked at the site where the Buried Goddess had been, and the unnatural streams of energy still teeming on the air. He couldn't believe what he'd just witnessed, nor could he deny it. Iam had shown himself, only, he was a hair too slow. Both great armies walked across the battlefield, as baffled as he was.

Alone, from the direction of the White Bridge, walked Rand Langley. His gaping eyes surveyed the gruesome scene from the thousands of dead soldiers on both sides to Muskigo. Tingur now held the rebel afhem, but he was beyond saving.

Rand knelt and pulled an arrow out of a man's back. Dread consumed his features as he stared at the blood on it.

"The Buried Goddess has returned…" Torsten answered, in utter disbelief of what he was saying. "And I don't know if we can stop her."

EPILOGUE

Burning flesh assaulted her nostrils. Nesilia couldn't feel the pain, but she could hear the agonized screams of her host deep within. Sigrid was anxious. Scared. Angry.

All of the things Nesilia felt when Bliss cast her down, and Iam left her in an eternity of torment.

Iam… How dare he show his face now!

Nesilia's nails dug into the dirt, continuing to burn from the light of dawn. The dirt turned to clay beneath her from the heat. Her skin flaked away to embers and whipped around her in the wind.

That spineless cur…

"Miss," a voice said. "Miss, are you all right?"

A hand tugged at her shoulder. She whipped around, screaming. Next thing she knew, a man's head hung limp from a crushed neck, the power in her host's fingers turning his spine to dust.

Nesilia then lunged for his collarbone, feeling Sigrid's hunger. She stopped herself just above the flesh, her mouth watering. She could feel her fangs sliding further from her gums, eager to feed.

"*No, my dear, Sigrid,*" Nesilia told the voice within. "*We won't let them make us what they want us to be anymore.*"

Nesilia stood, the man's body in hand, and stretched out her neck. Her body continued to burn away, but she was in no hurry. Iam showed his hand and battered her new form, but it took so much of his strength to do so. He was weak now. Susceptible.

"*They say they love us, and yet, here we are, left face down in the dirt,*" Nesilia said to Sigrid. "*Iam, your brother, Torsten Unger. They'll all stand witness to their failures!*"

She tossed the body aside, then heard whimpering. Leered to her left, she spotted a mother and her daughter, shrunk back against a covered wagon at the side of the road. The girl cried in her mother's arms. The mother tried not to.

Nesilia slowly approached them. She could taste ash in her mouth now, feel only warm bone if she licked at her lips.

She said not a word to the mother and child as she passed. She couldn't. Her tongue was too degraded, gobbled up by sunlight. Instead, she pulled what was left of her ravaged body into the back of the cart, and nestled beneath the shadow of its covering.

The woman finally unleashed a squeal and ran to her dead husband, and the child resigned to abandoned weeping. They couldn't see how better off they were. What he would inevitably do to them.

The horses started to move without Nesilia needing to coax them, like they could sense her will. And along the Glass Road, they rumbled in the loving embrace of shadow.

Her burned skin began to heal. Exposed sinew and muscles twisted back together again. Her whole body exhaled, but the panic of her host didn't wane.

"*They thought they had us,*" Nesilia told her. "*They were wrong. But no, that's not what it is. You're worried. About him. About Rand.*"

"*The way he looked at me...*" Sigrid answered, the voice small in the back of her consciousness.

"*Is the way they all look when they realize what they've lost,*"

Nesilia said. *"He doesn't love you. He can't love you. Iam didn't put love in them."*

"Maybe it was a mistake..."

"Like Kazimir made a mistake by seizing control of your fate? Like the men who tried to own you, but left you bleeding in the street?"

"They were yer followers who killed me. I remember now."

Nesilia smiled. Aloud, she said, "And they saw your weakness, dear. Exploited it, as they are meant to. But no longer. You've been purged of Iam's lies."

"I don't..."

"Understand? Of course, you do. You know it's true, my dear. You've given yourself to me. To resist is folly. I will give you the world."

Nesilia rose, her regenerated skin stretching to cover her figure like freshly boiled leather. Then she watched out the back of the cart as Pantego swept by, feeling as Sigrid's consciousness receded back, surrendering. A willing host, too broken by the world Iam forced her into to fight necessity. Unlike Sora.

Eventually, Nesilia found herself standing at the edge of Lake Yaolin, fully recuperated. The moons watched from high above, dancing behind clouds. The people of Yaolin scurried about, fixing up their city after Nesilia's worshippers showed them the error of their ways. They didn't even bother to stop her wagon, they were so distracted. So blind.

In Sora's body, Nesilia could have frozen the lake and walked across, but in her new one, she didn't need to. The world plied to her needs. She had worthy followers now. A wianu's tentacle bubbled to the surface and held flat for her at the edge of the water. She stepped onto it, then forward, and another rose to take its place in her path.

"Thank you, my pet," she said to the wianu. "The fallen ones can't hold you prisoner any longer. You can finish the task for which you were made."

All the way across the lake, the wianu helped her along. She could see the water stirring all around as more arrived from the Far North, free of the broken Citadel and the damnable upyr who'd used her creations for their own sinister means. They were the greatest threat to her in Pantego, and now they were finished, thanks to Whitney Fierstown's rashness and Kazimir's softened heart.

The wianu tentacle slithered up the coast of the Red Tower's lonely isle and delivered Nesilia to the gate. The oversized hunks of iron remained locked, but the tentacle reached into the space between them, then another, until they pried it open.

Aihara Na appeared in the entry, electricity crackling at her fingertips. She seemed weaker than ever, barely corporeal, after allowing Kazimir to defeat her. Nesilia could see precisely how it happened now, through Sigrid's memory.

Pathetic.

"You!" the old mystic growled. "I won't be beaten again!" Electricity seared forward. Nesilia extended a hand, the energy surged in her palm, then faded to a spark.

Aihara Na's eyes widened. "Impossible. Only your master could be so strong and he—"

"Is dead, you imbecile," Nesilia hissed. "It appears my faith in you was misplaced. You can't even recognize me, let alone protect my will."

The wianu pushed the doors open until they slammed against the inner walls. Nesilia strode in, and Aihara Na's spectral form soared up beside her.

"My Lady, Nesilia, it is you," she said. "Your new body—"

"Will suffice for now," Nesilia said.

"So, the upyr have finally been destroyed. Those meddlesome pests—"

"Defeated you," Nesilia finished for her. "The most powerful mystic left. Maybe, the only one left. I think I overestimated your part to play in this. Already, your new order is broken."

Aihara Na swooped before her. "I was betrayed. An acolyte under my tutelage opened the Well for them. One I thought was gifted. He's no longer with us."

"Show me."

"I'm afraid... there isn't much left of him to show."

"Not him!" Nesilia boomed. She knew the fate of the one named Kai, fed on by the very body she now inhabited. "Show me the Well."

"I... Yes, of course. Right this way."

Aihara Na led her across the hall, splotches of blood from her battle with Kazimir still staining the floor. Nesilia had trusted Aihara Na's strength, but it was obvious now she should have left the Ancient One with help. Freydis was a far more worthy second, fighting the upyr without fear or hesitation.

They descended the stairs, passed the training room. Nesilia peered in. Rows of her slaves stood, younger than the last batch she'd left Aihara Na with before sailing North. Their arms were gashed from blooding, learning how to draw on the magic of Elsewhere. With the last bar guai having shattered in the Citadel, they'd be forced to do so unaided.

"I've been training a new generation of mystics," Aihara Na said. "The intrusion was a minor setback, but these new ones... they are truly gifted. Plucked from their homes throughout the city."

"They don't look it," Nesilia said. They looked sallow, exhausted. Unworthy.

"Most mystics train for years. We don't have the luxury of time or even bar guais, but they will prove worthy of you, I swear it. We are to serve."

Nesilia couldn't manage more than a grunt of acknowledgment. She wasn't impressed. After the God Feud, the remaining power of the gods was claimed by some mortals, bound within the Well of Wisdom and Elsewhere. But it was clear now, the Mystic Order was useless.

"I must ask, what happened to your former host?" Aihara Na said.

"Thanks to you, breaking open the Citadel and freeing my pets cost much. The upyr were waiting, informed because you failed to keep the Well safe. Thanks to you, the bastard princess Sora lives, and I am this." She spread her arms and gestured to her pale, new body. "Thanks to you—"

Aihara Na dared to interrupt. "Then let me redeem myself. Let me hunt Sora down. She will join us, or she will perish."

"And tell me, Ancient One. What use would I have for you if I had her?"

"I… You…"

"It's no matter," Nesilia said with a hand wave. "She will fall with the rest. She's made her choice. Not a soul will ever know what she truly is. She'll die… forgotten."

They stopped in front of the tall stone doors on the bottommost level beyond which harbored the Well of Wisdom. Aihara Na positioned herself before them and spoke an enchantment. The doors shook, inscriptions on them glowing blue, then peeled open.

"What is it you wish to see?" Aihara Na asked.

Nesilia ignored her, pushing past. She stepped in, and the plants growing up the entry and around the waters wilted and blackened. An upyr was a corruption of its power, made by mortals long ago who didn't know how to handle it. Made after Nesilia was buried. When Iam left the mortals to their own devices—to war, and Cullings, and death.

She almost pitied the mortals. They, too, suffering his neglect when all they needed was a guide.

"Nesilia, your new body," Aihara Na said. "Perhaps you shouldn't be here. Perhaps I can help you see what you must."

"I see everything," Nesilia snapped. "Including your uselessness. The wianu are free. The cursed ones are destroyed. The mortals have weakened themselves beyond repair, and Iam right along with them. It's time to bring them to their knees."

She raised her head and glanced back at Aihara Na. Her wraithlike face wrinkled in confusion, truly showing her age.

"How?" she asked. "You said we needed to gather forces and eliminate threats quietly."

"My forces are all around us, can't you see? In the pubs where they drink and screw like rabbits. In the streets where they stew in their own filth. In you."

"What?"

Nesilia sneered. She raised her arm over the water and bit down on the wrist, learning the trick from Sigrid's memory of her fallen Maker. She opened the veins, feeling the pain but not stopped by it. Sigrid's consciousness roused and screamed out, but she was far beyond. Lost to Nowhere.

Her tainted upyr blood poured out into the water, but it wasn't enough.

"No, you mustn't!" Aihara Na cried out. "That much will—"

Nesilia raised her free hand and smacked the mystic across the face. Her nebulous body couldn't resist the touch of an upyr, and she flew into the wall.

Then, Nesilia bit into the other wrist, tearing more flesh and muscle and draining into the Well before she immersed herself fully. The power of the waters kept her wounds from healing, and the cursed blood continued to flow. The waters went red, then black.

"We damned you all to Elsewhere, but it was Iam who deceived," she spoke. "Deceived me! Join me and my pets, and we'll take back what was once ours."

She raised a bloody fist into the air, then drove it down, displacing the waters, and cracking open the bottom of the Well.

"No!" Aihara Na shouted again, but the shockwave held her back. "You promised me!"

"You shouldn't have failed me," Nesilia said. "You won't again."

She closed her eyes. She peered into Elsewhere.

"Elsewhere is empty."

She heard Kazimir's words echo in Sigrid's memory, but he was wrong. They were there but waiting.

She threw her arms open, and the water and her blood became one, circling her, flowing back into her veins as they healed. The ground beneath the Well continued to rupture, deep into the earth. Ages-old stone throughout the chamber shifted and freed.

"Damned men. Fallen gods. Be free," Nesilia said. "Serve me and the realm that was yours shall be ours again."

Spirits teemed forth from the rupture, beings trapped in Elsewhere. They weren't physical in this realm, but that didn't matter. As Aihara Na protested, one dove into her chest, her arms and legs twisting in unnatural ways as she was possessed.

Nesilia moved with the others, back to the gates of the Red Tower. She watched as they swarmed out over the city, laughing and screeching with glee. Free of the realm Iam built to contain them—the floodgates of Elsewhere were broken.

The wianu shook the lake's water in approval. Dakel un Ghastrin, Kazimir's rival extended up from the waters and wrapped its tentacles up the tower. Using them as a ramp, Nesilia climbed to the top of the structure where she could see all.

Horrified screams rang out across Yaolin as the spirits found unwilling hosts. They took over warriors, farmers, peddlers, everyone who, under Nesilia, wouldn't need to claw for a living. Cultists, hiding or locked away in Glass prisons howled with glee as possession came for them.

With her upyr eyes, she could see it all clearly: even Governor Philippi Nantby on the terrace of his mansion, fleeing a spirit of Elsewhere, only to trip and fall to his death. His wife wasn't so lucky.

"Now what?" a voice spoke behind her. It was reminiscent of Aihara Na but was deeper, more resonant, lilting with rage. Her eyes were milky white; her ethereal form, brighter and refreshed.

"Will you now kill me, too?" the spirit inhabiting Aihara Na asked.

"No, Bliss," Nesilia said. "Iam's lies corrupted you as it did many. It's time we buried our squabbles, and see this realm to its former glory."

"I'll settle for destroying the ones who took my forest from me."

Nesilia didn't answer. She just turned to look to the west, toward Yarrington and the seat of Iam, the screams of terror continuing to echo, and she grinned.

THANK YOU!

Thank you for reading *War of Men,* book five in The Buried Goddess Saga.

Thank you so much for reading War of Men by Rhett C. Bruno and Jaime Castle. We hope you enjoyed it as much as we enjoyed bringing it to you. We just wanted to take a moment to encourage you to review the book on Amazon and Goodreads. Every review helps further the author's reach and, ultimately, helps them continue writing fantastic books for us all to enjoy.

If you liked War of Men, check out the rest of our catalogue at www.aethonbooks.com. To sign up to receive updates regarding all new releases, If you liked this book, check out the rest of our catalogue at www.aethonbooks.com. To sign up to receive a FREE collection from some of our best authors as well as updates regarding all new releases, visit www.subscribepage.com/Aethon-ReadersGroup.

JOIN THE KING'S SHIELD

Sign up to the *free* and exclusive King's Shield Newsletter to receive early looks and new novels, peeks at conceptual art that breathes life into Pantego as well as exclusive access to short stories called "Legends of Pantego." Learn more about the characters and the world you love.

Did you know we have a Facebook group too? All the same perks as the email readers group plus instant interaction with Rhett and Jaime! The Official King's Shield Fan Club.

ABOUT THE AUTHORS

Jaime is the Audible #1 bestselling author of THE BURIED GODDESS SAGA. He lives in Texas with his wife and two kids. He enjoys anything creative, from graphic arts to painting. His office looks like the Avengers threw up on the walls.

Jaime has been writing since elementary school and is a bit of a grammar officer—here to correct and serve.

Rhett is a Sci-fi/Fantasy author currently living in Stamford, Connecticut. His published works include books in the USA Today Bestselling CIRCUIT SERIES (Published by Diversion Books and Podium Audio), THE BURIED GODDESS SAGA and the THE CHILDREN OF TITAN SERIES (Aethon Books, Audible Studios). He is also one of the founders of the popular science fiction platform, Sci-Fi Bridge.

SPECIAL THANKS TO:

ADAWIA E. ASAD	EDDIE HALLAHAN	KYLE OATHOUT
BARDE PRESS	JOSH HAYES	LILY OMIDI
CALUM BEAULIEU	PAT HAYES	TROY OSGOOD
BEN	BILL HENDERSON	GEOFF PARKER
BECKY BEWERSDORF	JEFF HOFFMAN	NICHOLAS (BUZ) PENNEY
BHAM	GODFREY HUEN	JASON PENNOCK
TANNER BLOTTER	JOAN QUERALTÓ IBÁÑEZ	THOMAS PETSCHAUER
ALFRED JOSEPH BOHNE IV	JONATHAN JOHNSON	JENNIFER PRIESTER
CHAD BOWDEN	MARCEL DE JONG	RHEL
ERREL BRAUDE	KABRINA	JODY ROBERTS
DAMIEN BROUSSARD	PETRI KANERVA	JOHN BEAR ROSS
CATHERINE BULLINER	ROBERT KARALASH	DONNA SANDERS
JUSTIN BURGESS	VIKTOR KASPERSSON	FABIAN SARAVIA
MATT BURNS	TESLAN KIERINHAWK	TERRY SCHOTT
BERNIE CINKOSKE	ALEXANDER KIMBALL	SCOTT
MARTIN COOK	JIM KOSMICKI	ALLEN SIMMONS
ALISTAIR DILWORTH	FRANKLIN KUZENSKI	KEVIN MICHAEL STEPHENS
JAN DRAKE	MEENAZ LODHI	MICHAEL J. SULLIVAN
BRET DULEY	DAVID MACFARLANE	PAUL SUMMERHAYES
RAY DUNN	JAMIE MCFARLANE	JOHN TREADWELL
ROB EDWARDS	HENRY MARIN	CHRISTOPHER J. VALIN
RICHARD EYRES	CRAIG MARTELLE	PHILIP VAN ITALLIE
MARK FERNANDEZ	THOMAS MARTIN	JAAP VAN POELGEEST
CHARLES T FINCHER	ALAN D. MCDONALD	FRANCK VAQUIER
SYLVIA FOIL	JAMES MCGLINCHEY	VORTEX
GAZELLE OF CAERBANNOG	MICHAEL MCMURRAY	DAVID WALTERS JR
DAVID GEARY	CHRISTIAN MEYER	MIKE A. WEBER
MICHEAL GREEN	SEBASTIAN MÜLLER	PAMELA WICKERT
BRIAN GRIFFIN	MARK NEWMAN	JON WOODALL
	JULIAN NORTH	BRUCE YOUNG